NORTHWOODS

NORTHWOODS

— A Novel —

Amy Pease

EMILY BESTLER BOOKS

ATRIA

New York   London   Toronto   Sydney   New Delhi

An Imprint of Simon & Schuster, Inc.
1230 Avenue of the Americas
New York, NY 10020

AT LAST
Music by HARRY WARREN
Lyrics by MACK GORDON
© 1942 (Renewed) TWENTIETH CENTURY MUSIC CORPORATION
All Rights Controlled and Administered by EMI FEIST CATALOG INC. (Publishing)
and ALFRED MUSIC (Print)
All Rights Reserved
Used by Permission of ALFRED MUSIC

First Emily Bestler Books/Atria Books hardcover edition January 2024

EMILY BESTLER BOOKS/ATRIA BOOKS and colophon are trademarks of Simon & Schuster, Inc.

Simon & Schuster: Celebrating 100 Years of Publishing in 2024

For information about special discounts for bulk purchases, please contact Simon & Schuster Special Sales at 1-866-506-1949 or business@simonandschuster.com.

The Simon & Schuster Speakers Bureau can bring authors to your live event. For more information or to book an event, contact the Simon & Schuster Speakers Bureau at 1-866-248-3049 or visit our website at www.simonspeakers.com.

Interior design by Jill Putorti

Manufactured in the United States of America

1 3 5 7 9 10 8 6 4 2

Library of Congress Cataloging-in-Publication Data is available.

ISBN 978-1-6680-1726-5
ISBN 978-1-6680-1728-9 (ebook)

In memory of my dad, who congratulated me on this book before I even wrote it

Author's Note

This book touches on issues that may be triggering for some readers, especially surrounding mental health and substance abuse. Please visit my website, www.amypeasewrites.com, for more details.

1

Eli North stripped off his clothes and waded into the water. The lake muck cushioned his feet, and, when he was in up to his chest, he rested his plastic travel mug on the water's surface and let his feet drift upward. He had always been good at floating.

The water had that mid-August feel, warm and slippery and heavy with microorganisms, and a flotilla of lily pads protected the tiny beach from water traffic. Not that anyone would be on the water at this time of night.

He tried to focus on the stars, the weightless sensation of floating. Meditation, they called it. A way to set aside negative thoughts. He put the mug to his lips and sucked the whiskey through his teeth so it wouldn't spill into his nose. His lip was split, only partially healed, and the fiery liquor lanced the wound open again.

Michelle had agreed to meet him after work, but she'd left before he had shown up, two hours late. It was a sad routine, making promises, breaking promises, and there was a part of him that had been relieved when she asked for a divorce in July. At least now they could both move on, her to something better, and him to a place where he didn't disappoint her all the time.

He thought of Andy.

Across the lake, somebody cranked up the radio. Etta James's voice slid over the water, a nice change from the usual shit-kickin' country coming from Dan Simons's cabin. *Classy with a* K was how Michelle had always described Dan. Eli took another sip of whiskey and winced at the pain on his lip, at the throb of the surrounding bruise.

At last
My love has come along
My lonely days are over
And life is like a song

The music seemed custom-made for the setting, as if it was to be sung only on dark summer nights, against the rustle of cattails and the plinking call of chorus frogs. Maybe the vacationers wouldn't mind Etta James. Maybe they wouldn't call to complain. Maybe tonight he could just get drunk and float. He lay there, floating, for a long time, long enough to notice that the music was playing on repeat, which suited him just fine.

Still, it came as no surprise when the scanner crackled from under the heap of clothes on the sand. People with lake houses weren't the type to let a noise disturbance go unreported.

"Eli, you there?"

He ignored the dispatch, vaguely wondered why he had bothered to bring the scanner to the beach in the first place, then breathed deeply and tilted his head backward until the water nearly covered his face. He relaxed his grip on the travel mug and let his arms and legs go limp in the soft, tepid water. The sound of the music was muffled now by the water over his ears, as if it was coming from another room, as if he had stepped away from a party. When the memories began to lap at the edges of his mind, he was ready for them, and pushed them away.

"Eli?"

The bark of the scanner broke his concentration and he floundered. Lake water poured into his nose and he choked, then scrambled to right himself. He coughed and sputtered and had just caught his breath when he noticed something pale bobbing among the lily pads several yards away, nearly concealed by the thick vegetation and heavy darkness.

He swam toward the object, but the waves from his forward motion pushed whatever it was deeper into the lily pads with each stroke. He stilled, treaded water just enough to stay afloat until the waves subsided, then ducked his head under the water and swam toward where the object had disappeared into the thick plants. Three kicks and he surfaced.

His travel mug, still nearly full. Bobbing against a lily pad.

He grasped the handle of the mug and was surprised to find that his hand was shaking, that his heart was hammering in his chest in a way that had nothing to do with the distance he had swum.

What had he expected to find, floating in the darkness?

With a twist of his hips, he turned and began to swim back to shore, holding his drink out of the water. He stumbled on the sand, caught himself, got up again. When he reached his pile of belongings, he eased the lid off the mug and tipped the rest of the contents into his mouth. He stood still for a long moment, the back of his hand pressed to his lips, then bent over to grab the scanner.

2

The shadows were thick along Lakelawn Avenue. Red pines had been planted by the thousands in tight rows across Wisconsin by the Civilian Conservation Corps during the Great Depression, and now they created a thick, eighty-foot-high wall between the county highway and the bumpy, potholed gravel road that led to Beran's Resort. Few plants grew in the dim understory of the pines, and the base of each trunk was bald and knotted, forming shadowy allées as perfect and precise as they were dark.

The sand in Eli's shoes chafed as he made his way from the parked cruiser toward the row of cabins. A campfire glowed in a backyard a little ways down the lake, and the flames illuminated a ring of people sitting in lawn chairs. Laughter and the pop and crackle of the fire mingled with Etta James, and none of the partygoers seemed to mind the music.

He thought of Andy again. His boy loved campfires—a born pyromaniac—and it wasn't until a few years ago that Eli and Michelle had been able to enjoy a campfire without fear of him falling into the flames. Now he himself was the one Michelle had to worry about, ever since he had stumbled, drunk, much too close to the neighbors' bonfire last Christmas. And his being burned to a crisp wasn't the only thing she was forced to worry about.

They're going to find you dead on the bottom of the lake someday.

The shore on this side of the lake was a zigzag of granite outcroppings and pine forest. Cabin Six was partially hidden from the road by trees, and from the water by a tall ledge of red granite. Through the pines, the windows of the cabin shone brightly.

Beran's Resort was picturesque, nostalgic, like something from a post-card; split-log cabins with red roofs and screened porches, stacked-rock firepits and tree-stump benches. There was a tiny beach with Adirondack chairs and racks of canoes, and a long, L-shaped pier with a westward view across Shaky Lake.

The parking space next to the cabin was empty, with two long scars in the gravel where a car had peeled out of the driveway. The music blasted through the open windows, and a light shone over the door. He paused in the shadow just outside the pool of light to take stock of himself. He wasn't drunk. Buzzed, maybe, but not drunk. His hair was still wet, his skin tacky with the lingering film of lake water. His uniform was rumpled and stale-smelling from sitting in a duffel bag in the back of his car, and the tan fabric hung too loosely on his large frame.

There was no doorbell, and nobody appeared when he knocked, so he let himself into the kitchen through the unlocked door. It was a small, homey space furnished with honey-stained knotty pine cabinets and a speckled linoleum floor. A Formica table, chrome with a bright orange top, sat in the middle of the room. All four orange vinyl chairs were pushed in. Nothing on the countertops. The refrigerator door was ajar and, upon further inspection, was empty and unplugged. No evidence of food or drinks.

The music was jarringly loud, like a smoke alarm in the middle of the night, but he resisted the urge to find the source and turn it off. The noise hid the sound of his movements, and for that he was thankful. It had always been the sound of his own movement that had scared him in Afghanistan.

"Sheriff's department," he shouted. "Anyone home?" He waited, and when no one came, he poked his head into the living room and looked around. He knew the moment he stepped into the room that the place was empty. The air had a slack quality, the indifference of uninhabited rooms. Plaid curtains puffed and sucked against the open window above a couch. A potbelly stove and empty log holder sat in one corner, and, in the other, a tiny gateleg table and chair, along with a bookcase full of old paperbacks and boxes of jigsaw puzzles. It was quaint and comfortable and completely empty. Not a single thing out of place, no personal belongings anywhere. He reached over to a nearby end table and ran a finger across the wood. A month's worth of dust, maybe more. He went quickly back to the kitchen and locked the door, then crossed to the other side of the living room, where another door led to a screened porch facing the lake. Strings of twinkle lights lit the space, but, like the rest of the cabin, there were no signs of life. He stepped back into the living room and locked the porch door.

He made his way systematically through each room of the tiny cabin, checked the closets, looked under the beds. Speakers were positioned throughout the house, and the source of the music was a radio in one of the bedrooms. Satisfied that the place was empty, he pulled the radio plug. His ears quavered from the shock of sudden silence. His lip throbbed, and when he touched it, his hand came away with blood.

"Shit." He found a dusty roll of toilet paper in the bathroom and pressed a wad of it against his lip, too hard, and winced. A stumble in the night, he had told everyone. Just part of learning the layout of a new apartment.

Outside, he heard the crunch of gravel.

"*Shit,*" he repeated. Eli looked for a trash can, thought better of it, then stuffed the bloody scrap of toilet paper into his pocket and rushed to open the kitchen door. There was a woman, walking away, barely visible at the far end of the unlit path. Her footsteps were muffled now by the cushion of fallen pine needles. She turned when she heard the door open.

"Excuse me, ma'am?" he called into the darkness. His voice was overloud, a shout in church. "Do you have a minute?" She paused for a moment, then walked toward him into the circle of light from the cabin. He studied her appearance. *Forty-something, dark hair, dark eyes, about five foot five, medium build. University of Chicago hoodie.* Her expression was calm but puzzled as she squinted at him in the half-light, and he was suddenly conscious of his bedraggled appearance and musty smell; if she noticed any of this, she hid it well.

"Thank god you came, Officer," she said, in a low, agreeable voice. "I was about ready to kill those people." She looked to the cabin behind him, then looked at his badge again and gave an awkward laugh. "I mean, you know . . . not *kill* them."

He smiled. "I'm Deputy North. Sherman County Sheriff's Department. Are you staying at this resort?"

She nodded and took a step closer to him. "My daughter and I are three cabins down," she said. "I thought we had the resort to ourselves until an hour ago." She took one hand out of her pocket and gestured at the cabin. "Until that started." She shook her head.

"You don't know the people staying here?" he asked.

"I didn't think anyone was here at all. We've been coming here for years, ever since my daughter was a baby, and I've never seen it this dead before. It's weird."

"How long have you and your daughter been here this summer?"

"Just a few days. Since Friday night. We come every August for two weeks before school starts."

No wedding ring.

He pulled out his notebook and pencil. "Can I get your name and contact information, ma'am?"

"Ma'am. Makes me feel old." The woman laughed and shook her head. She had an open, easy smile, something he hadn't been on the receiving end of in a while. Shaky Lake was a small town; everyone knew everyone else's business, and Eli's business could kill a good mood faster than a flat tire on the way to a party. "My name's Beth Wallace, and my daughter is Caitlin." She reached into her pocket and pulled out her phone, then peered at the screen and made a small noise of frustration. "The reception here is terrible, although that's probably a good thing. Forces Caitlin and me to put down our phones and actually talk to each other. She's sixteen, so that doesn't happen very often." She told him her number, then said, "If you can't reach me, try calling the owners, Mike and Kim, and they can track me down."

"You're going to be here for another week and a half?"

An expression he couldn't interpret flashed across her face, and even in the shadowy light from the porch, he could see a faint line appear between her brows. She nodded. "That's the plan."

Eli studied her for a moment. Something about his question had struck a nerve with her. He would have liked to learn why, but searching the property took precedence. He put his notebook back into his pocket and the fabric of his shirt shifted with the movement. He caught a whiff of his own smell and took a step backward from her, hoping that the night breeze carried away the evidence of his neglected hygiene. "Thanks for your help," he said. "I hope you and your daughter have a good vacation."

Eli watched as she disappeared through the trees, vaguely conscious of having spoiled her evening and not quite sure why. He looked at his watch. The night was very dark now. The stars shining over the lake earlier had gone, obscured by clouds. He went back into the cabin and walked from room to room, doing one last search, flipping off lights, locking doors. He went out onto the porch and unplugged the twinkle lights. It took a few moments for his eyes to adjust to the darkness, for his ears to grasp the rhythm of night sounds. It was almost eleven. He heard the shouted goodbyes and clatter of lawn chairs as the group he had passed earlier disbanded. The night went quiet.

God, he loved silence. Not silence, exactly. Just the absence of human noise. No voices, no radios, no motorboats, no rumble of helicopters or Humvees. These were the times when he loved Shaky Lake like it was part of his soul. He clung to these perfect summer nights when he was digging cars out of snowbanks or mopping puddles of dirty snowmelt off his mudroom floor. He would give anything to just sit there on the porch and take in the silence. The shiver of pine boughs in the warm air. The lapping of water against the rocks. The chirping and rustles of who-knows-what in the darkness. He *trusted* the darkness in Shaky Lake.

He pulled his flashlight off his belt and held it, unlit. The lake reflected what little light the night sky offered, and the glow was enough to see by as he moved silently down the pine-needled path to the water. A hollow bumping sound interrupted his thoughts, and he ducked into the shadow of the granite outcropping that still obscured the shore. He listened for a full five minutes before he was satisfied. No voices. No human movement. Just the sound of something he had known since his earliest memories— the sound of a boat against a dock.

Slowly, carefully, one foot at a time—he was still a little tipsy—he descended the path, then rounded the corner and saw the dock. A small aluminum fishing boat was tied to it, wobbling gently on the water in the near darkness.

The dock was rickety, and the peeled-paint boards sagged and creaked under his substantial weight; he nearly tripped on the uneven wood. He flipped on his flashlight and the aluminum hull of the boat was reflected back at him. The angle of the light and the depth of the boat kept the interior in heavy shadow until he was directly alongside it. He shone the flashlight into the darkness and there, crumpled in the bottom of the boat, was the lifeless body of a boy.

3

Eli jerked back as if he had been kicked in the chest, as if he hadn't seen dozens of dead bodies in his career. "Oh god, don't do this to me now," he said aloud. He stumbled, tried to right himself, failed. The back of his head slammed against the dock.

Blackness descended like a hood.

A memory, like shrapnel lodged in his brain, was knocked loose by the impact of his fall. Amanji this time, his shirt soaked with sweat, crouched in the cold, the muscles of his thighs seizing up as he waited for the echoes of the bombs to fade.

Then a slow, melting pain in the back of his head and the feel of something hard against his back. The air was cold and wet and thick. He opened his eyes with difficulty. His mind was strangely soft and there was a coil of something unpleasant in his belly. He ignored it. Ignored it again. All at once, he flung himself onto his side and began to retch. Softness turned to devastating pain, each heave like a hammer to his skull. Panic set in as he tried to regain his senses.

A boat.

Something about a boat.

Andy.

He scrambled to his feet, teetered, and nearly fell off the dock into the narrow slice of water between wood and boat.

Andy.

He threw one leg over the gunwale of the boat and his foot slipped. He fell hard again, chest-first against the gunwale, and just barely avoided hitting the aluminum with his face. He righted himself and dropped to his knees next to the still figure. His flashlight was gone, likely into the water when he'd fallen, and there was little light to see.

A boy. Dark hair, big-boned.

He reached for the boy and his hand met cold skin. He pressed two fingers against the boy's neck. Waited.

No pulse.

Andy.

The face was a pale oval against the dark floor of the boat, and Eli tried, and failed, to make out his features. He put a hand out and touched the boy's face. Later, he would remember the brutal force of his relief. A jolt of electricity to his spine, stunning and painful. His brain was slower than his body to realize what he was feeling on the cold skin.

Stubble. The facial hair of a teenager, not an eleven-year-old boy.

Not Andy.

Warmth poured through his body, an explosion of relief. The feeling was short-lived, however. A thunderclap of pain struck his head. He had tripped and fallen and hit his head. Hard. He touched the place where the pain was worst, but his fingers came away dry. He pushed the screen light button on his watch and discovered that nearly half an hour had passed since he had stepped onto the dock. Half an hour that he'd been unconscious. Not good.

He looked behind him and saw the outline of cabins on the dark shoreline. *Beran's Resort.* He remembered the woman he had talked to. Beth Something.

Music.

A boat.

A boy is dead.

Not Andy.

The air seemed to grow colder, and he shivered and rubbed at the gooseflesh on his arms. A car door slammed in the distance. He cursed and scrambled out of the boat, then onto the dock. He got to his feet and stood, legs wide, for a moment to be sure he wasn't going to fall over. From the top of the shoreline, he heard voices. A minute later, two flashlight beams bobbed around the outcropping.

"You standing there in the dark, Eli?" called Jake Howard, a fellow sheriff's deputy, as he made his way down the path. The dock shook from the man's bulk as he came to meet Eli next to the boat.

"Knocked my flashlight into the water like an idiot." He swallowed hard against the nausea and tried to keep his voice even. The dock shook again, more mildly this time. Through the glare of their flashlights, Eli could make out Jake's scarred face and, behind him, an older woman with short-cropped hair.

The woman propped a fist on her hip, looked at him, then shone her flashlight into the boat. "Shit, Eli."

"Sheriff. Didn't know you were on tonight." He gestured into the boat. "DOA."

Dead on arrival.

"I don't"—the sound of his own voice seemed to bounce around in his skull, jostling the words—"I don't recognize him," he managed.

She didn't respond at first, just looked around as far as the flashlight allowed. "You already checked the cabin?"

"Yeah. Noise disturbance call. When I got here, the place was deserted. No sign of anyone except the blasting music. Etta James."

She pinched her lips in thought. "Jake, go up and take another look. Call forensics."

"Got it, Sheriff." Jake nodded and headed up the path.

The sheriff wasn't much of a talker, and tonight was no exception. Eli waited for her to speak, and when she didn't, he began to describe the sweep in precise detail. "I spoke with a woman who's staying a few cabins down. She doesn't know the occupants of the cabin. Thought it was empty."

The sheriff's face was obscured by the darkness, and he wondered what she was thinking. She leaned over the boat and shone her flashlight at the boy again.

"I couldn't do much of an inspection without a flashlight," said Eli, "but he's—"

She walked to the end of the dock and stood, her back to him, for a very long time. Finally, she said, "Of all the kids for this to happen to—"

"You knew him?"

"I knew him." She turned and stalked past him to the shore. He followed her up the path to the cabin. It took all his concentration to keep his footing. His depth perception wasn't quite right, and pops of light floated on the periphery of his vision; he was also still a little drunk. The cabin lights were back on, and Eli could see Jake standing in the living room, scribbling something in a notebook. Eli followed the sheriff toward the building. When they reached the kitchen door, she turned and seemed about to say something. Instead, she peered at him and frowned. She pulled a penlight from her belt and stood on tiptoe to shine it in his eyes. He was over a foot taller than her, as massive as she was tiny. The light blinded him and he couldn't make out her expression. He reached to touch the lump on the back of his head but stopped just in time. She would notice the movement and ask more questions. Sheriff Marge North—his mother, his boss—noticed everything.

"Your eyes don't look quite right."

"Mom," he murmured, and pushed the light away. "I'm fine. Seriously."

She flicked off the light and crossed her arms, unconvinced.

"I promise you, I'm fine," he repeated.

She slid the penlight back into her belt. "It'll take the forensics company an hour to get here, and then it'll probably be morning before they have any useful information." She checked her watch. "The boy in the boat is Ben Sharpe. I'm going to see his mother now. Jake can supervise the scene. I want you to go home, get a little rest, and be back at the station at seven tomorrow morning."

"I'll come with you."

"No, I'll go alone."

Eli began to protest, but the look on Marge's face, not to mention the fact that he could barely stand, stopped him. He raised his hands in surrender.

"Good," she said. She put a hand on his arm and studied him one more time. Once again, she seemed about to say something, but instead just squeezed his arm and turned to go inside.

4

Michelle was the least crazy woman Eli had ever known. "That's why I keep her around," he had always joked. She was the one who held their family together when he was deployed, and even more so after he had come home. She was strong, but she was realistic. Andy had been eight years old when Eli was deployed. Old enough to understand, on a basic level, where his dad was going. Old enough to remember what his dad had been like before he went away.

Eli listened to the dial tone as he waited for Michelle to pick up, and each ring caused his head to throb more. He gripped the doorframe of the cruiser to steady himself and debated whether to hang up and get himself to the emergency room.

"Hello?" Her voice was thick, and he realized just how late it was. He shifted his phone to his other ear and looked at his watch. Almost midnight.

"Michelle? I—it's Eli. I'm sorry to call so late, but—"

"What is it?" The annoyance in her tone stung, and he swallowed hard.

"Andy. I just wanted to make sure he was okay."

"What are you talking about? Yes, he's okay," she said. She was quiet for a beat and then said, "What's going on, Eli? Has something happened?"

"I—I just wanted to make sure he's home." He paused. "We found a boy tonight, over by one of the vacation homes. Not Andy, of course, but I just wanted to—"

"He's fine. He's in bed, asleep," she said. "I heard him get up to use the bathroom a couple hours ago." She made a sound, something between a grunt and a sigh, probably to sit up. A wave of nausea swept over him and he pulled the phone away from his ear. He could hear her voice, faint and tinny. She was asking him something.

He took some deep breaths, then put the phone back to his ear. "I just needed to be sure."

"He's here. He's fine." There was concern in her voice.

"Can you have him call me tomorrow?" asked Eli. "I just want to see him. You know, give him a hug or something." He attempted a laugh.

"Are you okay, Eli? You sound sort of strange. Have you been—"

She thought he was drunk, assumed he was, and rightfully so. "I'm fine, Michelle. I just wanted to—" He lost his grip on the phone and it fell into the thick weeds beside the car. He cursed, then lowered himself to his knees and began to feel around for the phone. Michelle's voice, barely audible, came from somewhere farther into the weeds. The phone must have bounced and fallen toward the ditch. He clambered forward and yelped as a twig from one of the rangy, twisting mulberry bushes that lined the side of the road jabbed him in the face. He growled and pushed it away, only to have it recoil into his face again. Then he saw the glow of his phone screen a few feet to his left and managed to grab it and get to his feet. "I'm fine, Michelle. Not drunk."

She must have heard the edge of anger, of resentment, in his words, because she said in a flat, tired voice, "I'm going to bed now, Eli." The line went dead and he sagged against the car, wishing he had not called at all.

Cal

*C*alvin Wallace had never believed in love at first sight, but the first time he met Beth, it was as if he had recognized a familiar face in a photograph; as if, in a sea of faces that meant nothing to him, hers came into focus. Now his wife's face—a face he knew better than his own—wore a look of hurt and indignation that was only too familiar. He closed his eyes.

"Beth, please."

"You promised."

There was a note of detachment in her voice, an unsettling calm he'd not heard before, not in all the times they'd had this exact same argument in the past year. A jolt of alarm shot through him.

"I just have to go into the office for a few hours tomorrow morning," he said, and the pleading in his own voice disgusted him. "I should be able to leave in time to—"

Without a word, Beth turned away and walked down the hall. "Your father's not coming," he heard her say into their daughter's bedroom. Caitlin said something, but he couldn't make out the words.

Something awful twisted in his gut.

An hour later, when all the bags of beach gear and groceries were stowed in the back of the car, and the canoe strapped onto the roof, and the bicycles locked onto the rack, he stepped back and watched his wife and daughter pull out of the driveway and head to the cabin in Shaky Lake. When he waved goodbye, they didn't wave back.

5

Eli had never been good at hiding things from his mother. As a little boy, his face would give him away before he even had a chance to lie about whatever mischief he had gotten into. Even now, he thought she didn't know. Marge sighed and rubbed the back of her neck. It was aching more than usual lately, and she rummaged in the center console of the truck, searching for the bottle of ibuprofen she kept with her. When a few minutes of fumbling didn't produce the bottle, she gave up and slammed the console shut. Her thoughts turned back to Eli.

It used to be called shell shock or, more commonly, not talked about at all. But the governor's wife had recently taken on post-traumatic stress disorder as a pet project, and now Marge's doctor's office had posters everywhere, with a national hotline to call for support. She had been at the clinic that spring for her blood pressure checkup and scribbled the number down on a waiting room brochure when no one was looking. Months later, the brochure was still sitting in a stack of papers on her kitchen counter. She had reached for it so many times but could never bring herself to call. Calling the hotline felt like opening the door to something that had the potential to do more harm than good.

She had thought the job with the sheriff's department would be helpful. He was massively overqualified, of course, and she had hesitated to offer him the job. She didn't want to draw attention to how far he'd fallen. To go from being an elite investigator with the United States Fish and

Wildlife Service—one of fewer than two hundred such agents in the entire country—to being a sheriff's deputy in a sleepy northern Wisconsin resort town was a slap in the face, and she was loath to be the one to deliver the blow. She had watched him struggle to readjust to civilian life in the months after his return from Afghanistan, and not just because of his still-healing physical wounds. But gradually, week by week, he seemed to relax. To smile a little every now and then. To do the things he used to do—spend time with Michelle and Andy, go fishing at every opportunity, and tackle his Fish and Wildlife investigative work with the zeal of someone with an intrinsic need to get to the bottom of every unknown. Then he had been laid off. It wasn't his fault that his job was eliminated just six months after he returned from Afghanistan. But the timing could not have been worse.

She recalled the look on his face at Beran's Resort earlier that night. The sluggishness of his expression, the eyes that weren't tracking quite right. He had never been a heavy drinker, not even in college, but now . . .

The truck hit a pothole, and she winced and kneaded the back of her neck again. The ghosts of old injuries and decades of pushing herself too hard were starting to catch up with her now that she was pushing sixty, and it didn't help that her migraines had decided to return after a thirty-year hiatus. Retirement was starting to look more and more appealing. She knew that Tommy, her husband of twenty years, thought she should retire, though he never came out and said it. She had a selfish reason for offering Eli the deputy job; she needed him. She barely had the manpower to meet the law enforcement needs of Sherman County, even with him on the force. It had always been hard to hire deputies once applicants learned they would be working for a woman.

Something splatted against the windshield, and she squirted the washer fluid. The smear of lake fly carcasses momentarily clouded the glass, and she had to run the wiper blades a few more times before she could see clearly. It was at that moment that she reached the driveway to Rachel Sharpe's house. The trees along the driveway were perfectly styled and polished—professional landscaping rather than natural woods or red pine plantations—and the overall effect was like something straight out of a magazine. A minute later, the house came into view. Modern, stark white, like an alien spaceship that had landed in the middle of the woods.

Marge parked, moved her head gingerly from side to side, then got out of the truck and trudged up to the front door. After five minutes and four rings of the bell, a light came on inside the house, followed by a loud thud and, eventually, fumbling at the door.

Rachel Sharpe was clearly high. Her eyes were glassy, her pupils dilated into black pools. Her fluffy blond hair was stuck to one cheek, and a streak of dried saliva connected it all the way to the corner of her cracked lips. She was wrapped in a thick wool cardigan that was much too warm for the August weather, and her silk pajamas were crumpled and only half-buttoned. She smelled of dirty laundry and expensive perfume.

"Rachel, can I come in?"

The younger woman stared slack-faced, confused, before she understood who was standing on her doorstep. "Marge? Why are you . . ." Her voice trailed off and she tugged one hand through her ratty hair, as though the state of her hairstyle was what stood between her and presentability.

"Rachel, we need to talk. Can I come in?" The light in the foyer backlit the younger woman, shadowed her face, and Marge took a step closer to examine her more clearly. The initial look of confusion had shifted to something more wary. Fearful, even. Rachel pulled the cardigan more tightly around her and shivered, as if Marge were a gust of unseasonably cold wind. Marge, too, shook off a sudden chill that crept across the back of her neck. "It's very important, Rachel."

In response, the younger woman turned and stumbled down the hall, leaving Marge to follow her.

The house was gorgeous. Modern and rustic at the same time. Exactly what one would expect for a wealthy family's summer home. The pine floors reflected the light from simple, chic chandeliers, and the artwork was high-end and original. Abstract paintings in shades of white and tan and brown. Landscapes in hues of watery blue-gray, and rainbow-colored blown-glass sculptures on boxy pedestals. It was stylish, but with a flatness that suggested it had been purchased en masse by a designer rather than collected over the years. Marge followed Rachel into the open-

concept kitchen and living room, where the television over the fireplace
was playing some televangelist channel, on mute, and the cushions of the
sectional sofa were scattered on the floor. The room was lit only by the
television, and Marge was able to see through the floor-to-vaulted-ceiling
windows facing the lake. Unlike the steep, rocky shoreline at Beran's Resort, the backyard of the Sharpe house sloped gently down to the water,
the trees cleared to give an unobstructed view. Marge could see the dock
and boat lift, vague shapes against the blackness of the lake. No boat was
moored there tonight.

"Do you want something to drink?" Rachel's words were slurred, and
she didn't wait for an answer before she sank down onto the couch, her
back to Marge. Rachel had clearly been camping out there for a while, in
a nest of bed pillows and tangled blankets, the glass coffee table pulled
up to the edge of the couch. It was covered with dirty dishes, smudged
cocktail glasses, and an overflowing ashtray. Half a dozen prescription
pill bottles sat uncapped, and a few more were visible on the floor beneath the coffee table. A velvet-lined jewelry box, the sort that would
hold a huge diamond necklace but probably now held drugs, sat on the
glass, and there was a plate-sized splotch of something on the carpeting.
The room smelled of cigarettes and overripe fruit, and an overflowing
trash bag sat in the middle of the kitchen. The reflected light from the
television danced on the glass coffee table as the white-suited preacher
was replaced by an advertisement for expensive adjustable beds. It was a
familiar tableau—the mess, the drugs, the woman huddled on the sofa.
Only this time, Ben wasn't there. For the first time tonight, Marge's eyes
pricked with emotion. An image of the boy, lying so still in the bottom of
the boat, flashed through her mind. Witnessing violence and tragedy was
part of being in law enforcement, and she had survived nearly forty years
in her line of work by building and fiercely guarding a wall between her
own heart and soul and the suffering of others. Compartmentalization,
they called it.

It was Rachel who spoke first.

"I'm fine, Marge. I—I overdid it a little tonight, but I'll be fine." A
pause, then she looked over her shoulder at Marge and seemed to notice

the mess in the kitchen. "Ben was supposed to take the trash out this morning."

Marge's mouth was bone-dry, and she had to swallow a few times before she could speak. "Rachel, something very bad has happened." Her heart hammered in her chest and she gripped the back of the couch. "We found a boy who died, and I believe it's Ben." She watched the younger woman's face for a reaction. Horror or panic or disbelief. Something, anything, that mirrored her own emotions. Instead, Rachel just looked away and began to rummage through the jewelry box. Bottles scattered across the coffee table and onto the floor, but she paid no notice. With frantic, shaking hands, she pulled a plastic bag from behind the velvet lining. Marge circled the sectional until she stood in front of Rachel, then dropped to a squat and plucked the bag from her hand.

"When is the last time you saw Ben?" asked Marge, fending off Rachel's fumbling attempt to grab the bag.

Rachel seemed to realize that getting her drugs back was a lost cause. She sagged into the couch and wiped a sleeve across her nose. Her eyes brimmed with tears and mingled with yesterday's—or perhaps the day before that's—eye makeup, giving her a beaten-up look. "This morning." She rubbed her eyes and then sat, bent over, face in her hands. "He said he was going to go boating with a friend," she said, her voice muffled behind her hands.

"That's the last time you saw him? You're sure?"

Rachel began to rock back and forth, head still buried in her hands, and her breath came faster and faster. Marge sat down next to her on the sofa and put a steadying arm around the younger woman. She could feel the bones in Rachel's back and shoulders, sharp under the skin, birdlike and fragile. It occurred to Marge that she had never tried to learn more about Rachel, about her life, about how she had gotten to the point she was at—addicted to heroin and cocaine and who knew what else. It was always Ben who Marge had cared about. Ben, who had been forced to deal with his mother's overdoses and instability. There hadn't been much Marge could do for the boy over the years—he lived in Shaky Lake only during the summer—other than call to check on him when she could, and stop by the house from time to time. She had repeatedly called Ben's stepfather, Chuck, who was often back home in Minneapolis, and his response, in not so many words, had been to tell Marge to mind her own business. Ben's parents had always seemed like villains in the background through all of this, but looking at the woman in front of her, Marge saw something that hinted at what awful circumstances Rachel Sharpe might have faced in her life.

Suddenly Rachel's eyes rolled back in her head and she began to thrash and shake, beginning with her shoulders, then moving down to her limbs. She opened and closed her mouth, as if her air supply was being cut off. Marge knew it wasn't the first time Rachel had had a drug-related seizure—Rachel's cocaine addiction rivaled that of her heroin addiction—but it was disturbing nonetheless. She pulled out her phone and dialed, her fingers slipping on the screen so that she needed to redial twice before she got it right.

"Phil, I'm going to need an ambulance." She rattled off the address and a few details of the situation. The younger woman's shaking grew more sluggish, and after a few seconds, she went completely limp, like a marionette tossed in a corner. Marge took her by the shoulders and gently propped her upright on the couch. Rachel gave her a look of profound confusion. She seemed to want to say something to Marge, but the words came out as nothing more than the slow-motion gaping of a fish.

"Rachel, I'm here. Help is on the way."

Twenty minutes later, paramedics were loading Rachel, limp and confused, into the ambulance while Marge spoke on the phone with the emergency room doctor at St. Anne's Hospital. Once she was done, and the ambulance was gone, she trudged back into the house and proceeded to empty the contents of the little plastic bag of drugs—cocaine, from the looks of it—into the trash, tie up the bag, and haul it out to the can in the garage.

6

Eli shifted the car into drive and eased his way to the shoreline, where the gravel lot met the lip of the concrete seawall that protected the land from the lake. It was a straight drop down to the water—a good ten feet—with no barrier and another sixteen feet of water below it. The boat launch was deserted. He'd had to pull over twice on the drive from the cabin to vomit, and his ribs hurt from the force of retching. The pain was nothing compared to the agony in his head, though. It didn't take a neurologist to make the diagnosis of a concussion. Maybe making important decisions after a blow to the head wasn't the best idea.

He tipped his head back against the seat and considered all that had happened tonight, the questions of why and how. The noise disturbance. The boy in the boat. There had been a time when he would have been energized by such a puzzle, when his skills of investigation had been finely honed, underscored by his deeply ingrained need to discover the truth.

Marge could manage the investigation without him. She didn't need his help. Would be better off without it. Michelle, too. All he did was make things harder for her. Alarm bells sounded in a remote part of his brain. These were not safe thoughts.

How do those words make you feel?
Tired.

Too tired to put the car in park. Too tired to keep his foot on the brake pedal. Too tired to keep fighting for a life he might never get back. The alarm bells rang more loudly, and he opened his eyes. The nose of the car was so close to the seawall that he could see only water, not land, through his windshield. From across the lake, he heard the sound of a boat engine revving and the clatter and shouts of people loading up for an early morning fishing trip. It was a good hour before sunrise, but the eastern horizon had lightened to indigo. He heard the rustle and splash of birds taking their first swim of the day. He let go of the wheel and lifted his foot off the pedal.

His phone rang and he instinctively slammed on the brake. His car crunched to a halt on the gravel. He glanced at his phone, propped in the center console. His mother. He let it go to voice mail, then closed his eyes and took deep breaths until his heart stopped slamming in his chest.

Another ring.

Too tired.

In that instant, there was nothing in the world he wanted more than to sleep, which the rational part of his brain recognized as a classic symptom of a head injury.

His phone pinged. Marge again.

Call me ASAP. It's urgent.

Just a few more feet. He reached for the phone to turn it off, but it slipped through his hands and landed on the floor with a thud. He held up his hand and saw that it was slick with perspiration, then felt a sheet of sweat pour down his back and knew he was going to be sick. Just in time, he remembered to put the car in park, then pushed the door open and skidded onto his palms in the gravel. His phone rang again and he cursed.

The gravel dug into his knees as he turned and reached into the car for his phone.

"Hello?" He winced at the deafening sound of his own voice.

"Where are you? I'm at your apartment." Through the pounding in his head, he could hear a note of anxiety in Marge's voice.

"I'm—" He angled the phone away from his mouth and gagged, then braced a hand against his thigh and doubled over. His skin erupted in goose bumps that seemed to lift his sweat-soaked clothes right off his skin. "I'm fine." His voice sounded thick and decidedly not fine.

Marge was quiet for a moment. "You didn't pick up, so I was worried that—"

"I'm fine," he said again, then lowered himself to a seated position and leaned back against the cruiser. He dropped the phone again, fumbled for it in the early morning gloom, then put it back to his ear in time to catch the end of what Marge was saying.

"—which she says is completely out of character for her daughter."

"Sorry, can you say that again?"

A pause. "Are you sure you're—"

"Seriously, Mom."

Another pause, longer this time. "A woman named Beth Wallace just called to report that her daughter is missing."

Eli blinked. Blinked again and considered whether he had misunderstood. He touched the lump on the back of his head for the millionth time. He should definitely go to the emergency room. "The woman who's staying at Beran's?"

"Her daughter Caitlin didn't come home tonight."

Eli looked toward the lake. Beran's Resort was on the eastern shore, visible from here in daylight but now just part of the purple-black smudge of distant shoreline. He pictured Beth Wallace, smiling at him in the light from the cabin door last night. Bad things didn't happen to people like her.

He looked at his watch. Five o'clock. How long had he been at the boat launch?

"Caitlin left early yesterday morning to go boating," said Marge. There was a pause. "With Ben Sharpe."

Neither one of them spoke for a very long time, and it occurred to him that Marge was waiting for him to respond.

"Mom, I . . ."

"Eli, I need your help."

Her voice was low, with an edge of unease that he sensed had nothing to do with Caitlin Wallace. It was as if she'd read his thoughts, as if she knew what he had almost done just a few minutes ago. That was impossible, of course, but if she did know, she wouldn't want him working a case with her. Especially not a case like this. An eternity ago, he would have been up for the challenge, but now he was just too tired. He opened his mouth to tell her no. To tell her he was headed to the emergency room and that he couldn't work the case; head injury. She wouldn't argue with him, or guilt-trip him. She would tell him it was the smart decision. She asked so little of him.

He cleared his throat, but his voice still sounded scraggy and forced. "I'll be at the station at seven."

7

Eli's apartment sat above Trixie's Liquor on the last block of Water Street, just before the concrete curbs and paving dissolved into pot-holed gravel and then into pine forest. Shaky Lake had dozens of liquor-selling establishments, but Trixie's—owned and operated by a Hmong family for the past ten years—catered to the local crowd rather than the wine- and craft-beer-drinking vacationers. The front windows were plastered with discount offers for alcohol and tobacco products, and the dumpster behind the store was crammed with empty packing crates of Busch and Pabst and bottom-rail liquor. The gravel parking lot was dotted with tufts of crabgrass and tattered late-summer dandelions. It was bare in places where rainwater runoff had washed the stone away, leaving instead soft, sandy channels that squished under the tires of the cruiser as Eli pulled in. He wedged his way into his designated park-ing spot next to the dumpster and pulled up until the front of the car was four feet deep in the embrace of the feral crab-apple tree that hung over the parking lot. Eli leaned back in his seat and took in the scent of the damp morning gravel and the tree-house sensation of the crab-apple branches pressed thickly against the windshield. It was peaceful. He would have just rested in the car for an hour if he hadn't stunk like sweat and lake water.

The wooden stairway, newly built and still heavy with the scent of chemical weatherproofing agent, laddered its way up the exterior of the building toward a small landing. The gutter on the overhanging roof was twisted and punctured, probably from a fallen tree branch, and when it rained, the water dripped directly onto the stairway. Every time Eli went up or down it, he frowned at the prospect of ice-slick stairs this coming winter and made a mental note to talk to the landlord about getting the gutter fixed.

When he reached the top of the stairway, he pulled his keys from his pocket and nearly dropped them off the landing—his hands still trembled every time he opened his front door. Finally he managed to unlock the handle, the dead bolt, and the electronic keypad lock he had installed the day he moved in, then stood on the threshold and listened for a full two minutes until, satisfied that the place was empty, he entered and locked the door behind him. A memory came to him, unbidden, of the days when he never locked his front door.

The place was two bedrooms and nice enough so that Andy could stay if he wanted, which, in the month since Eli moved in, had not happened. The boy's room was furnished with a brand-new full-size bed and a matching nightstand and dresser; a flat-screen television and a Play-Station, still in their boxes, sat on the floor in the corner.

Eli locked the door and threw his keys on the kitchen counter, then began to peel off his clothes on the way to the bathroom. The hot water in the apartment was a little iffy, and he was forced to shiver his way through a lukewarm shower. Once done, he toweled off, feeling more exhausted than refreshed. He checked his watch and, seeing that he had an hour before he had to be back at the station, crawled into bed and wrapped himself in the threadbare wool blanket. He lay there, eyes closed, wet hair soaking through his pillow. The room was cold and his flesh moved across his bones in a wave of goose bumps.

The ache in his head wasn't quite as crippling now, and he played the scenes of the night over and over in his mind. No words, only images, like a silent film or a macabre picture book. Not like the nightmares he had suffered with each and every attempt at sleep since he had returned from Afghanistan. Those were anything but silent. Then, tentatively, as if analytical thoughts might worsen the pain in his head, he considered what he had seen tonight. He ran through possible explanations but kept coming back to what, to him anyway, threw doubt on the idea that the boy's death could have been natural or accidental. Thoughts that suggested there was more to this story; Etta James, the bright, wide-open, deserted cabin, and now Caitlin Wallace missing. The more he tried to organize his thoughts, the more they ricocheted back and forth in his brain.

He reached to the plastic storage tub full of clothes that served as a bedside table and picked up his watch, then cursed when he saw the time. He sat up too quickly and was struck with a wave of nausea. After a moment, his vision steadied and he was met with his own reflection in the cheap full-length mirror bolted to the back of the bedroom door. It had come with the place and was usually covered by his bathrobe. He avoided reminders of his own existence as much as possible these days. But the robe was crumpled on the floor beside the door, out of reach, and he was forced to watch himself stand up. Something made him pause and not look away. He was tall, wide-shouldered, capable-looking, with his mother's thick, coppery hair and acorn-brown eyes. His army buddies had mocked him as a pretty boy until they saw that he worked harder and more effectively than anyone else.

He reached over to flip on the overhead light and took a step closer to the mirror. His pupils contracted quickly and symmetrically to the sudden brightness. He checked himself for lingering effects of his fall; other than a brutal headache, a feeling akin to seasickness, and the suspicion that he might have cracked a rib, he decided he was more or less all right.

He had made a promise to Marge.

8

Eli looked around the conference room, if it could be called that. The windowless space was wedged between a boiler room and a matching pair of jail cells in a building that had once been a general store on Shaky Lake's main street. The building was picturesque on the outside, three stories high with a red-granite brick facade and white-trimmed windows. It was flanked on one side by the broad awning—striped in Green Bay Packers green and gold—of Coach's Sports Pub & Grill, and on the other side by the jutting, two-sided, charmingly dingy exterior of the Main Street Cinema. Shaky Lake's downtown had fared much better over the years than most small Wisconsin towns. There was a smattering of dead storefronts, but up and down the half-mile-long street were shops selling ice cream, high-end camping gear, pottery, locally produced wine and cheese, and overpriced clothing. Laminated signs in store windows advertised vacation property for sale, boats for sale, and all-inclusive guided fishing trips. Restaurants served everything from bespoke sandwiches to greasy-spoon fare to pricey steak to Chinese takeout. And, this being Wisconsin, there was tavern after tavern, their windows bright with neon lights in the shape of beer logos—Pabst, Schlitz, Leinenkugel's. The Shaky Lake Garden Club had an army of volunteers to plant and tend to the baskets of cascading petunias that hung from every third lamppost, and whiskey-barrel planters of geraniums and pint-sized fir trees sat next to wrought-iron benches at regular intervals down the street.

In contrast, the sheriff's station was decrepit and dated on the inside. The space smelled of damp wood and old plumbing, and the 1970s-era vinyl flooring was so heavily worn that it had begun to peel away from the floor, exposing what was undoubtedly asbestos. The actual station was in the basement, plus a dusty reception area on the first floor that was rarely staffed by anything more than a cheap desk bell and a sign that advised visitors to please call 911 with any emergencies. The second-floor occupant of the building was a small accounting firm, and above that were a couple of small apartments that Eli suspected were being used as illegal short-term vacation rentals.

The state of the sheriff's office was clear evidence that the taxpayers of Sherman County felt safe in their beds, as the county board of directors had gradually cut the department budget down to practically nothing. The entire staff consisted of himself, Marge, Jake Howard, and Phil Schulz. Enough manpower to do next to nothing. If asked about the skeleton crew she was given to work with, Marge would just shrug and say it was a good thing they couldn't afford more staff, because there wasn't enough room in the office for anyone else.

Eli fidgeted with his travel mug, which was filled with gas station coffee rather than his typical hair-of-the-dog concoction. It had taken all his willpower not to reach into his liquor cabinet this morning, but he knew that head injuries and alcohol were a very bad combination. His sheriff's department baseball cap hadn't fit over the goose egg on the back of his head, and he felt strangely naked without it. He felt Marge's eyes on him from across the room and glanced up to see her looking at him with knitted brows. Most people would look away, or at least look embarrassed at being caught staring, but when Marge's eyes met his, her questioning look seemed to deepen. She moved as if to come around the table to where he sat, but then stopped, her eyes going to something behind him.

Eli felt a hand on his shoulder and turned to find Jake Howard frowning down at him.

"How're you doing, man?" asked Jake. The smell of tobacco lingered on his hand from the cigarette he must have smoked in the parking lot just before coming inside. "That was an awful scene last night. Sorry you had to be the one to find him." He gave Eli's shoulder a rough squeeze and lowered himself into a chair.

Out of the corner of his eye, Eli saw Marge give him one long last look. Then she returned to where she had been standing at the head of the conference room table. Eli studied the plastic mug in his hands and didn't look at Jake. "I'm okay. I just want to get moving on this, you know?"

Jake nodded. "It's the waiting that messes with you."

Eli darted a quick look at him. Jake was a big guy, meaty in a way that comes naturally rather than from time spent in a gym. He spoke in a broad, rasping accent that was peculiar to the Upper Peninsula of Michigan and sounded how one would imagine a native-born Finn with a modest grasp of the English language might sound. He never wore a coat, and even on the coldest day of the year, wouldn't wear more than a long-sleeved shirt. In the summer, he was downright miserable and grumbled often about the absence of fresh lake air, by which he meant that deepest and coldest of freshwater bodies, Lake Superior.

Jake was the closest thing to a friend Eli had had since returning from his deployment—more than just a drinking buddy, although drinking always seemed to factor into their time together. He was a terrible fisherman, but, like Eli, he had been a soldier. Eli had asked Jake about his military service, his experiences, how he had dealt with the punishing heat of Iraq, and his friend had laughed. "The IEDs keep your mind off the weather." Jake was a few years younger than Eli, with a scar on his neck and the left side of his face where he had been hit with a roadside bomb in Fallujah. Eli studied it when Jake turned to look at his phone. The scar tissue was raised and extended from cheekbone to jawline, then slanted diagonally to the base of his throat. The skin was white in places, the stitching like the legs of a centipede, fanned out and fossilized. It gave the unsettling impression that Jake's head had been blown off, then simply stitched back on.

Marge leaned against the battered conference table and tapped a dry-erase marker against her thigh, then crossed the room to where Phil was slumped in a chair in the back corner, nursing a cup of coffee. He'd been on duty for a day and a half and looked awful. The skin on his already pale, pinched face drooped, and the bags beneath his bloodshot blue eyes seemed to have doubled in size since Eli had seen him the previous day. He and Marge spoke for a few minutes, too quietly for Eli to make out what they were saying. He knew Phil wanted him gone, that he kept Marge well-informed of the dispatches to Eli that went unanswered, of the missed shifts and whiskey fumes. Marge had never said anything to Eli about his job performance, or lack thereof, but he knew she would have fired him by now if he weren't her son. Most days, he wished she would. Years of surveillance experience had made Eli a world-class eavesdropper, but try as he might, he couldn't make out what Marge and Phil were saying, although Phil seemed to think that his scowling glances at Eli were going unnoticed. He couldn't blame the guy for hating him.

Marge said one last thing to Phil, something that left him looking petulant and even more exhausted than he had a few minutes ago. She returned to her place at the head of the table. "Let's get started." She slid a pair of glasses on and opened a manila folder, then pulled out a few sheets of paper and handed them out. "As you know," she said, with her typical lack of preamble, "a boy was found dead last night in a boat moored at Beran's Resort. He has been identified as sixteen-year-old Benjamin Sharpe, of Minneapolis." The way she phrased that last piece of information made Eli suspect that Marge herself had been the one to officially identify him. She turned to clip a photograph of the boy to the dry-erase board on the wall behind her. "Cause of death is still unknown at this time, pending the medical exam."

Eli forced himself to look at the photo of Ben Sharpe. It was a selfie, slightly blurry. The boy's dishwater-brown hair was worn a little shaggy in front, and there was a hint of stubble on his chin and a smile that showed a gap between his two front teeth. At first glance, the smile was unremarkable, forgettable, like a million other selfies. But just beneath the surface, something was off. A forced casualness, a nearly concealed hypervigilance in the boy's eyes, like a bodyguard in a crowd. The boy's gaze was directed toward the camera, and yet distracted. His arm was curled around the shoulders of a woman—blond and alarmingly skinny, with heavy makeup that made it difficult to judge her age. The two of them had the same pronounced V-shaped chins and hazel eyes, though her smile was tight-lipped, her eyes heavy with eyeliner and focused on something off-camera. In the background was a lake and a sliver of somebody else, a little off to the side. Eli squinted to see better, but the figure stood against the sun and was nothing more than a silhouette.

The photo was unsettling. Cryptic. Eli shivered and looked away, tried to focus on what Marge was saying. He couldn't help comparing his own mother to the fragile woman in the photo, clearly Ben Sharpe's mother. Marge wasn't beautiful, but her hair—the same russet color as Eli's—had only recently developed a strand or two of silver, and her smooth face belied her nearly sixty years. She was tiny but commanding, and a lifetime of being underestimated had given her an unshakable fortitude. Growing up, it had just been the two of them. His father—also in law enforcement—had been killed in the line of duty when Eli was three, and his memories of the man were nothing more than a handful of shadows. People were often shocked to learn that Eli, massive and imposing at six foot three, two hundred and fifty pounds, was Marge's son. The running joke was that she had somehow managed to give birth to a giant. "He was a lot smaller back then," she would say. "Must take after his father," they would say, to which Marge's perennial response was to change the subject.

"Ben Sharpe was last seen yesterday morning, around seven o'clock, by his mother, Rachel Sharpe." Marge gestured at the blond woman in the photo, then pulled another page from the stack on her desk and tacked it up next to Ben's photo. "His friend, a sixteen-year-old girl named Caitlin Wallace, is now missing. Her mother, Beth Wallace, called me around two this morning. She and Caitlin have been staying at Beran's Resort since Friday night. She said her daughter has gone boating with Ben Sharpe every day since they arrived, but last night Caitlin didn't come back. Mrs. Wallace hasn't been able to reach her by phone or email or social media. They're from Skokie, Illinois, a suburb of Chicago." The photo of Caitlin was of her standing between her parents, the three of them tanned and sporty, with a backdrop of what looked to be the Grand Canyon. The man Eli assumed to be Mr. Wallace wore a T-shirt emblazoned with WALK TO END ALZHEIMER'S. Caitlin's smile was wide, childlike, and goofy, though she was almost as tall as her mother. She had the same golden-brown hair as her father, and it hung in a long braid over her shoulder like a stem of wheat. It was a wholesome, happy scene. A loving family, with none of the tension, none of the uneasiness that pervaded the Sharpes' photo.

Jake leaned forward for a closer look at the photo. "That's Dad, I assume?" He looked at Marge.

She nodded. "Calvin Wallace. According to Beth, he was supposed to have come with them to Shaky Lake on Friday, but at the last minute, he stayed in Chicago for work." Marge uncapped her marker and made columns on the whiteboard. "As you all know, investigations of missing children must proceed without a waiting period. Phil reported Caitlin's disappearance to the NCIC and sent out an Amber Alert and missing person posters." She wrote a list of information on the board, bullet point by bullet point, then turned around. "I've come up with our investigation plan, and I think what will work best is— Oh, for god's sake, Jake, if you have something on your mind, just say it."

"Marge," said Jake, hands held wide, "how the hell are we going to investigate this? Just the four of us?" He looked around to see if Eli or Phil mirrored his concern. "I just don't see how—"

Marge put the cap back on her marker and held it up, cutting Jake off. "The county has agreed to pay for some outside help, so I've arranged for Wisconsin Forensics Solutions to process the scene. The volunteer search-and-rescue team from Eau Claire is getting started as we speak, and Chris at the DNR said they'll help with water search and do flyovers if we need them." She looked at Jake in a way that made it clear things weren't up for discussion. She leveled a finger at him. "You're doing door-to-doors. Phil is going to man the station and keep all the moving pieces organized."

She turned back to the whiteboard and transcribed names from her notebook onto it, a list under each child's photo. She put stars next to several names and then faced the deputies again. "These are the people we need to talk to first. Ben's and Caitlin's parents, of course, and also Kim and Mike Beran. I'm hoping this will at least give us a starting point. Eli, I'll need your help with interviews." She hesitated and seemed about to say something, then decided against it. He got the sense that she had been about to ask him whether he was okay with this assignment but realized before she spoke that to do so would imply that he might not be up to the job.

I'm not.

The department didn't exactly have a deep bench these days, though, and hopefully he was still better than nothing. He gave Marge a nod, then happened to glance at Phil and saw the expression of frank distrust on the other man's face. There was a beat of awkward silence, as if everyone was waiting for Phil to challenge the idea of Eli being given any amount of responsibility. Finally Marge continued.

"As Jake pointed out," she said, "we're only four people, not to mention that the day-to-day law enforcement needs of Sherman County aren't just going to wait until we've wrapped up this investigation." She sat and folded her hands on the table. "We need help, and the fact that this case has become a missing child situation means the FBI can get involved. They're sending Agent"—she checked her notes—"Agent Mason from Chicago, who will be here around six tonight."

Jake pulled a face. "Couldn't we just get some help from the Melvin County Sheriff's Department?"

"The FBI reached out to me, actually," Marge said. "Just after the missing persons alert went out for Caitlin Wallace. This was their idea, and I'm not exactly in the position to turn down help."

Jake cracked open a giant can of Red Bull and tipped it toward Marge, as if in a toast. "As always, Sheriff, I'm yours to command."

For the first time all morning, Marge smiled. "That's the spirit." She turned to Eli. "I need you to talk to Beth Wallace first, then Mike and Kim. Then you can—"

"Marge, are you sure this is a good idea?" said Phil. "Eli doing interviews?" He looked around the room, and his eyes grew defensive. "What? I'm just saying what we're all thinking. We can't afford to mess up this investigation." He met Eli's eyes. "No offense."

Every muscle in Eli's body went rigid. Phil's words were cutting, but his visible disgust was far worse. Before Eli could respond, Jake shot to his feet.

"What the fuck, man?" Jake's fists clenched at his sides. "That's over the line."

"Sit down, Jake." Marge held up a hand to silence him, then turned to the corner. "Go home, Phil. Get some rest." Phil looked about to argue, but his words died on his lips at the look on Marge's face. She was clearly losing her patience. "I want everyone back here at six o'clock tonight." She picked up her notes and folders, spun on her heel, and stomped toward her office. Without turning around, she barked, "Eli, get in here."

Eli was grateful for an excuse to walk away from Jake and Phil—he suspected they weren't done arguing yet—and followed Marge into her tiny office. He watched as she rummaged around in the old steel file cabinet in the corner.

"There they are," she said, and pulled two tape recorders from the lowest drawer. She slammed the drawer and the whole unit wobbled. "I knew we still had them."

She plunked them onto the desk. Ancient tape recorders, big as bread loaves, with scuffed black cases and yellowed donkey teeth for keys. Marge pressed experimentally on a faded orange button and the lid creaked open. "We'd have to find some blank tape cassettes—"

"Mom, these things are older than me." Eli flipped one of the recorders over and read the label. "Literally older than me." He set the antiquated device back on the desk. "Technology budget a bit tight these days?"

"A bit." She dumped the recorders back into the file cabinet and shut the drawer. "I'll save them for the next time the *Antiques Roadshow* is in town." She sat down at her desk and gestured for him to take the seat across from her, then began to dig around in her desk drawer.

He lowered himself into the chair. "Mom, I—"

Thwack. Marge slapped a notebook on the desk in front of him. "Now," she said, "let me tell you about Ben Sharpe." She was quiet for a moment, then said, "He was a good kid. A really good kid."

"How did you know him?"

Marge frowned. "His mom is . . . not well. Drugs. The first time she overdosed, he called 911 and I was first on the scene. He rode with me to the hospital. The poor kid was only eleven, scared shitless, trying to be brave. It was heartbreaking. After that, I gave him my number and told him to call me if he needed anything. I gave him some Narcan too, for when she OD'd again. Taught him how to recognize that she was overdosing, how to use the Narcan, how to position her so that she didn't choke on her own vomit."

"She overdosed again after that?"

Marge's frown deepened. "Multiple times, and that was just in the summers. Who knows what happened the rest of the year back in Minneapolis."

"Jesus."

"I made a point of checking on him and Rachel when I could. Here he was, just a kid, trying to keep his mom safe. He used to ride his bike all the way to Red River Falls because the public health clinic there gives out free clean needles for injection drug users." She propped her elbows on the desk. "I talked to Ben's stepfather, I called Child Protective Services, but nothing changed. There were times I almost scooped him up and took him myself. No kid deserves to go through what he went through. And now—"

Eli couldn't remember the last time he'd seen a look like that on his mother's face. Maybe never. He shivered.

"It's not your fault," he said, knowing she would never believe that.

She looked past him, her brows pinched. Then her eyes flicked to his. "I know Rachel Sharpe is suffering from addiction, but—" She shook her head.

Eli considered this a moment. "Do you think she may actually be responsible for Ben's death? In a literal sense, I mean?"

"I can't imagine her being violent," said Marge. "From what I saw last night, she can barely take care of herself these days."

They were both quiet for a moment. Then Marge cleared her throat and sat up straight in her chair. "It's frustrating. We have—what?—half a dozen overdoses a month in Sherman County alone, but we only have the law enforcement resources for damage control." She gestured to the file cabinet where the decades-obsolete tape recorders were stored. "No capacity for any investigation. For actually tracking down dealers." She pulled off her glasses and tossed them on the table, then rubbed a fist across her eyes.

"I wish I could have met him," said Eli.

Marge let out a long breath and stared at the ceiling.

"Look, Mom," he continued, "I know you don't want to talk about it, but maybe Phil's right." He leaned forward, put a hand on the desk, but she cut him off.

"I told you what I need you to do."

Eli took a deep breath, let it out. At this point, he would agree to anything just to escape the look on her face. He got to his feet. "Back at six?"

She gave a curt nod, then pushed the notebook and pen toward him. "Now go."

He reached for the notebook but stopped when Marge reached across the desk and grabbed his hand.

"Eli." She folded his big hand into her two small ones. Her face trembled, just for a fraction of a second, and then she squeezed his hand with surprising strength. "Don't be late."

9

Chuck Sharpe sat at the table in the interrogation room, elbows propped on the scuffed surface, chin resting on his folded hands. He looked up when Marge swept into the room. "Sheriff." He got to his feet and extended a hand. "Chuck Sharpe."

Marge shook his hand. "Dr. Sharpe. My condolences on the loss of your stepson."

He dipped his head. "Thank you." He waited for her to sit and then followed suit. The molded plastic desk chair, once white, was almond-colored with age, and it creaked and popped as he sat back down.

Marge set her folder and notebook on the table and studied him for a moment. He looked to be in his early fifties, balding, with the compact frame and leathery skin of someone who does triathlons in his spare time. He had a well-pressed appearance, as if he had just stepped out of a mens-wear catalog—purple-and-gray-checked button-down, navy linen sport coat, perfectly broken-in leather messenger bag resting against the chair leg. The planes of his lean face were sharp, the skin drawn so tightly over the bones that the hollows of his cheeks and temples were dark with shadows. She had learned through a quick internet search that he was a highly re-garded surgeon at the Veterans Affairs hospital in Minneapolis, and Marge was surprised to find that the arrogance she had expected from him—from any physician, really—was absent in his gaze and his posture. Instead, there was a stillness about Chuck Sharpe that she found difficult to interpret.

Marge pulled out her phone and set it on the table between them. "Dr. Sharpe, I'll need a statement from you, and then I have several questions to go through."

It was a fraction of a beat before he responded. "Yes, of course, Sheriff." He pressed his lips together and nodded. "I want to help in any way possible."

Marge hit the record button on her phone. "If you can please state your name and your relationship to the deceased."

"My name is Charles Sharpe. Ben was my stepson. I married his mother eight years ago."

She nodded. "And can you confirm your whereabouts yesterday between the hours of noon and eight p.m.?"

"I was in surgery all afternoon at the VA hospital in Minneapolis. Then I went home around eight. I'm sure there are people who can verify this."

"Hmm." She had, in fact, already confirmed his alibi with the hospital administrator. Airtight, with hospital security camera footage to prove it. She watched him carefully. "When is the last time you talked to Ben?"

"It would have been"—he paused, considering—"it would have been this past weekend. Saturday. We spoke on the phone."

"What did you talk about?"

"His mother." He shifted in his seat again. "I should probably tell you that Rachel and I are getting a divorce."

"You and Ben talked about Rachel?" Marge tilted her head to the side. "Can you be more specific?"

Sharpe traced a finger along a deep scratch in the table and didn't look up. "I decided to stay home in Minneapolis this summer, and I wanted to get Ben's opinion on how Rachel was doing. She has . . . health issues."

"What sort of health issues?"

He pulled his hand away from the desk and looked up, though he didn't meet Marge's eye. A tinge of color appeared on his face. "Rachel has substance abuse issues. She's getting care, but—"

"But?" asked Marge when he didn't continue.

"But things haven't necessarily gone smoothly all of the time."

"Were you and Ben close?"

For the first time, a flicker of emotion passed over his face. "Not as close as we—as I—should have been. He insisted on staying with Rachel this summer."

"Seems unusual for a teenager."

She thought of how Eli had come home from college in the summer to be with her, rather than stay in Chicago with his friends, before she had married Tommy. "His mother has struggled for the past . . . several . . . years, and he wanted to make sure she was okay. My work kept me away a lot"—he looked uneasily at Marge—"so Ben kept me updated when I couldn't be with her."

"Did it concern you that your wife frequently used drugs around Ben? That she overdosed, on multiple occasions, in front of him? In fact, she was intoxicated when I saw her last night."

His face went a shade whiter. "I—" He swallowed once, twice, and when he spoke, it was nearly a whisper. "Ben never told me that. He said"—Sharpe rubbed a hand across his mouth—"that she was going to her therapy appointments. That she was doing okay." He fixed Marge with a pleading look. "He said she was okay."

Marge had met countless liars, could smell them, and Chuck Sharpe was not lying. She felt a flash of anger. If he hadn't known what was going on with Rachel, it was because he didn't want to know, she decided. Instead, he had left it all on a young boy's shoulders and looked the other way. She set her hands, clenched into fists, in her lap before Sharpe could see them. She forced herself to relax.

"Does your wife have friends here? People she spends time with?"

"She's at the country club almost every day in the summer," answered Sharpe, still a bit pale, "so I'd imagine she has friends there. I don't know who they would be. Maybe some of the other doctors' wives?" He sounded skeptical, as though the idea of doctors' wives accepting his wife into their social circles was a dubious prospect, at best.

"Any extramarital affairs?"

He blinked at her, surprised by the blunt question. He made a moue of distaste. "Probably. She spends the summer in a bikini by the pool at the club." He shook his head. "To be honest, I didn't want to know. Our relationship hasn't been . . ." He paused. "Like I said, we're getting a divorce."

Marge chewed her lip, considering. "Doctor, I hope you don't mind me asking, but—how is it that you and Rachel ended up together? It doesn't seem like you have much in common." She thought of her own marriage to Tommy, born and raised on the South Side of Chicago.

He sighed. "Rachel was a nurse at the VA hospital in Minneapolis." He was quiet for a moment, and when he spoke, there was a hint of sadness in his voice. "She was a great nurse. Smart, compassionate. Someone who could do ten things at once without missing a beat."

"Did she have issues with drugs and alcohol back then?" asked Marge.

"She liked to drink. Nothing I'd consider extreme, though. But after we were married for about a year, she hurt her back at work. She had to take a leave of absence. She—she was given narcotic pain medication."

There was something odd about his phrasing, the passive voice. That she was "given" the medication. Marge raised an eyebrow. "Given by whom?"

He opened his mouth, hesitated, then said, "By—by her doctor. It was all completely appropriate. But"—he clasped his hands together—"she kept needing more. Higher doses, more potent drugs." He met Marge's eyes. "It was like she became a sociopath when she started using narcotics. Lying, cheating, stealing. Whatever it took to get more. Finally her doctor cut her off."

"And that's when the heroin started," said Marge. It was a story she had heard over and over again. So many overdoses, and they always seemed to start with a prescription.

His silence was acknowledgment. "It's why we bought the lake house," he said. "To be close to Wildwood Clinic. Rachel is in an addiction management program there. They're the best in the country."

"She had pill bottles everywhere when I went to the house last night," said Marge, "and I couldn't help but notice that one of them was Oxy-Contin." In the course of the past several years, she had become very familiar with seeing that particular drug in the homes of people who overdosed. "It had her name on the bottle, though. Surely she's not still being prescribed opioids."

He held up his hands. "I'm not directly involved in her medical care."

"Aren't her doctors at Wildwood aware of her other drug use?"

He looked thoughtful for a moment. "They must know. She always complains about the urine drug-screening tests. It's multiple times per week, she says."

"But"—Marge shook her head—"but they keep prescribing. It makes no sense." After a moment's pause, she said, "Do you prescribe opioids, Dr. Sharpe? You perform surgery, so I would imagine it goes with the territory."

His eyes widened and he spluttered. "Yes, but—what does that have to do with—"

She waved his question away. "I'm obviously not a healthcare provider, but it just seems strange that Rachel's doctors would keep prescribing her these strong drugs, knowing that she's using heroin."

"There's a new drug coming to market soon. A treatment for opioid addiction." His tone brightened at the slight detour from the topic at hand. "It's called Salvare, and they say it's a miracle drug."

She lifted a sardonic brow. "Sounds expensive." She thumbed through the notebook in front of her. "Rachel's currently at St. Anne's Hospital. I spoke with the physician an hour ago." She ran a finger down the page. "Dr. Kouris," she read. "Apparently, he's very familiar with her case. She's one of his most hands-on patients. He said—" She was about to continue when she happened to glance up at Sharpe.

The man's face was white, and splotches of red had materialized on his neck and jawline. He dragged the sleeve of his coat across his forehead and it came away damp with sweat. Marge stared at him, caught off guard by his sudden change in demeanor, by the unmistakable expression on his weathered face.

Fear.

"What was"—Sharpe moistened dry lips—"the cause of Ben's death?"

Marge considered how to answer the question, *whether* to answer the question. She felt a needle-prick of alarm, and that, combined with her anger—it was, she admitted to herself, anger—toward Chuck Sharpe made her want to keep from him the details of what had happened to Ben; made her feel as if he didn't deserve to know. Still, she reminded herself, he was the boy's stepfather, and, perhaps more to the point, she needed any and all information she could get if she was to learn the truth about what had happened to Ben.

"Autopsy results aren't back yet," she said, "but there were signs of head trauma." She hadn't mentioned that particular detail—she had been there when the paramedics removed the body, had seen the blood on the back of the boy's head—to Eli, although she would be hard-pressed to explain why.

The dismayed look on Sharpe's face grew worse, and it was a moment before he continued, his voice thick. "Do you mean that someone killed him?"

She made a noncommittal sound. "We can't be sure at this point." She set her hands on the table, mirroring his posture. For the next half minute, the only sound was the ticking of the cheap wall clock.

Marge spoke first. "Dr. Sharpe," she said, her voice soft, "what happened to Ben?"

It was a long time before he spoke, and when he did, his voice was shaky. "I don't know."

A pause. Marge kept her voice neutral, but her eyes were locked on his face. "Is there anyone who might have wanted to hurt Ben or Rachel?"

He swallowed hard and shook his head. "I don't know."

Marge tapped her pen on the table and gave him a questioning look, then stood up. She paced back and forth across the small room, eyes fixed on the floor. "Could Rachel have been involved, even peripherally? Debts outstanding to dealers? Reasons someone might kill Ben to punish her?" She turned back to look at him.

"No. I don't know anything about this, I swear." His lips were pressed so tightly together that they had gone nearly white, and his hands trembled. He blinked wildly, over and over again, and for a moment Marge wondered whether the man was going to pass out.

She sat down and reached across the table, considered putting a hand on his arm, then changed her mind. "Dr. Sharpe, are you ill?"

He shook his head and swallowed again, then took a series of deep breaths. Finally he recovered enough to speak. "I'm sorry, Sheriff. This has all been a terrible shock." He let out a slow breath. "You know, I *am* feeling a bit ill. Perhaps we can continue this conversation after I've had a chance to—" He put his hands on the table and began to stand when Marge spoke.

"Dr. Sharpe, a girl is missing. A friend of Ben's."

His head rocked back an inch at the interruption, and he sat back down.

"We think she was with Ben yesterday and that her disappearance may be related to his death. The girl's name is Caitlin Wallace. Have you heard of her?"

He opened his mouth, seemed about ready to answer in the negative, then paused. "Wallace? The name sounds familiar."

"Ben mentioned her to you?"

He shook his head and pursed his lips in thought. His color was improved, and the hives on his neck were fading.

"She's from Chicago," said Marge. "Vacationing at Beran's Resort with her mother." She looked closely at him. "Where have you heard the name?"

"I can't remember." He looked thoughtful for another moment, then shook his head. "I don't know. Maybe I'm imagining it."

"The Wallace family vacations here every summer," said Marge. "Caitlin and her parents, Beth and Calvin."

His face brightened. "Calvin Wallace. That's it. He's a drug rep, as I recall."

"Pharmaceutical sales?" asked Marge.

Sharpe nodded. "Orion Pharmaceuticals," he said. "They make chemotherapy drugs and medication to treat pain in cancer patients. I believe they make Salvare, too."

"You've crossed paths with Calvin Wallace before?" asked Marge. "Where?"

His brow pinched in thought. "It was—it was at the country club."

"Green Lake Country Club?" asked Marge. "Why would he be there?"

He lifted a shoulder. "I assume because of Wildwood Clinic. A lot of the doctors and administrators are members there." The shift in topic seemed to rally him and he straightened in the chair. "I remember it now. He was at the club with a couple of other people, and I overheard them talking about cancer treatment. About a new surgical procedure for pancreatic cancer. I couldn't resist butting into the conversation because, well"—he put a hand to his chest—"I was part of the research team that developed that procedure."

"You spoke with Calvin Wallace?" asked Marge. "What did you talk about?"

"Not much." He grimaced. "Rachel was getting a little rowdy—we were celebrating her birthday—and we had to leave. He gave me his business card, I think." He reached into the pocket of his blazer and pulled out his wallet, then rifled through it for a minute before he found what he was looking for. He handed the card to Marge, then sat back in his chair with a creak of the plastic.

The card was made of luxury card stock, blood red on one side, white on the other.

Calvin Wallace
Orion Pharmaceuticals
Senior Therapeutic Specialist
Chicago Sales Region

"I definitely remember him," Sharpe said. "Nice guy." The corner of his mouth quirked in a dry smile. "Of course, all pharmaceutical reps are *nice*. This would have been"—he thought for a moment—"June fifteenth. Rachel's birthday."

"And who were the people with him?" asked Marge.

"I don't know. We only talked for a few minutes, and I don't think they introduced themselves."

Marge studied him, studied the business card, then bent over to write in her notebook She looked up when she heard a sharp rapping at the door. Phil stuck his head into the room.

"Sheriff, hospital's on the phone." Marge nodded. Phil gave Sharpe an appraising look, then disappeared, leaving the door open a few inches.

Marge stood and gathered her paperwork. "I'm headed to the hospital," she said. "I need to speak with Rachel before you can see her." As she headed toward the door, she said, "Dr. Sharpe, I'd like you to stay in Shaky Lake. We'll need to speak again."

"Rachel will want to come home to Minneapolis as soon as possible," he said. Marge doubted that; suspected that Rachel returning to Minneapolis would have more to do with her husband's surgical schedule than anything else. Marge ignored his comment for now, watched as he straightened the sleeves of his sport coat, smoothed his nonexistent hair, and reached calmly for his bag. Any residual symptoms of his earlier agitation were gone.

"Thank you for your help, Dr. Sharpe. You'll be able to see Rachel once I have a chance to interview her at the hospital." She paused in the doorway and turned back to him. "Again, I'm sorry for your loss."

10

The Rose Unit at St. Anne's Hospital specialized in psychiatric and addiction care, and was as heavily fortified as any correctional institution Marge had ever seen. A great deal more fortified than the Sherman County Jail, although that wasn't saying much. There were locked doors and metal detectors, of course, but what made the unit nearly impenetrable was the labyrinth of hallways to get there, with its switchbacks and blind corners, unlabeled doors and elevators, and a bizarre approach to room numbering. It was impossible to find one's way in or out without a seasoned guide. Today's was a skinny, mop-haired nursing assistant with a protruding Adam's apple who probably drew the short straw when Marge buzzed to be let in. The young man was not a talker, and the silence gave Marge a chance to rehash her thoughts once more before seeing Rachel. As it stood now, her own heartbreak and anger—at Rachel, at Chuck, at whoever had killed Ben Sharpe—made it difficult to focus on the investigation, as did the harsh fluorescent hospital lighting that held the promise of a migraine. The stakes were too high to let her feelings take over, though—a life lesson she was still trying to master after forty years on the job. She considered the possibility that Rachel had had a hand in Ben's death. In no world could Marge imagine Rachel deliberately harming her own son. She was often intoxicated, of course, and a neglectful parent in Marge's eyes. But a murderer? Not possible. Who, then? The question sickened her, frustrated her, and she tried to bring her thoughts

more clearly into focus. Had Ben had an enemy, or was he simply a casu-
alty of someone else's war?

She thought of Eli.

There had been something about him at the meeting this morning.
An energy she hadn't sensed in him for a long time. Not quite a spark,
but something. Marge was not a religious person, but she had a vague yet
unshakable belief in a certain connectedness in the universe, that Ben's
death and Eli's life might be intertwined somehow. She didn't yet have
the words to describe this belief, and she would be hard-pressed to tell
anyone about it with any coherency.

A few steps ahead of her, the nursing assistant shouldered through
one last security door, and Marge found herself in the Rose Unit. The
wood-look vinyl floor was bordered with a rose vine pattern, and a styl-
ized image of a rose, wide as a supper-club serving platter, was inlaid into
the floor in front of the reception desk. The lighting was softer here, and
the air didn't crackle with electronics—IV pumps, breathing machines,
overly loud televisions—as it did in every other hospital she'd been in. A
fountain spilled softly from the wall on one side of the space, and on the
other a bronze sculpture of a climbing vine clung to the wall, punctuated with dozens of cut-glass roses, each inscribed with what she assumed
were the names of past patients or donors. The taciturn young assistant
walked off without a word and Marge approached the desk, where a
plexiglass partition stood between her and a gum-chewing woman who
was looking at her phone. Marge waited for her to look up. Nothing. She
cleared her throat. Still nothing. Finally she tapped on the glass.

"I'm Sheriff North and—" Marge broke off, realizing there was an intercom speaker. She pushed the button on her side of the partition and
began again. "I'm Sheriff North and I'm here to see Rachel Sharpe."

The woman—young, ponytailed—didn't set down her phone, just
gave Marge her best bored-student face and pushed the intercom button.
"I'm sorry, who are you again?"

"Sheriff North." She said the words carefully, more loudly, and tapped the
star on her chest. "Please let Rachel Sharpe know that I'm here to see her."

The woman gave a heavy sigh and reached for a nearby clipboard.

"You're going to have to—" But Marge had already turned around. While she waited, she surveyed the wall of roses and slipped her glasses on to read the etched inscriptions. Gifts made in memory of loved ones, gifts from various doctors and their spouses, from Wildwood Clinic, from local businesses, and from a handful of organizations that Marge vaguely recognized as pharmaceutical companies. She stood on her toes to read the inscription on a rose near the upper edge of the vine. *In memory of our daughter Melissa—where flowers bloom, so does hope.* Tears pricked in Marge's eyes and she cursed under her breath. Now was not the time. Blood began to pound through her temples—the point of no return for her migraines. Her medication was in the truck, and she weighed the feasibility of finding her way to the parking lot and back without having to deal with the nursing assistant again. Before she could make up her mind, the tin-can sound of the receptionist's voice through the intercom smacked her in the head. "Sheriff, Mrs. Sharpe is ready for you. Room twenty-four." With a sigh, Marge turned to nod at the woman—already vanished—then started down the hall that she hoped led to Rachel's room.

From the doorway of room 24, Marge saw Rachel doubled over in a vinyl-covered hospital chair, elbows on her knees, face buried in her hands. Her loose gray pajama pants were hiked above her knees, and the skin on her legs was raw from scratching. Her hair was pulled back in a ponytail that didn't quite mitigate the rat's nest on the back of her head, and from the smell of things, staff had been taking her outside for illicit cigarette breaks. She rocked back and forth, her breathing rapid and audible, even from the doorway. She glanced up when Marge entered the room, revealing a runny nose and a hairline dark with perspiration. For a moment, she went completely still. She came halfway to her feet, as if she would bolt from the room, then gave an embarrassed frown and forced herself back down into her chair. "Hello, Marge," she said, voice cracking. She groped for the tissue box at the foot of the bed and pressed a tissue to her nose, then sat with her eyes closed, seemingly trying to control her breathing.

Down the hall, someone began to shriek obscenities, and as the sound of footsteps hurried by, Marge stepped into the room and pushed the door shut behind her. The space was private and vaguely upscale. Nothing glitzy, but the furniture and bedding were a major step up from what Marge remembered when she had her knee replacement a few years ago. Abstract art in soothing tones hung on the walls, and the standard hospital paraphernalia—oxygen gauges, suction canisters, ominous-looking switches—seemed to be tastefully concealed by a faux wood armoire. Heavy drapes were drawn against the daylight, and it was stiflingly hot in the room. A breakfast tray sat untouched on the adjustable bedside table, and the smell of low-quality coffee and cold breakfast sausage lingered in the air.

Rachel stopped rocking back and forth and began rubbing her knuckles down her thighs, again and again. Her nose dripped and her eyes watered. Her frenetic sniffling and throat clearing cranked Marge's headache up another notch. "Hello, Rachel." She pulled a folding chair from its bracket on the wall, then situated herself across from Rachel, avoiding the harsh light near the sink.

Rachel wasn't wearing makeup, and it struck Marge that she had never seen her barefaced before. *So young.* Much younger, in fact, than Marge had realized. Early thirties at most. *A teen pregnancy.* Marge's throat tightened, and she swallowed hard before she spoke.

"Rachel, I'm so sorry for your loss." She reached across the space between them and put a hand on the younger woman's arm. "I can only imagine what you're going through." She peered at Rachel, gauging whether she was stable enough to be interviewed. Marge had dealt with enough people struggling with opioid addiction over the past several years to know withdrawal when she saw it. "I know it won't be easy, but I need to ask you some questions. Think you're up to it?"

Rachel put both hands onto her forehead and pushed the sweat from her brow into her bleached hair, then pressed the heels of her hands over her eyes and nodded. She let the hems of her pajamas fall and cover her legs, and slumped back in her chair.

Marge put her phone on the bedside table and hit record. "We think that Ben sustained a head injury. Did he have any medical conditions that could have caused a fall? Seizures? Fainting? Drug or alcohol use?"

"Not that I know of," said Rachel. Her voice was choked, and she began to bounce a knee.

"Can you think of anyone who may have wanted to hurt Ben?"

She was quiet for a long time, and Marge was just about to speak when Rachel straightened in her chair and wrapped her arms across her chest. "No. Everyone loved him," she said, no trace of irony in her tone.

"Could he have been involved with people or"—Marge hesitated—"situations that would put him in danger?"

Rachel leaned forward all at once and Marge flinched at the sudden movement. "Don't you think I would tell you if I knew anything?" She locked eyes with Marge. "He was my *son*." She drooped back in her chair again, then dragged a sleeve across her dripping nose in a way that blamed Marge for everything.

Marge shivered, and a wave of nausea hit her. If she could just get through this interview and get her migraine medicine . . . She forced her face into a calm expression and pushed on. "Let's go over yesterday's events."

At that moment, there was a knock on the door and a sliver of light from the hallway widened as someone came into the room. "Rachel, are you awake? Is it okay if I turn on the light?"

Marge turned toward the door to see a man emerge from the shadows. He had a white beard, full and luxurious and trimmed into a fluffy white triangle that extended all the way to his breastbone. The buttons of his white lab coat were pulled tight over his belly and his smile was warm and gentle, with a spark of intelligent curiosity. He stopped when he saw Marge, then looked to Rachel, his eyes wide with surprise. "Oh, I'm sorry, I didn't know you had a visitor," he said, in an accent Marge couldn't quite place. His eyes went to Marge's uniform and badge, and he looked embarrassed. "I'll come back."

"Is it okay if I talk to him for a minute?" Rachel asked Marge.

"Completely fine," said Marge. "Please, Doctor—"

"Kouris," he said. "Alexander Kouris, but please call me Alex." He crossed the room to her with a smile, arms extended, and for a moment, Marge thought he might embrace her. At the last second he put one hand alongside each of her shoulders in something like an air hug, then stepped back and turned to Rachel.

"This is Sheriff North," said Rachel. "She's here to talk about Ben."

He dropped his arms. "Ah, yes. Sheriff North, welcome. It's so nice to meet you, although"—his smile dissolved—"I wish it could have been under better circumstances."

"Doctor, I'm crawling out of my skin. I need something stronger." Rachel nearly yelled the words, and her face immediately reddened with chagrin. She folded her hands in her lap and looked down. When she spoke, her voice was shaky, just above a murmur. "Please," she said.

Kouris's eyes widened. "Oh my goodness. I didn't know you were—" He took a step closer. "Yes. My god, you are miserable. I see that now." He turned to Marge, then back to Rachel. "I'll ask the nurse to bring you something right away. A stronger dose, for the, er—" He gave Marge a sidelong glance.

"She knows," said Rachel.

He dipped his head. "Of course, of course." Rachel let him take her hand and give it a gentle squeeze. "I'll come back later, when you're more comfortable," he said, then nodded respectfully at both women and left the room.

Rachel scrubbed her hands over her face and took a series of deep breaths.

"I can come back," said Marge, when Kouris had gone.

Rachel shook her head, her face grim. "No. Once they give me the medication, I'll be too out of it to talk to you."

Marge frowned. "Are you sure?"

"Yes."

"Okay, then. Can you tell me what you know about yesterday's events?"

Rachel picked at the medical tape surrounding the IV on the back of her hand. "Ben was up early yesterday, around seven. He was making such a racket in the kitchen that he woke me up."

"Did the two of you talk?"

"He told me he was going out on the boat for the day with a friend." Rachel shifted in her chair, then pressed a hand to her lower back and grimaced. "He didn't say who, but I could tell it was a girl."

Marge raised an eyebrow. "What makes you say that?"

"Sixteen-year-old boys don't get up early unless it's for a girl."

Marge's lips twitched. "That's been my experience, too." She waited a minute, then pulled out a photo. "We believe Ben went boating with this girl yesterday." She handed it to Rachel. "Caitlin Wallace. Have you heard of her? Did Ben ever mention her?"

Rachel studied the photo for a long time. "So pretty," she murmured. When she looked back at Marge, her face was flat, emotionless. "I've never seen her. He probably made sure the two of us never met."

"Why do you say that?"

Rachel gestured to herself with a sweep of her hand, as if her physical appearance was Exhibit A of a failed motherhood.

"Oh." The word hung in the air between them, and the silence that followed seemed to confirm Rachel's proclamation. Marge continued on. "What about other friends? Anyone he spent time with?"

Rachel was quiet for a long time, clasping and unclasping her hands in an anxious rhythm. "The truth is, I don't know much about his life these past few years."

Marge felt a small, sharp pain in her heart, and the questions she was going to ask died on her lips. Rachel's words rang true, that she knew little about her son's comings and goings, of his passions and fears, of the life he led outside her orbit. But he did have a life of his own, and, if nothing else, it had included a pretty girl. Marge would have smiled at the thought if it hadn't been so tragic. She studied Rachel's bleak eyes, her twitching, feverish face, and felt an unsettling mixture of frustration and pity. In the hallway, the screaming had stopped, and in its place was a stifling silence. Marge stood and paced back and forth across the room, arms crossed. Her migraine was in full swing now, and the faint hum of the fluorescent lighting stabbed her again and again in the temples. All at once, her nausea flared, and she looked around the room for a trash can. Just in case.

From the chair behind her, Rachel spoke, her voice wire-tight. "I think back to—before Chuck. We had nothing but each other. I never knew from one day to the next whether we would survive. It was no way to live.

I thought I was protecting him by fighting my way up from—from where we were." She raised her chin. "I was wrong."

Rachel's words cut through the pain in Marge's head. She sat back down. "Rachel, you didn't *choose* addiction." She leaned into the words, willed the younger woman to believe her.

Rachel waved a hand dismissively, and Marge understood that she wasn't interested in arguing the point. Suddenly it was sweltering hot and the throbbing pain behind her eyes surged. Marge looked wildly around the room for a trash can again.

Rachel tilted her head. "Are you . . . there's the bathroom," she said, and pointed to a narrow door in the corner of the room.

Marge dove into the tiny bathroom and had just enough time to flick on the light and close the door before she was sick. She braced herself over the toilet and prayed that the noise of the bathroom fan covered the sound of her retching. When it was over, she stood up and felt a cascade of sweat pour down her back. She cursed, then untucked her shirt and dabbed at her back and underarms with toilet paper. This was the absolute last thing she needed.

When she was done, she tucked her shirt back in, took a few deep breaths, and pulled open the door to find Rachel standing there, a paper cup of water and a wet washcloth in her hand.

"Feel better?" Rachel handed her the water and washcloth.

Marge nodded, then took a sip of water and pressed the washcloth to the back of her neck. She let out a long breath. "Sorry," she said, then pointed to her head. "Migraines."

"I know the feeling."

"Once I, you know"—Marge gestured to the bathroom—"then it goes away."

Rachel nodded, and after a beat, she met Marge's gaze. Even through the withdrawal-induced agitation, the exhaustion apparent on every feature, those eyes held an appeal. Not for forgiveness, but for something else Marge couldn't quite make out.

Both women sat down and were quiet for a long time before Marge spoke. "I have a son too," she said. She looked away. "He's not well."

Rachel went noticeably still in her chair and waited for Marge to continue.

Marge cursed inwardly at her words. Why had she mentioned Eli? It was appallingly unprofessional. She set the empty cup on the counter and got to her feet.

"I'll be in touch. Call me if you think of anything, or if there's anything I can do." She reached to put a hand on Rachel's shoulder. "I'm so very sorry for your loss."

The hallway and reception desk were deserted when Marge left Rachel's room, and she hesitated for a moment before choosing what she hoped was the door that led to the hospital entrance. She was halfway down a long hallway when she heard a voice from behind her.

"Sheriff?"

She glanced over her shoulder as Dr. Kouris stepped out of one of the doors she had just passed. He smiled at her, wide and warm behind his fluffy white beard. "Do you have a moment?" he asked. Marge turned toward him and he made a beckoning motion, then disappeared into the room. When they had both stepped inside, he said, "Do you mind if I shut the door? A closed door can be anxiety-provoking for some, I know, but confidentiality is, of course, a top priority here."

"Closed is fine," said Marge, and she lowered herself into the well-worn leather chair in front of his desk. The room was small, or perhaps just seemed that way due to the hodgepodge of overflowing bookshelves and dinged-up file cabinets lining the walls, and the piles upon piles of books, medical journals, file folders, and loose paperwork covering nearly every horizontal surface.

He sat at his desk, and the rickety swivel chair creaked under the weight of his portly frame. He looked around the room and then back at Marge, his expression rueful. He pressed his hands together. "Please forgive the clutter. My wife doesn't let me make a mess at home, so this is my only outlet. I don't often have visitors here, but of course, these are exceptional circumstances." He laid his hands in his lap. "Now," he said, "Rachel has given her consent for you and me to speak."

Marge absorbed this with the skepticism she had developed after so many years on the job, and considered asking Kouris for proof of this supposed consent. Instead, curiosity got the better of her. What information could he possibly be looking for from her? And what information might he have that could help shed light on what had happened to Ben? She fixed a neutral expression on her face and waited for him to continue. Long seconds passed, and it became clear that he expected her to speak, to confide some details of Rachel's life outside the hospital, or even the specifics of the investigation. He was a psychiatrist, after all—a man accustomed to gathering people's secrets.

He cleared his throat. "I suspect you already know that Rachel struggles with substance abuse. She has experienced significant trauma in her life, and it has left her in a very weakened state. Now, with what has happened to her son—" He shook his head. "Her prognosis is not good."

Marge recalled her visit with Rachel. The woman had been in distress, that much was clear, but nothing about her had struck Marge as weak.

"I am meeting with her husband later today to discuss options," he continued.

Marge felt a pang of apprehension. "And will Rachel be involved in these discussions?" She suspected that was not the plan.

Kouris folded his hands together on the desktop and adopted the patronizing tone of teacher to student. "Addiction and mental illness can affect decision-making capacity, and sometimes—"

"She seemed fully capable of making her own decisions when I spoke with her a few minutes ago," she said in a slightly louder voice, as if making an official statement. One that would be written down and referred back to at some point, should questions arise about Rachel's competency. The idea of Kouris and Chuck Sharpe in charge of Rachel's fate carried more than a whiff of coercion, of toxic paternalism, both of which Marge disliked in the extreme. She deliberately drew attention to her sheriff's badge by pulling a pen and small notebook from her breast pocket, then fixed Kouris with a stare before slowly and conspicuously writing several lines on a blank page. Her performance had its desired effect.

"Oh no, Sheriff." Kouris held out his hands in something like self-defense, and she would be lying if she said she didn't enjoy the way the man's benevolent expression faltered. "Let me assure you that any inter-ventions will ultimately require Rachel's consent," he said. He seemed to realize he had backed himself into a corner, and his attempt to reverse course was almost palpable. "You see—"

Marge pocketed her notebook and pen and got to her feet. "I'm afraid I need to head out, Doctor, but I'll be sure to keep in close contact with Rachel during the course of the investigation." She could see that Kouris took her words as the warning they were.

I'll be watching you.

She nodded a goodbye and turned toward the door, then paused on the threshold to glance back at the doctor and found him watching her with a strange, calculating look in his pale blue eyes, as if she were a par-ticularly troublesome mathematics problem he was determined to mas-ter. She recalled the look of fear on Chuck Sharpe's face earlier when she had mentioned Dr. Kouris, and at that moment, it struck her that maybe she should be afraid, too.

11

Kim Beran smiled at Eli from across the desk of the resort's office and tugged her ruffly peasant top a little lower on her shoulders. The gauzy white fabric stood in stark contrast to her cleavage, bronzed and shimmering, maintained year-round with a tanning bed. Eli had to admit that it was quite a view. Not that Kim was his type. He looked away and busied himself with setting up the recorder on his phone.

"Hel-lo-o . . . Eli?" He looked up to find Kim staring at him. "Are we doing this or what? Because, believe me, I have *plenty* of other things to do today."

"Right, sorry." He hit record on his phone. "This is an interview with Kim Beran, co-owner of Beran's Resort." He set the phone on the desk and looked up. "Kim, as you know, the body of a boy named Benjamin Sharpe was found in a boat moored to your pier last night. Can you tell me what you know about this?"

Kim swished her long, blond, well-thought-out hair and looked down to inspect her manicure. She looked out of place in the room, with its knotty pine paneling and 1950s steel desk and file cabinet. Framed photographs, black-and-white and yellowed with age, hung on the walls—images of smiling picnickers beside Studebakers, kids in old-fashioned bathing suits proudly holding up strings of fish, white-haired couples in aluminum lawn chairs. A taxidermied lake trout hung on a carved wooden plaque above the window behind her, its mud-colored scales glossy and fissured from old shellac, and on either side of the window hung small, amateur oil paintings of white-tailed deer.

"I didn't really know Ben Sharpe," she said. She pursed her heavily glossed lips. "I know Rachel from the country club—she's there, I swear, every day—and I saw him there with her maybe twice." She sighed. "She must be freaking out."

"Can you tell me what you did yesterday?"

She folded her hands together on the desk. "I spent all morning at the antiques fair in Princeton, which was a huge waste of time, because they had nothing but junk." She shook her head and her dangling earrings chimed softly. "Things even my grandma would have thrown in the trash, and that's saying something." She sat back and tapped a finger against her chin. "In the afternoon, I went to lunch with my sister and then came home and spent, I swear, *hours* on the phone with a paint store in Minneapolis. Then Mike and I had date night at the country club." She gave Eli a kittenish smile. "It was the annual luau party—you know, mai tais, leis, coconut shell bras—" She leaned forward and smirked. "Mike likes to show me off."

Eli stared at her, unblinking, until she pouted and looked away.

"Anyway," she said, "we were at the country club—"

"Green Lake Country Club?" he asked.

She nodded. "From about five thirty to eleven."

Eli made some notes, then looked up. "And Mike? Can you tell me his whereabouts yesterday?"

She reached down to rummage in her enormous leather purse and pulled out a tube of expensive-looking hand cream. "He does CrossFit every morning, and then yesterday he golfed eighteen holes at the country club." She clucked. "He was *so sunburned.* I told him he's going to get all leathery if he doesn't take better care of his skin." As if to demonstrate proper skin care, she massaged the cream into her hands and smoothed it up both arms. The smell of coconut on warm skin drifted across the desk toward him, and his own skin grew warm. He gritted his teeth. "What time did Mike get home from golfing?"

Kim narrowed her eyes at him in something like amusement, as if she noticed Eli noticing her, then lifted one caramel-colored shoulder and let it drop. "Around four?" She slipped the cream back into her bag and sat up straight. "He showered and watched TV while I got ready. Then we left for dinner around five fifteen."

"So you and Mike were at home from about four to five p.m." He jotted this down in his notebook and then met her eyes. "Do you have anyone who can account for your whereabouts during this time?"

She looked at him, aghast. "We had nothing to do with"—she waved a hand toward the window behind Eli that looked out onto the lake—"what happened to that boy." A flush crept over her cheeks.

He laid a hand on the desk. "Easy, Kim. I'm not accusing you—either of you—of anything. I'm just asking a question." He gave her a reassuring smile, and after a moment, the panic left her eyes.

"Kim, do you have any idea who might have wanted to hurt Ben or his family?"

She looked away. "Didn't Rachel"—she fiddled with the stack of delicate silver bracelets on her wrist—"didn't she use drugs or something?"

"Do you mean you saw her using drugs?"

"No!" Her eyes flew to his. "I've just *heard* about her using drugs. I never saw any of that. Although she did drink quite a lot at the country club. I always wondered how she managed to stay so skinny, drinking all that alcohol. That stuff is *full* of calories." She smoothed her hands across her thighs, which were as smooth and tan as her arms, and barely covered by white denim shorts.

"Any suspicious behavior?" he asked. "Strange people hanging around?"

She shook her head. "Of course, I can't imagine she'd do any of that while I was around. I mean, it's *illegal*."

"And Rachel's husband? What do you know of him?"

"Chuck?" She shrugged. "He's nice enough. A lot older than her. Probably a sugar-daddy situation."

"Do you think Rachel may have been having an affair?"

The question seemed to amuse her. She looked thoughtful, and a smiled played across her lips. "She was certainly *friendly* with a lot of the men at the club—especially the bartenders—but I think it was just flirting." She sighed, as if disappointed. "From what I've heard, the club has a really strict policy about staff having those sorts of—interactions—with members. As for other members, I never saw anything that would make me think she was having an affair. Not that it would surprise me if she were. Her husband practically neglects her, and her poor son, too."

A sour taste rose in the back of Eli's throat. He knew all about being the neglectful husband and father.

"You mentioned seeing Rachel at the country club," he continued. "What about outside the club?" He turned to look out the window at the shoreline. "Her house isn't all that far from here." He turned back around and was surprised to see that Kim had gone still.

She licked her lips, then said brightly, "Of course we saw each other. Not all that often, but we would visit from time to time. She has *such* a gorgeous house. Just perfect for little get-togethers."

"Get-togethers?"

"Oh you know, just little cocktail parties here and there. Mostly people Chuck knew—doctors or whatever. She invited Mike and me a couple of times." She gave a nervous laugh. "I always felt like an idiot, because everyone would just talk about all this super-complicated medical stuff."

"Do you recall who you saw at these—get-togethers? Names, for example?"

"No," she said, and shook her head hard enough to make her earrings jingle again. "I would never be able to remember. I'm absolutely terrible with names. Besides," she said, "those parties were a long time ago. Last year." She leaned forward a little and lowered her voice. "Rachel and Chuck are getting a divorce. You should probably know that for your investigation."

Eli nodded. "Did you ever see any indication that things between them were violent or"—he searched for the right word—"unstable?"

She shook her head. "I don't think she would have let anything like that happen in front of people." She looked at her watch.

He shifted in his seat and picked up his pen. "I'd like to move on to another matter," he said. "Are you aware that Caitlin Wallace is missing? She and her mother are guests here at your resort, correct?"

She put a ring-spangled hand to her mouth. "Oh my god. I hadn't heard—" She looked away. A vein on her perfectly tanned neck began to pulse.

"How well do you know Caitlin Wallace and her family?"

Kim looked at him and swallowed. "They've come here every summer for a long time. Since before I knew Mike."

"Had you seen them since they arrived?"

She nodded. "They came late Friday night. Well, Beth and Caitlin did. I think Cal stayed home. I left the cabin unlocked so they could get in Friday night, and I stopped by on Saturday morning to get them checked in. Beth and I chatted for a bit. Caitlin was there, too, although she didn't really talk." She looked thoughtful. "To be honest, she seemed sort of . . . different."

"Different in what way?" Eli leaned forward and set an elbow on the desk.

Kim nodded. "She's always been so friendly. Cute and bubbly, you know? This time she was"—she paused, as if searching for the right words—"she didn't look good. Way too skinny, and pale, although that was probably makeup."

He frowned. "Do you mean she looked ill?"

"Not like she had cancer or anything, just—depressed, I guess."

Depression. He hated that word. As if anyone's psyche could be encompassed by some textbook term. An item on a list of medical conditions, like heartburn or arthritis. An insurance billing code.

Kim's eyes brightened and she sat up straighter. "She had a *tattoo* on her arm. I remember it clear as day because I was so shocked." She lowered her voice. "She's only sixteen. I don't think it's legal for sixteen-year-olds to get tattoos." She raised her eyebrows. "I could tell that Beth was pissed about the tattoo because it got *awkward* after I mentioned it."

"What was the tattoo?"

"A flower. It was bright red. I don't think it was a rose. Really pretty, actually, not that I said that to either of them."

"Did there seem to be any other animosity between Caitlin and her mom?"

She seemed to consider this. "I wasn't paying that much attention, to be honest." She waved a hand. "Anyway, I haven't seen them since Saturday. I've been so busy." She hesitated for a moment, as if debating whether to go on. "Mike and I are expanding our business focus now that his parents are both gone. You know, considering other possibilities for the property."

"This place has been a resort forever, hasn't it?" asked Eli.

Kim folded her hands together on the desk. "We've been—approached—about converting our resort into a rehabilitation facility." The great care with which she pronounced "rehabilitation" made Eli suspect it was a word she had learned only recently.

"What type of rehabilitation?"

She wrinkled her nose. "Drugs." She paused. "Treatment, I mean. Addiction treatment."

"A rehab resort," he said. He sat back and crossed his arms over his chest. "Interesting."

Kim nodded. "Patients will get the best care in a beautiful Northwoods setting. Very private and discreet." She dropped her voice conspiratorially. "Very high-end."

The idea of Mike and Kim Beran running a healthcare facility stretched the limits of believability, and he considered Kim's words with a twinge of uneasiness. All at once, it occurred to Eli that the typical sounds of a summer resort on Shaky Lake were absent—the slam of screen doors, the whoops and shouts of kids, the sizzle of meat grilling, the wet slap of someone jumping into the lake. He remembered what Beth Wallace had said to him last night—that she thought they were the only people at the resort.

Kim's voice rose with excitement. "When Wildwood approached us about converting it to a rehab facility, I'll admit I was really grossed out. I didn't want a bunch of, well, *those* people messing up the place. It just seemed creepy."

"But?" prompted Eli.

"But then they told us how much money—I mean, they told us how financially successful the rehab facility could be." She spread her hands. "And we just thought, well, why not?"

"Healthcare is a booming business," said Eli. He tried to keep his voice even. "What with the aging population and the opioid crisis." There was something to Kim's story, though it almost certainly had nothing to do with Ben's death or Caitlin's disappearance, and he instinctively wanted to know more. Unanswered questions never sat well with him.

Kim smiled brightly. "Exactly."

"Who approached you about this? You said Wildwood, but who, specifically?"

"It was like fate," said Kim. "Mike and I were at a wedding at the country club last fall, and we were just sitting at the bar when this man joined us. Bought us drinks. We got to talking, and he was super excited when he heard that we owned a resort on Shaky Lake. He said he had been looking for a place just like ours."

"Crazy," said Eli, his eyes wide. "Such a lucky coincidence. So was he a doctor or something?"

"Doctor?" asked Kim, puzzled. "No, he wasn't a doctor. He was—" She was cut off by a man's voice, harsh and sharp, from the door.

"Kim!" Eli turned to see Mike Beran standing in the doorway, a scowl on his face. He was as tan as Kim and wore a tight-fitting golf shirt. He was good-looking in a hyper-macho kind of way.

"Hi, baby!" Kim's voice jumped a few notes higher.

Mike didn't return her greeting. Instead, he let the screen door slam behind him and came around to sit on the edge of the desk, arms crossed. Eli ignored him and continued speaking to Kim.

"He was a what?" asked Eli. "This man at the wedding."

Kim glanced at Mike, then stood. She smoothed the edges of her blouse over her shoulders and said, "I have to run. I'm meeting the interior designer at our home to go over some options for bed linens." She smiled and let her hand graze the small of Mike's back as she slipped past him and out the door.

After Kim left, Mike didn't sit in the desk chair. He just leaned against the desk, stone-faced, arms folded like a nightclub bouncer.

"Something I can help you with, Eli?" he asked, in a decidedly unhelpful tone. "Because otherwise, I have a lot of work to do."

Eli considered his approach. He suspected that a textbook interview with Mike would get him exactly nowhere, and the last thing he needed was to get into a dick-swinging competition with the guy. He rested his arms on the chair, then let out a low whistle and looked around the room.

"Kim was just telling me about your plans for the resort. I can only imagine the amount of paperwork and red tape involved in turning this place into a rehab facility," Eli said. "Always some bureaucrat making it hard to run a business." He looked sidelong at Mike.

Mike's eyes sparked and he bobbed his head in agreement. He was a few notches higher than his wife on the intelligence scale, but that wasn't saying much. He went around the desk and lowered himself into the too-small chair. "Always some Madison liberal wanting to stick their nose into everyone's business."

"Ain't that the truth?" Eli shook his head.

"But you know what?" said Mike. He gave a wolfish grin. "There's not much paperwork involved in opening a rehab facility. Part of the appeal for us to convert the place, if I'm being honest." He paused and looked quickly at Eli. "It's totally aboveboard, of course."

"Hey, man, it's your property, right?"

"Damn straight. Wildwood Clinic has their big rehab center, but they're bursting at the seams. Not enough space for all the people who want treatment. I turn this place into a rehab facility and they'll all come running."

Eli considered this, then picked up his phone from where it sat on the desk. "Mike," he said, keeping his voice neutral, "we're investigating the death of Benjamin Sharpe, a boy whose body was found on your property last night." He gestured to the phone. "I have to record our conversation. Just protocol, of course."

Mike frowned. "I don't know anything about that."

"Of course not. But I'll need your help if we're going to have any chance of finding out what happened. Now," he said, sitting back, "can you tell me your whereabouts yesterday?"

Mike listed off the same information Kim had given Eli, leaving the same window of time—four to five p.m.—when they were home, just the two of them.

Eli considered this. "Does the resort have security cameras installed?"

Mike blinked. "No. Not yet, anyway."

Eli snapped his fingers. "Shit. Well then, I'm going to need your help figuring out who it was blasting music in one of your cabins around nine o'clock last night."

"How should I know?" asked Mike. "Kim and I weren't here."

Eli leaned back in the chair and crossed one leg over his knee. "The weird thing is, Mike, the music was coming from Cabin Six."

Mike was quiet for a moment, his face pinched with confusion. "But"—he hesitated, then shook his head—"that cabin is vacant this week."

"Then why did someone turn on all the lights, crank up the speakers, then disappear? See, it was the noise disturbance that led us to the boy."

Mike swallowed. "I don't—"

"So you're saying it wasn't you or Kim who turned on that music?" Eli sat back and folded his arms across his chest. "Who was it, then?"

A glow of perspiration appeared on Mike's face. "I have no idea, Eli. Somebody must have broken in. Kim and I were at the country club. Lots of people saw us there."

Eli watched as Mike dragged a hand across his sweaty forehead. "Another kid is missing, Mike. Caitlin Wallace. She was vacationing with her family here at your resort."

Mike's face went pale and his Adam's apple bobbed. Eli eyed him for a moment. "I'm concerned that there are things you aren't telling me." He lowered his voice. "Ben Sharpe was found on your property and the missing girl was staying here. This puts you and your wife in a difficult position, legally."

"You think we killed that kid? Are you serious?" Mike jumped to his feet and the steel chair nearly toppled over behind him.

"I'm not saying that," said Eli, holding up his hands. "I'm saying that there can be liability for accidents, et cetera, that happen on private property. Wisconsin law is heavily weighted toward victims in these situations." He cocked his head. "I assume you know that, given that you're working on converting this place into a healthcare facility."

Mike's forehead rumpled in confusion. He attempted to bluster back but failed.

Eli got to his feet and pocketed his phone. He gave Mike a smile and clapped him on the shoulder. "Thanks for your help, man." He headed toward the door, and when he reached the threshold, he turned and gave Mike a wave. "I'll be in touch."

12

Eli watched as Dr. Gina Hanson, the county medical examiner, bustled around the stainless-steel table where Ben Sharpe's body lay, covered with a white sheet. The air in the morgue was thick with the hum of refrigeration units and the low-frequency buzz of fluorescent lighting. The surge of energy Eli had felt after that morning's station meeting, and during his interviews with the Berans, had fizzled into a light-headed, twitchy state of pure exhaustion. He stared at the doctor beneath eyelids sticky with fatigue and didn't look at the motionless shape on the table in front of him.

"There was a head wound?" he asked.

"Two head wounds, actually."

Eli would have preferred to have this conversation over the phone, but Dr. Hanson had insisted that he come in person, and he had been too tired to protest. He knew her to be a sensible, efficient person with no use for the dramatic. The fact that she had insisted he come in person left him with a sense of foreboding he really could have done without.

"The wounds weren't accidental," she continued.

"Why do you say that?"

"There are two hematomas on his scalp and they overlap." She held her hands out in front of her, almost but not quite on top of each other, to illustrate her words. "So unless he fell repeatedly, in almost the exact same way, it's not feasible."

Eli thought of the boat, knocking gently against the dock, Etta James calling through the darkness like a homing beacon. He felt the faint but familiar ripple of interest that he refused to dignify with the name "hunch." Whatever had happened to Ben Sharpe, somebody had wanted him to be found. There weren't many plausible explanations for a scenario such as that, other than murder.

Gina interrupted his thoughts. "I estimate the time of death to be sometime between four p.m. and eight p.m. yesterday."

"No signs of a struggle?"

"No."

"So whoever killed him did it with two blows to the head, from behind, without warning," said Eli. He rubbed his eyes and tried to picture the scene. Marge had said the boat belonged to Ben, that he took it out on the lake almost every day. Eli was willing to bet that Ben would have manned the tiller, meaning he would be sitting in the stern of the boat, less vulnerable to attack from behind.

"No," the doctor said again. She laid her hands on the edge of the table and shook her head. "Ben Sharpe didn't die from head trauma," she said. "He died from a drug overdose."

Cal

*T*he office was the last place Cal wanted to be on a Saturday. He pushed his laptop away and got to his feet. The smell of onions from the remains of his sandwich wafted up from the trash can and mingled with the chemical smell left behind by the weekend cleaning crew. He looked at his watch and considered whether, if he left now, he could still make it to Shaky Lake tonight, and if it would even make a difference.

There was a light rap on his office door, and the ginger-haired head of his friend appeared.

"You poor bastard," said Kevin Allen. He stepped into Cal's office and closed the door behind him. "What're you doing here? You're supposed to be on vacation."

Cal sank back into his chair and tipped his head back against the leather. Kevin was his closest friend at Orion Pharmaceuticals. His closest friend, period. Any social life Cal had had outside work had dried up like an unwatered houseplant in the past couple of years. He gave a long, tired exhale and didn't look up when he heard Kevin take a seat in the armchair opposite the desk.

"Let me guess," said Kevin. "Kowalske wants something on his desk first thing Monday morning." Their boss, the CEO of Orion Pharmaceuticals, was not a man who valued balance in his life, or in the lives of his employees. His children were long since grown and his wife liked money more than she liked her husband; other than his obsession with racquetball, Bob

Kowalske lived and breathed work, and pity the employee who didn't share his fanaticism.

Cal scrubbed his hands over his face. He had learned that grumbling about work stress made him feel worse, not better. He lifted his head to look at Kevin, saw the look of sympathy on the man's freckled face. "Sales numbers. What else?"

Kevin groaned. "I feel for you. He's got me here running corporate assets reports. Wants to know how much money we've got tied up in factory equipment."

"Sounds urgent."

Kevin laughed. The two men were silent a moment.

"I'm guessing Beth wasn't thrilled that you stayed behind?" Kevin's words were facetious, but his tone was gentle. He was the only person Cal had confided in about the toll his job had taken on his family.

He forced a smile, despite the weariness. "I'm almost done," he said, then looked dumbly at the stack of paper on the desk in front of him. "Hopefully I can—I can . . ." He trailed off, unable to remember what it was he was going to say. His concentration was shot. Even the simplest information seemed to slide off the surface of his mind, unabsorbed.

Kevin got to his feet, leaned over to rest his palms on the desk. "Screw the reports, man," he said in a low but emphatic voice, as if wary of being overheard. "It's not worth it. Just go. Kowalske will just have to deal with it."

Cal thought of the large, comfortable house in the suburbs, the new car he planned to buy Caitlin for her birthday, the beach vacations and winter ski trips. Surely all of it was a worthwhile trade-off for the long hours, for the time spent on the road. He thought of the look on Beth's face last night. The way Caitlin had avoided his goodbye hug. The memory gave him a small, sharp pain in his heart.

"You're right," said Cal. He nodded and repeated his words, as if saying them again would bolster his conviction. "You're right."

Kevin pushed away from the desk. "Good." He grinned and went to the door, opened it, then turned back to look at Cal. "I don't want to see you back here until your vacation is over." His face brightened as an idea struck him. "I'll tell Kowalske you don't get cell phone reception at the cabin."

After Kevin left, Cal stared, unseeing, at a blank space on the wall of his office for a long time. He felt exhausted and his body ached; the half-digested sandwich sat heavily in his gut. He waited for his thoughts to organize themselves, as if waiting for a website to load on a slow internet connection.

Then the fax machine behind his desk came to life. Page after page spewed out until a half-inch-thick stack of paper sat, facedown, on the output tray. He reached over and picked up the stack, then flipped it over. He hadn't been expecting any faxes, especially over the weekend. The generic cover sheet had CONFIDENTIAL *printed in bold at the top of the page but was otherwise blank except for a message—written in a broad, scrawling hand:* AS REQUESTED.

13

At first Eli thought he must be hallucinating, that his exhaustion and the blow to the head last night had finally caught up with him. Dr. Hanson's words seemed to float just outside the boundaries of his awareness; he retrieved them with great effort.

Drug overdose.

"A drug overdose?" he asked. "But he was just a kid."

She frowned. "Fentanyl, probably. The toxicology results won't be back for at least a week, but I've been doing this job for longer than I care to admit, Eli, and I've gotten really good at spotting an overdose." She reached into a box on the rolling cart behind her and pulled out a pair of latex gloves. "These days, the inner arm is one of the first places I check in an autopsy. Let me show you something." She came around to Eli's side of the table and pulled back the sheet to reveal Ben's arm.

"Here's the injection site." She pointed to the inside of the elbow.

Eli tucked his hands under his arms to suppress a shiver—the air from the ventilation fan above him seemed to have grown even colder—then leaned over the table. The arm was smooth and white and crisscrossed with veins, like a slab of marble. There was a tiny purple smudge in the crook of the elbow, small enough that he was forced to lean over even farther to make it out. In the center of the bruise was a nearly imperceptible mark where a needle had punctured the skin.

"And this," continued Gina as she pulled the sheet a few more inches higher and rotated the arm, "is from the tourniquet." She indicated another bruise—a thin strip of discoloration on the inside of the upper arm—which was, again, so subtle that Eli would never have noticed it. She watched as he looked more closely at the site, and then she pulled the sheet back down. "He sustained blunt force trauma to the back of the head, but it's not what killed him. Don't get me wrong: it was probably enough to knock him out, but the damage to the head was . . ."

A throb of panic went through Eli's chest and Gina's voice grew fuzzy. He clenched his hands more tightly under his arms and gave a silent curse. *Not now.*

". . . so, assuming that the time of . . ."

A ring of black appeared at the edge of his vision, then grew thicker until all he could see was Gina, at what seemed like a great distance, still talking. His lips went numb.

". . . wouldn't make sense that . . ."

Dread hit him, low in the gut, and his eyes flew around the room, searching for something to focus on, something to tether him to reality before he was completely swept away. The vinyl floor tiles. The exit sign over the double doors. The open shelves containing stacks of white sheets and boxes of latex gloves. Nothing helped, and the overbright, antiseptic space turned ghoulish. Gina was still talking, but her voice was now completely drowned out by the blood whooshing in his temples, and she seemed not to notice the change in him. Desperately, he pushed back against the rising panic. If he could just hold himself together a little longer . . .

Then he looked at the exam table.

The edges of the white sheet began to stir, barely a shiver of movement. The blood in his temples surged, and the light in the room pulsed like a strobe, black and green-white, in time with his heartbeat. With each pulse, the edges of the sheet began to move more forcefully, until the entire surface undulated, and the blood screamed in his head. Then the feeling hit him like a thunderclap.

I'm dying.

The floor was suddenly too close and the walls of the room began to twist and recede.

I'm dying.

His knees crumpled and he groped for the edge of the table. The stainless steel began to rattle beneath his shaking hands, and all the muscles in his body went rigid.

I'm dying.

"Eli." Gina's voice cut through the whoosh of blood in his head, silvery sharp, then faded again. A blinding whiteness rolled across his line of sight and he let go of the table to rub his fists against his eyes to dispel the light. He opened his mouth to speak, but a clot of terror burst in his chest and he began to choke.

I'm dying I'm dying I'm dying.

There was a pressure around his shoulders and he felt himself moving, floating a few inches off the floor like a cartoon ghost. Any second now, he would hit the ground, hard. He felt something behind his knees, then a slight shove. He tumbled backward and didn't try to break his fall. Then, to his surprise, a soft landing.

He heard Gina's voice again, crackling in and out like a bad phone connection. "Need to . . . deep breaths . . . steady . . ." Her hands were on his shoulders, her face in front of him—there, then gone like the flicker of a film reel. He squeezed his eyes shut but the film reel kept spinning in his mind, a barrage of images.

Not now.

The whispering started behind him, just over his shoulder.

Do you remember us?

Sweat blossomed on his neck.

You've forgotten us.

He swallowed, over and over, against the scream rising in his throat.

Come back to us.

The voices begged, pleaded with him, louder by the second.

I'm dying.

Then, something cool against his cheek. A voice that eclipsed the whispering.

"Breathe, Eli." Gina's face shimmered, then dissolved again, like a mirage.

Just one breath.

He swallowed his scream, but still his breath wouldn't come. It was his brain that reached the surface first.

I'm not dying.

It was a lie, but he forced himself to think it again.

I'm not dying.

The vise around his throat loosened, a fraction of a fraction, but enough for one choking gasp to find its way into his lungs.

I'm not dying.

Another breath, stronger this time. Gina's face reappeared, corporeal, unwavering, and without another word, the specter behind him fled.

I'm not dying.

He repeated the words to himself, eyes closed, over and over, Hail Marys on a rosary. After what seemed like hours, he felt the first prickles of sensation return to his face, his fingertips. Air crept into his lungs.

I'm alive.

He opened his eyes. Gina leaned against the edge of the desk across from where he sat, a look of compounded concern and appraisal on her face and a bottle of water in her hand. At first he could only stare at her, but gradually, one pixel at a time, the room around him steadied and then came into focus, and the roar of blood in his head ebbed to a dull ache. He opened his mouth, unsure whether words would come out, but Gina spoke first.

"Drink." She twisted the cap off the bottle of water, placed it in his hands. It was only after he took a sip that she stepped back and resumed her place at the edge of the desk. "All of it," she said. He accepted the water without protest or thanks, and, for long minutes, the only sound was that of his lips on the bottle, the moist sound of his swallowing. He felt clammy all over, and when he looked down, the front of his tan shirt was dark with sweat, a bib-shaped patch of damp on his chest, and what he could tell was a matching one on his back. Embarrassment began to creep in on the heels of his gradually recovering composure. Eli shifted uncomfortably in his seat and considered what he could possibly offer Gina by way of explanation for what had just happened.

She picked up a box from the desk behind her and busied herself with opening it and rummaging around inside. Then, seeing him empty the last of the water bottle, she pushed off the desk and handed him what turned out to be a sleeve of Girl Scout cookies.

"Eat." Her tone was gentle, but it was clear that the monosyllable was a command, not an invitation. She looked pointedly at the cookies and then left the room, with a pause and a glance at him from the doorway to indicate that she would be back shortly. He watched her disappear into the morgue; a curtain had been pulled around the exam table that held Ben Sharpe's body, and the harsh fluorescent light over the table was switched off. He could hear but not see Gina at work somewhere in the large room—cabinets opening and closing, the sound of metal implements against metal countertops, the clack of computer keys.

He took a cookie and forced himself to eat as he examined his surroundings. The chair in which he sat was a tatty mauve armchair, far too small for his oversized frame, and vaguely seashell-shaped, like something from a 1980s department store lounge. The desk and attached bookshelf were standard-issue cubicle units, neatly stocked with important-looking books and a tidy stack of paper held in place by a *Game of Thrones* coffee mug. A corkboard, covered in a collage of family photos and lists of phone numbers, hung on the wall behind the desk. He took another cookie, though the first one had tasted like mint-flavored sawdust.

Drug overdose.

Gina's words emerged from his still-fuzzy brain, a welcome distraction. Marge had said that Ben Sharpe would ride his bike to Red River Falls to get clean needles for his mom's heroin habit. The boy had known about heroin, had access to it, and had the gear to use it. But Eli recalled the photo of Ben with his mother—his restless watchfulness, her vulnerability. There was a dissonance to the idea that Ben used drugs.

From the other room came the sound of water spraying from a faucet, then another metallic clank, and a moment later, Gina returned, wiping her hands on a paper towel. Eli started to get to his feet, but she put a hand out.

"Not yet," she said. "You're just starting to get your color back." She tossed the paper towel in a trash can and took a seat behind the desk.

Eli swallowed against the food that was attempting to creep back out his gullet. He cleared his throat once, twice, until he was reasonably certain that only words would come out. "Gina—"

"The last thing either of us needs is for you to pass out, Eli." The corner of her mouth lifted in a half smile. "There's no way I could get your gigantic carcass off the floor, and I'm pretty sure you don't want me to call 911 for assistance."

He managed a smile. "Marge would not be pleased."

Her eyes softened, and amusement touched the edges of her voice. "You two tag-teaming this case?"

"Not if she hears about this."

Gina moved the stack of papers and the coffee mug to the side and shoved a large textbook into the bookcase, then folded her hands together and rested them on the desk in front of her.

"You want to talk about it?"

His heart gave a thump of alarm. The color *was* returning to his face, he knew, but there was no way, not even the slightest possibility, that she took it for anything less than his total mortification.

She waited in silence for him to respond. If he said nothing, it would be confirmation that there was, indeed, something that needed talking about. He brushed a crumb off his lap and, in looking down at himself, again saw the state of his shirt; stiff and heavy with sweat, hanging slack from his shoulders and bunched in a pile of extra fabric against his too-lean abdomen. His normally substantial legs—"rugby thighs," as Michelle had always referred to them—were shrunken to the point of lankiness beneath his pants. "I'm just tired," he said, addressing the sleeve of Thin Mints. "And—I'm not going to lie—finding the boy last night was a shock."

He felt her eyes on him but didn't look up. From the other room came a *ding*, like the sound of a toaster-oven timer, and he felt a flash of hope that she might leave again to tend to something in the morgue. Anything that could extricate him from this situation, this conversation.

Instead, Gina said, "I've known you since you were a kid, Eli. Maybe I'm just the medical examiner now, but I'm still a doctor. You don't look well." He looked up to find her studying him. She set an elbow on the desk and leaned toward him. "When was the last time you slept? I mean *really* slept?"

The thought did not escape him that talking to a doctor might be a good thing, and though she now specialized in caring for the dead, he knew Gina Hanson had always been a very good doctor. Her eyes moved in a swift zigzag from his face to his baggy clothes to his left hand, and rested for a second on his ringless fourth finger before coming up to meet his gaze again. He couldn't blame her for her concern, but if he answered one question, she would ask another, and nothing productive would come from heading down that path.

"Seriously, Gina. I'll be fine." He took a deep breath and let it out with a puff. "Nothing Thin Mints can't fix." He gave a wobbly smile and avoided her eyes. "Thanks for the refreshments."

She gave him a dubious look and seemed about to press the issue further, but he spoke before she could say anything.

"You said Ben probably died of an opioid overdose. Did the autopsy suggest he was a habitual drug user?"

"He didn't have any scarring on his veins that would suggest repeated injections. I checked everywhere. His feet, his groin. Even his gums. Nothing."

Eli winced. "His gums? Jesus."

She ignored his exclamation. "Second, he was almost certainly right-handed. The right-hand pocket of his shorts was more worn, he had more calluses on his right hand, et cetera."

"The injection site was in his right arm."

She nodded. "I'm not saying it doesn't happen, but it would be unusual for someone to inject themselves in their dominant arm unless it was the only option. Some people who use injection drugs run out of good veins, but, like I said, he didn't have scarring."

"Is that why people inject in their—" He pointed to his mouth.

"Sometimes. But sometimes it's to hide their illness." She paused, and her gaze flicked to Eli, then away. "We all deal with pain in our own way."

Instead of responding, Eli took another cookie.

"I won't have the toxicology results back for at least a week," said Gina, "but I wanted to get you the important information right away."

Eli got to his feet with careful deliberation. "Marge is talking to the boy's family. I'll let her know about your findings." He ground the heel of a palm against one eye, then looked at his watch. "Sorry to get you out of bed so late last night, Gina. I owe you."

She nodded in acknowledgment of his thanks, but then her expression clouded. "Promise me you'll get some rest, Eli. Even if it's just a couple hours."

He forced his face into a repentant smile. "I promise." The falseness of the words echoed in the small room.

"I'm serious." Gina came around the desk and put a hand on his arm to stop him as he moved toward the door. Before Eli could form a response, a door opened somewhere on the other side of the morgue and a pair of voices entered, one low and heavily accented and one with the gossipy singsong of a college student. Gina glanced past him through the doorway, annoyed at the interruption. She turned back to him, and there was a tightness around her mouth that suggested there was much more she wanted to say. She regarded him in silence for a moment longer, and then her expression eased.

"It was good to see you, Eli. You let me know if there's anything I can do to help." A pause. "With the case."

A wave of weariness hit him broadside, and Eli braced against the wobble in his knees. He felt himself smile at Gina, heard a voice issuing from his own mouth with what he hoped was a polite leave-taking, then turned and headed toward the door.

14

The FBI had clearly sent the rookie. The woman seated in the far corner of the conference room could not be more than twenty-five years old, with dishwater-blond hair pulled back in a ponytail and a swath of freckles across her nose, all in stark contrast to her horn-rimmed glasses and black blazer. She sat with her laptop balanced on her knees, fingers flying over the keyboard, with the intense expression of an overachieving student. She was small-framed and short enough that, when seated, only her toes touched the floor. Eli's heart sank. They needed someone with experience, someone to elevate their investigation. The last thing they needed was to babysit the new kid.

Marge met Eli's eye from the head of the conference table, and she smiled. "Feel better after some rest?"

He let out a long breath. "Much better." It was the truth. After he left the morgue, he had managed to drive, nearly blind from exhaustion, to his apartment and make it through the door just in time to set an alarm on his phone, stagger to his bed, and collapse. His sleep had been dreamless and intense, with the sharp edges of a blackout rather than the gradual transitions of sleep. If it hadn't been for the blare of his alarm, he might have slept for days. He found, when he sat up in bed, that he felt alert. No grogginess, no sickening feeling of having woken too soon. A quick shower, a change of clothes, and four fingers of whiskey had him feeling refreshed and ready to work.

"Food's here." Phil appeared at the conference room door carrying a stack of pizza boxes, and a plastic bag full of bottles of soda hung from one skinny arm. He might have looked somewhat better since Marge had sent him home this morning, but all the rest and relaxation in the world couldn't make Phil Schulz look healthy. His skin was ashen no matter how much time he spent in the sun, though Eli could remember only about a dozen times when he'd seen the man wear anything but long-sleeved shirts and pants, even at the height of summer. He carried a faint odor of camphor and menthol from the Bengay cream he used on his hands, which were gnarled and stiff due to early-onset arthritis. Eli suspected Phil's perpetually sour expression and impatience were owed at least partly to his chronic pain. He seemed to subsist entirely on coffee and cigarettes, though he had recently quit smoking, which only added to his ill temper. He was clever and observant, beyond what one might expect from a small-town dispatch officer, and had a need for thoroughness and attention to detail that bordered on compulsion.

"Thank god!" Jake jumped up from his seat across the table from Eli and took the boxes from Phil. "Come to Papa," he crooned. He set the boxes down and began to flip open lids and push boxes to the center of the table. He peeked inside the largest box and slid it to Eli. "Here's yours, buddy. As requested."

Eli had a slice in hand even before the box came to a standstill. He was absolutely starving, and the first bite was the only moment of enjoyment he'd had in longer than he cared to admit. Okay, maybe the second moment. There was Kim Beran's cleavage.

He supposed he should consider himself lucky that the incident at the morgue had happened in front of Gina Hanson. Anyone other than a doctor would have thought he was having a seizure or a heart attack rather than a panic attack, and he almost certainly would not be sitting in this meeting, or likely even be involved in the investigation anymore.

A drug overdose.

He looked at his watch—six thirty. Almost twenty-four hours had passed since he had found the body, and he felt a gnawing sense of impatience, which, to be honest, was an improvement over everything else he had been feeling for the past month; a whisper of what things had been like, before.

Andy hadn't called him back today, and Eli suspected that Michelle hadn't told him about their phone conversation last night. He had considered going to the house after his interview with the Berans that morning, but then Gina had called him, and after his breakdown at the morgue, he was in no shape to see his son. He took a long drink from his gigantic bottle of Mountain Dew, then lifted the lid off the pizza box and grabbed another slice. From the corner behind him came an unfamiliar voice; low, for a woman, with the slightly scratchy quality that comes on the tail end of a cold, and an unmistakable Chicago accent.

"You're going to eat that entire pizza?" Everyone turned to look at the FBI agent, who had been silent, busy with her work, since before Eli, Jake, and Phil arrived. Somehow, she had faded into the background of the room so completely that Eli—Phil and Jake, too, judging from their startled expressions—had forgotten she was there.

The agent blinked. "What? I'm just saying . . . it's an eighteen-inch pizza"—she craned her neck to get a better look inside the box—"covered in meat." She shrugged. "It seems like a lot for one person."

"What the—" Jake gaped at her. "How is that any of your business?" He turned and looked at Eli with a *Can you believe this?* gesture, then looked back to the agent. "It's probably the only thing he's eaten in two days." He shot Eli a smirk. "Other than whiskey."

It took a moment for Eli to decide that Jake was joking. He forced a laugh. "Got to soak up the booze with something, right?" He hoisted a slice and held it up in salute to the woman. Her eyes were unreadable behind her glasses, but the tilt of her head left him fumbling for excuses. "I'm not—" He directed an uneasy look at Marge, who watched the exchange without a change in expression. "He's just giving me shit. I don't actually—"

The agent lifted a shoulder, let it drop, then looked back to her keyboard, dismissing him with a finality that left him feeling mistreated, as if he hadn't been given time to defend himself against whatever it was she saw wrong with him.

Marge shot an impatient look at Eli and Jake over the top of her reading glasses. "Let's get started." She got to her feet, a fraction more slowly than she had that morning, and pulled off her glasses. She looked as composed and focused as always, but the lines at the corners of her eyes seemed deeper, and her lips were pinched tightly. She rubbed a hand against the back of her neck as she always did in the aftermath of a migraine, then pointed her glasses at the FBI agent in the corner.

"First, let me introduce Agent Mason with the Federal Bureau of Investigation. She's going to be helping us with this case. She's been with the bureau for ten years, and for the last two years has been with the Critical Incident Response Group based in Chicago."

Eli did the calculations in his mind. FBI applicants had to be at least twenty-three years old, which would make Agent Mason at least thirty-three years old, likely older if she was part of CIRG. He didn't bother to disguise his reappraisal of her appearance—he was still annoyed at her pizza comment—and found that, even under more careful scrutiny, she looked unsettlingly young.

The agent lifted a hand and glanced around the table. "Alyssa. Hi."

"As I said this morning," continued Marge, "Agent Mason is here as a result of the missing child investigation for Caitlin Wallace, which I'm considering, at least at this point, to be connected to Ben Sharpe's death." She finished introductions, then picked up her notebook and flipped to a blank page.

Alyssa put up a hand. "*This* is the entire sheriff's department?" She looked around the table, and though Eli avoided her gaze, he could see a level of annoyance in Phil's and Jake's expressions that mirrored his own.

Phil draped an arm over the back of his chair and gave her a sardonic look. "Sorry to disappoint."

Marge turned to Alyssa with a mild expression, a testament to her self-control in an increasingly tense atmosphere. "Unfortunately, Sherman County has a very small budget for law enforcement."

It occurred to Eli that Marge had likely not slept since yesterday.

"Eli," said Marge, her voice edged with fatigue, "why don't you give us the update on the autopsy? What did Gina have to say?"

Eli took quick stock of his stomach and decided he was still hungry. He grabbed another slice of pizza. "Nothing is official yet," he said around a mouthful of food, "but Gina believes that Ben Sharpe was given a lethal dose of intravenous narcotics sometime between four p.m. and eight p.m. yesterday."

For a moment, the room was silent. From the lobby upstairs came a jingle and a surge of street noise as the front door opened, then laughter and excited chatter and the sound of feet disappearing up the stairs to the higher levels. Eli waited for everyone's eyebrows to lower before he went on.

Alyssa spoke before he could continue. "What do you mean, 'given'?" She had been in the process of slipping her laptop back into the messenger bag at her feet, leaning halfway over in the too-tall chair, but froze at Eli's words. The hem of her shirt shifted upward with the motion of leaning over, and he noticed something on the skin just above her waist. A cluster of puckering in the skin, pinker and shinier than the surrounding flesh, that disappeared upward beneath the fabric to hint at the possibility of more. Eli knew gunshot scars when he saw them. She straightened in her chair and tugged her shirt down to conceal the scars again.

He cleared his throat. "Well, Gina found—"

Jake interrupted him. "The toxicology results are back already?" He frowned. "That seems . . . fast."

Eli turned to Marge. "This is all based on bodily evidence. An injection site, a tourniquet bruise"—he ticked off the items on his fingers—"the location and pattern of the head wounds."

He told them what Gina had said: the nonfatal head wounds, the injection site, the lack of any other signs of habitual injection drug use. They listened without interruption, and then Alyssa scooted her chair closer to the conference room table. She gave Eli a dubious look from her new position an arm's length away. "This all seems . . . speculative. An overdose is one thing, but the idea that someone attacked him and then injected something into his vein . . ." She frowned. "It's an incredibly strange way of killing someone."

Eli turned to Jake. "Was any drug paraphernalia found at the crime scene?"

Jake didn't answer right away; he seemed to be following his own train of thought, and it was a moment or two before he replied. "No. Nothing." He didn't open the folder of documents in front of him.

"Not in the water near the dock?"

"I've read the report," interjected Marge. "They did an intensive search in the water near the shoreline, in the cabin, the whole resort property. No drug paraphernalia."

Means before motive.

It was an investigative tenet that had served Eli well his whole career. Start with the *how* and let it guide you toward the *who* and then the *why*. He took another slice of pizza. "So Gina must be right. Ben couldn't have injected himself elsewhere, then safely docked the boat on the pier at Beran's by himself. No drug paraphernalia means someone else injected him."

"Did Gina have any guesses on what drug was used?" asked Jake.

"She suspects it was fentanyl."

Jake nodded. "Fentanyl is easy to find, a hundred times stronger than heroin, takes less than five minutes to kick in."

"Ben Sharpe was sixteen years old," said Eli. "Just a kid, but nearly full-grown. For someone to pick him up and move him from, say, land to a boat would take significant strength, or else two people. But if he was killed *in* the boat, there would be no need to move the body. No need for strength, no need for more than one person."

"So who was in the boat with him?" asked Jake.

"Caitlin Wallace, for one," said Marge. "Both Beth Wallace and Rachel Sharpe said the kids were going boating together yesterday morning."

"The opportunity was there," said Eli, "if Caitlin wanted to hurt Ben, and the means were certainly within the abilities of a teenage girl. Physically, I mean. Ben was attacked from behind. No time to react or protect himself."

"Or," said Alyssa, "there could have been a third person in the boat."

Cal

*C*al *flipped through the pages of the fax, a full-length report of research trial data on Salvare, Orion Pharmaceuticals' new drug, due to launch next month. Salvare was going to be the answer to the opioid crisis—a prescription drug that counteracted the dangerous effects of opioids. No more drug abuse, no more overdoses, no more ruined lives and loved ones gone too soon. Salvare. A play on "salvation."*

He had seen the trial data dozens of times. Had formulated eye-catching graphs and charts of the trial results for the presentations he had given to healthcare providers, hospital systems, pharmacies, and various movers and shakers of the medical community. He could recite the numbers from memory. Didn't even need the PowerPoint slides anymore. And really, there wasn't much to say about Salvare, other than that it was truly a lifesaving drug. There were a handful of research trial participants with mild side effects, but nothing serious. The drug had sailed through the review process at the Food and Drug Administration, and, despite the cynicism Cal had developed over the past five years peddling expensive prescription drugs, he was genuinely proud of Salvare, and hopeful for what it could do to reverse the ever-increasing devastation caused by opioid addiction.

He scanned the columns and charts, paragraph after paragraph of dense clinical language. He was about to toss it into the shred box, chalk it up to a misdirected fax, when something on one of the pages caught his eye. It was an asterisk, highlighting the start of a handwritten bracket that extended down the entire page and onto the next several pages. He studied the bracketed information more closely. It was a list of research trial participants, identified only by assigned numbers and date of birth. It was the same list he'd seen over and over again, only this time there were lines through some of the entries. A lot of the entries, actually, with numbers scrawled next to them. Cal looked back and forth between the entries and the handwritten numbers. Participant number, date of birth, then another eight-digit number. He stared at the page in his hand for a long time, then reached for his computer.

15

It was just past twilight, and the tavern windows along Main Street glowed with neon beer signs and backlit bar counters. Patrons spilled out onto the front steps to smoke in groups of two and three, and the sounds of classic rock and drunken laughter drifted through the open windows. The buoying effects of Eli's afternoon sleep and glass of whiskey had faded, leaving him feeling drained and weary. He was very conscious of the pain that lingered on the back of his head where he had hit it last night, and of the greasy food in his stomach.

Agent Alyssa Mason's car was too small for him. Perfect for the dense Chicago streets but incompatible with his oversized body. He leaned away from her and rested an elbow on the open window frame in an attempt to create more space between the two of them, and thought of the flask of whiskey in the glove compartment of his car. It had been a mistake to let her drive them to Beth Wallace's cabin, and he wondered whether Marge was making a mistake sending the agent along with Eli when he interviewed Caitlin's mother.

He imagined himself inside one of the bars along Main Street; the feel of a cold bottle of beer, slick with condensation, the smooth, shellacked wood of the bar counter, the press of people as they shouted their orders to the bartender over the loud music, and the scent of beer and fried food and women's perfume. He let out a breath.

"You want me to drop you off somewhere?" Alyssa asked.

Eli turned from the window to look at her. "What?"

"That was a pretty deep sigh." She glanced at him. "And you're hanging out the car window." The traffic light reflected off her glasses and hid her eyes, but he heard the amusement in her voice. Until now, she hadn't said anything beyond asking whether he wanted the windows open or the air-conditioning on, and Eli had begun to think they would be making the journey to Beran's Resort in silence, which suited him just fine.

The light turned green. Alyssa accelerated, only to slam on the brakes to avoid hitting a grizzled couple wearing black leather Harley-Davidson jackets as they darted across the street in front of her. She swore under her breath and aimed her hand at the car horn.

"I wouldn't do that if I were you," said Eli, his tone mild. She shot him a look, which he ignored. "Not if you want to get to Beth Wallace's cabin anytime soon. Drunk bikers love a fight." He gave a cheerful wave to the couple as they stumbled past the car and into the bar across the street, then to a family with three teenage kids, and finally to two women dressed in extremely short jean shorts.

Alyssa drummed her fingers on the steering wheel, and when everyone finally went past, she hit the gas with a little more force than necessary. Soon the liveliness of downtown gave way to county highway, the darkness punctuated here and there by rural taverns and illuminated private driveways that disappeared through the woods toward the lake. The water wasn't visible from the road, but he could smell it, could feel the cooler air that gathered on the lake's surface and spilled onto the shoreline and in through the car windows. He looked across to where Alyssa sat, tugging her lower lip in contemplation, her hair whipping across her forehead and the nape of her neck where the wind had blown it free from her ponytail.

The speed limit on this stretch of the county highway was only forty miles per hour. The road's wealthy lake homeowners didn't want to dodge highway-speed traffic when pulling out of their driveways with their trailered luxury watercraft or behemoth SUVs. The slower pace mitigated the roar of wind through the windows of Alyssa's car just enough that she didn't have to shout.

"How do you feel about me leading the interview with Beth Wallace?" she asked. She glanced at him, then back at the road.

He considered the idea. Marge evidently intended for them to work together on the case, and watching Agent Mason in action would give him the opportunity to gauge her skills.

He started to respond, but at that moment, his phone lit up.

Andy: Mom said u called.
Andy: maybe we can fish tomorrow after we mow the lawn
Andy: ???

Eli's heart did a little flop, and he grinned and texted a response in the affirmative. He and his son hadn't fished together all summer, a fact that gnawed at him constantly. Until this summer, and with the exception of his time spent overseas, Eli and Andy had fished together at least weekly since Andy was a toddler, even in the winter. He smiled at the memory of two-year-old Andy, bundled in a snowsuit, mittened hands holding his fishing pole as he pulled a walleye through a hole in the ice; of the candy that Andy would convince him to buy when they stopped at the bait shop for night crawlers; of letting him stay up past his bedtime to fish just a little longer in the midsummer twilight. Even this past winter, on days when it was all Eli could do to get out of bed—to perform the basic activities of daily life—he had managed to get out on the ice with Andy on weekends. Gradually, though, the one or two cans of beer he'd brought along with his fishing tackle were replaced with flasks, and then travel mugs of liquor, until the day in early May when he had driven the car into a ditch on the way back from Moon Lake. Neither he nor Andy were hurt—a tiny ding in the front bumper of his car was the only physical evidence of the crash—but the effect on his family was devastating. It had marked the breaking point in his crumbling marriage, and though Andy had forgiven him immediately, had even jumped to his defense against Michelle's anger, Eli was left feeling as though he was a danger—rather than a father—to his son.

Alyssa's voice broke through his thoughts. "Is that okay?"

They had reached the turnoff for Lakelawn Avenue, and as the car slowed, the humid night air poured through the windows, heavy and fragranced with pine and smoke from distant campfires. Eli looked over to find Alyssa staring at him, and he struggled for a moment to remember what she had been saying.

She must have noticed his puzzlement. "Is it okay if I lead the interview?" she repeated. If she was becoming impatient, she hid it well. "Unless—"

"There it is," interrupted Eli. He pointed to a painted wooden sign ahead on the right. "Beran's Resort." He leaned forward to peer through the windshield. Alyssa slowed and turned down the gravel driveway. "Belongs to Mike and Kim Beran," he continued. "I spoke with them this morning." He pointed through the window into the blackness. "Beth's cabin is the third one down." The cabin he had searched last night was now dark and silent, delineated from the landscape only by yellow crime-scene tape. Alyssa stopped the car in front of the empty cabin, then looked across Eli and through the passenger-side window. Her eyes flicked over the scene—the cabin and the yard and the view of the lake beyond. To his surprise, she put the car in park and turned off the ignition. He was about to tell her she had stopped in front of the wrong cabin when she got out of the car, shut the door quietly behind her, slipped under the crime-scene tape, and headed toward the path that led to the water.

The soft slap of lake water against rock, the creak of weather-beaten aluminum, a blot of darkness in the bottom of a boat.

The memory of last night's scene, and with it, a whisper of panic. He couldn't risk a repeat of what had happened in front of Gina Hanson in the morgue today. If he sat here in the car, safely out of view of the shore, maybe he could fend off the panic. He swallowed, over and over, until his throat hurt and his mouth was bone-dry. He tried to reason with himself. The boat and its passenger weren't there anymore. Besides, if he didn't follow the agent to the water, she might ask him why, or worse, she might come to her own conclusions.

What finally got him out of the car were the mosquitoes. Agent Mason had left the windows down and taken the keys, leaving him defenseless against the steady influx of the bloodsucking insects. Both his travel mug of whiskey and his can of bug spray were sitting in the center console of his own car, useless to him now. For the second time, he cursed himself for letting her drive. He slapped a mosquito on his neck, one behind an ear, two more on his arm, then jumped out of the car and shut the door behind him. The mosquitoes weren't much better outside the car, and he swatted at the cloud of them. It would be better by the shore. He headed toward the path and had reached the granite outcropping halfway down when he heard the dock creak. The sound sent a shard of ice down his spine, and he put a hand against the rock to steady himself, then pressed his other hand to his chest as if he could channel the stability of a thousand-pound chunk of granite straight to his heart. He heard Alyssa's footsteps on the dock, and then it was quiet again. He forced himself to move forward. As he came around the corner of the outcropping, he saw her standing at the end of the dock, her gaze fixed to a point farther north along the shore. She looked down suddenly and pulled her phone out of her pocket. She studied the screen for a long time, as if reading a text, then put it back into her pocket. She was too far away, and it was too dark, for him to make out her expression, but for a moment, she pressed the heels of her hands against her eyes.

Minutes passed, and then she took the phone back out and tapped something onto the screen, then put it back into her pocket. She must have noticed her messy, windswept hair, because she tugged the elastic off her ponytail and went through the process of smoothing and pulling her hair neatly back again. She glanced at her watch, then looked toward shore and stopped short when she caught sight of Eli standing at the corner of the outcropping. He felt a stab of embarrassment at having been caught watching her, and gave an awkward wave.

"Want to see the cabin?" he called, loud enough for her to hear, but low enough not to disturb the general stillness. He had a finely tuned sense of how sound moved across water, how it bounced and slid over the surface differently, depending on the wind, the temperature, the current. He had grown up surrounded by water, after all. A hot, humid, windless August night required little more than a murmur to carry the sound of his voice all the way to where she stood. Any louder, any sharper, and it would have sounded like a shout, but the resulting huskiness of his voice lent an uncomfortable intimacy to the scene. He took a step back into the shadow of the massive stone beside him.

Agent Mason responded by making her way back to shore and up the steep path toward him. "It's not locked?" she asked, then suddenly slapped herself on the neck. "God, these mosquitoes are vicious." She looked at her hand and then wiped it against her pant leg. She continued up the path until she was a few feet away from him, close enough to see the key in his hand. She was a good foot shorter than him—she had to tilt her head way back to meet his eyes—with skinny shoulders and a too-long neck. His grandma would have said she was liable to blow away with a strong gust of wind; the bullet-wound scars Eli had seen earlier suggested otherwise.

"Kim gave me a key," he said, then stepped aside as she pushed past him. "Don't they have mosquitoes in Chicago?" he called after her.

As if in response, she slapped the back of her shoulder in two different spots and spouted a string of curses. "Just hurry up," she snapped, and jogged the rest of the way to the top of the path. When he reached the back door of the cabin, she was already standing in the screened porch, both hands busy scratching at her mosquito bites. He unlocked the back door and followed her inside, then flipped on the lights.

Agent Mason turned in a slow circle in the center of the living room, taking in the cozy, rustic space, as Eli himself had last night. Aside from the mess of fingerprint powder everywhere, it was just as untouched as it had been the last time he saw it. Without comment, she went into the kitchen and turned on the light. While she did that, he headed to the hallway and peeked into the bathroom and bedrooms. He was standing in front of the radio in the bedroom, staring at the plug where it dangled off the end of the dresser, just as he had left it last night, when Alyssa joined him.

"This place is straight out of a movie," she said. "I can see why people make the trip all the way up here." It occurred to him that the North-woods of Wisconsin might be an entirely new experience for her. Her

Chicago accent was thick, and there was something about her blunt manner and scrawny appearance to suggest that she might have grown up in a part of Chicago where paid vacation time—vacations in general—was not a commonplace occurrence. A place only the most ambitious, the canniest, could leave behind. She left the room again and he could hear her open the closet door in the bedroom across the hall.

Some morbid part of him wanted to hear Etta James again, to see what the music might do to him; a poke-the-bear impulse. Not with the agent there, of course. Not to mention that the CD wouldn't be in the player. It would be sealed in an evidence bag, sitting in a box, locked in Marge's office, safely tucked away. There was fingerprint powder residue on the outlet and plug and top of the radio. He turned the radio around and saw more fingerprint powder on the control panel, then put the radio back in its place. He stared at it for a long time.

Agent Mason reappeared in the doorway. "We should probably get going." She watched as Eli bent over, grabbed the plug, and inserted it into the outlet. The radio came alive: a blinking twelve o'clock on the display and the sound of the CD drive waking up. Then, to Eli's astonishment, a disc slid out from the slot on the front of the radio, the slim plastic suspended halfway out like a wafer held out by a priest at Communion. An offering. Fingerprints were visible on the shiny surface of the disc. They had clearly not been powdered and collected. The hair rose on the back of his neck. Agent Mason crossed the room and looked over his shoulder.

"Tell me that's not—" she said, appalled.

He carefully took the disc from the radio, one finger through the center opening to avoid leaving fingerprints, and held it out for her to see.

At Last: The Best of Etta James.

She stared at the disc, wide-eyed. "The sheriff told me the forensics company wasn't great, but . . ."

"Maybe Jake forgot to tell them about the music," said Eli, though the idea was highly unlikely. Jake was smarter than he seemed, and meticulous with his work.

"Still," she said. She took another look at the CD, and to his surprise, she let out a puff of laughter, an exhale of warm air he could feel against his shoulder. "I couldn't believe it when the sheriff told me about the noise disturbance call. Someone blasting jazz music . . ." She shook her head, still smiling, and took off her glasses and began polishing the lenses with the hem of her shirt. She took a step back, but she was still close enough for him to see now, with her glasses off, evidence of her true age. A hint of darkness beneath her eyes, faint lines at the corners of her eyes, a softening of the skin above and below her eyelids. She was wearing a trace of makeup, and it looked as though she had just applied lip balm. He glanced away before she could notice him looking at her mouth. She slid her glasses back on and, to Eli's alarm, met his eyes and lifted one brow almost imperceptibly, as if she knew he had been studying her, as if to ask, *Seen enough?* and then disappeared into the living room. Once she was gone, he let out a breath, then pulled the radio plug from the outlet a bit more roughly than absolutely necessary and switched off the bedroom light.

The agent turned when he came into the living room. She had been looking out the front window in the direction of Beth Wallace's cottage, and she let the curtain drop back into place as he leaned a shoulder against the doorframe. "Anything I should know before we talk to her?" she asked, without the slightest trace of the awkwardness he felt.

"I only talked to her for a few minutes last night," said Eli. "Before I found the body." He scratched the mosquito bite on his neck as he searched his memory. "She was friendly. No red flags. There was something Kim Beran said, though, about Caitlin getting a tattoo."

She cocked her head and waited for him to continue.

"It was a tattoo of a red flower. *Not* a rose."

Her brow creased slightly. A round red welt had developed at the base of her neck where a mosquito had bitten her, and the sight of it made his own mosquito bites itch even more. He shoved his hands into his pockets and went on. "Kim mentioned that Caitlin's appearance had changed since last year."

"How so?" asked the agent. For a second, she was distracted, and her hand dipped into the pocket where he had seen her put her phone. He paused a beat, waited for her to take out her phone, to respond to the text or call she had clearly gotten, and when she didn't, he went on.

"You saw the photo of her at the station." It wasn't a question, and he didn't wait for an answer before he went on. "My guess is that photo wasn't taken recently. Kim said she was pale, skinnier, more withdrawn than last summer." He gave a half smile. "Kim Beran may not be the brightest bulb on the tree, but she has a very good eye for appearances."

She met his eyes then, and the crease between her brows deepened. After a long moment, she nodded. "You're thinking . . ."

He buried his fists deeper into his pockets. "Yeah. Maybe."

The agent sucked in a breath and let it out with a heavy sigh, then pulled the curtain aside again and looked at Beth Wallace's cottage one last time before turning back to Eli. "Let's go."

16

The half-empty plastic bottle of rum pinched and crackled in Beth Wallace's hand as she poured the liquor into a glass. She took a sip, then straightened in her chair and cradled the glass like it was hot tea on a cold winter's day. "Can you repeat the question?" she asked. Her dark hair was wet from a shower and she was dressed in a loose white top and pajama shorts. The air in the cabin was stiflingly humid. An ancient floor fan oscillated back and forth across the kitchen, providing little relief from the heat. Eli's shirt was heavy with perspiration, and he plucked and tugged at the fabric as inconspicuously as possible. His temples pulsed with headache; he desperately needed a drink.

"I was asking you how your relationship with your daughter has been lately," said Agent Mason. Her face was flushed and strands of hair clung to her neck despite the breeze from the fan. Twice she had to push her glasses up to wipe perspiration from the bridge of her nose, and the hollow at the base of her throat shone with moisture. In contrast with her overheated appearance, however, was her demeanor. Calm and unhurried; soothing, like a damp washcloth on a feverish forehead. So far, he felt good about handing her the reins to the interview.

"It's been a little"—Beth's voice caught—"a little rough lately." She looked away too late to hide the shimmer of tears in her eyes. The vintage aluminum-and-vinyl chair creaked as she shifted in her seat and tucked one foot beneath her. The space was nearly identical to the kitchen in the other cabin. Knotty pine and Formica and linoleum, but made all the more welcoming by the bag of hamburger buns and jars of baked beans and pickle relish on the countertop, and the stack of dishes drying on a towel next to the sink. Beth tugged the neckline of her shirt up to wipe her eyes, then looked back at the agent. "She's a teenager," she said, her voice steadier. "It's—it's a hard time for any kid."

Eli could smell Beth's drink—the sugary-sharp aroma of rum—with every oscillation of the fan, and he forced himself to look away from the bottle on the kitchen table. Instead, he studied Beth's face: pale, smudged with shadows, eyes unnaturally bright, her good-natured smile from last night replaced with something heavy and inward. She plucked at a loose thread on the hem of her shorts. "Caitlin would have let me know if—" Her fingers trembled. She squeezed her hands together and set them on her lap. "She would never have just left."

The painted glass shade of the old light fixture overhead lent a sepia tint to the kitchen table, and to the faces of its occupants, like an old photograph. Eli thought of the photos he had seen earlier that day in Kim Beran's office. These cabins were meant for good memories. Cards around the kitchen table on too-hot nights. Brownies and beer and swim-suits drying on the porch rail.

"Has there been anything bothering her lately?" asked the agent. "School? Friends?" She kept her eyes fixed on Beth. "Any mental health issues?"

Beth reached for her drink, swirled the liquor around in her cup, then set it back on the table without taking a sip. She sat up straight and ad-opted the matter-of-fact tone of a patient answering a doctor's questions in the exam room; a stoicism that comes from having to say overly inti-mate things to a stranger. "She's seeing a psychiatrist for depression and anxiety."

"Is she taking any medication?"

Beth narrowed her eyes, and Eli thought for a moment that she might decline to answer the question. "She takes Zoloft for depression."

"And has it been working?"

At first Beth didn't respond, just returned the other woman's stare.

Finally she said, "Agent, do you have teenagers?" She didn't wait for a response. "Because if you did, you'd understand that the last thing they want to do is talk to their parents about their feelings." She wiped a hand irritably across her damp forehead and looked away.

Agent Mason was unfazed. "Street drugs? Alcohol?" She looked down at her notebook and scribbled something Eli couldn't make out.

"No."

The word was too loud and hung in the air like smoke after a fire-cracker. The agent looked up. "Caitlin has never used drugs or alcohol?" The skepticism in her tone was unmistakable.

Beth wiped more tears from her eyes, one after another, with the back of one hand. Something like anger flared in her gaze, and when she spoke, her voice was tight with emotion. "She's a good kid." She looked at Eli, as if asking him to be on her side. Eli knew from his own experience that Agent Mason's interviewing techniques were spot-on. Eliciting emotion—genuine emotion—in an interview yielded the best information. Unexpressed emotions, even positive ones, chafed if left inside, like a pebble in a shoe. The agent's subtle provocations were expertly done.

The agent laid her pen on the notebook. "I'm not here to pass judgment on you or your family, but if we're going to find Caitlin, I need more help from you."

Beth seemed to take several steadying breaths, then picked up her glass and emptied the contents into her mouth. She pressed the back of her hand to her lips, and Eli was struck with the memory of last night on the beach, when he too had tossed back the lukewarm dregs of a strong drink before getting to unpleasant business. She set the glass on the table and said, "Caitlin wasn't herself last fall. Cal and I knew something was wrong, so we took her to see a psychiatrist in October. They did a urine drug screening as part of her workup and"—she squeezed her eyes shut and put her hands over her face for a long moment, then dropped them to her lap—"the test was positive for opioids."

The sweat on Eli's back went cold. He looked at Agent Mason, but she was laser-focused on Beth. The image of Ben Sharpe's pale arm—the puncture site, the nearly invisible bruises—flashed in his mind, quickly replaced by the picture of Caitlin that Kim Beran had painted. Pale, with-drawn, bearing no resemblance to the girl in the photo. What had they—Caitlin and Ben—gotten themselves into?

"What opioids, specifically?" asked the agent.

"I don't remember."

The agent raised a brow. "Are you sure? Urine drug screenings are usually very specific."

"I'm not a healthcare professional," snapped Beth.

"But your husband is."

Beth frowned. "Cal isn't a healthcare professional. He's—"

"A pharmaceutical salesman. I know. Prescription opioids, I believe." A new sharpness had entered the agent's voice.

The sense of general uneasiness around the table tightened into some-thing darker, and Beth folded her hands in her lap and returned the other woman's look.

"I was freaking out," said Beth. "Cal is more levelheaded. He kept track of the medical details."

"What did you and your husband do after you discovered that your daughter was using drugs?"

Beth twisted a diamond ring—a ring that had not been there last night—around and around on her left fourth finger. "We got her into psychiatric treatment, and she did really well. No more drugs. She was in a better mood, doing well in school." Then her face clouded.

"But?" prompted the agent.

Beth seemed to weigh her next thoughts carefully. "It sounds like no big deal, but about a month ago, Caitlin got a tattoo on her arm." She drew a deep breath and let it out. "I don't know where or how she got it. She refused to tell us. It was"—she hesitated—"it was a tattoo of a poppy."

Agent Mason seemed to pointedly avoid Eli's gaze. Their speculation about the significance of Caitlin's tattoo had been correct, and little plea-sure did it give either of them.

Opium.

"She swore it didn't mean anything," continued Beth, "but I—I didn't believe her. She's young, but she's smart. She knows the symbolism of poppies, that opium comes from poppies. Ever since she was little, she always wanted to know everything about everything." Her lips trembled in what seemed to be an attempt at a smile. "Each new fascination, she'd read and study whatever she could get her hands on." She smiled, and Eli was surprised to see genuine warmth on her face. He thought of the version of Beth Wallace he had met last night: easygoing, funny.

"I told Cal we needed to get her in to the counselor again, do another drug test." The words began to tumble out of her, and her pale cheeks grew flushed. "He told me I was overreacting and it became this, I don't know, this power struggle between the two of us. And the whole time, Caitlin swore up and down that she wasn't using drugs. That it had been a onetime thing." Her words grew faster. "Then the clinic back home didn't have any openings, and I figured coming to Shaky Lake would get her out of . . . of"—she waved a hand—"whatever it was she might have been involved in. But then this happened, and—" She leaned an elbow against the table and buried her face in her hand. Eli glanced at Agent Mason, the expression on her face giving nothing away. The air in the room became even more oppressive, if that was possible, and it was a long time before anyone spoke.

"And how is Caitlin's relationship with her father?" The agent's words startled both Eli and Beth after the long silence.

Beth's mouth twisted. "Cal and Caitlin don't always get along."

"What do they disagree on?" asked the agent.

"Like I said, she's a teenager. They disagree on everything." Across the kitchen, the fan started clicking violently.

"Cal works long hours," continued Beth. "It's stressful for all of us." Neither woman seemed distracted in the least by the noise from the fan, and Eli got up to examine it. He waited for Agent Mason to press the issue of Caitlin's relationship with her father, but she didn't.

"Your husband works for"—he heard the agent flip open a file folder and shuffle the papers for a second—"Orion Pharmaceuticals."

Beth said nothing.

"Quite the salary, I see." The hint of provocation was back.

Eli glanced back at the table and saw Beth's expression blacken. She folded her arms over her chest. "What does my husband's salary have to do with my daughter's disappearance?"

Agent Mason put up a hand. "I didn't mean to offend you. It's standard practice in a missing persons case to get a very thorough picture of their home life."

The kitchen window was closed against the mosquitoes that had been infiltrating the cabin via a torn screen, and Eli looked through the windowpane into the darkness beyond. He imagined the scene in the kitchen as it should have been. The Wallace family on vacation. Beth tidying up the kitchen for the night, Caitlin rummaging through the cabinets for snacks, Calvin leaning against the doorframe with a beer in hand and a tattered paperback spy novel tucked under his arm.

The fan began to wobble stiffly, precariously, back and forth on its long stem, like a penguin trying to navigate a downhill slope. Eli turned away from the window toward the fan, and after a smack of the gearbox and a good yank on the oscillator pin, the old machine quieted down and began blowing stale air around the room again. He slipped back into his chair.

Agent Mason acknowledged his return with a glance, then tucked a damp strand of hair behind her ear and turned her attention back to Beth. "Can you tell me more about your husband's employment with Orion?"

Beth pursed her lips. "Seems like you know quite a bit already."

The agent looked down at the file folder. "I know dates of employment, that sort of thing, but what I'm trying to understand is"—she paused, thoughtful—"the *vibe* at Orion. Maybe that's not the right word. What is it about your husband's job that compels him to work so much that it's become stressful for your family? He must be away from home a lot on sales trips."

It was a line of questioning that took Eli by surprise, and he studied the agent with a newfound curiosity. She seemed to know more about the Wallace family than he would have expected.

Beth's face went blank. "The work he does at Orion is very important."

"More important than his relationship with his daughter?"

For a moment, Beth didn't respond. Her lips pressed into such a thin line that they disappeared, and her eyes glittered. "What do you want me to say?" snapped Beth. "That it's the money?" She looked from the agent to Eli and back again, then held up her hands as if in surrender. "Yes, his salary and bonuses are excellent. Yes, the company car and phone and credit card are amazing."

A new vision of Beth Wallace appeared in Eli's mind. A wealthy, privileged woman with a luxury car and an inattentive husband.

"But," continued Beth, "you need to understand what it was like before Orion." She dropped her hands and, after a moment, stood up and began to do an uneasy circuit around the room, like an automated vacuum cleaner patrolling for dirt. "Ten years ago, during the recession, Cal got laid off and couldn't find a new job. My teacher's salary alone wasn't enough to pay the bills, and we lost our home and had to move into an apartment. We had to make up excuses to Caitlin's kindergarten teacher about why she couldn't go on field trips, or contribute to classroom fundraisers. We sold our wedding rings. We ate expired food. Needless to say, we certainly couldn't afford to come up here anymore." She fiddled with the dish towel tucked through the handle of the refrigerator. "And then it got worse. A perfect storm of expenses all at once. Cal broke his leg and needed surgery. My position at work—I was a sixth-grade teacher—was eliminated due to budget cuts."

Eli knew that feeling. A job, a career, eliminated for the sake of a budget.

"Our apartment building had a fire." She waved a hand in front of her, as if to dispel the memory as one would a cloud of smoke. "Nobody was hurt, but we lost nearly everything. We hadn't been able to afford renter's insurance." In the shadows along the perimeter of the room, Eli saw her pale face grow red with agitation. "For a while, we lived in motels, and for a few weeks, we even lived"—she paused, then, with a strangled sound, dropped back into her chair—"we lived in our fucking *car*."

Eli's eyes had been following her around the room, and as he looked at her, he tried to digest what she had just told them. Here was yet another version of this woman and her world. He thought of the photo of the Wallace family on the board at the station. The happy, comfortable, successful family in the photo was a snapshot in time that seemed less and less a reflection of the reality of their life.

"We survived by cashing in all of our retirement investments and racking up huge credit card bills," continued Beth. "Eventually, things got a little better. Cal got a job teaching at the local technical college. I got a job at a grocery store that offered health insurance, but"—she shook her head—"all that debt."

"Then, out of the blue, he was offered a job at Orion?" asked Agent Mason. She ran a finger down the page in front of her. "He has a business degree. How did he end up in pharmaceuticals?"

"He ran into an old college friend at a White Sox game," said Beth. "The guy worked for Orion and knew of a sales position opening up. He told Cal to apply, that he didn't need to have a science or healthcare background, that they would teach him what he needed to know on the job. He applied and Orion called him the next day."

Agent Mason sifted through her notes again. "And he's been there for"—she peered at a page in front of her—"six years. It must have been quite a relief for him to get that job, after all your family had been through."

"Cal and I swore never again, that Caitlin would never have to go through that again."

The agent gave a sympathetic nod, and there was a moment of silence as she picked up her notes and placed them into the folder, then clasped her hands together. The fastened kitchen window, stiff with age, creaked with a sudden change in air pressure, and the first drumbeats of rain struck the glass. From his position at the kitchen table, Eli could see into the living room. The plaid cotton drapes had up until now hung limply in the open windows, but with the change in the wind, the fabric billowed into the room with each gust.

Agent Mason gave Beth a long, measuring look, and the eyes that stared back were red-rimmed, drooping with exhaustion. Beth was trying, Eli knew, to keep it together, to stay levelheaded and calm, because to give in to her fears would mean acknowledging that the worst had happened, that something terrible and irreparable had happened to her child.

"Mrs. Wallace," began the agent, her voice so quiet that Eli had to lean in to hear over the sound of the fan and the rising wind, "where is your husband?"

Beth glanced at Eli and held his gaze a beat, her eyes asking him something he couldn't understand. In the other room, a newspaper flew from the coffee table to the floor and landed with a smack, and the sound of rain on the screens grew louder. Nobody moved. A shadow passed over Beth's face. When she spoke, her voice was hoarse and unsteady, and she met Agent Mason's gaze with something like despair.

"I don't know."

17

Eli should have gone home. He should have gone home and gotten a good night's sleep after such a long day. He should have listened to his body, wobbly with exhaustion. Instead, he listened to his idiotic mind.

Alyssa—she had corrected him when he addressed her as Agent Mason on the drive back to the station from Beth Wallace's cabin—pulled herself onto the red-and-black pleather seat next to him at the bar. "Wow, the barstools don't even wobble. Classy."

Babe's Bait and Tackle might have sturdy barstools, but classy it was not, which suited Eli just fine. Part fishing shop, part gas station, part convenience store, with a tavern in back for those who didn't want to get drunk in front of their families. The drop ceiling was sooty from the days when smoking was allowed in bars, and the walls were clad with dark faux-wood panels. Sagging banners for Bud Light and Smirnoff Ice and Captain Morgan vied for wall space with smudged mirrors and framed posters of long-retired Green Bay Packers players, and above the bar was a taxidermied ten-point buck. The air was thick with grease from the deep fryer, mixed with the smell of bleach and the sour odor of spilled beer. It all felt like home to Eli, but it occurred to him, looking at Alyssa in her simple yet polished clothes, stylish glasses, and full set of teeth, that he had made a big mistake bringing her here.

He directed her to a two-person high-top in the darkest corner of the already dark space. She seemed to consider setting her messenger bag on the floor but then decided against it. The speckled linoleum was yellowed and cracked with age, and a few stray crumbs and a straw wrapper lay on the floor beneath their table. Eli dragged a third stool over to the table and gestured that she could put her bag there. He had been surprised and not a little alarmed when she had taken him up on his offer of a drink after the interview with Beth Wallace. He was just trying to be hospitable, which, in Wisconsin, almost universally involved alcoholic beverages.

"I guess I didn't need to bring this thing," she said, with a wave toward the bag. "Force of habit." She had changed clothes at the hotel. Instead of her blazer and pants, she wore dark jeans, a fashionably loose gray T-shirt, and black leather sneaker-type shoes that probably cost as much as his car payment.

He held up the drink in his hand. "What can I get you?" It was his second drink, fourth counting the two shots he had when he first arrived. The alcohol now coursed soothingly through his bloodstream, restoring his function like a battery charger.

Alyssa peeled the laminated drink menu that was stuck with who-knows-what to the table and scanned the options. Eli considered suggesting they go somewhere else, somewhere less depressing, but decided against it. Parading an FBI agent around town would probably not be helpful to the investigation. Worse, everyone would assume she was a rebound girlfriend and word would get back to Michelle. Not that Michelle would care, but the last thing he needed was more scrutiny in his life. A light flashed from the pocket of Alyssa's jeans. Her phone again. She didn't react, other than to put a hand in her pocket and push the phone deeper inside. Her expression didn't change, but her shoulders tightened in a way that reinforced his suspicion that the calls she had been ignoring all evening were not work-related. The liquor in his system told him it was completely appropriate to ask her who she was ignoring, and he was about to do exactly that when he felt an arm around his shoulders.

"You've lost weight, baby." A woman's voice. The warm smell of powdery perfume and cigarette smoke.

"Hey, Connie." Eli smiled and leaned into the woman's embrace.

The woman gently pushed him away and held him at arm's length, a frown on her thin, wrinkled face, then squeezed her hands down both of his arms. Her frown deepened. "Do I need to be worried about you?" Her voice sounded like the rumble of a far-off lawn mower, low and rough from decades of cigarette smoke and alcohol.

"Connie, this is Alyssa Mason," he said, nodding to where Alyssa sat.

Connie spun around. "Oh." She scanned the younger woman's face. "Nice to meet you, Alyssa," she said, her voice careful. She held out her hand, and Alyssa shook it with a polite smile. Connie turned back to Eli with a questioning look.

"She's here to help with the case," he said. "Marge brought her in."

It was a beat before Connie responded, and he knew she, too, was wondering what had possessed him to bring Alyssa to Babe's. Finally she patted his arm. "Smart woman, your mother."

Eli's eyes shot to Alyssa; it occurred to him that she might not know he was Marge's son. He squirmed on his barstool as if caught in a lie. There was a flash of amusement in her eyes before she made a show of turning her attention back to the drink menu.

Connie turned to Alyssa and set a faded brown hand on her arm. "What can I get you, honey?"

Alyssa looked up from the drink list and tapped it against the table a few times, lips pursed in contemplation. He hoped she liked mass-produced domestic beer and bottom-rail liquor. Babe's was a stranger to the craft beer scene, and the "Shiraz" and "chardonnay" on the drink menu, he knew, were boxed wines far past their prime. Alyssa pointed at Eli's drink. "I'll have what he's having."

Connie raised an eyebrow, and one corner of her heavily lipsticked mouth kicked up. She nodded at Alyssa. "I'll have Ray bring it over." She frowned and grasped Eli's chin in one hand, turned his head from side to side. "So handsome," she said, a hint of sadness in her voice. "Some food, too. On the house." She put her arm around his shoulders again. "I won't have you wasting away."

Eli let her give him another hug, and once she had walked away, he turned back to Alyssa to find her staring at him.

"What?" he asked.

She narrowed her eyes. "Do you have cancer or something?"

"What? No."

"Then why is everyone"—she waved a hand in search of the right word—"babying you?"

"*Babying* me?"

"Asking about your sleep, feeding you—" She pushed her glasses higher on the bridge of her nose and looked him up and down. He resisted the urge to straighten his shirt. "You don't look like you're wasting away. You look like a Disney prince."

Her observation seemed more criticism than compliment, and he was thankful that the dim lighting hid the flush that sprang to his face. He struggled to find a response. There really was no good way to explain to a virtual stranger that his life had fallen into ruin, and that everyone in Shaky Lake knew all about it. "They're not babying me, they're just—"

"Drink for you, miss," grunted the bearded, round-bellied bartender as he tossed a cardboard coaster on the table and set down an extremely alcoholic-smelling cocktail, followed by three baskets of various fried foods. There was a rumpled, nearly empty pack of Marlboros in the breast pocket of his worn, too-tight BABE'S BAIT & TACKLE polo shirt, and he smelled strongly of underarm deodorant. He put a hand on Eli's shoulder and gave him a grim smile. "How you doing, man?" he said, in what he seemed to think was a conspiratorial whisper. "Hanging in there?" He ignored Alyssa. "Been a while since we've seen you. Connie was starting to worry." He hung an elbow on the side of the table. "You know how she is."

Eli ignored the spark of curiosity in Alyssa's eyes and gave the man what he hoped was a reassuring smile. "It's all good, Ray. I've just had a lot on my plate this summer."

"I know how that goes," Ray said. "Women." The word conveyed equal parts annoyance and bewilderment. He clapped Eli on the shoulder and glanced at Alyssa for the first time. "No offense, miss." He stabbed a finger into Eli's chest. "You need anything, brother, you know where to find me." He pushed away from the table. "I mean it. Anything."

When he had gone, Alyssa picked up the drink in front of her and sniffed it experimentally. She didn't seem to be bothered in the least by Ray's performance.

She took a sip of her drink and grimaced. "Jesus."

He grinned at her for the first time since they had met. "Strong?"

She shuddered. "I haven't had a drink that strong since high school."

"Yeah, well, welcome to Wisconsin." He drained his own drink and lifted the empty glass in a signal to Ray for another. "You want something different?"

She ignored the question and took another sip. "What *is* this?"

He pointed to a chalkboard behind the bar. "Two-for-one Korbel mixers tonight."

She stared at him blankly.

"Brandy." He nodded at her drink. "That one's a double."

She made a face. "I guess that's what I get for trying to keep up with you."

"I appreciate the effort," he laughed, "but please don't. Marge would kill me."

Alyssa studied his face. "She doesn't look old enough to be your mother." She paused. "Not that you look—"

"She was pretty young when I was born. It's why she and my dad got married."

"Oh." There was no awkwardness in her tone, but she seemed momentarily at a loss as to the proper response to this remark. Thankfully, Ray materialized again. He slid a drink across the table to Eli, then turned to Alyssa and nodded at the drink in her hand. "Takes the rust off, don't it?" He elbowed her and winked. "Don't know what Eli was thinking, ordering you something that strong." He took a step back and looked her over. "You look like you'd be a cheap date." Eli considered, then abandoned, the idea of punching him, and Ray must have recognized the look on his face, because he took another step back and held out his hand in a conciliatory gesture. "No offense," he said, for a second time. He looked back and forth between Eli and Alyssa. "I just meant"— he waved a hand in the general direction of her chest—"she don't have much meat on her bones."

"Thanks for the drink, Ray," interrupted Eli loudly. He watched, jaw clenched, as Ray fled to the bar. Then he turned to Alyssa with an apology on his lips, only to find her laughing merrily behind the rim of her glass.

"He's not wrong," she said. She plucked a maraschino cherry from the plastic cocktail spear in her drink and popped it into her mouth. "These are *pint* glasses, you know." She wiggled her straw. "And these things are for milkshakes, not cocktails."

He ignored the observations. "Sorry about that. Ray's a good guy. He just doesn't have much of a filter."

"Don't worry about it." She took one last sip of her drink, then set it down and wiped her hands on her thighs. "Anyway," she said, "who's Babe?"

Eli's brows came together. "Babe?"

"Babe's Bait and Tackle."

"Oh," he said, grateful for the change of topic. "Babe the Blue Ox." He pushed his own drink away and rested his elbows on the table. "You know the legend of Paul Bunyan, don't you? The mythical lumberjack?"

Alyssa shook her head and shrugged to convey her nonrecognition.

"Eight feet tall, could clear an entire forest in a day?" He paused a beat, and when she shook her head again, he looked at her in astonishment, then leaned forward and pointed to the wall behind her. "See?"

She turned to look at a poster that hung there. "Paul Bunyan Days," she read. The words were compilations of log illustrations, arranged to create letters, and the bearded, brawny figure of Paul Bunyan, clad in buffalo plaid and stocking cap, axe tucked into his belt, stood astride a broad landscape of bare stumps. She pushed her glasses up farther on her nose. "Logrolling competition. Axe-throwing contest. Pancake and Porky breakfast." She squinted at an illustration of a powder-blue ox at Paul's knee. She turned back and looked at Eli. "Babe pageant?"

"Babies, not women in bikinis."

"And that's less weird?"

"More adorable than weird."

She looked at him doubtfully.

"You missed it anyway," he said. He reached for his drink. "That poster is from last year."

She laughed, and he felt himself relax a fraction. "Didn't you see the twenty-foot-high Paul Bunyan statue when you got into town?" he asked.

"Is that what that was?" She shook her head. "Shaky Lake is . . ."

"Cheesy?"

"I was going to say charming."

He waved a finger in a circle above his head to indicate their shabby surroundings. "Oozing with charm, this place."

She laughed again. "So," she said, "how long have you been with the sheriff's department?"

"About six months."

"And before that?"

He jiggled the ice in his newly replenished drink and took a sip. When he looked up, the inquisitiveness in her face had not waned. He suppressed a sigh. "Army. I spent two years in Afghanistan."

Her face went still. "Combat?"

He nodded. Took another sip of his drink.

"And before that?"

"You're really good at asking questions. Maybe you should join the FBI."

She smiled, but there was a wariness in her eyes.

He cleared his throat. "US Fish and Wildlife Service. I was a Special Investigations warden for fifteen years. I joined the army after 9/11 but spent most of that time in the reserves."

Her eyes widened; it was the first hint of excitement he had seen from her so far. "Wow, Fish and Wildlife positions are some of the hardest federal law enforcement jobs to get," she said. "You must have been *good*." The moment the words were out, she bit her lip. "I mean—" She opened her mouth. Closed it. "I didn't mean to imply that you're not—"

He waved away her apology, then drained his nearly full glass and set it on the table a little harder than he had intended. "My position was eliminated six months after I got back from my deployment." He didn't want her to think he'd lost his job due to poor performance. He had loved his job. He still missed it every single day. Alyssa was right; US Fish and Wildlife was a big deal. Wildlife trafficking was one of the most lucrative illegal activities on the planet; a multibillion-dollar industry. Maybe illegally imported mitten crabs or poached bear gallbladders weren't as dramatic-sounding as smuggled heroin or cocaine, but the criminal operations were often just as organized and dangerous. Now, as a small-town sheriff's deputy, he was little more than a traffic cop, or a glorified bouncer. Phil would send him to crimes in progress—bar fights, domestic disputes—and his massive physical presence alone was often enough to put an end to the situation. Jake had worked for a private security company—an incredibly dull job, per his report—before moving to Shaky Lake, and he adored breaking up a good bar fight. But the department didn't have the manpower or resources to investigate much of anything, and Eli suspected that the only reason Marge was taking part in the current investigation was her personal connection to Ben Sharpe. She could have farmed out the whole thing to the FBI rather than collaborate.

"I'd be interested to hear your thoughts on the case so far," Alyssa said, and he got the impression that she was trying to make amends for inadvertently insulting him. "That was a good catch back at the cabin, finding the CD."

He ran a hand across the overlong stubble on his jaw. "Whoever played the music in the cabin did it with a very specific purpose," he said. "They wanted the body to be found."

Cal

*C*al closed his laptop. *Hours had passed since the fax arrived; the sun had set and the natural light in his office had shifted to shadow, then to night. For a long time, he sat in the darkness and went over the information again and again, like an equation he had long ago solved, afraid that he had made some elementary error. It had taken hours and what probably constituted hacking to find the full names of each study participant with a handwritten number by their name. After that, it hadn't taken long to realize what the eight-digit numbers represented.*

Dates of death.

Cal had scoured the internet for obituaries, news articles, public records, and social media posts. Two hundred thirty-six people in the research trial, dead. Nearly 10 percent of study participants. Yes, people in the general population were dying from opioid addiction. There were bound to be study participants for whom Salvare just wasn't enough, for whom the treatment was too little, too late. He knew the statistics, had recited them again and again in presentations to doctors and pharmacists, and try as he might, he could come up with only one explanation for the fact that study participants were ten times more likely to die than others who were addicted to opioids.

Salvare was killing people.

18

Eli knew he was snooping. Alyssa's phone lay facedown where she had left it on the sticky bar table while she used the restroom. There was a buzz, then a halo of light on the table around the phone, announcing an incoming call. He glanced at the restroom door, across the bar but safely in his line of sight. He tipped the phone on its side to see the screen.

Jason

No last name. A contact close enough, perhaps, not to need further identification, like *Mom*.
Or Michelle.
The caller hung up, and a bubble appeared on the screen showing four missed calls from *Jason*, plus three texts from him.

Call me when you get there.
You okay?
Will you please just call me?

He set the phone back on the table, exactly where she had left it. A moment later Alyssa emerged from the bathroom and made her way back to the table.
From across the room came an eruption of shouts and drunken guf-

faws as Ray and a pair of men with the beaten-leather look of highway workers played dice at the bar. As Alyssa climbed back onto the barstool, the air-conditioning kicked up a notch, and the breeze from the vent above their table intensified and blew wisps of hair free from her ponytail. She pressed her hands between her knees and shivered, and he could see goose bumps erupt on her pale arms.

He got halfway to his feet. "Want me to have Ray turn the AC down?"

"It's fine," she said. "Another sip of this drink and I'll be sweating." She raised the glass to her mouth with one hand and reached for her phone with the other, then stopped mid-sip when she saw the screen. Eli pretended to watch the rowdy game of dice at the other end of the room.

"Sorry, do you mind if I step out for a second?" she asked.

He turned back to her as if he had forgotten for a moment that she was there. Then, "No problem. Take your time." He watched her walk to the door. In her street clothes, she didn't look so scrawny, so adolescent. He shook his head to dislodge the thought.

Several minutes later, Alyssa reappeared. The rain must have picked up while she was outside, because the shoulders of her shirt were damp; she pulled off her glasses to wipe away raindrops, then looked at her watch. "God, it's almost midnight." She reached for her bag. "I should really get going," she said, and gave him a smile that, even in the dim room, looked forced. He wanted to ask her what was wrong, but his head felt suddenly fuzzy, and he stared at her blankly for a moment. It occurred to him that he was very, very drunk.

The front door swung open and two young women entered, along with the sounds of sudden heavy rain sweeping across the parking lot. Their hair and thin shirts were plastered to their skin from the rain, and they panted with laughter as they made their way into the bar. As if on cue, the song on the jukebox switched to a racy country song Eli didn't recognize, and the women squealed and twitched their hips in time to the beat. He watched them scan the room, then stop abruptly when they saw him in the corner. As drunk as he was, he could make out their predatory smiles and the way they arched their backs a little, slowing their steps as they headed toward the bar. They seemed not to care in the slightest that

Alyssa was with him, or that he was probably fifteen years their senior. The taller of the two leaned over the bar a bit farther than necessary to order a drink, then fingered the hem of her tank top where it had ridden up to reveal several inches of her lower back. Her friend adjusted her bra strap and glanced back at Eli. Exhaustion and a dull sense of depression washed over him, and he got to his feet. Alyssa watched him closely as he planted himself firmly against the table.

"You're right," he said. "It's getting late. I'll walk out with you." He was good—too good—at disguising intoxication, but whether it was from the exhaustion or the pain in his head, he pushed himself away from the table and immediately lost his balance. He fell heavily against the leather-backed stool Alyssa had recently vacated, and it scraped loudly against the floor and began to tip. Too late, he tried to catch himself and instead toppled over with the stool. He landed hard, facedown, his chest against the metal stool legs, then bounced onto the grimy floor. The impact knocked the wind out of him, and he lay there on the floor for a full five seconds before he caught his breath.

"Oh no!" he heard Alyssa exclaim. He looked up and saw her leaning over him, hand extended. He blinked at her hand for a moment, then got slowly to his feet without her assistance. "I'm *so* sorry," she said, loud enough to be heard throughout the bar, even over the music. "I tripped you. I'm such an idiot!" She bent over and picked up the stool and set it upright, then took a few steps forward and put her hands on his upper arms. "I'm really sorry," she said again, her voice still resonant, then turned around, shamefaced, toward the appalled faces of everyone in the bar before turning back to him. She was very close, and he could smell the sweetness of maraschino cherry on her breath as she tipped her head way back to study his face. Eli's heart thundered in his chest, both from the impact of the fall and from his mortification at having fallen in the first place, and perhaps from other reasons he chose to ignore. Her back to the crowd, Alyssa's expression turned appraising. "You okay?" she asked quietly, businesslike, with no hint of embarrassment. He glanced over her shoulder and saw that the onlookers had fallen for Alyssa's ruse and returned to their own affairs. His gaze connected with Connie, who was staring at him with a deep-cut groove between her black-lined eyes. He looked quickly away from Connie and managed a nod at Alyssa.

"Good," she said, then took a step back. "I'm going to go," she murmured, "and you're going to finish all that food"—she glanced to the now-cold food on the table—"and drink a couple glasses of water, and in an hour, you're going to go home and get some sleep." She slung her messenger bag over her head and onto one shoulder, then gripped the strap with both hands where it angled across her chest. "I'll see you tomorrow." She turned and headed toward the doorway, but halfway there, she turned and looked back over her shoulder. She smiled at him with what looked like genuine warmth. "Thanks for the hospitality." Then, before he could respond, she turned and pushed her way through the glass door and out into the rain.

19

D an Simons was sitting in his front yard drinking a beer when Eli drove up. The morning sun had not yet crested the dense row of windbreak pines that shielded Dan's house from the road. Eli couldn't remember what time he had gotten home last night. Couldn't remember the drive home, if he was honest, but once home, he had lain awake for hours, thoughts flickering deep in his subconscious. Facts that wouldn't rise to the surface, ideas that came and went in a flash of tantalizing silver, like a fish vanishing in lake weeds. He had awoken in a damp tangle of sheets with a crushing headache—a hangover rather than head trauma this time, thank god—and with a single concrete thought lying next to him on the pillow, like a coin from the tooth fairy.

Heroin.

Marge had called before he had a chance to turn the idea over in his mind, so he kept it to himself for the time being and instead spent the next forty-five minutes mulling things over in the shower, until the hot water tank ran dry and the spray turned lukewarm, then piercingly cold against the back of his neck. When he finally turned off the tap, he stepped onto the bath mat with a bad case of the shivers, but with an idea. A next step toward an explanation for what had happened and, just maybe, a chance of finding Caitlin.

Dan watched, eyes half-open, as Eli made his way across the patchwork of weeds and sunburnt quack grass that some might call a lawn.

The scent of clover and the oregano-like aroma of ground vine were surprisingly refreshing. Even if his visit to Dan Simons turned out to be a dead end, at least it got him out of bed. Eli hadn't called ahead; Dan wouldn't have picked up the phone anyway. Their rapport didn't go nearly that far. By the time Eli reached where Dan was sitting, his shoes were drenched from the damp vegetation, and they squelched with each step. He could see why the other man hadn't bothered to wear shoes at all.

Dan was skinny and flabby at the same time, with pale, almost translucent skin where a shirt should have been, and dark, leathery arms decorated here and there with faded tattoos. He held court in a decrepit lawn chair that looked like it was held together by nothing more than duct tape and stubbornness. He wore old cargo shorts and a tattered straw cowboy hat, like something left behind after a Kenny Chesney concert. He looked Eli over with good-humored contempt.

"You look like shit, Eli."

"Good morning to you, too, Dan." Eli had left his car windows open last night in the rain, and he realized just now that his backside was damp from the soggy, musty upholstery. He pulled his phone out of his back pocket and crammed it into the breast pocket of his shirt, where it sagged and wobbled stupidly in the thin fabric. On the drive here, he had fantasized about never having to see Alyssa Mason again. At least she was gracious enough not to text him this morning to see how he was doing. He still had no idea why she'd covered for him last night.

"What have I done now, Deputy?" Dan leaned back in the chair and stretched his legs in front of him. Despite his skinniness, he had a round face and wide shoulders that hinted at the meaty guy he had been years ago. He was just a couple of years older than Eli, early forties, but time had not been kind to him. Eli had been there the day Dan got expelled from Shaky Lake High School for taking a swing at the principal, a swaggering, smug-faced bully of a man. He had seen the look—not anger or fear, but relief—on Dan's face afterward, as if he had won a bitter fight, and banishment was his reward. After that, Eli had seen Dan only rarely, at the bait shop, and then not at all for years. According to Marge, he had been in prison for the better part of his twenties and had spent his thirties in the clutches of heroin addiction. It was one of the reasons Eli had decided to pay him a visit this morning.

"Got some time to talk?" Eli propped his fists on his hips and squinted past Dan toward the faded brown cabin behind him. The front windows and door were shaded by fabric awnings, limp and tattered after fifty-plus years of wear, the original stripes nearly indistinguishable. The concrete pad in front of the door was cracked and uneven and lush with weeds, and a couple of warped two-by-fours had been nailed together to form a rickety front step. A snow shovel and stacks of mismatched bricks rested against the house on one side of the steps, and on the other was a row of tomato plants in orange ten-gallon pails. "We could go inside if you want."

Eli saw something move in the shaded patch of weeds below Dan's chair. A fuzzy brown head emerged; then a Labrador retriever puppy wiggled out and promptly did a face-plant into an overgrown patch of clover before settling itself in front of Dan's feet.

"She's not quite house-trained," said Dan as he scooped up the puppy and balanced it on his lap. He looked at Eli. "So maybe we can stay outside for now."

Eli felt a wave of homesickness. He had left a dog behind when he moved out, in addition to a wife and a son. A shout of laughter and the rev of a boat engine drifted from the lake beyond Dan's cabin, and Eli pictured being out on the water with Andy. Eli hadn't taken his boat out once this year. Hadn't even cleaned it and prepared it for use.

Eli took a step toward Dan. "That's a nice-looking dog," he said. "What's her—"

"What can I help you with, Eli?" Dan smoothed a wisp of puppy fluff on top of the dog's head, then held up his beer can and wiggled it at Eli. "As you can see, I'm busy."

Another lawn chair lay in the weeds, and Eli reached for it, shook it open, and lowered himself down. The aluminum legs creaked under his weight. "We're investigating a murder. A kid named Ben Sharpe. Did you know him?"

Dan nudged the puppy off his lap and fished a pack of cigarettes and a lighter from the pocket of his shorts. He lit the cigarette and took a long puff, then picked a speck of tobacco from his tongue before he responded. "Talked to him a couple times. Wouldn't say I knew him."

Eli pulled a stem of clover from the lawn and began to pull out the tiny plug-shaped petals. "We found him dead in his boat on Tuesday night, moored over at Beran's." He glanced up and met Dan's eyes for a moment, then looked away.

"Don't know nothing about that." The man tapped the ash from his cigarette into the grass and nudged the puppy with a bare foot, then winced when she attacked his ankle. "Maisy!" He scooped her up into his lap again and shook a finger at her. *"No biting."* He clucked and shook his head, then looked at Eli.

Eli smirked. "Never thought of you as the fatherly type."

"Are we done here?"

Eli grinned and rubbed his tired eyes, then pulled his notebook and pencil from his pocket. "As long as I'm here, I should probably go through the motions." He flipped to a blank page in his notebook, then set it on his knee, pen poised. "Where were you on Tuesday between, say, noon and eight p.m.?"

Dan took one last draw from his cigarette, then bent over the arm of the lawn chair to stub it out. "Home."

"The whole time?"

"The whole time." He chugged the rest of his beer, and when he was done swallowing, he let out a rather theatrical belch.

"Can anyone corroborate this?"

"Just her." Dan curled his arm around the puppy and bent to kiss her wet brown nose.

Eli chewed on his lip. "I probably shouldn't do this, but could I pet her? It's Maisy, right?"

Dan paused a moment, then held up the squirming puppy and passed it to him. There was a flash of anxiety on his face, there, then gone. He grunted a laugh. "Michelle kicked you out and kept the dog, huh?"

Eli shot him a look, then tossed the pen and notebook in the grass and took the puppy. "My new place doesn't allow dogs."

"Ah."

Eli pressed his cheek against the dog's soft head and took in the smell of puppy breath and dog shampoo. He smoothed her rolls of puppy fat and yelped when she reached up to bite his ear. "She been out fishing with you yet?"

The corner of Dan's mouth twitched. "The little shit jumped off the boat the other day. Had to get her a life jacket."

Eli snorted. "She's got you whupped already." He scratched the puppy behind the ears and let her gnaw his hands for a moment, then handed her back to Dan and picked up the notebook. Just then the morning sun crested the tree line along the eastern edge of the property and hit Eli squarely on the back. He wiped at the back of his neck and considered, then rejected, the idea of moving his chair into the shade. It might not hurt to sweat the residual alcohol from his body before he saw Andy.

"Don't take this the wrong way, Eli, but you look like you could use a drink." Dan set the puppy on the ground, fished an unopened can of beer from the small cooler under his chair, and held it up.

Eli gazed longingly at the beer. In that moment, he ached with something other than just a craving for a dose of alcohol. How many times had he sat in a rickety old lawn chair on a bright summer day, beer in hand, fishing pole at the ready, dog by his side? He waved away Dan's offer. "I'm good, thanks."

"Worried I'll tell Marge?"

Eli attempted a smile. "Something like that." Then, "When was the last time you talked to Ben Sharpe?"

Dan lifted his hat and scrubbed a hand through his hair. "A few days ago. Would have been Sunday. Dumbass hadn't tied his boat down right, and the thing floated halfway to my place before he noticed. I took out my boat and brought it back for him. Showed him how to tie it down right."

"Was anyone else with him?"

"Some skinny blond girl." He made a face. "Just stood there while the kid and I did all the work."

The men sat in silence for a while, then Eli spoke. "I never met Ben Sharpe. Marge said he was a nice kid. What was your impression of him?"

Dan looked confused. "Impression? I don't know, that he was a kid too stupid to tie his boat down right."

Eli thought for a minute. "Could he have been, you know, *on* something? Drugs?"

Dan shook his head. "No." He pronounced the word with perfect certainty. "He was . . . I let him pet Maisy."

"And the girl?" asked Eli.

"She just sat there on the dock looking bitchy. She wasn't on anything either, except maybe the rag."

"Any idea who she was?"

"No idea."

Both men watched as the puppy began to dig up an anthill a few feet away. Sand shot out in all directions. "What about Ben's mom, Rachel? Do you know her?"

Dan crossed an ankle over one knee. "Yeah, we've been dating for a while now."

Eli sat upright in the chair. "Really?"

Dan snorted. "Fuck no." He rested an elbow on the back of the lawn chair. "I don't associate with those country club types."

Eli lifted an eyebrow. "You mean *they* don't associate with *you*."

Dan shrugged.

Eli plucked his sunglasses from where they dangled on the neckline of his shirt and pushed them onto his face. He had never met Rachel Sharpe, had only the photograph from the station to go on. Her husband was rich, that much he knew, but the woman in the photo was not. Not really. She had money now, clearly. A huge lake house, a country club membership, a high-quality boob job. But something haunted her. He had recognized the look because it was the same one that greeted him in the mirror on the infrequent occasions when he was forced to look at himself. Bad things had happened to her; they still whispered in her ear, still clung to her. And now her boy was gone. What would he himself have done if it had been Andy in the bottom of that boat? Eli suppressed a shudder and thanked god for the dark sunglasses that obscured the expression in his eyes.

"Rachel Sharpe looks fancy," said Dan, and then, as if he had heard Eli's thoughts, "but she ain't right in the head." He reached for another cigarette, lit it. "Not that I judge her for it. Addiction is—" He shook his head. The metallic buzz of cicadas swelled and filled the silence as Dan seemed to struggle with what to say next. "You tell Marge," he said finally, then paused, put his cigarette to his mouth, and then lowered it again without taking a draw, "that someone needs to keep an eye on that girl."

"Rachel, you mean?"

Dan nodded. "She don't have much to live for now, does she?" He cloaked the profundity of his words with a rough tone and a scowl, but Eli recognized the truth in what he said. He didn't need to imagine the sort of experiences Dan might have had to give him knowledge about such things. Then, in a highly effective change of subject, Dan leaned over the arm of his lawn chair and hocked a massive loogie into the weeds. "Anyway." He dragged the back of his hand across his mouth before taking a long drag on his cigarette. He turned to looked at the puppy, who had given up on the anthill and was at that moment engaged in a fierce battle with her own tail. "Maisy, get over here." He snapped his fingers and the dog looked up, then barreled over to him.

Eli would have liked to ask Dan more about Rachel, but it was clear that he had said all he was going to say about her. He changed course. "We found the boy because of a noise disturbance call, and at first, I assumed you were the one blasting the music." He leaned forward, elbows on his knees. "That's how you usually go about getting my attention, isn't it?"

Dan's surly expression broke into a self-satisfied grin. "I have no idea what you're talking about, Deputy."

Eli ignored that. "Thing is, as you know, the music wasn't coming from your house this time. It was coming from a cabin at Beran's Resort, near where the body was found. Around nine o'clock Tuesday night. I assume you heard it. That's not all that far from your house. Hell, I could hear it halfway across the lake."

Dan reached down to pet the puppy and didn't look at Eli. "I went to bed early on Tuesday. Once I'm out, I'm out."

Eli, who had heard a thousand rehearsed answers, found the response too pat, too fluent. He didn't challenge Dan on the matter, though. The answers Eli was seeking didn't necessarily come in the form of words. He let the silence between them lengthen until he realized that Dan must have had plenty of experience being interviewed by law enforcement. He knew the tricks—the awkward silences, the baiting questions—and, unfortunately for Eli, he knew how to disappoint his interrogators.

"Dan, the boy died of an opioid overdose."

The man's face was shielded by the brim of his hat as he bent over to pet the dog, but at Eli's words, his hands stilled. He didn't look up.

"Somebody knocked him out and injected him," continued Eli, his eyes locked on Dan. "And that girl you saw with Ben on Sunday? Her name's Caitlin Wallace and she's missing. She was last seen with Ben on Tuesday, right around the time we think he was killed."

Dan seemed transfixed by the weeds beneath his feet. He was quiet for a long time, then, "I told you, Eli, I don't—"

"Look, we both know you're not a killer." Eli ran his thumb along the side of his notebook, ruffled the pages like a deck of playing cards, then stuffed it back into his pocket. The heat from the sun grew more intense on his back, and the skin on his neck prickled with the promise of a sunburn. By August, he was usually as brown as an acorn from being out on the water or working in the yard or taking the dog for long runs, but not this summer. He watched as Dan straightened in his chair, saw the tension in the cords of the man's neck and the way he worried a thumb across the knuckles of his other hand.

"So who killed him?" asked Eli. The question was sincere, not a provocation.

"I don't know." Dan's face was taut with obstinance.

You know something.

Eli barely managed to keep the words inside his head. Instinctively, he knew that pressing Dan would be a mistake. The man had no reason to trust Eli and every reason to believe that he would get the raw end of whatever happened if he agreed to talk. As much as he dreaded ever laying eyes on her again, Eli wished Alyssa were here. She was clearly very good at her job. Beth Wallace hadn't told them the whole story last night.

Eli was sure of it. But what she *had* told Alyssa was the absolute truth, and it was a whole lot more than she had intended to say. Last night Alyssa had asked questions as if she already knew the answers, had presented as fact what surely could only, at that point, be speculation. Eli had his own speculations as to how Dan Simons fit into all that had happened in the past two days, and it was going to take all his patience to let Dan's story ripen before plucking it from him. He looked at his watch, more for an excuse to break the tension between the two of them than to determine what time it was, but noticed with a start of alarm that he was due to meet Andy ten minutes ago. The boy had finally convinced his mom to let him mow the lawn, and Eli had promised to teach him how to use the mower today.

"Shit," he said, and got to his feet. "I've got to run." He noticed with some satisfaction that Dan looked discombobulated by the sudden end to the conversation. It was confirmation that there was more the man wanted to say. Eli pulled a business card from his breast pocket and tossed it on the lawn chair where he had been sitting. "Call me if you think of any information that might be useful." He paused. Smiled. "Or, you can always blast some of that shitty music you like and wait for the neighbors to call in a noise disturbance."

Dan scowled. "You make it sound like the Bat-Signal."

"Your words, not mine," said Eli. He stooped down to scratch the puppy behind the ears. "Bye, Maisy. Don't be too hard on your old dad." He straightened the dog's too-big leather collar and stood up. Then, with a departing nod to Dan, he started back to the car.

20

Marge craned her head out the window of the truck and swore at the dark tangle of old-growth trees and impenetrable bracken that lined the road. She turned off the GPS and twisted around to look out the back window. How had she lived the better part of sixty years in Sherman County and never visited the Green Lake Country Club? She had done some research last night before bed and come up nearly empty-handed. No website. No advertisements. She'd had to search municipal records just to find the address. What little she could learn about the place came from a Wisconsin travel blog, last updated fifteen years ago, that listed Green Lake Country Club as the former Northwoods hideaway of a Prohibition-era mob boss from Chicago.

She hadn't told anyone she was going to pay a visit to the country club today. She didn't have a good explanation for why she had even decided to come. Curiosity, mostly, after talking to Chuck Sharpe about the place. Now, sitting in her truck on the side of a no-name road, gas light on empty, surrounded by nothing but trees, she considered whether maybe she had better things to do today. Visit Beth Wallace, for one. She had called Caitlin's mother first thing that morning to update her on the search, to offer reassurances that they were going to the greatest lengths possible to find Caitlin, and to suggest again the idea of assigning a liaison officer to stay with Beth in the cabin. The neighboring Melvin County Sheriff's Department owed Marge more than a few favors, and

she knew they could be easily persuaded to lend her one of their deputies. This last part she did not share with Beth. No good would come
from her knowing how pathetically short-staffed the Sherman County
Sheriff's Department was. Beth, to Marge's disappointment, had refused
the offer of a liaison officer, and now the idea of Beth sitting alone in the
cabin, mere yards away from where Ben Sharpe's body had been found,
had turned up the volume on the whine of anxiety that formed the backdrop of Marge's state of mind.

She drummed the fingers of one hand against the steering wheel,
looked one more time in the rearview mirror, and decided she must have
driven past the entrance. She didn't bother to make a U-turn, just put the
truck in reverse and cruised backward down the deserted road until she
saw what she had, on her first pass, assumed was the driveway of someone's remote cabin. Then she noticed the security camera mounted on a
nearby tree, and a nearly concealed pair of boxes, one on each side of the
driveway, that she recognized as laser motion detectors, and she knew she
had found the right place.

She started down the driveway, which soon divided into a smooth
blacktop boulevard, the center strip lush with the kind of plants that didn't
survive Wisconsin winters. Palms, canna, banana trees, riots of orange
and hot-pink flowers. The kind of plants that require an army of land-
scapers and a lot of money. Art deco lampposts arched across both sides
of the boulevard. Impressive in the morning light, undoubtedly magical
at night. The heavy forest came right to the edge of the pavement, and the
effect was like traveling through a tunnel toward some strange, mysteri-
ous destination. When she finally reached the gate—an art deco master-
piece capped with intricately carved stone pine cones—she half expected
to find that she had been transported to an entirely different world, as if
she had crossed into the Land of Oz.

To her surprise, given the clandestine flavor of the place thus far, the
beautiful iron gate was open wide, with no evidence of electronic con-
trols or intercoms or keypads. It would ruin the wonderland effect, she
supposed. However, barely visible in the canopy of the beech trees and
aspens that skirted the gate was another set of security cameras, and a

discreet sensor cord stretched across the paved surface from column to column. Her arrival would not go unnoticed.

The main building was directly across from the gate, over a circular expanse of crushed gravel, and the wide-open space was punctuated in the center with a large tiered fountain, ringed with yews clipped into perfect topiary balls of various sizes. The structure was Tudor Revival, all stucco and timber-framed gables and mullioned, leaded glass windows. Charming in a fairy-tale sort of way. Closer to the building, the tropical plants were mixed with clusters of red geraniums, all marshaled into neat pathways by low yew hedges. The flagstone path diverged here and there to create shady bowers and patios, furnished with black wrought-iron tables and chairs. A silver-haired woman in tennis clothes sat on a patio to the left of the front door, sipping coffee and flipping the pages of a very thick magazine.

Marge parked the truck at the far end of the gravel lot, next to a beat-up brown Subaru station wagon, the only other non-luxury car, and made her way to the front door. The woman on the patio subjected Marge to the kind of brazenly critical stare that only people of a certain tax bracket felt entitled to give, and proceeded to watch as Marge approached the front door as if she were a dangerous wild animal that had wandered into the backyard. It struck Marge that Rachel, for all her faults, was not a snob.

The door was a massive slab of oak, heavy and dark and very old, banded with iron strips at the hinges and topped with a small window decorated with wrought-iron grilles shaped into curlicues. It fit with the fairy-tale style of the building, but it reminded Marge that the building had originally been built as a fortress during Prohibition. Though she had, until five minutes ago, been wholly unacquainted with the place, there was something about the Green Lake Country Club that made her uneasy. Ghosts of a violent past, perhaps. She glanced to her left to find the silver-haired woman still staring at her, all the Botox and fillers in the world unable to smooth away the disdain in her expression. Marge turned her attention back to the door. Something about the tableau in front of her made it clear that one did not simply open this particular door and stroll inside. There was a mother-of-pearl doorbell to the side of the entrance, and she pushed it. Her conjecture from earlier, that she had been surveilled since the moment she turned off the main road, proved accurate when, mere seconds after she rang the bell, the door opened.

The man was thirtysomething, of medium height and slim, with dark hair above a high forehead, and a clean-shaven, angular face. He wore a mud-brown vest, matching tie, and gray wool pants, and the sleeves of his crisp ice-blue shirt were rolled to his elbows, with a white linen dish towel thrown over his shoulder as if he had just come from polishing the silver. The foyer behind him was a large vaulted space, paneled in honey-stained pine, with a huge fireplace set into one wall, clad floor to ceiling in fieldstone and topped with a mantel crafted from what was likely an ancient, colossal pine tree. An enormous chandelier made of deer antlers hung from the ceiling, and the furniture and decor, though obviously of high-end stock, managed to evoke coziness and a certain seductive nostalgia—a continuation of the fairy-tale experience that gave Marge a better understanding of why people would pay small fortunes to belong to the Green Lake Country Club.

"Good morning. Welcome to Green Lake Country Club." The man at the door smiled and held out a hand to Marge. His expression was solicitous and warm, and his handsomeness and polished appearance seemed custom-made for the high-end space. If he held Marge in the same condescending disdain as the woman on the patio, he had the good training to hide it.

She shook his hand. "I'm Marge North, with the Sherman County Sheriff's Department." They seemed to be the only two people in the large room, though she heard the chink of glassware and the soft hum of conversation coming from a doorway at the far end of the space. Still, she kept her voice mild and not so loud as to draw attention to herself. "I'd like to speak with the manager as part of an investigation."

The man glanced at her badge, and it was a beat before he spoke. "Sheriff, I'm so sorry, but Mr. Gilson, the owner and general manager, is out of town to attend to a family emergency. I'm the assistant manager, Andrew Doherty." He gave a little bow and an apologetic smile, then gestured toward an open door adjacent to the front entrance. "Let's talk privately." Despite his courteousness, Marge sensed he was keen to get her out of view as quickly as possible. Not that she blamed him. Law enforcement on anyone's doorstep is never a good look.

He led Marge into a well-appointed room, with a gleaming wooden desk and sideboard, antique rugs, and a pair of overstuffed leather chairs arranged in front of an unlit fireplace. The room was lined on three sides by tall pine bookcases, generously stocked, and over the finely carved pine mantel was a large, antique-looking piece of framed art.

Doherty followed Marge a few steps into the room and paused, hands clasped solicitously. "Can I get you some coffee, Sheriff? I've just made a fresh pot."

She smiled. "I'd love some, thank you." She'd had her morning coffee hours ago, but Andrew Doherty didn't need to know that.

He gestured at the leather chairs. "Please make yourself comfortable."

When he'd left, rather than sit, Marge went to the fireplace. The mantel was tastefully styled with framed black-and-white photographs and various objets d'art, in keeping with the vintage Northwoods aesthetic, and the piece over the mantel that had caught her eye turned out to be a faded topographical map of the country club and surrounding property. She took a step back to take in the entire piece. The boundaries of the Green Lake Country Club property extended much farther than she had realized; all the way from the southern and western shore of Green Lake to the northernmost sliver of Shaky Lake's shoreline. Clusters of zigzag lines seemed to illustrate wooded areas, which covered most of the western and southern sections of the property. She had learned in her research last night that the country club boasted an eighteen-hole golf course, and despite the massive acreage of the property, she imagined that much of the forest was now gone. She leaned closer to the map to see the date, faded to the point of near illegibility, in the lower right corner: 1929.

"Pretty amazing, isn't it?"

Marge barely managed to suppress a cry of surprise at the sudden interruption, and she turned to find Andrew Doherty standing just inside the doorway, a tray balanced on one hand. He extended his other hand in a pacifying gesture. "I'm sorry to startle you." He pulled the door shut behind him. "Your coffee," he said, and set the polished silver tray, laden with a steaming cup of coffee and various silver vessels, on the antique steamer trunk that served as a coffee table. He joined her in front of the fireplace and put his hands in the pockets of his perfectly pressed trousers in a casual manner. "Those are the original plans for the estate from the twenties. A lot of people think Green Lake Country Club—it wasn't a country club back then, of course—was built by Al Capone, but it was actually—"

"Joe Aiello. Yes, I read about that." She took a sip of the coffee. "Capone's enemy, as I recall?"

Doherty raised a brow, impressed. He pulled his hands out of his pockets. "There was a nasty feud between them, and this was Joe's hideout after the Valentine's Day Massacre in 1929. Back then it was just a big piece of wilderness with a log cabin." He gestured toward the zigzag areas on the map, then pointed to squares spaced at regular intervals around the perimeters of the property, like watchtowers on a fortress wall. As though reading her thoughts, he said, "Joe wanted the place to be impenetrable, with lookouts at each of those buildings, but, ironically, he was murdered in Chicago before they could be built. In the end, the only building that was ever completed is the one we're standing in now."

Marge nodded with interest, then turned her attention to an old, blurred photograph on the mantel of a man in a three-piece suit and flat-brim bowler hat, leaning on a shovel, a trace of a smile on what might have once been a handsome face. He had the soft jawline of a man entering middle age, with unusually wide-set eyes and fleshy lips. He stood next to a small pile of dirt, a symbolic groundbreaking of his new fortress, with several similarly dressed men standing uneasily in the background. All around him were massive trees, punctuated with clusters of stumps where workers had started to clear the heavy forest.

"The legend," continued Doherty, "is that Joe Aiello survived the murder attempt." He took a few steps back and leaned against the edge of the desk. "There are photos of him, shot dead in the street, but some people say it was staged, that he faked his death and escaped to Green Lake and lived the rest of his days in hiding."

Marge lowered herself into one of the leather chairs. "That's quite a story. Is it true?"

Doherty laughed. "Parts of it, I'm sure. It certainly adds to the mystique." He looked around the room. "Not a bad place to hide." He left his perch on the edge of the desk and sat in the chair opposite Marge. "Now." He steepled his hands in front of him. "What can I help you with, Sheriff?"

She busied herself for a moment by adding a small spoonful of sugar and a dash of cream to her coffee, then stirred while she carefully considered her next words. Doherty waited patiently, with an amiable concierge-like smile on his face. Marge took an unhurried sip of coffee, then finally said, "We're investigating the death of a teenage boy named Ben Sharpe and the disappearance of his friend, a girl named Caitlin Wallace."

Later, Marge would turn over and over again in her mind the way Andrew Doherty's face went carefully blank at her words. She might have expected shock, or horror, or maybe even disgust in response to such disturbing news, and the lack of expression on his face was, in itself, an expression. A shade drawn too quickly across a window. A fraction of a second later, his brows snapped together and he leaned forward slightly. "I'm very sorry to hear that."

His words and the troubled look he now wore were sincere, and Marge very nearly decided that she had imagined his puzzling initial reaction. She was convinced, however, that what she had told him—one child dead, another child missing—had taken him by surprise, and not in an abstract sense. Ben Sharpe, Caitlin Wallace. One or both of these names were meaningful to him in some way.

"I understand," she said, "that Ben Sharpe and his family were members here?"

She watched him carefully for a reaction over the rim of her coffee cup, but he seemed to have regained his composure. "Yes," he said evenly. "Rachel and Chuck Sharpe's son, I believe. I remember meeting Ben once, earlier this summer." He paused, then said with what Marge recognized as genuine pathos, "I really liked him. We talked about baseball." He glanced at Marge and the corner of his mouth rose. "I'm a big White Sox fan, and he cheered for the Twins."

"You're from Chicago?"

He bobbed his head. "Born and bred." He shoved his hands in his pockets again and she heard a faint metallic jingle as he clasped and un-clasped what must be a ring of keys.

"Do you have any idea who might have wanted to hurt him or his family?"

He pressed his lips together and stared into the middle distance for a moment, then said, "I don't, although I haven't been here long enough to get to know our members very well." Another clink of his keys. He answered Marge's next question before she could ask it. "I've worked here since mid-May. The previous assistant manager—" The flicker of his ex-pression was like the shiver of an animal's flank when a fly touches it. "He had health issues, and, well—" He waved a hand to indicate that whatever issues the man had, they had not been compatible with the job.

Marge had never received formal investigative training beyond the police academy, but she had learned to let people tell their stories in their own way; the untrammeled flow often revealed details, apparent inconsequentialities, that would later provide invaluable fragments of in-formation. She had come to the country club today with no real expecta-tions, just an urge to see what all the fuss was about. But now she couldn't shake—couldn't ignore—Andrew Doherty's moment of hesitation at the mention of Ben Sharpe and Caitlin Wallace. He had made a mistake, and she studied his face to see whether he knew it and, if so, whether he saw that she knew it, too.

He drew a breath and moved back a few inches in the chair. "Do you mind me asking how the boy died?"

Marge lowered her coffee cup to her knee. "We found him in a boat on Shaky Lake. It was moored to a dock at one of the resorts. We don't have all the details yet but we believe drugs may have been involved."

"Narcotics?" The crease between Andrew's brows returned.

"We believe so."

He hesitated. "And the missing girl? What was her name again?"

"Caitlin Wallace," she said. "Sixteen years old."

"Wallace." He folded his arms across his chest and fell quiet. "It's not a name I recognize," he said, then got to his feet and went around to the far side of the desk, where he pulled a laptop computer from a drawer. "Do you know her parents' names?"

"Calvin and Beth Wallace, from Chicago."

He typed and scrolled for several minutes, then finally looked up and shook his head. "Nobody named Wallace."

Marge pulled out her phone and scrolled until she found what she was looking for. It was Calvin Wallace's employee photo from the Orion website; he was handsome, with golden-brown hair and a tan that looked real. He was seated on a box in front of a white background, one arm on his knee, suit coat open, the top button on his shirt undone. A perfect combination of attractiveness and approachability. She held up the phone and Andrew came around the desk, laptop balanced on one hand, to peer at her screen. "Her father is a salesman with Orion Pharmaceuticals," Marge continued. "I understand a lot of your members are in the medical field, what with Wildwood Clinic nearby. Could he have come here as a guest?"

Andrew looked at Calvin's photo for a long time, then returned to his seat, set the laptop on his knee, and began typing again. After a long moment, he looked up from the keyboard and shook his head. "I checked our guest registry, and I don't see—" He stopped talking with an air of having said a little more than he had intended. "Sheriff, privacy is very important to our members and their guests. I shouldn't have—" He cast her an uneasy glance and seemed to struggle with what to say next. "I want to help," he said. "Sincerely, I do, but—" His hand went suddenly to the pocket of his vest, and Marge could see the outline of a phone through the tweed. He looked even more awkward for a moment.

"Do you mind?" he asked. "I think this may be Mr. Gilson calling."

The phone had neither made a sound nor, as far as she could tell, even vibrated, and she suspected that there was not, in fact, a phone call, and that Andrew Doherty was simply trying to get rid of her. She made to stand. "I should be going anyway."

"No," he said emphatically, and put a hand out. "Please, stay. I'll be back shortly." With that, he reached into his vest pocket and made his way out of the room, shutting the door completely behind him. No sooner had the door clicked shut than she was in motion. He had left the laptop, half-open, on the chair, and, propitiously, the computer had not been idle long enough for the screen to lock. She pulled her reading glasses from her pocket. On the screen was a list of what looked like dates of service and charges. She glanced at the door and listened for a moment, but the thick wood muffled any sound that might otherwise be audible from the foyer.

She scrolled through the list. Names of individuals, names of companies, all with records of money spent and goods or services rendered. Bar bills, golf games, dinners, overnight stays. A spreadsheet of schmoozing, as it were. She scrolled through screen after screen until her heart began to beat faster in anticipation of Doherty's return. And then, there they were. Entries going back to last summer, multiple charges per month. All on an Orion Pharmaceuticals credit card, with no names attached.

She used her phone to snap several photos of the computer screen, then arranged the laptop as Andrew had left it. At the last moment, she locked the screen and sprang to her feet. When Doherty returned seconds later, she was standing at the fireplace, studying a carved wooden bust of a Native American man. She turned as he entered.

"I apologize for the interruption, I—"

She put up a hand. "Don't worry about it." She looked around the charming, luxurious room one more time, then said, "I've got to be going, anyway."

He nodded and clasped his hands behind his back, once more the graceful, well-trained servant. "I wish I could offer you a tour of the property," he said, "but with Mr. Gilson gone, I'm afraid there won't be time for me to do the place justice." He reached into his breast pocket, pulled out a slim silver case, and flipped it open. "Here's my card. Please don't hesitate to call if there's anything I can do for you." A shadow passed over his handsome face. "The investigation, too. If I can be of help in any way—"

She pulled out her own card and pressed it into his hand. "You've been most helpful, Mr. Doherty." Then, with a nod, she turned and headed toward the door.

21

Bella wasn't a wolf, of course, but the massive, shaggy gray dog, with her quiet, lupine watchfulness was mistaken for one often enough that she'd been shot at a couple of times when she'd wandered out of the yard. Since then, Eli had outfitted the oversized Siberian husky with a thick blaze-orange collar to identify her as a pet, rather than a backyard menace. The dog watched, panting, tongue lolling, from the cool garage as Eli and Andy puttered with the lawn mower on the hot driveway.

"You read the manual, right?" asked Eli. He planted himself against the garage doorframe and crossed his arms across his chest. His morning interview with Dan Simons had sobered him up, both by virtue of sweating out the residual alcohol in the heat of Dan's front yard, and because the man had—unintentionally, perhaps—given him some answers. First and foremost, it was clear to Eli that Dan Simons had not killed Ben, that the man, in fact, had a certain amount of fondness for the boy. Next, Dan seemed absolutely certain that Ben hadn't used drugs, which supported Marge's assertion. And finally, it was clear to Eli that the man had more to say; something he hadn't told Eli that morning but clearly wanted to get off his chest.

"I couldn't find the manual," said Andy. The boy's face and arms shone with sunscreen. He wore a pair of banged-up fishing sunglasses Eli recognized as his own and a baseball cap he had gotten in Little League that spring. The sight of the cap tugged at Eli's heart. He had attended exactly two of Andy's baseball games this summer and had been drunk for both of them. He managed to push the memory away for a moment.

"That's strange," said Eli, "seeing as how your mom told me she gave it to you last night after dinner."

Andy muttered something and looked away.

"Hmm?"

He rolled his eyes. "Dad, seriously."

Eli pushed away from the doorframe and joined Andy next to the old push mower. "You know how mad your mom would be at me if you got your leg chopped off?" Eli wasn't sure how much angrier Michelle could be with him than she was already, especially since she was adamantly opposed to Andy mowing the lawn.

"He's only eleven," she had said. "That's too young, even for a push mower."

"He's mature for his age," Eli had said, though both he and Michelle understood that Andy had been forced into accelerated maturity by having an absent father for two years, then, far worse, by having another year and counting of a father who couldn't even take care of himself, let alone his family. In the end, Michelle had grudgingly agreed to let Eli show Andy how to use the mower, on the condition that Eli be there, on time and sober, the first few times Andy mowed. He'd been late today, admittedly, but he hadn't had a drop of alcohol since last night.

"I'll read the manual tonight," said Andy. "I promise."

Eli pulled his sunglasses off, wiped the sweat from his face, and then put them back on. Michelle had been making her legendary pineapple habanero salsa when he'd arrived, which meant she was either hosting guests at the house or going to a party that night. He had started to ask about her plans but stopped when it occurred to him that her social life was no longer any of his business. She was still young and beautiful, not to mention smart and funny, and surely it was only a matter of time before another man—a better man—took Eli's place. At the thought, bitterness had spread in his chest, black and heavy like oil, and he had fled to the garage before he could do or say something he might regret.

Eli squatted down next to the machine. "Did you check the spark plug?" he asked.

"Yep," said Andy, touchingly excited by the simple act. He picked up the small metal tube and held it up like a trophy. "And the air filter. They're both in pretty good shape." Eli had to swallow a smile at the seriousness of the boy's tone.

The air filter was, indeed, in good shape, for the simple, ugly reason that Eli hadn't used the lawn mower more than a handful of times all summer. Michelle had offered to take over lawn duty in the spring, but he had told her no, dragged himself off the basement couch, mowed half the lawn, then given up and left for Babe's, returning well after midnight. Two weeks had passed before a rare burst of energy had coincided with an even rarer hour or two of sobriety, and he mowed the whole lawn. The grass had gotten so long that the yard looked like a harvested alfalfa crop when he was done, striped with clippings that grew yellow and dingy within hours. Again, Michelle had volunteered, then demanded, to take over lawn maintenance, and like an asshole, he had barked at her. "Stay in your lane," he'd said. "I'll get to it when I get to it." He remembered the specific shade of red her face had turned. She'd walked away and remained tight-jawed and silent the rest of the day.

For weeks after that, she had said nothing about the lawn. Just looked the other way at the shin-high grass, paid the fine from the city when the grass grew higher than allowed by municipal ordinance, then mowed it herself one evening after Eli had left for the bar. He had noticed the newly trimmed grass when he arrived home late that night and had said something rude to her—he couldn't remember what, having been extremely drunk—before stomping downstairs to the basement, where he slept off a massive hangover until late morning and missed work in the process.

That had been a few days before she confronted him in the kitchen, a month ago now, and told him she wanted a divorce. Her expression, her tone, her mannerisms during the conversation still haunted him. All anger seemed to have gone and been replaced with a freshness that told him loud and clear how relieved she was at having finally chosen to rid herself of him, of the terrible burden he had become. He hadn't argued, had just nodded like a feckless idiot, though the pain in his chest had been so terrible that he had wondered whether it was possible to die from a broken heart. He had finally driven her away. He hadn't tried to, truly. They had been together for nearly twenty years and had loved each other with a singular devotion and passion that most married couples would never experience. She'd taken in stride his two-year absence when he was deployed, and had taken care of his lingering physical wounds when he finally returned home after the long hospital stay. She was a nurse. Caring for people was what she did. She had been understanding and patient, and her devotion and passion hadn't waned. She knew, instinctively rather than as a result of anything Eli actually told her, about the scars he bore in his mind, and the need to alleviate the pain with alcohol. She'd convinced him to get counseling at the Veterans Affairs hospital, had been so happy and so hopeful when he'd agreed, until he'd come home after one session and declared that he was never going back again. She'd tried to remain hopeful, and when she'd finally given up hope, she'd tried to be stoic, for Andy's sake, until the day she had found Andy sweeping up shards of glass from a mirror Eli had knocked off the basement wall when he was drunk, while Eli lay passed out on the floor in the basement bathroom. The boy had tried to hide his tears. Had tried to pretend it was no big deal. Eli knew the incident had been Michelle's breaking point, the point at which staying married to him was doing more harm than good to their son. It broke Eli's heart that Andy, in the wake of the announcement of their separation, had tried to broker a peace deal between the two of them. Had tried to take the blame for the ever-worsening friction. Had tried to come up with a routine, a system, that would make living together in one house still possible.

That was a month ago, and this was the first time Eli had returned to the house he had called home for so many years. He'd seen Andy a handful of times, at Marge's house, since then, and the guilt he felt about the entire situation, for everything he had put his family through, weighed on him so heavily that, if anything, his bad behavior had only worsened since moving out. The one benefit of leaving his home, however, was that nobody had to see him passed out on the bathroom floor. Nobody had to clean up the broken glass, or empty the trash bin of drained liquor bottles, or see the holes in the drywall left by his fist or his foot.

He rose to his feet, and as he stood on the driveway and watched Andy chatter on about various lawn mower–related things—and reflected on the horrible father he had become—he felt a familiar shiver pass through him; his lips grew numb and his skin suddenly felt a size too small. Andy's voice receded into static, and Eli was in the process of deciding how best to exit the scene—the last thing he wanted was for Andy to watch him disintegrate—when he felt Bella's warm, wet nose against his hand, and the not unsubstantial weight of the gigantic dog leaning against his leg.

As a kid, Eli had had his own dog. A mutt someone had foisted on Marge, one Eli had fallen in love with at first sight. He had named him Leonardo, after his favorite Teenage Mutant Ninja Turtle, and he and the dog had been like siblings. Closer than brothers, even, as Eli had confided in Leo all the insecurities and bewilderment of an adolescent boy without a father, and, in later years, had looked to for validation of life goals that others dismissed as pipe dreams. He was, to put it mildly, a dog person. Had his new apartment allowed dogs, and had Andy not loved Bella equally as well as Eli, he would have taken the gigantic beast to live with him without a second thought.

Bella snuffled and nudged Eli's hand, harder now, and the feel of the dog's muzzle against his skin seemed to interrupt the cascade of sensations that he knew could very well end with him on the ground. He managed to run his hands along the scruff of the dog's neck and down the sides of her face, and a few moments later, Andy's voice and the lawn mower and the hot driveway came back into focus. Eli squatted to let the dog lick his face until he felt the panic begin to recede, and by the time Andy spoke, he felt more or less all right.

"Grandma said you're investigating a murder," Andy said.

For a moment, the sudden change of topic was disorienting, as though Eli had just awoken from a heavy sleep in an unfamiliar bed. He blinked once, twice, then said, "That's right." The last thing he wanted to do was tell his son about the death of a boy not all that different from himself. Still, he could see curiosity on Andy's face. His son had always been fascinated by Eli's profession, beyond what one would expect of a kid his age. Eli had had little to no investigative work since coming home from his deployment, but Andy could recall Eli's past cases with an almost astonishing degree of detail, though he had been no more than eight years old at the time. He had inherited his father's inquisitiveness, his need to discover the truth of any given situation. Eli knew he should change the subject, but he could see that Andy was eager to learn more about the case, and there were few opportunities these days to make his son happy.

Eli stood up and rested a hand on the dog's shoulder. "A vacationer was killed."

"A teenager, right?" Andy sat back on his heels on the cement and looked up at Eli. "And his girlfriend is missing, too."

In the end, Eli settled on giving the boy a whitewashed account of what had happened thus far, no more than what one might hear on the five o'clock news. Andy pressed him with questions—excellent questions, Eli thought with pride—until he could get no more information from his father and turned his focus back to lawn mower training.

"Safety, above all," reiterated Eli, after he had reviewed the lawn mower safety rules at least three more times. "I don't care if the lawn looks like crap, as long as you're safe."

"It won't look like crap and I promise I'll be safe."

"And read the manual tonight."

Andy set a hand solemnly over his heart. "I promise."

Eli bent over to give Bella one last pat, then herded the dog back into the house and returned to the driveway.

"Okay," he said to Andy. "Start it up."

22

There you are," said Marge. She let the heavy door swing shut behind her and made her way along the outside of the building to where Phil leaned against the brick wall. He looked up from the unlit cigarette in his fingers and shifted his sunglasses to the top of his head. The skin of his narrow face hung loosely over his cheekbones and jaw, as if all the fat had been sucked out, and his jutting nose was all the more prominent in contrast to his receding chin. He wore his usual sour expression, as well as long sleeves and pants over spider-thin limbs, despite the August heat.

"Raccoons are back," he said, and nodded in the direction of the overflowing dumpster at the far end of the parking lot. The station shared the space with the movie theater next door, and the scents of burnt popcorn and rancid peanut oil wafted from that establishment's dumpster. Its plastic lid was warped—one end curled up to create a gap between lid and metal—and trash was scattered on the gravel alongside. "Lionel's too cheap to get it fixed. Now we're going to have to keep our car windows shut." He looked once more at the cigarette in his hand, sighed, then tucked it into his breast pocket.

"Where is everyone?" asked Marge. From the back deck of Coach's sports bar next door came a shriek of microphone feedback and the clatter of wheels across the wooden boards. The deck and beer garden, newly renovated that spring, were tucked behind an equally new privacy fence that shielded customers from the dusty, uninviting parking lot and blocked the view of non-patrons who might want to watch the Tuesday and Thursday night outdoor band concerts without paying for drinks.

Marge checked her watch. Just after noon. Rachel had been asleep when she had called her room at the hospital earlier that morning. Or at least, that was what the front desk person said. Marge would have to stop by in person after the meeting to see how she was doing.

Phil stretched side to side, then cracked his shoulders. "Jake's with the dive team. Don't know where the other two are." He looked past Marge in the direction of the sports bar, where shouted instructions mingled with the sound of patio furniture being rearranged. She felt a pang of guilt. Phil rarely took time off, the victim of circumstances where a profound staffing shortage collided with an unshakable work ethic. His girlfriend, Jenny, worked nights as a nursing assistant at a retirement home in Red River Falls, and in the handful of times Marge had seen her, she had looked just as bedraggled and thin and worn as Phil.

"Heard Eli was at Babe's till closing time last night," he said, in a casual tone that did not match the tightness around his lips and the rigid set of his jaw.

Marge didn't quite manage to suppress her sigh. "Phil—"

The early afternoon sun cleared the building and flooded the patch of gravel where they stood. Marge took a step closer to the building into the sliver of shade that remained and watched as Phil put his sunglasses back on. She knew exactly what he was going to say.

"You're not doing him any favors by protecting him, Marge."

As if she could help it.

Phil and Jenny didn't have kids—something about a congenital condition that ran in her family—and Marge could never find a way to explain to Phil the primal need of parents to protect their young. If she had, Phil would have no doubt pointed out that Eli wasn't exactly young anymore. She shook her head. "He's a good investigator."

"He *was* a good investigator."

"What do you want me to say?" she snapped. She was as aware as anyone that Eli's job performance had gone from bad to worse to untenable since she had hired him six months ago. The unanswered dispatch calls, the unreliability, the drinking.

Into the silence that followed her question came the sound of tires on gravel as Alyssa's car came down the narrow driveway. Phil glanced at the car and took a step closer to Marge.

"I swear this isn't personal, Marge. I just don't think—"

"We need him."

Phil's eyes widened. "You can't be serious." He looked around, as if the building or the parking lot or the dumpster might offer a translation of her thoughts. "He's a *liability*. Especially now." He turned and stomped away from her, then came back. "I didn't want to have to tell you this, but"—he hesitated, his mouth twisted in frustration—"the noise disturbance call. It came in around nine on Tuesday night."

Marge opened her mouth, but Phil continued before she could say anything.

"I called Eli right away, since he was on duty. Took a while, maybe twenty minutes, before I could get ahold of him. He said he'd check things out right away. Then . . . nothing. He didn't answer the radio, didn't answer his phone. Finally, I called you at eleven thirty when I hadn't heard from him. I didn't know what else to do."

Her stomach did a painful flip, and she recalled the way Eli had acted on Tuesday night at Beran's.

Your eyes don't look right.

"I feel for him, Marge. I really do, but—" He fell silent, but his expression remained belligerent.

She put a hand on Phil's shoulder. "Do you trust me?"

He was quiet for a moment. "I think Eli is your blind spot."

"Do you *trust* me?"

She saw his thin jaw clench, and when he didn't say anything, she felt a ripple of alarm at the thought that he might answer in the negative. She couldn't afford to lose him.

Finally he heaved a loud sigh, then said, in a tone that could only be described as grumbling, "Fine."

She gave his arm a gentle punch. "The f-word, huh?"

He didn't laugh, and instead pulled his sunglasses off again and polished the lenses on his sleeve. Marge turned from him and squinted across the parking lot. Alyssa seemed to be talking on the phone, car windows rolled up, engine still running. Marge turned back to Phil. "I had an interesting visit to the Green Lake Country Club this morning," she said, the words a peace offering.

He grunted.

"Quite the place," she went on. "Ever been there?"

He slid his sunglasses back into place, but not before Marge saw the flicker of interest in his eyes. "I'll bet they loved seeing you on their doorstep," he said.

"The manager—sorry, assistant manager—was nice enough. Andrew Doherty. He gave me some very useful information, although I'm not sure whether he intended to or not."

One of Phil's brows rose over the top of his sunglasses.

"First," she continued, "he knows who Caitlin Wallace is. I'm sure of it. He knew Ben Sharpe, of course; the Sharpes are members there, after all. But Caitlin—" She rubbed the base of her neck; she ought to get out of the heat before she ended up with another migraine. "He acted like he'd never heard of her or Calvin Wallace or Orion Pharmaceuticals." She pulled out her phone and showed Phil the photos she'd taken of the spreadsheet on Andrew Doherty's laptop. "But here they are. Transactions on a credit card belonging to Orion Pharmaceuticals. Dozens of them going back at least a year." She pointed to the screen. "Four transactions last month alone. Alyssa says that Calvin Wallace is Orion's sole sales agent for all of Illinois, Wisconsin, and Minnesota, so most, if not all, of these charges were almost certainly made by him. His whole job is to schmooze with medical people. There's no way Andrew Doherty hasn't crossed paths with him at the country club." She filled him in on the clandestine nature of the place; the hidden location, the heavy surveillance. "They keep track of anyone and everyone who sets foot on the property."

"So why is the guy lying?" asked Phil.

"Good question." Lies, she knew, didn't serve a purpose unless the truth was felt to be dangerous. She pursed her lips, and Phil waited in silence as she considered her next words. "The thing is, he *wanted* me to see these transaction logs." She looked once more at the photo of the spreadsheets, then put her phone back into her pocket. "At the time, I thought he was just careless, leaving me alone with the unlocked laptop. But he was *too* careless, you know?"

Phil stared at her, nonplussed. "Why the hell would he do that?"

She spread her hands in a helpless gesture. "I can only come up with one explanation."

Phil crossed his arms over his chest. "He knows something and wants us to know, too."

She nodded. "And damned if I can figure out what it is."

23

Eli pulled off his Sherman County Sheriff's Department T-shirt and tossed it into the back seat. He stank of motor oil and grass clippings, and though Michelle had offered to let him use the shower before he left the house, he could tell she wanted him gone as quickly as possible. She was, as he had suspected, having friends over that night. There hadn't been enough time to stop at his apartment before the meeting at the station, but in a stroke of rather pathetic luck, he still had a plastic bin of clothes in the trunk of his car that he hadn't gotten around to carrying upstairs to his apartment. The rumpled but clean white T-shirt sat on the passenger seat, and he had just leaned over to grab it when Alyssa materialized outside the open passenger window and leaned down to say something. She froze when she saw his bare torso, then gave a little squeak and turned her back to the car window. "Um—"

"Sorry!" He grabbed the clean shirt and yanked it on as quickly as possible, then sat for a moment, eyes closed, contemplating the perverse irony of the situation; that he had been dreading seeing her again, and now, when the terrible moment arrived, it was to find him disheveled and half-naked. The car interior still smelled of damp—earthy and fungal, like a forest floor—and grew more stiflingly hot with each second that passed in the blazing heat of the parking lot. He wondered if the ass of his pants was still wet. He ran a hand through his hair, sniffed his armpits, and reassured himself that at least he stank only of lawn mower, not of booze or body odor. He sighed heavily, opened the door, and got to his feet.

Alyssa whirled around to face him. "Sorry," she said, and waved a hand vaguely toward his midsection. She had exchanged her glasses for a pair of sunglasses that obscured any expression in her eyes, but he could see that she was a bit red in the face. "I didn't mean to—"

He spoke at the same time. "It's no big—"

They both fell silent, as if to reboot the conversation, and after a tidy pause, Alyssa spoke. "I checked out the Paul Bunyan statue. Very impressive." She smiled, and Eli saw that they were going to attempt normal conversation. Before he could respond, she went on. "These mosquito bites kept me awake all night, though." She scraped her nails over a pink splotch on the side of her neck, as if to illustrate the nature of her complaint. "You might have warned me. I would have come prepared."

"It's our state bird."

"What is?"

"The mosquito."

She stared at him a moment. "Clever."

Eli was surprised to hear a laugh escape his throat, and a dry smile tugged at the corner of Alyssa's lips. Then, from around the building, came the sudden, violent, vaguely musical screams of the Dropkick Murphys. Music and the smell of cigarette smoke spewed from the open windows of Jake's truck as it hurtled down the driveway and across the parking lot to the far corner, where Eli and Alyssa stood. They watched as he killed the engine, hopped out of the truck, and slammed the door shut.

"Hey, kids," he said, his face corned-beef red with sunburn from being on the water all morning. He pulled the remnants of a cigarette from his lips, tossed it on the gravel, and ground it out with the sole of his boot. He paused and looked back and forth between the two of them, once, twice, then grinned, as if he had thought to make a smart remark but decided against it. He picked up the cigarette butt and reached through the open window of his truck to drop it in an empty fast-food cup, then went around to the tail end of his truck and dragged out a large plastic cooler. He hoisted it onto one shoulder with a grunt. "Glad I'm not the only one who's late."

"We're not—" began Alyssa, with a frown at her watch.

"I'm just giving you shit," called Jake, from the other side of the cooler. "Eli, you want to grab the rest of the food?" Jake swung around to point at a large box in the truck bed, and Eli ducked just in time to avoid getting hit in the head with the cooler.

"*More* food?" Alyssa shifted her bag onto her opposite shoulder and went to survey the box, packed full of white cardboard carryout containers and a bag of plates and utensils. "There's enough food for at least twenty people in here."

Jake turned to her and pulled himself up to his full, considerable height, then patted his belly with his free hand. "What is it about Eli and me that says 'light eater'?"

She glanced between the two men, then shrugged. "Fair enough."

Jake hitched the cooler more securely on his shoulder, then swung back around and headed toward the station door. Eli nodded in the direction of the box of food. "The Chinese restaurant down the block donated it."

"They *donated* it?"

He inclined his head toward Jake's truck. "The car dealership in Red River Falls donated two trucks, and we get all our uniforms made for free by the lady who runs the clothing shop down the street." He paused. Why the hell was he telling her this?

Alyssa stared back at him, appalled.

"I suppose it's not exactly kosher—"

Eli saw himself reflected in the lenses of her sunglasses, wrinkled shirt and all. His hair was standing up in front from when he had changed shirts, and he looked away and ran a hand across his head. It came away damp with sweat. He wiped his palm on his shorts and braced himself for a lecture on civic corruption.

Instead, Alyssa turned to the bed of the truck and moved to pick up the box. Eli got to it first, and she let him take it without protest.

He turned for the station door and heard her slam the tailgate closed. "Why isn't there more money?" she called. "It's not like Shaky Lake doesn't have a tax base."

He turned around to find her leaning against the back of the truck. The box of food was heavier than it looked, and he lifted it up and rested it on his shoulder. "The county board of directors makes the budget," he said. "Every year Marge tries to convince them we need more funding, but they always find some reason they can't afford it."

She was quiet for a long moment, and he could tell from the set of her lips that she was carefully processing this piece of information. "How can you even meet the basic law enforcement needs of the county?"

"We can't."

Silence.

He waited for her to share her thoughts, but after another beat of quiet consideration, she straightened and pushed past him toward the building. "I'll get the door."

Marge was on the phone in her office when Eli and Alyssa arrived in the conference room, and everyone took her temporary absence as an opportunity to eat. Phil was in his usual position in the corner, arms folded across his chest. He looked pointedly away when Eli entered the room, and Eli knew he had been talking about him to Marge. About what, specifically, was less clear, and for a moment, Eli considered confronting him. Asking him what his problem was. He knew, however, that Phil would be more than happy to answer that question in great detail, in front of everybody, and the only thing stopping him was his loyalty to Marge.

Jake looked up from where he was rummaging around in the cooler. "God. Finally. What were you guys doing out there?" he asked, not expecting an answer. He looked from Eli to Phil and frowned, then pulled a can of soda from the cooler, wiped away the crushed ice that clung to it, and handed it to Phil. "Here. Have some caffeine." For a moment, Eli thought Phil might refuse, that even Jake's peacekeeping efforts could not assuage the man's anger. Thankfully, after a moment of hesitation, Phil reached for the can and muttered something that vaguely resembled an expression of gratitude.

No sooner had Eli set the box of food on the table than Jake began to pull out containers and line them up neatly. He laid out paper plates and plastic forks and napkins; then, as if the thought had suddenly occurred to him, he turned to Alyssa. He propped his fists on his hips and frowned at her. "You're not going to call Eli fat again, are you?"

Eli darted a look at Alyssa and saw Jake's amusement mirrored in her expression. Years spent in the FBI had no doubt taught her the art of working with men in close quarters, that giving each other shit was the bedrock of professional camaraderie. She shot Eli a lopsided grin.

"Shut up, Jake," Eli muttered. He opened a take-out container—shrimp stir-fry—then grabbed a fork and a wad of napkins and took a seat at the far end of the table.

He felt it the moment he sat down—pinpricks of sensation, like the first, nearly imperceptible drops of rain before a storm. He checked his watch.

Twelve hours.

A ripple of irritability that had nothing to do with Phil or Alyssa or Jake lapped at the edge of his consciousness, and he laid down his fork. He searched his mind for where he might have stashed some whiskey at the station, came up with nothing, then considered making a quick run to his apartment.

Twelve hours without alcohol.

He needed a clear head for the meeting, and he had a couple of hours, maximum, before the jitters started. Just a shot of something, maybe two, and he would be fine. He could be back in fifteen minutes, could tell everyone he just needed to change his shirt. They might even believe him.

Not Phil. Eli recalled the look on the man's face when he had arrived. He knew that Phil would see Eli's excuse for the lie it was, and he would not let it go unchallenged this time.

His thoughts were interrupted when Marge appeared at her office door. She looked at Jake. "Do you have the report?" she asked.

Jake straightened in his chair. He had been leaning over to say something to Alyssa—something funny, judging from the smile on her face—

and he reached for a file folder on the empty chair next to him. He waved it at Marge. "Got it."

She went to the cooler and pulled out a bottle of water. "Want to give us the gist?" Eli could tell from the crease between her brows that she had one of her headaches. He thought back to what he had just told Alyssa about Sherman County's lack of law enforcement funding; how the burden of that fell on his mother's shoulders—shoulders that had carried more than her fair share for a very long time. He'd wager that he had become the heaviest part of that burden.

"We got the fingerprint report back," said Jake. He wiped two cans of Mountain Dew dry with a napkin, then passed one to Alyssa and slid the other across the table to Eli. "Forensics found about a million different fingerprints in the boat, including Ben's and Caitlin's."

"And the cabin?" asked Marge.

He shook his head. "There wasn't much. The resort's cleaning crew does a very thorough job." He leaned back and balanced his chair on its back two legs. "The only valuable information we got were fingerprints in the boat from two very interesting people. First, our friend Dan Simons."

Eli looked up from his unopened can of soda. "I talked to Dan this morning and he says he helped Ben with his boat last weekend." He noted the looks of surprise on Jake's and Phil's faces. They had clearly assumed that Eli had spent the morning sleeping off a hangover. He didn't look at Alyssa.

"What else did Dan have to say?" asked Marge.

Eli opened the soda and took a sip. The jolt of chemical sweetness provided him a momentary reprieve from the next wave of irritability. "He felt strongly that Ben didn't use drugs. He seemed one hundred percent certain of it and I didn't push him for an explanation."

"Dan Simons did time for drug charges," said Phil, addressing Marge. "If he says Ben was clean, I believe him. He would know."

Marge turned back to Eli. "Does he have an alibi for Tuesday?"

"No alibi. Just a puppy." Marge looked at him questioningly, and he went on. "Her name's Maisy. He bought her a *life jacket*." Jake laughed, and both he and Phil nodded, as if this fact provided all the information they needed to determine whether or not Dan Simons was a killer. Marge, too, gave a satisfied nod. Alyssa, he noticed, did not offer any objection to the idea that having a puppy absolved Dan of suspicion of murder.

"He knows something, though," continued Eli. "He was waiting for me to show up asking questions. He even had a lawn chair ready for me."

And a can of beer.

He looked at Marge. "I don't think it would take much to get him to tell us more. Maybe a lot more."

"Maybe he would be willing to come down to the station later and talk to me," she said.

"He's always liked you," said Eli.

Marge grimaced. "I'm not so sure about that. Who do you think the arresting officer was when he ended up in federal prison for narcotics trafficking?" She went over to the spread of Chinese food and dished some onto a plate, then sat at the head of the table. For a few minutes, everyone was quiet while they ate. Alyssa hadn't yet taken any food and was busy at her laptop.

"Simons did five years and got out in 2006," said Alyssa. She scanned the information on the screen, then looked up. "Nothing since then. No arrests, no charges. Not even a parking ticket." She looked at Marge. "I can get more specifics on the trafficking case but it will take some digging."

Marge nodded. "Good." She looked at Jake. "What else?"

Jake swallowed a mouthful of food, then cleared his throat. "Forensics also identified prints in the boat from a guy named Russell Kovach. He was in federal prison until about six months ago, and now he's on parole in Hudson."

Marge looked at Alyssa and was about to say something, but the younger woman was already typing. Alyssa peered at the screen. "Extortion and witness tampering. And before that, narcotics trafficking in the early 2000s." She scanned the screen, her lips moving wordlessly; she typed, scrolled, typed some more. Then she looked up. "It was the same case."

"The same case as what?" asked Marge.

"The same narcotics trafficking case for both Simons and Kovach." She adjusted her glasses and looked at the screen again. Frowned.

Typed some more. She put a hand to her chin and looked up. "They were associates."

The room was quiet for a moment, and something unsettling curled through Eli. Jake let out a low whistle.

Alyssa looked back at her computer screen. "It was a huge heroin bust in 1999. A drug ring out of Chicago. Simons did five years, Kovach eight."

Eli's earlier certainty, that Dan Simons wasn't capable of hurting Ben Sharpe, evaporated. He saw his thoughts reflected on the faces seated around the table.

"I knew there were others involved in the trafficking ring, of course," said Marge, "but I didn't know names. Kovach didn't live around here, that much I know."

"I'll get ahold of Kovach's parole agent," said Phil.

"Good." She looked at Eli. "I need Dan Simons here this afternoon, tonight at the latest."

"Sheriff," said Alyssa, "I have something you're going to want to see." She pulled a document, covered on both sides with densely packed type, from her bag and handed it to Marge. "That," she said, "is Caitlin Wallace's cell phone record."

Cal

*T*he Hotel Allegro was a newly restored art deco gem, just six blocks from Orion's downtown Chicago office. The lounge area was dimly lit, and the plush carpeting and velvet furniture deadened the sounds of conversation. Cal resisted the urge to page through the document another time, fumbled with his watch, glanced at the newspaper, scrolled mindlessly on his phone. It was nearly ten p.m. Beth and Caitlin hadn't answered his calls.

"Sorry I'm late, Cal."

He jumped at the sound of his friend's voice, then let out a sigh of relief and got to his feet. "Kev." The two men clapped each other on the back and sat down. "Thanks for coming."

Kevin Allen raised a freckled hand to the cocktail server and, after ordering a whiskey, leaned toward Cal. He was dressed in a Boston College T-shirt and a White Sox baseball cap "I'm not exactly dressed for the occasion," he said, looking around the lounge, then back at Cal. "What is it, man? You look like you've seen a ghost."

Cal opened his mouth to speak, closed it. Tried again.

"Cal, seriously, what's wrong?" The cocktail server arrived and Kevin accepted the glass of whiskey with a murmur of thanks, then took a sip.

Cal reached into his messenger bag and pulled out a stack of paper. "This showed up on my fax machine today." He handed the document to Kevin.

Kevin looked at him questioningly, then scanned through page after page. He looked up at Cal and shook his head. "It's Salvare data. So what?"

Cal reached forward and took the paper from Kevin, then flipped through the pages until he found what he was looking for.

"Here," he said, and slapped the document back into Kevin's hand with unintended force. The sound of paper on flesh was loud, and he quickly glanced up to see whether anyone in the lounge was looking at them. He reached into his bag and handed Kevin a folder. "I looked up every one of the trial subjects with a mark through their name. I don't technically have access to study participant information—not even names or dates of birth— so I'm sure I broke more than one confidentiality law by accessing this data."

He watched as Kevin paged through the documents in the folder— printouts of obituaries, death notices, social media screenshots, and a spreadsheet with all the information Cal had collected since the fax had arrived earlier that day.

Kevin looked up, two lines between his brows that hadn't been there before. "This has to be some sort of mistake," he said.

"It's not a mistake." Cal heard the wobble in his own voice, felt the woolliness in his brain, and gritted his teeth. He needed all the self-possession he could manage. "They falsified the research data."

Kevin stared at a point beyond Cal's shoulder. He seemed to be trying to fathom what he had just heard, to work it out in his head, and long seconds passed before Cal could see him putting it all together in his mind.

"Kev," he said, with the last shred of patience he could muster, "Salvare is coming to market in two months, and when that happens, people are going to die. We have to go to the authorities."

Kevin blinked at him, dazed, then looked down at the faxed document he still held in his hand. "Who sent this?" he asked, his voice just above a whisper.

"I don't know."

"Who else have you told?"

Cal shook his head. "Nobody. You're the only person I trust."

24

Marge scanned the pages containing the Wallace family's cell phone records.

"Sorry it took me so long to get this," said Alyssa. "The family's cell phones are all paid for by Calvin Wallace's employer and it took a lot of . . . convincing . . . for them to give me the call log."

"Let's hear the highlights," said Marge.

"Caitlin called her father's phone three times on Tuesday," began Alyssa. "At 4:06, 4:09, and 4:12. Each call lasted less than ten seconds, so I think we can assume she didn't reach him."

"No calls to her mother?" asked Eli.

Alyssa shook her head. "There are about a dozen calls from Beth to Caitlin on Tuesday but nothing in the other direction. At 4:20, there was another call from Caitlin's phone that lasted three minutes. This time, it was to someone named Tyler Mattson." She looked at her computer screen. "His Facebook page says he's twenty-six, not in a relationship, lives here in Shaky Lake." She looked around the table and was met with shrugs of nonrecognition at the name.

"Why would Caitlin be calling him?" asked Marge. "Could they have been friends?"

"Other than Tuesday afternoon, she had never called him before," said Alyssa. "Nobody in the family had. At least not from their cell phones."

"There's always the possibility that someone else had Caitlin's phone and used it to place the call," said Eli. "The person who killed Ben could have taken it from her and called a conspirator. Maybe that's Tyler Mattson."

Marge drummed her fingers on the table. "I'll follow up with Mattson. Phil, you and Agent Mason can deal with Russell Kovach."

Lunch, it seemed, was over.

25

Tyler Mattson's knee hadn't stopped bouncing since he had climbed into Marge's truck, and his forehead shone with perspiration despite the icy blast of air-conditioning in his face. Beyond him, through the passenger-side window, Marge saw a curtain twitch in the bay window of the shabby but tidy little house behind the Piggly Wiggly grocery store. She couldn't blame Tyler's mom for snooping; Marge had, in fact, made a point of interviewing Tyler in plain view of his own house, which the twenty-six-year-old shared with his mom. The look of abject terror on the young man's face when Marge had knocked on his front door and asked to speak with him was not the look of a cold-blooded killer, of someone who could plan and carry out a murder such as what had happened to Ben Sharpe. It was, however, the look of someone with something to hide.

"You look a little overheated," she said mildly.

Tyler made a strangled noise at the back of his throat, then wiped one large hand across his temple, then onto his shorts. He seemed transfixed by the dashboard in front of him, and his averted gaze gave her an opportunity to study his appearance. He was tall, with the overly muscular upper body and thin legs of someone who spends a good deal of time pumping iron at the gym, and a good deal of money on protein shakes and bodybuilding supplements. He was deeply tanned; too young, still, for his skin to turn leathery. His close-cropped blond hair was mostly covered with a baseball hat, and he was dressed in black basketball shorts and a stretched-out tank top. His left earlobe was pierced and his arms were littered with the sort of garden-variety tattoos one might expect from a twentysomething man. If he weren't trembling like a frightened rabbit, Tyler Mattson would have been the embodiment of a small-town beefcake.

"I understand you work at the Green Lake Country Club," said Marge. She was careful to keep her tone mild, but, nevertheless, his face—the left side of it, anyway—went rigid with alarm. She could sympathize; when Alyssa had tracked down the man's tax records to find out where he was employed, it had come as a shock that Tyler Mattson worked at the very place Marge had visited that morning. Even now, she was filled with trepidation.

Tyler's Adam's apple bobbed once, twice, before he nodded.

"Yep." He cracked his knuckles, then seemed to have noticed his bouncing knee and stilled it with obvious effort.

Marge gave him a moment to elaborate, and, when he didn't, she said, "Can you tell me what you do there?"

"Um—" He tucked his hands under his thighs and seemed to give the question long consideration. Finally, he settled on "Landscaping, mostly."

"Mostly?"

"Just—landscaping." The knee started bouncing again.

There was a long silence as Marge considered her approach. Tyler seemed about two minutes away from jumping out of the truck and running, and if that happened, she would be forced to take a harder line with him, to arrest him, even; it was a scenario unlikely to be very constructive. She decided to cut to the chase.

"Do you know a girl named Caitlin Wallace?"

The knee relaxed and Tyler looked at Marge for the first time. "The missing girl from the news? It's all my mom's talked about for two days." He shook his head. "I don't know her, though."

"She vacations here every summer with her parents at Beran's Resort. Calvin and Beth Wallace?"

He shook his head again. "Never heard of them."

The front door of Tyler's house opened, and his mom stepped onto the front stoop in nothing but a faded pink tank top that was just barely long enough to qualify as a dress. Her poorly feigned nonchalance as she lifted the lid of the metal mailbox made it clear from whom Tyler had inherited his utter lack of a poker face. Through the truck window, Marge met her eye and the woman froze for a moment, then scurried back inside. Marge rubbed the back of her neck and stifled a sigh of impatience.

"Tyler, you seem really uncomfortable. Is there something you want to get off your chest?"

He pressed his lips together so tightly that they nearly went white, and he stared even more fiercely at the dashboard.

"Is it something to do with the country club?" she ventured.

Silence.

"Oh, for Christ's sake, Tyler, you might as well tell me."

He let out a puff of air, then sucked it back in, as if he had been drowning and had finally managed to fight his way to the surface. "It's just weed, I swear," he gasped.

Marge raised a brow but remained silent.

"I sell it." He darted a glance at her, then flinched, as if he expected her to take a swing at him. "Not a lot, though."

It was all Marge could do not to roll her eyes. How this kid managed to engage in illegal activity was beyond her. "And who are your . . . clients?" She cocked her head. "People at the country club?"

For a moment, she thought he might throw up. The knee started bouncing double time, and his silence was confirmation. "I see," she said. "And do you sell to anyone outside of the country club?"

"Don't need to."

"Business is booming there, is it?"

A hint of a smile crossed his mouth before he realized it. He frowned and cleared his throat. "No comment."

This time, she did roll her eyes. "Where do you get your product?"

He hesitated. "My buddy grows it in his barn."

"Your buddy."

A pause. "My cousin."

She studied him for a moment. "Is marijuana really all that you're selling?"

He looked at her then, eyes wide. "Yeah, I swear."

Marge hadn't thought of it until now, but maybe Rachel Sharpe didn't have to go very far to get her drugs. "Is there anyone who might be selling something else at the club?" she asked. "Heroin? Cocaine?"

Tyler chewed the inside of his lip, then said, "Not that I know of. Stuff like that, though—the hard stuff, I mean—is a whole different ball game. I don't get involved in that kind of shit."

"Does Mr. Gilson know you sell marijuana at his club?"

Tyler shifted in his seat and cracked his knuckles again. "It's possible," he said to the dashboard. "He's there all the time, so . . ."

All the time, except when law enforcement shows up.

"If you don't know Caitlin Wallace," she asked, getting back to the matter at hand, "why did she call you on Tuesday afternoon, right about the time she disappeared?"

Tyler's faced crinkled in confusion, and he pulled his phone from his pocket. He tapped the screen a few times and then seemed to remember something. He looked up.

"I didn't have my phone on Tuesday afternoon. It died that morning and I gave it to Mr. Gilson. He gave me a new one on Wednesday morning."

Marge recalled Eli's theory that someone else had used Caitlin's phone to make the call. If that was the case, the person on the receiving end might not have been Tyler Mattson at all. It might have been Mr. Gilson, the elusive country club owner, or possibly Andrew Doherty. Marge struggled to digest this information. Finally she said, "The club provides you with a phone?"

Tyler grimaced. "All staff get one. It sounds cool, but it's actually a pain in the ass. Mr. Gilson wants to be able to reach us at any time."

She paused for a long moment, then pointed at his phone. "Show me your GPS settings."

She watched over his shoulder as he scrolled through screens on his phone until he reached the settings. "There." She jabbed a finger at the screen. "My guess is he gives you phones so he can keep tabs on you."

Tyler stared at the screen, slack-jawed. "He *spies* on us?"

"Haven't you seen all the surveillance equipment at that place? Besides, I suspect it's become basic corporate practice to use company-provided electronics to monitor employees."

He shook his head. "That's so fucked-up." He tapped the screen and opened the GPS settings.

Marge put out a hand to stop him. "No. Leave everything as is."

There was a flicker of movement outside Tyler's window, and Marge looked up to find an elderly, violet-haired woman peering myopically at the truck from the sidewalk. It occurred to her that the fewer people who saw her with Tyler Mattson, the better. She leaned forward and gave the elderly gawker a smile and a little wave, and, to her relief, the woman stooped to pick up the squirrel-like dog at her feet and hurried away.

Marge turned to face Tyler directly. "Look," she said, "you're not in trouble for the weed." She shot him a look. "Yet." She paused. "Are you familiar with the term 'confidential informant'?"

His eyes went wide. "You want me to be a CI?"

"You've admitted to criminal wrongdoing, haven't you?" she asked. "Dealing drugs carries a pretty stiff penalty. Five years? Ten?"

Despite the implied threat, Tyler's expression brightened, and Marge suspected that the young man's notion of criminal intelligence was based entirely on cop shows. Any concern for his own safety took a back seat to his excitement. She wished she felt more optimistic about Tyler's ability to keep a secret, and she had more than a twinge of guilt for possibly compromising his safety by involving him.

"First things first," said Marge. "Tell your mom we talked about a recent bar fight. That you were a witness and I needed your help figuring out who did what. Next—and this is the most important part—don't breathe a word of this conversation to anyone. I don't want anyone else to know that you and I spoke. Not your girlfriend, not the people at the country club, and *especially* not your boss. If I hear otherwise, you'll be in jail." She pursed her lips and considered her next words. "Keep doing what you've been doing at the club. No changes in your routine. No changes in your behavior."

"Just act natural, right?"

"Right." She pointed at his phone. "When you're not at work, leave that thing at home. Most importantly, I need you to let me know right away if you see or hear anything out of the ordinary." She saw the gleam of excitement in his eyes, like a small boy with a toad in his pocket, and she worried whether she might be making a big mistake.

She put a hand on his arm. "I don't want you to *do* anything," she said firmly. "Just keep your eyes open." She flipped open the center console of the truck and pulled out her wallet. "Buy a burner phone at Trixie's Liquor. You know where that is?" He nodded and she handed him some cash. "Don't buy it anywhere else, and call me when you get it." She pulled a business card from her wallet and handed it to him. "Don't carry the burner on you either. Keep it hidden in your car or your house."

For the first time since she had said the words "confidential informant," a shadow crossed his face, and she thought for a moment that he might change his mind. Then he nodded and pushed open the door of the truck. He got out, then turned back to Marge.

"You can count on me, Sheriff."

26

Jake poked his head into the interrogation room slash broom closet, and the excitement on his face was immediately replaced with devastation. "You didn't bring the puppy?" He stood limp-shouldered in the doorway. "The fuck, Simons? It was the least you could do."

Dan Simons scowled at Jake from across the rickety table where he sat. "I'm not bringing Maisy to a place like this." He looked at the wall and muttered something about animal abuse.

Marge looked at Jake. "I promise I'll buy you a puppy when all this is settled."

The smile returned to Jake's face. "Really?"

"No. Now go make yourself useful." Marge waited until Jake had left, then shut the door and took a seat at the table. Eli was camped out in front of a laptop in the conference room, scouring the internet for information on anything related to the Green Lake Country Club, Tyler Mattson, Andrew Doherty, and the elusive Mr. Gilson. Marge knew it had taken Eli some coaxing to convince Dan to come to the station, and, in the end, she suspected Dan had agreed out of pity for Eli. Dan Simons knew as well as anyone in Shaky Lake how far Eli had fallen in the past year, and he himself seemed to be a man well acquainted with rock bottom.

Dan tugged at the front of his faded black Metallica T-shirt. The air-conditioning was broken again, and the heat and humidity had begun to trickle into the subterranean lair that was the sheriff's station. "I already told Eli I don't know anything," Dan muttered, and crossed his arms across his chest, a hand tucked into each armpit. There was a tattoo on his right forearm, brighter and newer than the rest; a black coffin, emblazoned with an all-seeing eye, scarlet drops of blood, and what looked to be a date. The death of a loved one, perhaps, although to Marge's knowledge, Dan Simons was an unflagging loner, and had been for as long as she could remember.

It had been nearly twenty years since the last time she'd sat across this battered steel table from him. She didn't regret her actions back then, not exactly. He had been dealing drugs—heroin, cocaine—in the community she was sworn to protect. She hadn't had a choice. Still, she couldn't help feeling responsible for what she saw across the table now. It wasn't the scruffy clothes or overgrown beard, or the scowl on his face, or the insolence in the way he slumped back in his chair. It was his eyes that sent a stab of something like shame through her. They were the eyes of a man twice Dan's age, of a man who had lived through eighty, ninety years of hard times and didn't care one way or another if he saw another sunrise. She could have looked the other way, all those years ago. Could have pulled him aside and said, *Keep selling drugs in Shaky Lake and I'll arrest you*. He'd been so young then. Instead, she'd arrested him. Would she have done the same thing had she known what it would lead to, or that one day she might need his help? To her dismay, she felt a prickling behind her eyes and looked quickly away. She was just overtired, she told herself. Stretched too thin. She cleared her throat and pretended to search for a pen in the stack of file folders.

Dan leaned forward a little. "We just gonna sit here?"

Marge felt a flash of irritation with herself, with her discombobulation, and looked down at the pen she always wore clipped neatly into the breast pocket of her shirt. She pulled it out and set it on the table next to her paperwork, then clasped her hands together, businesslike, on the table. "Let me start," she began, "by saying that you're not here because I think you did something wrong."

"Very kind of you." He tipped his head back slightly, as if from boredom, and looked at her down the bridge of his crooked nose.

Marge resisted the urge to clear her throat. She flipped open one of the folders and pulled out a sealed evidence bag. "In fact, it's actually quite the opposite." She laid the clear plastic bag on the table and pushed it toward Dan. "Look familiar?"

Dan's bland expression, his disinterested manner, didn't change, but blotches of color appeared on his throat, like a poker-game tell, visible even through his rough, patchy neck beard. He gave the bag only the briefest of glances, but it was clear he knew what it contained. He said nothing.

Marge tapped the CD through the clear plastic.

At Last: The Best of Etta James.

"Your fingerprints are on it," she said, "and I don't think I have to tell you where we found it."

More silence.

"The music was what led us to Ben Sharpe's body," Marge said.

Dan stared at the disc, and his trademark scowl slid into something darker. A sort of fatalism settled into his features. "I suppose I should ask for a lawyer now."

Marge put the evidence bag back in the folder. "A young girl is missing and it's already been over forty-eight hours. I have zero good leads. Every hour that goes by takes us that much farther from finding her. Please, Dan. I know you don't owe me anything, but I really need your help."

He crossed his arms more tightly across his chest and looked at Marge with an expression eloquent with contempt. She saw the bone-deep bitterness of the continually overlooked, the pushed aside, but there was something about him beneath the saturnine facade that she found touching: a fierce pride, a vulnerability.

Marge leaned forward and propped her forearms on the table. "Here's what I think happened." She held up a hand to quell his protest. "You don't need to say anything." There was a loud *thunk* from the wall behind Dan's chair as the air conditioner came to life, then Jake's voice in the hall, a whoop of celebration. One of Marge's file folders blew open from the sudden gust of air through the vent, and she clamped her hand down on it just in time to prevent papers from flying everywhere.

"I think," she continued, "that you came across Ben Sharpe's body on Tuesday night. You were out on the water and saw his boat on the dock. Eli tells me that Ben wasn't great at tying his boat up and you'd helped him before."

Dan's expression clouded, but he stayed silent.

"But when you got to the boat," she continued, "you saw—"

"He was already dead," he snapped, his voice full of gravel.

A pause. "Why didn't you call 911?"

His mouth twisted in something like pain. "He was past saving." He looked away. "And I ain't doing time again."

"So you blasted some Etta James—nice choice of music, by the way— and waited for someone to call in a noise disturbance." It wasn't a question.

He scowled. "The CD wasn't mine. It was already in the player when I got there." He gave a humorless smile. "Nothing like a good noise disturbance to get Shaky Lake law enforcement riled up. Got to keep the vacationers happy, right?"

"Only you forgot to wipe your prints off the CD."

He didn't say anything, but Marge could see the rise and fall of his chest, the pulse of a vein in his neck. Her conjecture had been correct, it seemed. But Dan's admission, such as it was, that he had found the boy and called for help, albeit in an unconventional way, didn't offer any further clues as to how Ben had died, and by whose hand.

"Ben was—" Dan cleared his throat. When he went on, his voice had lost all of its sarcasm, its aggression. "Most kids are shit, but he was—" He pressed his lips together tightly and shook his head. The blotches of redness on his neck spread to a full flush. He cleared his throat again, then put his hands on the table and began to stand. "Are we done here? Maisy probably has the house torn up by now. She's not used to me being gone."

Something tightened in Marge's throat, and it was a moment before she could speak. "There's something else," she managed.

Dan frowned at her warily and slumped back into the chair.

"We found fingerprints in the boat from a man named Russell Kovach." She raised a brow. "An old friend of yours?"

"Friend?" he scoffed. "Like hell."

"He was in prison until late last year," said Marge. "Why would his fingerprints end up in Ben Sharpe's boat?"

"No idea," said Dan. "I haven't seen or heard from the piece of shit in years, and thank god for that."

She gave him a questioning look. "Why?"

"He's not somebody you'd want to meet in a dark alley." Dan's words were flippant, but there was a very real anxiety in his tone. His hands, she noticed, were clasped so tightly together that his knuckles shone white in the harsh fluorescent lighting.

"Meaning?"

Dan hesitated for a long moment. "Just because he didn't go away for murder doesn't mean he didn't kill people."

Marge had done a quick internet search on Russell Kovach after the station meeting that afternoon. The man's mug shot had sent a shiver through her; he was pale, bald, thick-necked, with a horseshoe mustache of indeterminate color and a tilt of bored amusement on his thin lips. Even through lazy, half-closed lids, there was a snakelike watchfulness in his eyes, a terrible leisureliness, as though he had all the time in the world in which to strike, and when he did, he would show no mercy.

"What exactly was your business relationship with Kovach?" she asked.

"I reported to him. I was low-level in the organization, but he was closer with the big guys."

"Big guys?"

"Russell Kovach is a thug. He works for people who don't want to get their hands dirty."

It wasn't the first time Marge had considered whether Ben's death might have been drug-motivated, what with Rachel's drug use. Retaliation for debts outstanding, perhaps. Punishment for wrongdoings. She recalled what Rachel had said to her yesterday.

Don't you think I would tell you if I knew anything? He was my son.

Marge smoothed the rumpled edge of one of the file folders and thought for a moment. She hadn't specifically asked Rachel if anyone might have been trying to hurt *her*.

She turned her attention back to Dan. "Were you asked to give evidence against Russell Kovach or anyone else?"

Dan laughed. "Yeah, I was asked. I told them to go fuck themselves. I wasn't looking to get murdered in prison. Or out of prison, for that matter."

"Would Kovach have come to Shaky Lake to find you?"

"I don't know why he would," said Dan. "Our business relationship is long over and I'm out of the game."

Marge pulled her notebook out and skimmed through it. "He completed his sentence for drug trafficking in 2011, then got sent up again for witness intimidation and extortion in 2016. That case was retried last year—newly discovered evidence or something—and he was acquitted."

"'Newly discovered evidence,' huh?" Dan scoffed. "Sounds about right." He leaned forward and tapped a finger on the table. "That motherfucker is guilty of every crime he's ever been charged with, and a whole lot more. If he got out early, somebody's pulling strings."

Marge looked at him skeptically. "You said Kovach was somebody's thug, and you're suggesting that this 'somebody' was able to get him a new trial and get him acquitted?" She shook her head. "Sounds like something out of a movie."

He sat back in his chair and shrugged.

Marge stared at him for a long time, then picked up her pen and scrawled some notes in the notebook. She closed her various file folders and notebook and stacked them into a neat pile.

"There's somebody," she said, "who's going to want to talk to you."

He tilted his head back, and after a moment, he addressed the ceiling. "You want my help." He shook his head slowly back and forth. He met her eyes then, and his face was tight with an emotion she couldn't identify. "Fine," he said, his voice harsh. "But just so you know, I'm only doing it for him. For Ben."

27

Eli saw the fear on Beth Wallace's face the moment she opened the door; the same fear he had heard in her voice an hour ago on the phone.

I need to talk to you, she had said, and he hadn't asked her why, had just saved his work on his laptop and left the station. Everyone else had already gone home, and he was surprised to find, when he emerged onto the parking lot, that it was much later than he realized. His internet research hadn't yielded the results he had been hoping for. For Tyler Mattson, he had found a disorderly conduct charge from a softball game brawl in May and a handful of old mentions in Shaky Lake High School sports articles. The search for Mr. Michael Gilson turned up page after page of baronial professional photographs and accolades for his extensive philanthropy and advocacy in the realm of healthcare equity, which Eli found amusing, considering the man ran one of the most expensive, exclusive clubs in the country. On Andrew Doherty, he found nothing.

"Thanks for coming," said Beth. The planes of her face glowed a warm, golden color, lit by the rays of the setting sun, which poured in through the west-facing living room window, but her lips were pulled tight and her eyes met his for only the briefest of moments before she looked past him to search the encroaching dusk outside. She turned without a word toward the kitchen, and he followed her into the unlit room and sat at the table in the gloom while she moved in the shadows along the edges of the room, shifting things on the counter, pouring glasses of something. Their mutual silence lent a strange air of intimacy, as if they had long been close friends. He was thankful he had taken the time to go home before coming to see her. His hair was still wet from the shower, but at least his clothes were clean, and, thanks to the beer he had chugged the moment he'd gotten home, his hands and mind were relatively steady. It occurred to him now that he should have eaten something.

Beth flipped on the light over the kitchen table and sat down. Her face was tense, as though she was listening, and she gripped two juice glasses half-full of something that was not juice.

She sat and pushed a glass toward him. "Scotch."

The word was a command, and, without protest, he put the glass to his lips and took a sip. His eyes widened. It was very, very good scotch, the likes of which was not sold at Trixie's Liquor. His unexpected pleasure must have registered on his face.

"It's Cal's," she said. "I brought it along in case he decided to join us." The words had a bitter edge that she seemed to regret the moment they were out. Calvin Wallace had not, it turned out, decided to join his family in Shaky Lake. Beth's words to Alyssa last night had felt like a confession. An argument on Friday night, an angry ultimatum—she would leave him if he didn't come to Shaky Lake on Saturday—a tense parting. And then silence. Cal hadn't answered her calls. She had even called the next-door neighbors. Gone, they said. Left Sunday morning and never came back.

Eli had been horrified. He had thought Michelle asking him for a divorce, asking him to move out, had been excruciating, but the idea that she would simply walk away from him, just leave without a word, was too terrible to contemplate.

Beth took a sip of her drink, then set it on the table. She traced the rim of the glass with her forefinger. "Somebody's been watching me," she said. Her tone was guarded, as if she was bracing herself for what he might say in response: skepticisms, glib reassurances. He was, in fact, swearing inwardly at himself for not considering more seriously the idea that Beth herself might be in danger. It had been a careless mistake.

She seemed to misinterpret his silence as distrust. She fixed him with a hard stare. "I'm not crazy."

"No."

The monosyllable seemed to satisfy her. She shifted in her chair and pulled a knee up. A thread of damp night air curled in through the window as the heat of the day gradually withdrew, and a loon called from across the water. The meager light from the fixture overhead picked out the cords of Beth's neck as she swallowed.

"I couldn't sleep last night and I went to open the bedroom window a little wider. I saw a light in the woods—like the light from a cell phone—maybe fifty feet away from the cabin." Her hands clasped and unclasped in a nervous rhythm. "At first, I thought maybe it was Caitlin, that she had found her way home. I couldn't see anyone, just the light, so I called for her through the window." She rubbed a hand against her temple. "Pathetic, I know, but"—she took in a deep breath, let it out in an unsteady stream—"I'm not ready to give up hope."

He would have taken another sip of scotch if he thought he could bring the glass to his lips without his hands shaking. The muscles of his legs tensed involuntarily, as if to stand, as if determined to flee, to escape somewhere he could turn on every light and lock every door.

She wrapped her arms around her raised knee. "After I called out, whoever it was disappeared. This morning, I looked outside the bedroom window and the pine needles were—well, I could tell that someone had been standing there."

The image flashed in his mind: Beth, standing in the darkness, looking out the window, as something terrible circled the cabin, closer and closer every moment.

"You should have called me," he ground out. The image of her dropped from view, to be replaced with one of himself, falling-down drunk at Babe's last night. He gripped the seat of his chair and focused on Beth's face.

She ignored his comment and, instead, tossed back the rest of her drink and got to her feet. She went to the countertop and reached for the bottle of scotch, then turned to face him. She leaned against the countertop, her face hidden in shadows. She was quiet for a long time, long enough for the last rays of afterglow to disappear below the horizon and turn the kitchen window mirrorlike against the darkness outside.

"Deputy, are you married?"

Her voice was quiet, barely more than a murmur, but for some reason the question shocked him like a blow from behind, a falling bucket of water. For a moment, he couldn't respond, and when he recovered enough to speak, the words were sour in his mouth.

"Separated."

She considered him for a moment, then pushed away from the counter into the light and sat back down at the table; the moist air in the room shifted with her movement, and the silence between them lengthened into something uneasy and disconcerting. She put a hand to her head and rubbed her fingertips against her scalp, as if to dispel a headache, but the fissure between her eyebrows only deepened.

"I think Cal might be having an affair."

Eli waited in silence for her to elaborate.

"Maybe all these extra hours at work are"—she made a helpless gesture with her hand—"just an excuse. He's on the road a lot, too. There would be plenty of opportunity for . . ." She gave an embarrassed shrug.

Eli considered this for a moment. "What would that have to do with Caitlin's disappearance?" He thought back to last night's interview. How much of what Beth Wallace had told Alyssa had been the truth and how much had been, maybe not lies exactly, but half-truths, omissions?

"I don't know. I just . . . I just thought you should know."

Eli took a sip of his scotch; as he put the glass to his mouth, some of the fiery liquor spilled against his lips. The cut on his lower lip was just barely healed, and he rubbed a thumb gingerly over his mouth, then set the glass back down on the table.

"You're not safe here," he said. "There are still a lot of unknowns in this case"—a terrible understatement—"and if someone is watching you, it means you could be in danger."

Beth stood suddenly, and the abrupt movement, the sharp scrape of the aluminum chair against the floor, startled him. With great effort, he kept his seat and stared up at her through the slant of yellow lamplight. She turned away from him and began to pace. The gray fabric of her tank top was black with sweat along her spine and at the small of her back.

"I'm not leaving," she said. She turned to glare at him. "What if Caitlin comes back and I'm not here?"

Eli didn't point out the very real possibility—one he had been doing his best to ignore—that Caitlin might never come back. "We'll have someone watch the cabin," he said. "We'll know if she comes back."

"No offense," Beth said, a touch of frost in her voice, "but I don't get the sense that you have the manpower for that. Besides, I have my pepper spray." When his expression turned skeptical, she looked at him as if he was utterly clueless. "I'm from *Chicago*," she said, slowly, as if explaining something to a backward kindergartner.

Eli saw the expression on her face and knew that he could not dissuade her from staying. "I want you to call me right away if anything happens, or even if something just doesn't feel right. I don't care if it's the middle of the night."

"Thank you for coming over, Deputy."

"Eli."

She nodded but didn't say his name. "I promise I'll call you."

"I still think you should stay in a hotel. I'm sure there are—"

She put up a hand. "I'll be fine."

He said good night, and at the door, he turned back to look at her. She didn't look fine. She looked gaunt and undone. Unrecognizable from the woman he had met two nights ago. He would surveil the cabin despite her protests, he decided. His instinctual need to protect her, to keep her from harm, would keep him awake and alert as long as necessary. These days, sleep was something he preferred to avoid anyway.

Cal

*C*al was being followed. He was sure of it. It was late Sunday afternoon
and he had sat for hours at Starbucks that morning, waiting for Kevin
to arrive so they could come up with a plan on how best to proceed with
turning over the information Cal had found to the authorities.

Kevin never showed up.

Cal looked in the rearview mirror and saw the same black Escalade, just
a couple of cars behind him, still there, even through the warren of downtown Chicago streets. It was only when the Escalade followed him on the
Dempster Street exit toward his home in Skokie that he realized. The car.
His phone. They belonged to Orion. The luxury of a company car and cell
with the tight leash of GPS tracking software.

He pulled a U-turn on Dempster on a red light, nearly causing an accident, but he succeeded in losing the Escalade for just long enough to double
back onto I-94, this time back into the city. He knew it was just a matter
of time before the SUV, or another Orion vehicle, showed up behind him
again. He wove his way on and off exits and down the winding streets of
commercial districts before coming to a stop at an empty school parking lot
on the well-traveled street in front of the entrance to the Cook County Forest
Preserve. He dialed Beth but hung up before he finished entering the phone
number. Orion was probably monitoring his calls.

The need to speak to his wife, to make sure she and Caitlin were safe,
nearly overwhelmed him, and he fought to stay calm as he stood on the

street corner. The stop-and-go traffic inched along, too heavy to cut across the street. Each second he stood there, waiting for the walk light, brought him closer and closer to sheer panic. Finally the traffic stalled enough to risk stepping out. A pickup truck idled at the front of the line, and he used the opportunity to drop his phone into the open truck bed as he wove through the stopped cars. At the entrance to the forest preserve was a line of shiny red bicycles, available to use for a couple of hours at the cost of a few dollars. The machine only accepted credit cards, and he hesitated. His company card. Bad idea. He fumbled through his wallet for the travel rewards card Beth had given him at least a year ago and prayed that it was already activated. He breathed a sigh of relief as the kiosk light flashed green. He pulled the bike from its charging station and pedaled into the park.

The forest preserve was meant to be a slice of wilderness in the heart of urban Chicago, spanning out to the suburbs, and he was thankful for the heavy tree cover and lack of fellow park-goers. He pedaled as quickly as he could in the fading light and turned into his neighborhood just after sunset.

From his vantage point behind his neighbor Mitch's garage, he could see his own house. No lights on, no car in the driveway or on the street. Seemingly deserted. But he knew they were there somewhere. Waiting for him. Searching his house for copies of the document. For evidence of Orion's terrible crimes. The strap of his messenger bag had worn his shoulder raw miles ago, and he pulled the bag frontward over his chest and reached inside. It was still there. Fax cover sheet, the document, the folder. The originals were tucked into the hidden compartment in his basement safe.

He had been an idiot for not taking the Salvare data to the FBI right away, for trusting Kevin Allen. His only thought now was getting to Beth and Caitlin before Orion did. He'd make sure they were safe, then go to the FBI. It wouldn't be easy getting to Shaky Lake without a car, but on the long bike ride to his house, he had come up with a plan.

Mitch's house sat kitty-corner to his own. An impressive two-story Tudor that dwarfed Cal's mid-century modern ranch. Far too much house for a ninety-year-old widower to take care of on his own. Cal had begun help-

ing with upkeep a few years back. Snowblowing and mowing to start with. Then work got too busy. He knew that Mitch had moved to an assisted living facility a couple of months ago, and he hoped that the locks hadn't been changed yet.

Cal fished the key to Mitch's house out of the hiding spot beneath a fake rock near the garage entrance and let himself in. The place was musty from being closed up, but Cal collapsed into the leather couch in the front living room. He adjusted the blinds so that he could see his house through the window, then sat there in the dark for an hour before his growling stomach sent him into the pantry. He knew there was no going home. Not now, anyway.

After he had eaten a can of beans and some stale crackers, he made his way to the garage. The keys to Mitch's titanic Buick sedan were on the shelf by the door, and he prayed as he put the key in the ignition. To his relief, the car started up right away and the gas tank was half-full.

He looked at his watch. It was nearly midnight. He turned off the car and went back into the house. Mitch's land telephone line and internet had long been disconnected, which left Cal without any means to contact Beth. He rummaged around in Mitch's drawers and found a few dollars' worth of coins. That plus the twenty dollars he had in his wallet was his only cash.

He gathered up what was left of Mitch's food and some musty clothing from the older man's closet and threw everything in the car. The Buick was a boat to drive and would burn through that half tank of gas in no time, but he silently thanked Mitch for being there for him. This time, he was the one who'd needed help.

The car lights would attract the attention of anyone watching his house, so he pulled out of Mitch's driveway with the lights off, only switching them on a few blocks and a few turns later. He passed the Skokie police station and considered going to them. Maybe they would help him. Help Caitlin and Beth. But maybe he would spend the rest of the night trying to explain things to them instead of driving to Shaky Lake. He looked at his watch again. If he sped, he could be there in six hours. Then he could go to the police, once he knew his family was safe.

The interstate traffic was sparse this time of night and he made good *time. The fuel light on the Buick came on just before the Belvedere Oasis, the last pit stop before he made it to Wisconsin. He pulled into the fueling area, took the travel rewards credit card out of his wallet, and inserted it into the gas pump scanner. Out of the corner of his eye, he saw another vehicle pull in. It was a black Escalade. How could they have found him? He glanced at the gas meter. He had managed to get a few gallons of gas, at least. He yanked the pump handle out of the tank opening and jumped into the Buick. He slammed on the gas and skidded out of the station through a side driveway, then barreled past the Escalade toward the on-ramp.*

As he drove, he thought frantically about the ways Orion could be tracking him. He kept one hand on the wheel and one eye on the road while he dug into his pockets. The messenger bag. A gift from his boss last Christmas. He reached over and dumped the contents of the bag onto the passenger seat. He tried as best he could to keep the car on the road as he clawed through the papers and other office debris. All the while, the pounding in his chest grew. His search turned up nothing, and, frantic, he exited the freeway onto a county highway. The cracked and potholed road took him farther and farther into the dark countryside. He constantly scanned his rearview mirror for lights, and after half an hour of turning and weaving his way along the graveled side roads, he pulled into a short, muddy driveway that led into a cornfield. He checked the gas gauge. The distance-to-empty light indicated that he had perhaps ten miles' worth of gas left. He turned off the car and got out.

The Escalade couldn't have followed him this closely just by sight. There was no way. He had dodged and backtracked over and over again. They must be tracking him some other way. At this rate, he knew it was only a matter of time before they caught up to him. He pulled off his shoes, then his shirt and jeans, combing every inch of them in an effort to find a tracking device. He went through the papers strewn about in the passenger seat and felt every inch of the briefcase.

Then he found it. A tiny metal tracker. No bigger than a pencil eraser, wedged into an inner corner of the briefcase. He held the tracker and stared at it for a long time. The cold predawn air settled between the high cornstalks, and he shivered. Then he put his clothes and shoes back on and neatly gathered up the documents from where they had been strewn on the floor of the car.

Ten miles' worth of gas left. Enough to get him to a road that led somewhere other than a cornfield. He tossed the tracker as far into the cornfield as possible and got back into the car. He clutched the wheel, looking into the rearview mirror every few seconds for car lights.

He didn't see the deer until it was too late. Three does suddenly appeared in his headlights, and he swerved to avoid hitting them. The last thing he remembered was the crunch of gravel as his car left the road.

28

Jake was already there when Eli got to Babe's, his scarred face creased in the smile that always got him free drinks when Connie was working. He glanced over as Eli came through the door, and his grin widened.

"Speak of the devil," boomed Ray from behind the bar. "We were just talking shit about you, Eli." He set a bottle of High Life on the bar in front of Jake, who smacked the seat of the barstool next to him as an invitation for Eli to sit.

As much as he craved a drink, Babe's was the last place Eli wanted to be at the moment. Not that Ray or any of the usual patrons of the bar would hold last night's drunken stumble against him, but the thought of facing more of Connie's worried glances was highly unappealing. Jake, however, was not a person who asked for much, and when he had called Eli and asked his friend to join him for a drink, Eli was loath to let his friend down.

Eli headed first to the bathroom. When he returned, a beer had materialized on the bar for him. He dropped onto the chair and took a sip, then another in quick succession. High Life wasn't his typical beer of choice, and the drink tasted even more sour than he remembered.

Jake swiveled his stool to the side and propped an elbow on the bar. "How did it go with Caitlin's mom?" he asked, his voice as low as possible over the music from the jukebox and the general clatter of the bar. Eli looked at him in surprise. "Beth? How did you—"

Jake waved away the question. "I swung by your place to see if you wanted to get a beer, and your car wasn't there. You weren't at Babe's, so I figured, where else would you have gone?" The corner of his mouth twitched. "From what Alyssa says, Beth Wallace seems to think you walk on water."

Eli stared at him, confused. "She—she *what*?" He shook his head. She had called him, asked him to come over, that much was true. *Still.* "I guarantee she doesn't think I walk on water," he said. "Last night Alyssa played bad cop and I played good cop, so of course Beth wasn't going to reach out to the bad cop with more information."

Jake straightened on his barstool. "What did you two talk about?"

Eli felt a thread of unease pass through him, and he hesitated. It felt wrong, somehow, to disclose to another person what Beth had shared with him. A betrayal of her confidence. Which was ridiculous, he told himself. Beth was not a friend, she was a vital part of an investigation, and he needed to share every piece of information with his team if they were going to find Caitlin.

"She thinks someone's watching her."

Something slid over Jake's ruined face, then off again, like rainwater, and the bottle of beer he balanced on one knee wobbled and began to tip. He managed to right it, but not before some of the contents sloshed onto his jeans. He swore and reached for a handful of napkins from the dispenser an arm's length away. Eli considered whether his friend might be drunk.

Jake looked up from the wad of napkins in his hand. "In Chicago?"

"Here in Shaky Lake, at the cabin." Eli set his drink down, then proceeded to give Jake the details of what Beth had told him: her refusal to seek safer lodgings and his plan to stake out her cabin.

"Did you tell Marge?" asked Jake.

"Not yet."

Jake looked at his watch. "What do you need me to do? I can head over there anytime."

"No," said Eli, "I'll keep watch tonight."

Jake looked concerned. "You sure? If someone was outside her cabin last night, they might make their move tonight. We could go together."

Eli shook his head. "I can handle it. And at least one of us needs to have some brainpower left over for tomorrow."

Jake looked doubtful. "Couldn't Marge convince her to go to a hotel?"

He shook his head again. "Not a chance." He took a sip of his beer. "Also, she thinks her husband is having an affair."

Jake looked at him, brows raised.

"She feels like he's keeping secrets from her. His business trips get longer and longer. He stays later and later at work. No concrete evidence, though." The two men drank in silence for a few minutes. Jake drained the last of his beer and got to his feet.

"I'm going outside for a smoke. Want to join me?"

Eli didn't smoke, but he welcomed some fresh air. Sometime in the preceding few minutes, his temples had begun to pulse—the beginnings of a headache—and he followed Jake readily to the deserted back parking lot.

"I'm not going to lie," said Jake, after he had lit a cigarette and taken a few long, deep drags. "This case is getting to me. It all sits a little differently here"—he put a hand over his chest—"when it's kids, you know?"

Eli nodded. They both knew it was an understatement.

"There were kids involved when"—Jake hesitated, shook his head, seemed on the verge of changing the subject—"*this* happened." He waved a hand absently at the scar on his face and didn't meet Eli's eyes. If Jake's experiences were anything like his own, they were not memories meant to be spoken out loud. There was a long silence, and then Jake spoke.

"Eli"—he spoke without inflection, without looking up—"do the dead ever talk to you?"

At first the words didn't register. Eli saw Jake's mouth move and sounds come out, but there was a delay, as if the words had to swim upstream against a strong current to reach Eli. He thought of the voices in his own dreams, who spoke to him every night. Pleaded with him for help. Asked him why their homes were being burned with their families still inside, why their daughters were being taken and returned broken, or not returned at all, why they did as they were told and still ended up with a bullet in their brain. In his dreams, he apologized. He explained. He begged for forgiveness. But still they talked.

"I—" Eli stopped. His throat was tight. "Yes."

Jake took a drag on his cigarette. In the light from its glowing tip,

Eli could see the fissures that darkened his friend's forehead, the deep grooves on either side of his mouth. He waited for Jake to continue, to elaborate. It had never occurred to him that the dead might haunt anyone else besides him. That maybe he wasn't alone.

Eli pulled his hands from his pockets, slowly, not wanting to ruin the fragile thread of connection Jake had just extended. He studied his friend's face for a long while in the darkness, deciding whether perhaps he had imagined Jake's words.

"I thought I was . . . ," Eli said, finally. "I thought it was just me." He heard the tremor in his own voice, the rattle of air flowing harshly through his own chest.

Jake shook his head. "No."

For a moment, Eli couldn't process this information, could do little more than stay upright as the notion careened through his brain, as it ricocheted against the inside of his skull.

I'm not alone.

The realization struck him like blinding sunlight after being too long underground. Bright and dazzling, but painful. Still, the warmth was there, spreading across his neck and down his shoulders.

Not alone.

Jake shrugged. "I know you've been struggling." The lines of his face were stark in the semidarkness, and his eyes glittered with intensity. Then he looked away and took one long, final drag of his cigarette. "If you ever need to talk"—he tossed his cigarette butt to the ground, stepped on it, picked it up—"you know where to find me." Then he fixed Eli with a grin. "On one condition."

Eli felt as if his heart were stuck somewhere between his tonsils, threatening to burst. He scrubbed a hand over his face. "Anything."

Jake jerked his chin at the door to the bar. "One game of pool before you stake out Beth Wallace's cabin?"

Eli responded without a moment's hesitation. "One game."

29

Eli awoke in a slab of warm sunshine to the sound of pounding. It struck him that the noise had been going on for a long time, and that the angle of the sun through the window was sharper than at his usual waking hour, or, more accurately, the hour at which he typically gave up trying to sleep.

He opened his eyes warily and looked around. He was in his own bed, at least, and not lying on the bathroom floor or sprawled in the back seat of his car, both situations with which he was all too familiar. He pulled his arm from the tangle of sheets to check his watch, only to find that his wrist was bare. When he looked for his phone, it, too, was nowhere to be found.

God, why was he so sore?

Every muscle in his body ached. Had he been in some sort of accident? It felt as if he had run a marathon in his sleep last night. He looked down to inspect himself for injuries, just as he had after passing out on the dock after finding Ben Sharpe's body. His head, too, ached as it had that night, but a cautious exploration of his scalp didn't reveal any bumps or tender spots. Just the thought of getting out of bed made his bones hurt worse, so he lay there, disoriented, staring at the dust motes that floated gently in the morning sun, conscious of the knot of worry taking shape in his chest. Before he could piece together his thoughts, the pounding on the door was replaced by his mother's voice.

"Eli!"

More pounding.

"Eli, open up!"

A rattle of the doorknob, a muffled curse, then more pounding.

He heaved himself out of bed in one agonizing movement and promptly toppled forward onto his hands and knees. The fall knocked the air from his lungs like a punch to the chest, and it took him a moment to catch his breath. A sickening warmth spread through his body and he knew he was on the verge of passing out. He eased himself forward until his forehead rested on the floor, as if in genuflection—like the Afghan men at their morning *salah*—and he crouched there, eyes closed, and waited for the room to stop spinning. One thing was clear: he was terribly, devastatingly hungover and, apparently, still a little drunk.

Marge shouted his name again, more urgently this time, and it occurred to him that she might use the battering ram if he didn't answer the door. He opened his eyes and forced himself into a kneeling position.

"Coming!"

He knew the moment the shout left his throat that he had made a terrible mistake. At the force of it, the pain in his head exploded and it was all he could do not to vomit.

He cursed, which only brought with it a second wave of nausea. He gagged, then scrambled to his feet. It had been a very long time since he'd felt this wretched, which was saying a lot. He rummaged through the plastic bin of clothes at his bedside, pulled on a pair of sweatpants, and staggered to the door. His tongue was shriveled and stiff, and he would have rinsed his mouth in the bathroom sink if he had had even the slightest confidence he could do so without falling again.

The sunlight in the living room was painfully bright, and for a moment, he thought his eyes were playing tricks on him. He stared dumbly at the electronic display pad on the wall adjacent to the front door, then at the door itself. He blinked once, twice, then rubbed his eyes and looked at the keypad again.

The alarm system. The electronic dead bolt. Both unarmed.

He shuddered. He must have been very, very drunk last night to leave himself unprotected, and to have no recollection of how he'd gotten home. He reached for the cheap brass doorknob—at least he had remembered to lock *that*—but missed; his hands were as slick as sticks of butter.

"Just a minute," he croaked.

He worked to open the knob lock with the awful deliberation of the very drunk, until finally, he threw open the door to find Marge standing there, fist poised to strike another blow on the door. Her jaw dropped at the sight of him.

"What the hell happened to you?" Her words came out in a gasp, and Eli heard an underlying note of panic. His earlier supposition, that she was just moments away from getting out the battering ram, had likely been correct. How many mothers were forced to use battering rams to make sure their adult children were safe? The thought was too depressing to consider, and he pushed it aside.

"What time is it?" His voice was sonorous and rubbery, as though he were at the midpoint of a particularly nasty case of strep throat. He held up a hand to shield his eyes from the searing morning light.

"It's nine thirty," said Marge. She had steadied her expression and her voice, and he felt a tug in his chest at the obvious effort that simple undertaking had cost her. "I called you a dozen times," she said. To an outside observer, she was a mother scolding her teenage son for staying out past curfew and for sleeping so late as to miss the school bus.

She stepped past him into the apartment. He turned to follow her, stumbled, bounced off the doorframe, then planted himself firmly against the arm of the ratty sofa next to the door.

His phone was on the floor near the kitchen door, and she picked it up and examined it. "Your ringer is on." She turned to look at him, started to hand him the phone, then hesitated, as if she were having second thoughts about giving a child a pair of scissors. "How did you not hear me when I called?"

He scrubbed his hands over his face. Tried to remember last night. Failed. He had a general idea of how much alcohol it took for him to get blackout drunk. It must have been a very long night of drinking, indeed, to bring him to his current state. He couldn't think of how to answer her question—he wouldn't insult her with a detailed explanation of how he had come to be falling-down drunk at nine thirty in the morning, even if he *could* remember a damn thing from last night.

Marge set his phone on the coffee table and came to stand directly in front of him. She pulled the penlight from her belt and shone it in his eyes, one at a time, then took a step back. Her visible disgust was more painful than a slap.

"You're drunk."

He opened his mouth, then shut it again. There was nothing he could say—no excuse, no protest. He turned away and was suddenly desperate for a glass of water—something stronger, if he was being honest—but didn't dare attempt to walk to the kitchen and was too ashamed to ask his mother to get him something to drink. Second only to a glass of virtually any potable liquid, what he wanted most in the world at that moment was for his mother to leave.

He cleared his throat. "I'm really sorry, Mom." The words fell like a pile of horse dung into the space between them, and he winced. "Just give me half an hour and I'll—"

"It's Beth," said Marge. The words were an accusation.

He stared dumbly at her. For a moment, the name didn't register.

Beth.

He ground the heels of his hands against his eyes. Images, shadows from last night flitted at the edge of his memory, like bats in the treetops over a campfire. Beth Wallace. A dark kitchen. A bottle of scotch. She had been afraid, but of what? He had made her a promise, but what had it been?

Suddenly he remembered. His eyes flew open, but before he could speak, Marge continued.

"The cabin burned down," she said. "She got out but the smoke inhalation was pretty bad." He saw the strain on her face before she turned away.

"*What?*" Eli stared at the back of her head, slack-jawed, as if she had just confessed to cannibalism. He put a hand to his temple and considered seriously whether he might be dreaming.

Beth.

He had promised to keep her safe. Had promised to be there at a moment's notice if she needed him. Had even made a promise to himself that he would keep watch over her all night, and the night after that if necessary. And now—

"Where is she?" he demanded.

Marge turned back to him and hesitated, then, "Ascension Hospital in Chippewa Falls," she said. "St. Anne's Hospital was full."

His memory of the visit to Beth's cabin last night flooded back to him in its entirety.

"Somebody—" He swallowed hard and attempted to get the words out with some semblance of coherence. "Somebody was watching her. She told me last night."

Marge frowned. "Why am I just hearing about this now?"

"I was going to call you last night, but—" He paused, struggled to remember. He had had a good reason for not calling Marge, he was sure of it. "I talked to her at the cabin, and then I went to—" He stopped again, embarrassed.

"Babe's." She crossed her arms over her chest. "Jake told me, although I practically had to beat it out of him."

Jake.

Jake might know what had happened last night. If he could just talk to Jake . . . Eli reached for his phone on the coffee table but fumbled it and watched stupidly as it bounced off the table and onto the floor. The movement set him off-balance and he swayed, then just barely managed to lower himself onto the sofa before falling.

Marge North was not given to fits of temper—anger wasn't an emotion she considered particularly constructive—but now her eyes blazed and her lips were pressed into a thin, pale line. Without another word, she grabbed him by the elbow, dragged him to the bedroom, and deposited him on the bed.

The pain, the blinding sunshine, the churning in his gut—it was too much. The last shreds of lucidity in his brain dissolved and he closed his eyes. When he opened them again, it was to the sight of his mother standing over him with a glass of water and an inscrutable expression on her face that was infinitely more alarming than anger.

She handed him the water and two small pills. "Aspirin," she said, her voice tight. When he had swallowed the pills, she propped her fists on her hips. "Get some sleep, Eli. I'm taking you off the case."

"*What?*" He scrambled halfway up in bed, his elbows propped behind him on the mattress. "Absolutely not. I didn't—I don't know what happened but I promise—" When he tried to sit all the way up, she stopped him with an outstretched hand and a shake of her head.

She set his phone on the bed beside him. "I'm sorry, Eli."

He started to protest but stopped when he met Marge's gaze. Her smooth, still-youthful face was drawn, and her brown eyes, so sagacious, so kind, were now dull and ringed with shadows. It wasn't anger he saw in her eyes, or disgust. Instead, he saw resignation, sadness, and the one thing he had never, ever thought he would see in her eyes, even through the hell of this past year.

His mother, his champion, had given up on him.

30

Eli was lying flat on his back on the floor of his bedroom when his phone rang. He reached for it and held it up in front of him. The screen was shattered—he must have dropped it last night—and something flashed behind the cobwebs in the glass. A word. A photo below.

Michelle.

He didn't need to look at the photo. He had it memorized. Every last detail. Her dark eyes. The broad, bright, beaming smile on her lips—it had been Andy's eighth birthday party—the dark hair that had escaped her ponytail and hung in wisps against her cheeks. She had called him exactly twice since he'd moved out a month ago, and he felt a stab of panic that perhaps Marge had told Michelle about what happened this morning, that Marge had taken him off the case. He sat up.

"Hello?"

"Eli, it's me," said Michelle. "Andy's had an accident. I called 911, but—" Her voice was calm, but tight with fear, and then muffled as she pulled away from the phone to say something to Andy. Then, "Please, Eli . . . come quick." He could hear his son's cries in the background.

"I'm on my way," he said, already halfway to the door.

———

By the time Eli pulled into Michelle's driveway, the last of the fog in his mind was gone, though his head and body still ached with a strange intensity, like no other hangover he'd had before. The hot, still air was filled with the oily scent of scorching blacktop. Up and down the street, neighbors puttered with Weedwackers or tinkered with their cars in their driveways. The sweet, ticklish smell of freshly mown grass hung in the air, and he knew with terrible certainty what had happened.

"Michelle!" he shouted, and sprinted around the garage.

"We're back here!" Michelle's shout mingled with Andy's cries.

All thought of his own state of mind, his own state of being, vanished. He crossed the yard in half a dozen strides and skidded to his knees in the grass beside Michelle. She, too, was on her knees, Andy pressed tightly against her chest. The lawn mower lay tipped on its side a few feet away, and he forced himself to look away from the dark substance on the grass beneath it, and the wheel rim, painted a bright scarlet.

"What happened?" Eli gasped.

"It was the lawn mower. He reached into it while the blade was turned on." Michelle's phone rested in the grass at her side, its screen and her left cheek both smudged with blood.

The boy's face was ashen and his eyes were glazed with fear and pain. There was something off about the way his legs sprawled out in front of him, the way his feet in their grass-stained sneakers were all akimbo in the newly shorn grass. A cluster of synapses fired in some primitive section of Eli's brain and he drew a deep breath, then exhaled harshly. He couldn't afford to lose it. Not now. Andy needed him. In the distance, he heard the first whine of sirens.

Andy whimpered when he saw Eli. "Dad!" He choked on a sob, then said, "Dad, I'm sorry. I'm sorry." He sagged against Michelle, and his newly developed Adam's apple bobbed again and again as he swallowed. His eyelids sagged shut. Something tore in Eli's chest, something vital, and he wondered briefly whether a man could die from it.

"Don't you worry, buddy," he said, his voice gravel. "It's no problem at all." It was as massive a lie as he had ever told.

"We're here, baby," said Michelle, "You're going to be just fine. I know it hurts." She looked up at Eli, then down at Andy, wordlessly directing him to examine the boy. Her self-possession was something marvelous to behold.

He repositioned himself on the grass to get a better look at Andy, then froze. At first his brain couldn't register what he was seeing. An abstract painting. A collection of shapes and colors with no recognizable meaning. The all-too-familiar sense of impending doom flickered in his belly. He must have paused for a moment too long, because he heard Michelle's voice prodding him.

"Eli," she whispered, eyes wide and questioning. She looked pointedly at Andy again, then back to Eli.

He willed himself to look again, to push back against the rising dread. He had seen people bleeding on the ground countless times, an awful yet familiar experience. The front of Michelle's shirt was heavy and stiff with blood, and the arms that held Andy were smeared red from her fingertips to above her elbows, like crimson opera gloves. Her hand was wrapped tightly around Andy's wrist, but the amount of blood made it difficult to tell where her hand stopped and Andy's began. The metallic, iron-rich smell was strong enough to lean against, strong enough to taste. A prickling sensation hit Eli in the mouth; a thousand needles poking into the soft tissue of his lips, tongue, and inner cheeks. He tried and failed to swallow away the sensation. Tried and failed to fill his lungs with air. He met Michelle's eyes, and she must have seen that something was wrong, because her face creased with concern and something else he couldn't decipher. She said something to him, asked him something, but he knew it was too late. Her words were a foreign language, garbled and nonsensical.

The air seethed and crackled around him, the trees that edged the yard seemed to undulate, and the expanse of lawn around him brightened from green to neon yellow to white. The tingling in his mouth sharpened, dulled, then sharpened again, then radiated across his face until it smothered him, like a mask without holes, before spilling down his throat, down his neck, until he couldn't move. He blinked, over and over. There was something important he needed to do, to see, if only he could remember what.

A deep gray wave rolled slowly, invitingly, across the lawn, and the idea of letting it wash over him was seductive. He didn't want to open his eyes anymore. Didn't want to see whatever it was that had terrified him. Something soft and spongy and sweet-smelling cradled his head, his back, his legs, and a remote part of his brain registered it as freshly mown turf. He heard Michelle's voice one last time; then the wave rolled over him and he let go.

———————

Time passed; hours, maybe. Then, a sickening softness in his head. A flicker of shadows through closed eyelids. He squeezed his eyes more tightly shut and willed himself back under the gray waves.

More time, then voices. Over him, around him. Shouts. Sounds of re-assurance. Then the scrape of metal on metal and sirens receding. He lay perfectly still and waited for the clamor to move on and leave him in peace under the waves, cool and soothing on his face. Then he felt some-thing beneath his neck, behind his shoulders, buoying him up and out of the waves. He struggled desperately against the upward pressure and heard a plaintive sound that he registered as his own voice.

"Eli?" A voice, muffled, as if trying to penetrate through water.

Something soft against his face.

"Eli." Clearer now. Closer.

A face materialized in the center of his vision, then vanished again.

A shove. Grass against the side of his face. A jolt of brutal pain in his gut and suddenly he was wide awake. He retched into the grass. An arm wrapped tightly around his shoulders, a hand on his back.

"You're okay, honey." His mother's voice. She rubbed his back as if he were a little boy with the stomach flu.

He tried to sit up, but she stopped him with a gentle push to the shoulder.

"Give it another minute," she said. "Take your time."

His shirt hung from his shoulders, stiff with sweat, and overlaying everything was the ripening scent of frightened animal flesh, like some-thing that would waft from a tannery. Marge shifted the arm she held around his shoulders.

"Andy. Mom, is he—" He twisted around to look at her, and the move-ment made his vision go black for a moment. He clutched a handful of grass to steady himself.

Marge made a soothing gesture with her free hand. "He's on his way to the hospital. Michelle is with him."

"But is he—will he be—"

"He'll be okay." She was quiet for a while, and Eli finally looked at her. "The lawn mower."

Marge nodded.

"It's my fault," he said.

The beat of hesitation before Marge responded hit him like a knife to the gut. When she finally spoke, her tone was decisive and commanding. "It's not your fault, Eli."

He knew she was lying.

———

Half an hour later, Eli stood pressed against the wall in a hallway of the St. Anne's Hospital emergency department and sipped from a lukewarm bottle of Pepsi that he wished were whiskey. A steel-sided cart of medical supplies opposite him mirrored the lower half of his body, the sight of which added to the strange sense of disembodiment he had felt since seeing Andy bleeding in the grass. All he wanted to do was sleep—it was like that after every panic attack—or at least that was what his body was begging him to do, while his mind could think of nothing but his son. He had managed—after using Michelle's shower, changing into some clean clothes, drinking multiple glasses of water, and eating three granola bars—to convince Marge he was capable of driving himself to the hospital, but he questioned the wisdom of that choice now as he fought to stay upright against the wall. The rubber hospital floor appeared disturbingly near at hand.

So tired.

The privacy curtain inside the glass door of the exam room was pulled aside enough that he could see Michelle, perched on the edge of the gurney, Andy's uninjured hand clasped between her own. The other side of the room was obscured by the curtain, and Eli took a couple of steps to the left to get a better vantage point. Andy was calm now, drowsy and quiet from whatever they must have given him for the pain. His injured hand was hidden beneath the bedclothes, the color had returned to his face, and Eli took it as a good sign that the boy didn't seem to be hooked up to any machines or oxygen tubing. Still, Eli hung back from the door in fear of how his traitorous body might react to seeing his son's wounds again.

Michelle leaned over, murmured something to Andy, and pushed a stray piece of hair from his eyes. Eli must have made some sort of movement, because she turned to look at where he stood, just outside the doorway. Her face turned icy.

So terribly tired.

Her lips trembled and she looked away for a moment, then back at him. "Feeling better?" He heard contempt in her voice, rather than concern.

No, he wanted to say. In that moment, he imagined how it would feel to tell her the truth. To tell her exactly how he felt, exactly what was going on inside his seriously messed-up mind. Maybe she would understand, or at least hate him a little less. Or maybe she would only hear excuses, a shameful attempt at avoiding responsibility. She crossed her arms and looked away, but not before he saw the look of disgust on her face. He looked at Andy, who lay now with closed eyes, his chest rising and falling in the deep rhythm of sleep. As painful as it was to see Michelle's revulsion, Eli would not leave without seeing Andy. Without making sure his son was safe.

Eli had just built up the mental strength to walk into Andy's room when an athletic, ponytailed woman with a line of pagers clipped to her gray scrub pants swept past him into the room.

"Well," the woman said to Michelle, without a greeting but with a tone of authority that announced her as the doctor, "his index and middle finger are fractured, and we had to suture some pretty deep cuts, but there's nothing six weeks in a cast won't fix." She looked down at Andy with a baffled, almost amused expression, then smiled when he opened his eyes. "You're a really tough kid, you know that?"

"He's not going to lose any fingers?" asked Eli from just inside the doorway. He couldn't bring himself to approach the gurney, for fear that he'd lose it again. The doctor turned around, noticed him for the first time. "Dad, I assume? No, he won't lose any fingers."

Michelle avoided Eli's gaze, jaw clenched. The doctor looked back and forth between Eli and Michelle, then shifted uneasily. "I can assure you, he's going to be fine. I—" One of her pagers chimed, and she plucked it from her waistband with obvious relief, glanced at the device, then tucked it into the pocket of her scrubs.

"The nurse will be in shortly to put on the cast," she said, already backing toward the door, "and then Andy can go home. I'll send him out with something for pain, and he'll need to see his doctor in a couple days." She met Eli's eye and said, as if she knew exactly what had happened, as if she knew whose fault all of this was, "No more lawn mowers for a while, Dad."

After the doctor left, Eli approached the gurney, careful to avoid looking at Andy's bandaged hand, careful to ignore the nameless feeling that swelled in his chest. For a moment, they were silent. Voices of staff and a cacophony of chimes and alarms floated through the open door. Then Andy turned to look at him, and in his awkwardness, Eli tapped the boy gently on the shoulder and said, with false lightheartedness, "Didn't mean to get you in so much trouble."

Andy smiled at that, then shut his eyes again. Eli glanced at Michelle and found her staring at him, eyes hard and angry.

"You were drunk, weren't you?" she asked, her voice low.

"No."

She gave a sharp, bitter laugh.

"No," he repeated. "I swear. In fact—"

She held up a hand. "Save it, Eli." She waved a hand at the bottle of soda he held. "You walk in here with a bottle of who-knows-what and think I won't realize?" She glanced down at Andy and saw that he had fallen asleep again. She lowered her voice to a harsh whisper. "You can't even keep your shit together to help your own son."

She was right. Completely, undeniably correct, and what could he possibly say in his defense?

Something shifted in the corner of the room and whispered to him now, urged him to consider again how far he'd fallen. Thirty-nine years and nothing to show for it but the tatters of a family. A young boy in a hospital bed, hurt and broken because of what he, Eli, had done. Because of what he had not done, and what he understood now he could never do again. The specter in the corner crept closer, directed Eli's eyes to the woman who would never again be his. Jeered at him for thinking there was anything left for him in her heart. Eli had long felt that his soul was in pieces, like a puzzle, and that Andy and Michelle each held one of them. Only when the three of them were together would the pieces fit into place and become whole.

"I think you should leave," Michelle was saying. "We'll manage without you." She gestured to Andy, asleep on the gurney, but Eli knew she didn't just mean they would manage without him in the emergency department. He understood, then, that she was casting off her piece of the puzzle. Andy's too.

There were things he wanted to say to her, but his throat was too tight for words, so instead he came around to the other side of the gurney, leaned down, and kissed her temple. He felt the flutter against his lips of the blood pumping beneath the surface of her skin, and for a fraction of a second, he considered pulling her into his arms. Just once before he left.

Instead, he stood up and set a hand on her shoulder. "You're an amazing mother, Michelle." His throat closed again but he willed the words out. "I've never told you this, but the thing I'm most proud of, in my whole life, is the fact that you chose me, all those years ago." He squeezed her shoulder and took a step back. Her dark eyes softened a bit, and she looked at him with concern.

"Will you be all right?" she asked, and Eli realized that she expected him to say yes.

So he did.

31

The north side of Shaky Lake was rimmed with bluffs of red granite, and, as it was part of Red Cliff State Park, the area was undeveloped aside from hiking trails and a few scenic overlooks for drivers to stop and admire the view. Eli had chosen the highest and most remote of these spots, with no guardrail between the gravel parking space and the cliff face a hundred yards in front of him. He patted his breast pocket and felt his phone, then opened his eyes long enough to turn it off.

He closed his eyes again, leaned his head back against the car headrest, and called to mind the house in Al Jalil.

It had been late in the day, the waning sunlight dimmed by heavy, low-hanging clouds. The weather had warmed since the previous day, still cold, but without the frigid bite of the past few weeks, and a blanket of fresh snow covered the barren, broken landscape. Eli had brought a bag of Hershey's Kisses for the village children, who had grown accustomed to his squad's visits to the tiny town perched on the side of the Spīn Ghar mountains, and who would surely be out playing in the streets. It is a universal pleasure to be the first to leave tracks in the snow. Still, he knew his squad was not welcome there, the women disappearing into doorways as he passed, the men pausing in their work to stare at him, tight-lipped and hard-eyed.

Eli knew the moment they got out of the Humvee that something was wrong. Even more wrong than usual.

The snow.

It was pristine, flawless, without a single footprint. No children had ven-
tured outside to play in the perfect white streets. There was no sign that
anyone had stepped one foot out of their homes since the snow began. Eli
looked at his watch. It had been nearly four hours since the snow had fallen,
and still it lay undisturbed. He had grown up in a small town, had spent
many solitary hours in the woods, so he knew what normal quiet sounded
like. The silence in Al Jalil was anything but normal that afternoon.

Eli opened his eyes, and the cold mountain silence was replaced by
the view in front of him of Shaky Lake in all its summer exuberance. The
leaves on the aspen trees outside the car window quivered and sighed as
a gust of wind crossed the bluff, carrying with it clouds like popcorn and
the scent of lake water and pine needles.

A man in the Veterans Affairs therapy group he had attended last year,
a man with overbright eyes and a trembling mouth, had described the
lightness he felt each morning, how he woke every day with the knowledge that the worst had already happened. Eli had hated the man instantly.
Knew he was lying. The truth was that all of them, for the rest of their
lives, would be trapped in a moment that had gone, or worse—trapped in
the moment just before the worst happened.

His squad broke into groups of two or three and made for the houses of
the handful of villagers they knew. The door of Aalem's faded cement house
opened when Eli knocked, though the man opened it only enough to show
half his face. There was a very long pause before he opened the door all the
way and gestured for Eli and his partner to enter. Hospitality was sacrosanct
in Afghan culture. The villagers had invited the US soldiers into their homes
many times before. Aalem and a younger man Eli knew to be his son moved
to arrange seating on floor cushions for Eli and his partner. Once they were
settled, Aalem sat at the low table and his son retreated to the far corner of
the room.

"Chai?" asked Aalem, and at Eli's nod he placed cups in front of the
soldiers and poured the tea. Only after a few minutes of quiet sipping did
Eli speak to the man in Pashto, beginning with the universal topic of the
weather. Yes, Aalem had managed to fix the leaky front window before the
snowfall. Yes, he had enough coal for the bukhari *and oil for the lamp. Eli*

exchanged glances with his partner while Aalem bent to light the lamp. Once lit, the oil lamp threw its amber glow over the table. The shadows in the rest of the mostly windowless room seemed to lengthen and shift, and the effect only added to Eli's uneasiness.

Eli took another sip of his tea, then said, "There are no footprints in the snow." He attempted to keep his tone neutral, conversational, his expression mild, as though he were still discussing the weather. Something flickered at the back of Aalem's gaze, but he responded smoothly.

"The cold keeps us inside today."

"But, friend," said Eli gently, "it's warmer than usual, and the snow is not deep."

Aalem was silent, his eyes fixed on the teacup he passed back and forth between his hands. In the shadows at the far edge of the room, Aalem's son uncoiled himself from his cushion with catlike ease and stepped forward. Eli shot a look at his partner that warned him not to make a move.

"We are not here to make trouble, but I need to know, Aalem. Why have people not come out of their homes today?"

The older man pressed his lips together, and his eyes seemed to sink deeper into his face, like boot buttons sewn into creased leather. He moved his teacup to one hand, and Eli saw the other hand make a nearly imperceptible gesture to his son. Eli's heart sped up and he heard his partner shift on the cushion behind him. He knew that if they didn't leave now, they wouldn't be leaving this house the same way they'd come.

He rested his hands on the steering wheel. The feeling in the streets of Al Jalil, the terrible stillness in Aalem's home, the feeling of impending doom—it was here with him. Had never left. The feeling that something terrible was coming still hung about him, coiling like a python over his shoulders.

Aalem's son stepped closer to the lamplight and Aalem gestured angrily, unsuccessfully, for him to sit. Then, a thud from the next room. Eli and his partner shot to their feet at the same time as Aalem. The man stepped in front of the doorway into the next room, hands held out in a soothing gesture.

"It's just my wife," Aalem said. "She was sleeping and must have woken up. I will bring her here." He turned away, toward the door.

"Stop."

The man turned slowly, carefully, and pressed his hands together. "There is no trouble, friend. It is just my wife."

Eli held out a hand and the man stopped talking. His weathered face sagged, and Eli could see him take a deep breath before stepping back from the doorway. He nodded at Eli to proceed.

Eli looked back at his partner, who stood with his weapon pointed toward the ground. The hallway to the bedroom, where the sound had come from, was long for such a small house. About eight feet, and the opening at the far end was hung with a thick, patterned kilim. The rug fit snugly in the door opening, and no light escaped around the edges. Eli flipped on his headlamp. Outside the doorway, he listened, then called in his best, clearest Pashto, "Madam, please come out. We are not here to hurt anyone. I would like to speak to you." He waited several minutes, then repeated his request, only to be met with silence.

"Please, friend, it's nothing. Just my wife," Aalem called from his position at the other end of the hall.

Eli put a hand to the kilim and was about to push it aside when he heard the soft but unmistakable click of a safety lever being released. Whoever was on the other side of the doorway had a gun and was preparing to use it. Eli slowly removed his hand from the kilim and, without turning around, signaled to his partner. He waited until he heard the quick movement of the other man and felt him enter the hallway a few feet behind him. Eli dissected the problem in front of him—a process that always calmed him. Objective, critical thinking. If this, then that. Risk versus benefit. Sifting and winnowing to reach the correct answer. The correct next step. He took his own weapon in hand, released the safety mechanism, and pulled back the rug.

And that was where his memory ended. He knew there was more. That he had entered the cold, dim room and something had happened. He had the scars to prove it. The medals to prove it.

He shuddered, then squeezed his eyes shut tight. He didn't want to remember. Knew he couldn't live with himself if he did. But his strength—his ability to fend off the memories and fight for what he'd once had—was dwindling and had now come to an end.

In his moments of clarity, of sobriety, since he'd returned home, he had tried to find a way forward. To find the correct next step. Toward what, he didn't know. He had gotten it wrong again and again, though. He had exhausted all other options, and only one was left. It was shameful. He knew it would hurt people who loved him, but it was his last resort. He considered, then discarded, the idea of leaving a note.

He drew a deep, steadying breath and opened his eyes. The lake was gorgeous, welcoming and safe. He reached for the shifter.

The crunch of tires on gravel startled him as a car pulled into the small lot. He kept his head down to avoid looking at the new arrival. He would just wait while they admired the view, snapped a few pictures, then went on their way. It was a distraction. He'd been distracted from his plans before, but this time he would not change his mind. He heard a car door slam and the sound of footsteps in the gravel, and suddenly, she was there in the passenger seat next to him.

"So," she said, and buckled her seat belt, "where are we going?"

"Mom—"

The skin below her eyes was dark from weariness, the creases in her forehead as deep as knife scars, and she wore the no-arguments expression he had seen so many times in his life. "Because you're going to have to take me with you," she said.

"I—" He shook his head, then was quiet, his head sunken a little between his shoulders in frustration. Marge had never been an overbearing mother when Eli was growing up, had managed to find the halfway point between protective and controlling. Aside from the fact that he had wanted to climb *everything* since he was old enough to crawl—baby gates stacked two high at the door to the basement stairs—she said he had always been an easy kid. Still, like any parent and child, there were moments of conflict. Of resentment, on his part, anyway, when she thwarted his plans—backflips off swings, riding a sled tied to the bumper of a friend's car, jumping off the bluffs into the lake.

He had the same feeling now, of his good, sensible plans being shot down by a mom who just didn't understand. They sat in silence for a very long time before he looked at her. She sat with her arms crossed, as if she was chilled, and it took a few moments before Eli understood that she was waiting for him to do something. He looked down to find that his foot was on the brake and the car was in drive. His hands gripped the steering wheel but he didn't feel the smooth surface, as though the hands belonged to someone else. He waited and watched. He shifted in his seat and his foot stumbled off the brake pedal. The car lurched forward before he slammed on the brake. Marge went completely still.

He knew she was only trying to help. That none of this was her fault, that, in fact, he was what he was *despite* all she had done for him. It only made him angrier, and he smacked a hand against the steering wheel. With a growl of frustration, he jerked the shifter into park and collapsed back against the seat.

Marge spoke first, her voice soft but inevitable.

"Tell me, Eli. Please."

He turned and studied her face, the features so familiar, her expression gentle but unyielding. He searched for a way, any way, to give her what she was asking of him, but couldn't. He dropped his eyes and stayed silent.

"Okay," she said. "I'll go first."

Eli's brows shot together, but Marge continued before he could speak.

"I've told you about your father. How he died."

He nodded but didn't speak.

"I didn't tell you the truth," said Marge, directly addressing the travel mug resting in the cup holder. "I didn't tell anyone the truth, and I never have. Not in all these years." She rubbed her forehead. "He died in the line of duty. That was the story. But the truth is, it was my fault." She met Eli's eyes.

"Your father was—" She paused. "He was abusive. I knew it when I married him. I was young and pregnant and I decided that it was more important for you to have a father. I promised myself I would change him, for your sake. I had complete confidence that I could make things work, and I believed that for a long time. I believed it even through the— the violence. I've always thought of myself as a tough person. That I can handle pain. And I could, but it got harder and harder to hide the bruises, the broken bones."

"Broken bones?" Eli nearly shouted.

She reached over and took his hand. "I told myself it was worth it. And it was for a while. He was so happy to have a son, and he loved you so much. But then, when you were three—" Her voice caught, and she worked to steady it. "When you were three, you did something that made him mad. Colored on the wall or something, like every three-year-old does. He just snapped. He held a pillow over your face." She wiped her eyes with the back of one hand. "You tried to get away but you were just a baby. I tried to stop him, but he wouldn't listen. When he got into a rage like that, nothing I said or did could stop him. I took my gun out of the wall safe where we kept our service weapons and I pointed it at the back of his head." Something about the words, the description of the actions she'd taken, seemed to steady her. "I told him I'd kill him if he didn't stop. And I meant it. I was ready to do it. To this day, I don't know if he believed me. But he stopped. Took the pillow off your face and leaned over and tickled you, as if it was all a game." She wiped her eyes again and took a deep breath. "Some people are born without a human conscience. That was your father, and I needed to be sure that this would never happen to you again." She looked straight into his eyes, didn't try to hide her anger, her ferocity. "We were serving an arrest warrant together one night, soon afterward. This was when we lived in Chicago, and it was the type of situation you go into expecting the worst. For every firearm an officer had, the suspects had three, and they were a lot more likely to use them."

She was quiet for a moment. "Everyone accepted it as a terrible accident, but the truth was, I knew where the suspect was. Saw him in a mirror as we came up to the door of the room where he was hiding. Your father didn't see him, but I did. And I let him walk into that room. I let your father walk right into the suspect's line of fire and I knew the suspect would shoot." She laid a hand on his arm. "The thing that was hardest, that stuck with me for a very, very long time, was the guilt. But it wasn't guilt for what I had done, it was guilt that I didn't regret what I had done. That I would do it again in a heartbeat." She examined his face. "I thought I must be a monster. A murderer, even. The thought gnawed at me for years, until I told Tommy what had happened, and about the—the abuse."

She hesitated, and when she spoke again, her voice was careful. "I'm not saying it's as simple as telling someone, and I know that what happened to me isn't the same as what happened to you."

"Mom—"

She reached to his face and cupped a hand under his chin. "Eli, do you know what the great joy of my life is? The thing that lets me live with myself, with the memory of what I did, of everything that happened? It's the fact that you, *my* son, possess more natural kindness than any person I've ever met. I was afraid you would be like him. That any day I would see something in you that scared me." She smiled and put her hands on either side of his face. "But it never came. And here you are. So loving and *so* strong, bearing so much pain." She wiped a tear from his cheek. "It wasn't your fault."

He looked away. "I'm not who I was . . . before," he said. "I'm not sure I ever will be, and I can't keep asking everyone to carry my weight."

"You make it sound as though loving you is a decision," said Marge, with a smile. "You believe that we'll be happier if you"—she gestured to the lake—"go away. But it doesn't work that way. Wherever you go, you take us with you, and you can't just slip out while we're looking the other way."

Eli started to protest, but she pushed a hand against his chest. "Andy loves you desperately, and, despite what you may think, despite everything, Michelle still cares for you." Her face crumpled, but she didn't turn away or hide her tears. It was a long time before she could speak, and her voice was thick with emotion when she began again. "I don't know what to do, Eli." She swallowed once, twice. "Loving you is clearly not enough." She put a hand out to stop his protests. "You need help from someone else. A professional."

He wanted to tell her he'd tried that already. That, if anything, the therapy sessions had made things worse. He squinted at the lake in the distance, but this time his eyes skimmed across the water—its depths had seemed so inviting minutes ago—to a point on the far shore, impossibly far away. Beyond reach.

"I can't make you do anything you don't want to do, even if I *am* your mother." She smiled, though her eyes still shone with tears. "But maybe, just this once . . ."

She was offering him a life raft. A directive from a mother to her child. Something that didn't require him to think about what might lie ahead, something to simply keep him afloat a little longer.

Do as you're told.

Something began to shimmer from deep inside his chest, dazzling and painful, like the reflection of midday sun on water. Too bright to look at directly. He struggled for a moment to speak. It was as if all his strength, all the tension in his body, had left him. Just melted away from his head down to his feet and onto the floor of the car, leaving him wobble-kneed and defenseless, like a small child.

"Okay," he said. The thought of dredging up what he had been trying so hard, for so long, to contain was terrifying, but he would do anything for her. For his mother, who loved him.

She leaned across the center console and kissed his cheek, and he felt her smile in the kiss. She held her cheek pressed to his for a beat, then leaned back into her own seat, still smiling.

"Let's go," she said. She unbuckled her seat belt. "And, honey, how about you let me drive?"

32

It was early evening when there was a knock on Eli's door. After Marge had brought him back to his apartment that afternoon, he had crawled into bed, exhausted, shaken by what he'd nearly done. If, later, someone had asked him if he had slept, he would have said no, not at all, but the gathering darkness beyond his window was evidence that more time had passed than he realized. He held his breath and listened, but the knocking stopped, and he decided that it had just been a dream. He rolled back over and pulled the rough blanket more tightly around him, not yet ready to get out of bed, despite the rumbling in his stomach and the increasing pressure in his bladder. It had been his habit since childhood to take inventory of the details of the day each night before bed. This tendency to rehash things, to examine and re-sort and identify areas for improvement in everything he did, had given him a thirty-year bout of insomnia but the undeniable advantage over most other people in virtually every endeavor. His ability to reflect and regroup—to remember—had been one of his greatest strengths. But since Al Jalil, he could no longer browse through memories as if he were looking for a shirt in a familiar closet. It was as if there were yawning crevasses between the floorboards.

The sodium vapor light that illuminated the liquor-store parking lot flickered to life outside his window, announcing the arrival of dusk, and the humid air from outside carried with it the smell of clove cigarettes and the clatter of beer bottles in cardboard boxes being loaded into a car. Brandon, the youngest son of the Khang family, who owned Trixie's Liquor, ran the shop on Friday nights and was partial to bass-heavy trance music, which bellowed out into the night air with each customer's coming and going.

Eli sat up and swung his legs over the side of the bed with the intention of getting up—maybe to the bathroom, maybe to the kitchen, where a bottle of something strong was waiting for him. He stared at his own reflection in the mirror on the back of the door. The shadows had grown thick in the room, and all that illuminated the space now was the harsh green-blue light coming from the parking lot. It lit him from behind, obscuring his face in the mirror, so that he saw only the silhouette of his head, shoulders, and back. A paper cutout of a man. He stood and approached the mirror slowly, warily, not sure what he would see, not sure he wanted to see. His face appeared in the mirror, and he studied it as if it were a photo of a stranger. Methodically, out loud, he began to describe what he saw in the most objective of terms. Face shape, hair and eye color. Then the items in his room. Bed, robe, water glass. A precise, orderly assessment of his surroundings, of his situation. It calmed him, like a favorite lullaby. He relaxed his shoulders and let his hands rest lightly at his sides, felt the fabric of his boxer shorts against his fingertips. One memory. Just one. Surely he could handle that. He closed his eyes.

The gentle scrape of a boat, Ben Sharpe's boat, against the dock. The soft, rhythmic splash of lake water against the rocky shore. The peaceful night air. A shape in the bottom of the boat. The feel of the gunwale beneath his hand as he lowered himself into the boat, then the feeling of stubble and cold skin when he touched the boy's face. A dead boy. Not Andy.

He opened his eyes, stared at the calm face reflected in the mirror, and recognized it as his own. No racing heart. No shaking or shivers of panic. He put a hand to his chest and felt his skin—warm, dry. He was debating the wisdom of trying again, of reaching back for another memory to see what would happen, when a knock sounded again on the front door. Marge, come to check on him. He rushed to the living room, sensitive to the fact that he had given his mother every reason to assume the worst if he didn't pick up the phone or answer the door. He had made her a promise that afternoon.

"Coming!" he shouted. He disarmed the alarm and unlocked the double locks as quickly as possible, then threw the door open to find Alyssa standing there in the half darkness. The exterior lamp on the landing outside his door was supposed to turn on automatically at dusk, to provide enough light to use the stairs with a modicum of safety, but it must have burned out. The inside of his apartment was equally unlit. Her glasses flared red with the reflection of the taillights of a car pulling out of the parking lot, and he couldn't make out her expression.

"What are you doing here?" he asked, rude in his confusion.

Her teeth flashed white in the darkness. "Hello to you, too." She swept past him into the living room, instantly located the switch plate on the wall between the living room and the hallway, and flipped on the lights. They both shielded their eyes at the sudden brightness.

"I was beginning to think you lived in your car," she said, her back to him. She craned her neck to look into the kitchen and down the hall. "This place is depressing as hell."

Eli let out a small puff of laughter. "How do you really feel?"

"After seeing this? Depressed." She turned around, and they both seemed to realize at the same moment that he was wearing nothing but underwear.

"Shit," he said. "Just give me a—" He dove into his bedroom and pulled on a shirt and some jeans and then, on further thought, put on socks and boots. If he could just, for once, not find himself stripped bare, literally or figuratively, in front of her, it would be a huge step in the right direction. An uncomfortable intimacy had developed between the two of them, and it only added to his constant sense of dread. It would be unfair to attribute any blame to her in this regard, seeing as how he was the one constantly giving her glimpses of himself she most certainly did not want to see.

From the kitchen came the rustle of plastic bags and the thud of something against the countertop, then cabinets opening, closing, and the rattle of the silverware drawer. The door of the fridge was lined with bottles of beer, and there was a glassy clank as she opened the door. He breathed a prayer of thanks that she was far too short to see into the cabinet above the fridge where he kept his liquor. He went across the hall to the bathroom and did his best to look and smell like a sane person—toothpaste, deodorant, a wet hand through his hair—rather than someone who had spent the better part of the day descending into madness.

He returned to the kitchen to find a bottle of Gatorade, uncapped, and a cereal bowl filled with Goldfish crackers laid out on the counter in the pass-through opening between the kitchen and the living room. Alyssa was perched on a kitchen stool.

He affected a look of disappointment. "What, no apple slices?"

She gave him a half smile and pulled her messenger bag from her shoulder. Her pale hair was loose for a change, and damp. She smelled of toothpaste and shampoo, and her skin had a fresh-scrubbed look. He dragged the other stool from beneath the countertop overhang and set it as far away from her as possible without actually moving into the living room.

"I heard you were under the weather," she said.

He reached for the bottle of Gatorade and took several long pulls of the salty-sweet green liquid, not because he was thirsty, but to give himself a moment to find a way to change the subject. His brain was sluggish, likely due to his ill-timed evening nap, or the general stress of the day, or the fact that he hadn't had any alcohol since that morning, and the best response he could come up with was to wipe his mouth with the back of his hand and say, "Something like that."

He braced himself for a full shakedown, an interrogation into the whys and wherefores of him sitting in the dark in his underwear rather than leading the investigation of a dire and time-sensitive case. To his surprise, she changed the subject.

"You missed all the drama at the station this morning. Jake and Phil got into a huge argument, and Marge had to break it up." She shook her head in astonishment. "Your mom was such a badass. I would never have guessed. It was spectacular."

Eli felt a pang of apprehension. Any disharmony in the Sherman County Sheriff's Department inevitably boiled down to something he'd done, or, more likely, had not done. "What were they fighting about?"

"Jake was defending your honor." She cocked her head. "He does that a lot, I've noticed." She paused, seemed a bit embarrassed, then said, "Phil was questioning your, um, competency, and Jake freaked out. Called Phil a bunch of unflattering names. Marge kicked them out." She pursed her lips. "*Very* dysfunctional."

He drank the rest of the Gatorade and waited for her to continue. If he kept quiet, maybe he could get through this visit without slipping any further in her estimation. But to his growing panic, she stayed quiet, and he recognized with a sinking heart that she was employing one of the most effective ways of getting information out of somebody—silence. He made his best attempt to deliver a solid return serve.

"So, you're here because . . . ?"

"You know, you're not a very good host." She pushed the bowl of crackers toward him and eyed him severely until he took a handful and began to eat. She made a sound of disgust. "Here I am, babying you. Just like everyone else." She smiled, but there was a flash of anxiety in her eyes.

"You don't have to—" he started.

She waved his words away. "I had some time to kill." She watched him eat for a minute, then got up and went to the fridge. "How's your son?" she called, pulling out another bottle of Gatorade.

He thought of Andy, bleeding and terrified, the look of weary disdain on Michelle's face, and he turned toward the living room window, not sure whether he could prevent his thoughts from registering on his face. Too late, he realized that his body language was far more telling than his expression to someone like Alyssa, who noticed everything and interpreted it with a canniness approaching clairvoyance. He turned back to accept the Gatorade she proffered, then cleared his throat and did his best impression of how a normal dad might act when his son had a very close call; relieved, but with a hint of boastfulness, as if to highlight the extraordinariness of the situation, the fact that *his* son was extraordinary. "He's going to be okay. Two broken fingers." He attempted a chuckle. "Not too bad considering he stuck his hand into the mower while it was running."

"Must be made of some pretty tough stuff," she said. A pause. "Like his dad."

The comment caught him off guard and he studied her, trying to decide whether he had imagined the provocation in her tone. Was she baiting him?

"What do you mean?" he asked, then inwardly kicked himself for so easily falling into her trap.

Alyssa looked down at her hands where they fiddled with the strap of her messenger bag, and he was surprised to see a flash of uncertainty on her face before her loose hair fell forward to hide it. She was quiet for a long moment, and when she looked up, she didn't meet his eye.

"Your scars—" She waved a hand over the left side of her own chest, darted a quick look at him, then away again. Her gaze roved around the small space—the wall behind him, the bowl of crackers, the tips of her shoes as her feet swung gently from the stool. "I saw them when you were changing your shirt in your car yesterday."

He bit back a curse. The tattered state of his body was the absolute last thing on earth he wanted to talk about, not because of vanity or embarrassment, but because he knew it was a topic that could open a door he kept firmly closed. Plus, the scars reminded him of Michelle. She had worked hard to heal those scars. Eli attempted to deflect Alyssa's inquiry.

"He gets his toughness from his mom, not from me," he said lamely.

She nodded. "Of course, but—" She paused. "I did some research."

Shit. He opened his mouth to stop her but she wasn't looking at him, didn't see the look on his face.

"I read about what happened," she continued, her voice careful. "In Afghanistan."

He went absolutely still. "A lot of things happened in Afghanistan."

"In Al Jalil, I mean," she said. Her eyes bored into his, pinning him down with the same mercilessness she had employed with Beth Wallace. She was, he knew, well aware that she was venturing into dangerous territory, but she seemed unfazed, utterly prepared for whatever he might do or say. He folded his arms across his chest and responded with silence.

"A Purple Heart, the Medal of—"

He closed his eyes. "Don't."

"Look, maybe it's none of my business."

"It is *absolutely* none of your business," he snapped. He opened his eyes and saw that her expression, if anything, had become more resolute at the harshness of his words. He got up and stalked past her into the kitchen, where he opened the cabinet above the fridge and pulled out the first bottle he found—Hennessy, with a bright orange CLEARANCE label. Why did an FBI agent he'd known for two days think she had the right to interrogate him? The right to judge him? He got a glass from another cabinet, yanked the cap off the bottle, and poured a large amount of the deep amber liquid. Alyssa followed him, stood in the narrow kitchen doorway, and watched as he drained the glass in one swallow. His anger flared and he could tell that she noticed it. She put a hand on the doorframe but didn't take a step back. He was about to tell her off, tell her to leave, when she spoke, her voice soft, almost a murmur.

"It's bad, isn't it?" she asked.

A sliver of ice slid down his spine. Michelle had asked him the same question, once. Just once, and he had rounded on her like a threatened animal, then spent the rest of the night wide awake, shaking, in his car in the driveway while she cried in the bed they used to share.

He swallowed hard against the sudden heaviness in his throat. "I don't know what you're talking about."

"You know what I'm talking about."

He was suddenly struck by a bone-deep weariness, and it was all he could do not to sink to the floor. Instead, he took a step back and propped himself against the wall. The cheap wallboard creaked under his weight. He had set the empty glass on the countertop a moment ago but realized he still held the bottle. The countertop was now out of reach, forcing him to stand there, a bottle of liquor in one hand, like a curbside drunk. "What did my mother tell you?"

"Nothing." She took a careful step toward him, hands extended slightly, as if she were approaching a large, unfamiliar dog.

"She sent you here to check on me?" His words contained an accusation, although of what, and to whom, he couldn't say.

"No," she said. "I had to convince her to give me your address. I just—" There was a long moment of hesitation, and he imagined that he saw her lips tremble. "Eli, you are *seriously* not okay."

He considered leaving. Simply pushing past her and walking out of the apartment. But in the two days he'd known her, he already recognized that Alyssa was not the sort of person to let things go. To leave questions unanswered or problems unsolved. He considered his other options. Belligerence, maybe. Silence. In the end, he chose to lie.

"I'm working on it," he said, then made what he knew was a ridiculous show of setting the bottle back on the counter, of rinsing out the glass and setting it neatly in the sink, as if he were just tidying up after a quick glass of orange juice.

She narrowed her eyes. "You're lying." When he didn't respond, she turned and went to look out the living room window. He followed her for reasons he couldn't explain, or maybe just preferred to ignore, and watched as she stood, back toward him, fingers drumming against her crossed arms.

The music from the store below went abruptly quiet, followed by a heated exchange of voices, and then resumed at an infinitesimally lower volume. The Friday night liquor store traffic was reaching its peak, and from the parking lot came the sounds of slamming car doors and shouted requests for one type or another of alcoholic drink to whomever was buying that night. He thought for a moment that he might have made her cry. Her already narrow shoulders were curved forward, arms wrapped tightly around herself. Then she looked up at the window, and as if she had conjured it like a sorceress, the wind outside gusted suddenly. The cheap mini-blinds clattered violently, and a mass of cold air blew into the room. He saw her shiver, then relax her arms to the side. When she turned around, her face was smooth, neutral, utterly in control. "One thing."

"What?"

"I want you to tell me one thing. Anything you want. About what happened over there." She sat on one end of the sectional sofa and pointed to the opposite side, indicating that he should sit.

He shoved a hand through his hair, then said in a choked voice, "Why do you *care*?"

"Because"—she made an exasperated noise—"you're a human being."

It wasn't a real answer.

"I don't know what you—"

"Your memories are crushing you, Eli. I'm not going away until you give me something. Anything."

He hesitated a moment, then decided that resisting her would be about as useful as commanding lava to flow backward. He lowered himself onto the beat-up, groaning sofa with a strange feeling in his gut that had nothing to do with the large glass of fiery alcohol he had just consumed.

The wind began to pick up outside and the first spits of rain hit the glass, hit him through the open window. There were exclamations and shrieks of laughter from below as liquor store customers exited the building or their cars to find themselves in the opening beats of a thunderstorm. Neither Eli nor Alyssa moved to close the window above the couch, just eyed each other warily in the too-bright overhead light fixture. Then, in a way that had him seriously considering whether she could be a mind reader, she got up, flipped on a small under-cabinet light in the kitchen, then turned off the light in the living room.

"There," she said, settling back onto the couch. "Much better."

He reached over and shut the window. The only sound in the room was the muffled, throbbing bass line coming from the store below. Alyssa's small, dark-clad body seemed to recede into the shabby brown upholstery, and her face was sphinxlike in the dim half-light. It was as if she had stepped away, and in her place she had left a toy, a doll, for him to tell his troubles to, like a traumatized child. It struck him that perhaps one of the reasons he had resisted counseling was that he was terrified of being on the receiving end of anyone's pity, or, worse, their smug self-composure.

But with her, it felt so black-and-white. She was simply investigating his past experiences, and to him, investigation and interrogation were comfortable, familiar concepts.

"I killed a boy," he heard himself say, without preamble.

Silence. A ghost of a nod from the other end of the couch.

"In Al Jalil. I shot him." The words fell from his mouth like marbles. Smooth and solid and uniform, like an official report. "Intelligence got word that the village was harboring a member of the Islamic State, a new recruit, and we were sent to capture him. Ghafur, grandson of a man named Aalem. I had met him before, at his grandfather's house, the previous summer, before he joined up. He was young, maybe fourteen. I remember thinking I might be able to"—he searched for the right word— "convince him to leave the IS. We went to Aalem's house and I found Ghafur there, hiding in a back room. He shot me."

"And you returned fire."

"I did."

"You were injured."

"One shot through my left arm, that's all. The rest of it"—he waved a hand over his hidden, scar-riddled chest and arms and abdomen— "came afterward." He paused, suddenly short of breath. Sweat trickled between his shoulder blades, and he felt his face go numb. He closed his eyes and tried to control his breathing, then felt the couch cushions move as she sat beside him, felt her arm across his back. They sat in silence for a very long time, then she moved her hand to his shoulder and gripped it gently.

"I'm sorry that happened," she said. "Thank you for telling me."

He took a breath and let it out on a long sigh. It was the first time he had said the words out loud. The people who had been in that house on that snowy evening were all dead now. He couldn't remember what he'd told his commanding officer in the debriefing. He was in and out of surgery for weeks after the battle, sedated and disoriented, and when he was alert enough to give a report, he found that he couldn't remember anything beyond the rug in the doorway of Aalem's back room. It wasn't until months later, in the military hospital in Maryland, that the memories of what had happened began to stir, and the terrors, the nightmares and hallucinations and blackouts, began.

"Eli?" She had moved to the middle of the sofa, out of arm's reach, and he felt a profound sense of gratitude at the gesture.

"Hmm?" He felt a bit wobbly, as if he had just crossed the finish line of a race for which he hadn't trained, and braced his elbows on his knees.

"I think Caitlin Wallace is alive."

33

Alyssa dug through the greasy paper bag and pulled out a burger. "I can't imagine how expensive it must have been for your mom to feed you, growing up. You're an only child, I hope?"

He smiled as he unwrapped the first of three Big Macs. The McDonald's parking lot was barely visible through the sheets of rain across the car windows, and Alyssa's parked car shuddered each time a semitrailer whooshed past on the half-flooded highway frontage road. The windows were open a crack and the car was turned off. Despite the cooler air the storm had brought, the inside of the car was warm and humid; womb-like and restful. He would be content to sit here all night. Only the growling in his stomach prevented him from dozing off. To his relief, Alyssa made no comment on what they had discussed at his apartment, and instead, they ate in companionable silence. He had laid one terrifying memory—one of many—on the table and survived. Doing so had left him with a strange sense of anticlimax, and of uncertainty. Had he made a mistake in telling Alyssa? Had he opened a door that was best left shut? The thought sent a fresh thread of panic through him, but he pushed it firmly away.

Alyssa finished her burger and crumpled the wrapper. Wordlessly, he fished some napkins out of the bag and handed them to her. She wiped her hands, shifted the ring on her left fourth finger to wipe underneath, then moved it back and twisted the band until the diamond was centered on her finger.

"So," started Eli, pointing at her ring, "who's the lucky guy?"

Alyssa didn't answer directly; she seemed to be following her own train of thought, and after a moment replied, "Sorry, yeah." She fiddled with the ring and smiled. "His name is Jason. We just got engaged."

Eli instantly regretted raising the topic, because his next thought was of Michelle, of how he had proposed to her. "Congratulations," he said, with a brightness he hoped sounded authentic. Then, for some idiot reason, because he clearly hadn't told her enough about himself for one evening, he said, "I proposed to my wife—well, soon to be ex-wife—on a wilderness camping trip."

She held out the used napkin and he took it and shoved it into the bag. "That sounds romantic," she said.

"I dropped the ring in the lake."

She snorted. "Smooth."

"Fucking expensive. I hope Jason did a better job."

She looked down at the ring, twisted it again. "It was at a White Sox game, on the Jumbotron. He's all about the grand gesture." By the merest flicker of her facial muscles, Alyssa managed to convey what she thought of grand gestures.

"Not your thing?"

She shrugged. "It made him happy, so that made me happy." She rearranged herself in her seat and leaned against the door. She curled one leg under her and drummed her fingers softly on her knee. They spoke at the same time.

"How's the burg—"

"Is your fiancé—"

"Sorry," they said in unison, and there was a moment of awkward confusion before she waved a hand at him. "You go first."

"Oh, sorry." He crumpled his burger wrapper and wiped his hands on a napkin. "I was just asking if Jason is FBI, too."

She laughed, as if the idea was preposterous, but he caught a whisper of something not at all humorous in the sound. "He's an engineer at Boeing."

There was a telltale little tightening around her lips, and he recalled the phone calls she had ignored the night she arrived in Shaky Lake. He suspected that Alyssa's fiancé might not have been pleased by her sudden departure from Chicago. It was not a line of conversation Eli wished to pursue.

"He's a rocket scientist?" he asked. "You're going to marry an actual rocket scientist?"

He was relieved when she grinned. "Technically, yeah."

"Damn. Well done." He unwrapped another burger and took a bite. "Want to know what I did for a living when Michelle and I got married?" He paused, held up a finger while he finished chewing, then said, "I chopped down trees." He swallowed another bite. "Sometimes they even let me cut the trees into smaller pieces."

"You were a lumberjack?" The diamond on her ring flashed as she held her hand over her mouth to stifle a laugh. "Did they make you wear flannel shirts and suspenders and carry a big axe?"

"Keep your fantasies out of this."

She snickered.

"Hey, I was quite a catch," he protested. "Two-time all-American log-rolling and boom-running champion."

"That's not a real thing."

"Ask anyone. I'm a legend."

She laughed and shook her head, then rolled down the car window and stuck a hand out. The rain had stopped. "Thank god. I was starting to sweat," she said. She ran a finger across the fogged windshield, opened the rest of the windows, and nodded to the McDonald's entrance behind him. "They probably think we're a couple of kids smoking weed in here."

Or a couple of kids making out.

The thought was immediately followed by a wave of mortification, as if he had said the words aloud. She was the closest thing to a mind reader he'd ever known, but if she had guessed his thoughts, she did not acknowledge them. Instead, she reached into the back seat and pulled her laptop out of her bag, then flipped it open and balanced it on her knee. He busied himself by unwrapping his third Big Mac.

"I talked to Dan Simons," she said. "Interesting guy. He opened up a huge can of worms, though." She typed for a few seconds, then looked at Eli. "Which is fine. In fact, nothing gets me up in the morning like an open can of worms."

"Wow, okay," he said, around a mouthful of burger.

"I believe"—she paused for effect—"that Russell Kovach is the tip of a very large iceberg."

"You're mixing metaphors."

She put a hand up to silence him. "Kovach has an alibi. Video footage of him a hundred miles away from the scene of the crime. He's not involved. Case closed."

"Except the fingerprints in the boat," said Eli.

She lifted a shoulder, let it drop. "Fingerprints alone won't get you charged, let alone convicted, if you have a good lawyer." She paused. "Do you mind if I . . . ," she said, and gestured to the glove box.

Eli's knees were already pressed to the dashboard and his legs left little space for movement, but he set his food down and attempted to open the glove box.

"Just—" She made a shooing motion at his legs and reached across him to extract a packet of wet wipes from the compartment. Then, as if she hadn't just draped herself across his knee, she straightened up, pulled off her glasses, and began to wipe off the lenses. She settled back against the door and resumed speaking. "Kovach has a good lawyer. A *very* good lawyer."

The car was a few sizes too small for Eli to begin with, and the windows weren't letting in enough cool air to mitigate the stuffiness. Worse, he was beginning to realize how starved he was for human interaction, as if with his confession to Alyssa, he had been released from solitary confinement and wanted to be best friends with the first person he saw. The last thing he wanted was to weird out a female FBI agent in an enclosed space.

"Do you mind if we stand outside for a while?" he said.

"Oh," she said. "Okay." She put her hand out the window again. Then, satisfied that it still wasn't raining, she opened the door and got out. The nearby picnic tables were soaking wet, so they just leaned against her car.

"I did some research on the lawyer," she said. "Charles Dawson. He has a private practice in Red River Falls. From what I can tell, he works on a sort of freelance basis for Wildwood Clinic. Mostly lawsuits against health insurance companies who don't want to pay their bills."

"And yet he's representing a violent criminal." Eli's curiosity sparked. Fingerprints that shouldn't be there. A lawyer who didn't fit the crime.

Look for the things that don't belong.

Alyssa's face was bathed in the yellow light of the McDonald's Golden Arches and her expression was eager. Excited. As if they were playing a game of Hot and Cold and he was one step away from discovering the hidden item.

It took him half a beat to organize his mind. To meet her at the point she was trying to make. "You think the surveillance video of Kovach is fake?" he asked. "That Kovach's alibi is fake?"

Alyssa broke into a huge grin. She reached through the open window to set her laptop onto the car seat, then gave him a backhanded slap on the shoulder. "I *knew* you were good." She gave an almost delighted sigh, then said, "I looked through the video last night. Kovach is a custodian at a medical clinic in Hudson, and the video from Tuesday is eight hours of him moving around the building, cleaning, emptying trash cans, that sort of thing. He makes an appearance in front of each security camera. Nice, long pauses, like clockwork."

Eli pictured her typing away at her computer last night, immersed in her work, while he was getting blackout drunk at Babe's. With effort, he pushed the thought aside. "What about the time stamp on the video?"

"I called the company that does security for the building. They keep each video for a month, and it's all super organized. Tuesday's video is date- and time-stamped the same way as all the others."

"But you still think it's fake because Kovach's movements are a little too perfect."

She nodded. "It's just a hunch at this point. I still need to go through the footage in more detail and talk to potential witnesses."

"You think Kovach was in Shaky Lake on Tuesday, and that he killed Ben."

"I do."

"To what end?"

She drummed her fingers on the roof of the car. After a moment, she said, "Truthfully, I assumed Caitlin was dead. That we just hadn't found her body yet. And blowing a hole in Kovach's alibi wouldn't change that. But after what happened to Beth Wallace last night—"

"The fire," said Eli. He thought of Beth in her kitchen last night, a mere twenty-four hours ago; the fear on her face, the way she had confided in him and trusted him to keep her safe.

"The fire inspector said someone put chunks of rubber tire in the wood-burning stove in her cabin," said Alyssa. "The smoke was terrible, but there wasn't much in the way of open flames at first. Those cabins have smoke detectors and Beth was able to get out and call 911." She began to pace again. "Whoever set the fire," she said, "wasn't trying to kill her. They were trying to scare her." She stopped, turned to him. "This was never about Ben Sharpe. It's about Calvin Wallace. Somebody is trying to find him, to lure him out from"—she paused—"wherever it is he's gone. They kidnapped his daughter and left Ben Sharpe's body at Beran's Resort as a message, then when Wallace still didn't show, they moved on to his wife. It was meant as a second warning."

She stopped talking, braked almost visibly, with an air of having said more than she had intended. A look of unease passed over her face. He recalled their interview with Beth Wallace two nights ago, the surprising amount of information Alyssa had already known regarding the Wallace family, and now, the efficiency with which she had analyzed all that had happened in the past couple of days. She was an excellent investigator, but Eli recognized now what he hadn't earlier: Alyssa Mason had come to Shaky Lake armed with information that predated Ben Sharpe's death and Caitlin Wallace's disappearance.

He shot her a look of compounded surprise and appraisal but stayed silent.

"I—" Alyssa began, with an unfamiliar awkwardness in her tone. She leaned back against the car again, farther away from him this time. After a long moment, she turned to him but didn't come any closer. "Look," she said, a tinge of defensiveness in her tone, "there are things I can't discuss with you. It's nothing personal, I just—"

"Nothing personal," he repeated. There was a pause as his words fell between them. Alyssa's eyes were unreadable behind her glasses, but he saw that whatever was on his face had her taking a step back.

He should be angry. She was withholding information from him, from Marge. She wasn't collaborating with them; she was using them. But he found it wasn't anger that burned hot across his cheeks, that pulsed faster beneath his skin. It was mortification; the realization that he had made a terrible mistake. He had trusted her with information that was very personal, indeed. He had revealed more to her than he had been willing to reveal even to himself. The food he had just eaten churned in his gut, and he swallowed hard. A damp fist of wind swept the parking lot, pressing his eyes into their sockets. Alyssa's hair blew across her face and she shoved it back. Her lips were flattened into a straight line.

"Have you told Marge the whole story?" he asked.

"I've told her everything I've told you," she said, her face rigid with a strong emotion he could not identify. "Everything that's relevant to finding Caitlin." She turned away.

The ensuing silence became overlong. Thunder rumbled again from the west, and a gust of wind shook the small car. Alyssa turned and, to his alarm, crossed the space between them and put a hand on his arm. She gave him a long, penetrating look. He could tell she was measuring the extent of the damage she had caused; she knew enough to recognize that she had betrayed his trust. He was trapped against the side of the car, or he would have moved away.

"It's not that I don't trust you," she said. "I do. The sheriff too. It's just—"

"You do what you need to do," he said, with an exaggerated brightness, so she might understand the extent of her betrayal, so she knew, going forward, that their relationship would be nothing more than the simple esprit de corps of two professionals with a common mission.

He didn't wait for her response; he just looked at his watch, then headed around the back of the car toward the passenger door.

"We're late," he said. He pulled open the car door and glanced across at her once more before lowering himself into the car. She stared at him, but her face was in shadow, backlit by the glow of the McDonald's sign, and he couldn't read her expression. For a moment, he thought she might speak, but then, without another word, she pulled open the car door and got inside.

Cal

Cal opened his eyes and saw the pockmarked surface of a drop ceiling, like something from an outdated office building. Could he be at work?

The thought sent a ripple of panic through him, and he didn't understand why. He tried to sit up but found that he couldn't. With a growing sense of alarm, he brought his hands to his neck and felt a sharp pain in his left arm. Where his hands were expecting to feel his face, they were blocked by a wall of hard plastic. He scrambled up in the bed, clawing at the ring around his neck. An alarm sounded from somewhere over his left shoulder, followed shortly thereafter by the sound of a door opening.

"Wait! Wait, you need to lie back," said a woman's voice.

"Beth?" he asked. His head felt heavy and he stumbled on the word.

"Sir, you need to lie back down," said the voice. "Your neck."

He slumped back into the bed but kept his hands on the neck ring. The woman took his left arm and he let her straighten it out. Over the wall of plastic around his neck, he could make out the top of someone's head.

He moved his tongue around in his mouth. It was so dry. After a few seconds, he attempted to speak.

"Where—" he started. He could barely get the words out through his tight, chapped lips.

"You're in the intensive care unit," said the nurse. She moved closer so he could see her face. "You were in a car accident. A pretty bad one."

His mind grasped to put together the pieces. Beth. Caitlin. Orion. He tried to sit up again. The document. Where was the fax?

The nurse gently but firmly pushed him onto his back. "Sir, it's not safe for you to move around yet. You've just come out of sedation and—"

"What day is it?" he asked.

"It's Friday," she said, and glanced at her watch. "Five thirty p.m. You were airlifted here early Monday morning." She smiled. "We were pretty worried about you there for a while."

"Airlifted?" he asked.

"You're in Madison. University of Wisconsin hospital," she said.

His thoughts swirled, and he forced himself to concentrate.

"My bag," he said.

"Your what?"

"My bag," he said. "Where's my bag?"

She gave him a strange look. "Locked up in patient belongings. You wouldn't let it go when they picked you up, apparently. The ER waited until you passed out and then locked it up." She studied him. "Do you remember any of that?"

He tried to shake his head, but the collar prevented his movement. "No," he said. "I don't remember any of it."

"You're going to be okay, but you're going to be here for a while." Her eyes opened wider. "Oh, I forgot. We don't know your name. You had that bag but no wallet, no identification, no phone. We've been calling you John Doe."

"Calvin," he said. "Calvin Wallace."

"Glad to meet you, Calvin," said the nurse. "I think there's some paperwork for you to fill out, now that you're awake." She used a remote control on the arm rail of his bed to turn on the television. It was high enough on the wall that he could see the screen, and it was tuned to what looked like the local news. "I'll put on some television for you while I figure out what the protocol is."

He remembered just before she closed the door. "My bag," he said. His mouth and tongue were leather-dry, and he licked his cracked lips. "Can you bring it to me?" He saw her skeptical look. "Maybe just set it on the table? I promise I won't sit up in bed."

"Sure," she said. *A few minutes later, she was back with the bag and what looked like a child's sippy cup. "You pulled your IV out. I'll put it back in later, but, for now, you need to drink something."*

After she left the room, he groped for the bag. He felt a thick stack of paper and yanked it from the bag. There it was. AS REQUESTED. *He held the document high over his face and thumbed through it. Everything was there. He stuffed it back into the bag and set it on the bedside table.*

He forced himself to take some deep breaths, then watched the TV screen while he sipped what turned out to be apple juice. The meteorologist was standing in front of a radar screen, gesturing this way and that. The sound was down too low to hear, and he was about to close his eyes when he saw the banner scrolling across the bottom of the screen. It was an Amber Alert, the universal code for a missing child. He squinted to get a better look at the words and watched the banner cycle through three or four times before he believed what he was reading. Caitlin. Caitlin was missing.

May be in the company of father Calvin Wallace, 48, under suspicious circumstances. *His photo, the one from Orion's website, scrolled next to a photo of Caitlin.*

He watched in horror as the banner rolled by, again and again. He had to get out of here. He had to find Caitlin. As soon as people realized who he was, the police or FBI would detain him. What if they didn't believe his story?

He felt around on the bed rail and found the TV volume button. He turned the volume up loud enough to mask the sounds of his movement. First he took off the neck brace. He moved his head experimentally and found that, though it was stiff and achy, it seemed to be stable. He sat on the edge of the bed for a few seconds until his vision cleared. He felt like he had been hit by a truck, and he saw for the first time that his left leg was in an air cast that extended from ankle to mid-thigh. He wiggled his leg around and found that it was painful but functional. He carefully unbuckled the brace and felt around on his leg. The skin was purplish-red and crisscrossed with cuts and scrapes. He flexed his knee a few times before attempting to bear weight on the leg. When he did, the pain in his knee was breathtakingly sharp. His brain was foggy, and he fought back a wave of nausea. He knew the nurse would be back any minute, and she would put him right back in his brace. He couldn't take the chance of this happening, but he didn't know what to do. Then, over the loudspeaker, a voice announced, "Code blue: Medical Response Team to room six-two-four on the sixth floor." He could hear movement outside his room as the announcement was played twice more, then loud voices and the sound of rolling carts and hurrying feet. This was his chance.

He picked up the messenger bag and limped out the door. Nobody was at the nurses' station outside his room, and he didn't see anyone in the hallway between himself and the illuminated exit sign. A warm-up jacket with the UW hospital logo hung on the back of a chair, and he shrugged it on and continued toward the exit. Shelves in an alcove contained clean hospital gowns and, to his relief, a stack of scrub pants. He pulled a pair on, gasping with pain and nearly losing his balance. Just then he heard the grind of the heavy metal exit doors opening, then voices coming around the corner. He quickly ran his hand through his hair in his best attempt to tame his bed head. Then, keeping his head down and doing everything he could to avoid limping, he hurried past the two staff members and out the door.

He headed toward the front door of the hospital, trying to blend in with the crowd of patients and visitors and staff members. So far, nobody seemed to notice his limp, his disheveled appearance, or his bare feet. He had no idea how he was going to get to Shaky Lake with no car and no money. As he came to the front door of the hospital, he saw a desk labeled VALET. His heart thumped. Nobody was standing at the desk, so, with a quick glance around, he opened the cabinet, left slightly ajar, behind the desk and scanned the keys hanging there. He grabbed a set and hurried out the front door. The tag said L78, and, looking up at the five-story parking complex, he prayed that L stood for "lower level." He spotted the stairs and half hopped his way down. He glanced behind him to see if anyone had noticed him. He found the car more quickly than he had anticipated. A maroon Pontiac sedan that had seen far better days. It started on the first try, and he was relieved to see that the tank was nearly full. Enough to get to Shaky Lake. The clock on the dashboard read six o'clock. He pulled out of the spot and managed to get out of the parking ramp by going the wrong way down a driveway that wasn't blocked by a ticket gate. After half a dozen wrong turns, he found the on-ramp to the interstate and was on his way to his family.

34

The old brick walls of the police station were thick enough to muffle the sound of cars traveling down Main Street, and of people shouting and laughing as they made their way from one downtown tavern to the next. Many times over the years, Marge had left the station only to discover it was pouring rain, the sound having been deadened by the tons of hundred-year-old timber and brick surrounding the station.

Not tonight. The humid evening air had turned into an unsettling wind, then rain, then the worst thunderstorm Marge could remember.

Everyone sat at the conference table in the basement of the station. The power was still on, but Phil had brought some camp lanterns and extra flashlights just in case. It was late, after nine o'clock, and the front door was locked.

Marge was currently doing her best to avoid clucking over Eli like a mother hen. Phil and Jake were on opposite ends of the table, studiously ignoring each other, and Eli was looking over Alyssa's shoulder at something on her laptop. Marge didn't smell any alcohol on him tonight, but then again, she never had before. She thought of Rachel Sharpe, of what addiction had done to her and her family. A good family, with the best intentions. She had seen the Rachel who lay beneath the layers of addiction and depression and lord knows what else, and it was that person, smart and caring, who suffered all alone, deep inside the disaster. She hadn't known Rachel before this had happened, not really, but she knew Eli like she knew her own soul. Knew what he used to be like. Strong and steady. A protector. Someone to be relied on to get things done, to have the answers, to keep his cool when things were difficult. Someone who laughed and fished and sat around the campfire with those he cared about. She knew he was still there, beneath the pain, in the darkness. But could he ever pull himself back out? It was clear, after sitting with him in the car on the cliff, that he couldn't do it by himself, and that it was only a matter of time before he found his way back to the cliff, or a gun, or a rope. No, he needed more than just her love. She wasn't so delusional as to think she could help him all by herself.

She studied him as he and Alyssa talked. He had more energy than the last time she had seen him. A glimpse of his old self. It had been the right thing to do to allow him to return to the case. She had sat in on Alyssa's interview with Dan Simons, heard all the things that shifted the investigation from a dead boy and a missing girl to something much bigger, much more opaque. The truth was, she needed Eli for this. Phil ran the dispatch, and while Jake had his private security background, it had been more brawn than brains. Jake and Phil did great law enforcement work, but they weren't investigators. The cases Eli had cracked while working for the US Fish and Wildlife Service were legendary, though not exactly glamorous.

A tremendous crash of thunder struck.

"Jesus Christ," said Jake, ducking his head. His face was pale, and it was a few seconds before he looked up again.

"You okay?" asked Marge.

Jake took a few long breaths. "As long as that's thunder and not an IED, I'm good." But after a few minutes, he was still ashen, and she could see his hands trembling on his lap.

Marge fiddled with the cap of her pen as she considered the state of her deputy. "Why don't you head home, Jake?" She frowned at him. "You look like you could use some rest."

"I'm okay, Marge, seriously."

She brushed aside his comment. "We're almost done here anyway." Alyssa had updated the team on the developments related to Russell Kovach, and beyond that, there wasn't much more to be said. Marge had decided to keep her conversation with Tyler Mattson to herself for the time being. Another roll of thunder sounded from above, quieter this time. She looked at Jake, considered whether she should drive him home. Some of his color had returned, but, even across the conference table, she could see the sweat on his forehead. She jammed the cap of her pen back on and tapped it on the table in Jake's direction. "Be back tomorrow morning," she told him, "with an update on the search efforts." He looked as though he might argue, but instead got to his feet with a long exhalation and, with a wave at everyone, departed.

———

"God, the look on his face," said Phil, once Jake was gone. He picked up a flashlight from the table and fiddled with it. "Sometimes I forget what he's been through." He took his hat off, rubbed a hand across his scalp, then put his hat back on.

"You could give him a pass once in a while," said Marge.

"I know."

Marge was about to continue with the meeting when there came a sound from upstairs, barely audible through the sounds of rain and wind and thunder.

They all exchanged looks, and then Phil stood up. "Sounds like someone's at the door." He left the room, and a few minutes later, he returned. "Marge, you have a visitor." Behind him limped a man dressed in what looked like soaking-wet pajamas, hair plastered to his pale, haggard, unshaven face. He was racked with shivers—Marge could hear the man's teeth chattering from across the room—and he looked on the verge of passing out. Another massive thunder crash reverberated through the building and the lights flickered, then steadied again. A puddle of rainwater had begun to form beneath the visitor, and she saw with astonishment that the man's feet were bare. The man seemed about to speak but swayed and teetered and nearly fell, until Phil caught him by the arm and lowered him into a chair.

The visitor shuddered and took a gasping, choking breath, looked back into the shocked faces that surrounded him, then finally spoke.

"My name," he said, "is Calvin Wallace."

35

Tonight would go down as one of the more bizarre nights of Marge's life. Calvin Wallace had appeared like a specter in the night, with a story so far-fetched that it could only be true. He had refused to go to the hospital. Had, in fact, demanded to be taken to see Beth at the hospital in Chippewa Falls, nearly an hour away, and spirited her out of her dark hospital room before a doctor could be called to sign her discharge papers.

"We aren't safe here, Beth," he had said. Marge had been there with him, had felt the fear radiating from him like a blast from a furnace. He was badly injured, that was clear. His left leg was hideously swollen and bruised—broken, probably—and the whites of his eyes were tinged with the reddish brown of broken capillaries, now four days healed. His thick hair had been shaved on one side of his head, and a long, angry red slash along his scalp was held together with staples. Beth, her voice hoarse from the smoke inhalation, had cried with relief to see him and then climbed out of the hospital bed and into her clothes without hesitation.

Now, at nearly two a.m., Marge sat at the foot of the motel-room bed and listened as Cal recounted the events of the past week. He was propped up on a stack of pillows against the headboard of the king-size bed, his left leg elevated on another pillow. The overlarge sweatpants and T-shirt, borrowed from Eli, gave him a shrunken appearance. Alyssa stood in the corner nearest the bathroom, half in shadows, outside the circle of light from a lamp on the dresser.

"Salvare was going to change everything," said Cal. "An end to over-doses."

A miracle drug.

Chuck Sharpe's words echoed in Marge's memory.

"That was our slogan," continued Cal. "I must have said those words ten thousand times in the past year to doctors, pharmacists, rehab facility owners, public health officials—anyone who cared about the opioid epi-demic. I told them Orion was going to fix the problems that other phar-maceutical giants had created when they peddled newer, stronger, more addictive opioids to unsuspecting people. Those companies had lied, but not Orion." His tone was harsh, his mouth twisted with bitterness.

"Cal," murmured Beth. She moved a few inches closer to him on the bed and rested her hand on the back of his neck.

"Then I got the fax." He nodded toward the sheaf of paper in Alyssa's hands, now crumpled and torn, that had set in motion all that had trans-pired in the past week. "I have no idea who sent it, or if it was even meant for me. Maybe someone sent it to me by mistake. 'As requested' was all it said on the cover sheet, but I hadn't requested any research data. I had my own copies of it, anyway." Car lights flashed by the motel-room window and Cal went a shade paler than he already was.

Marge gave him a reassuring look. "Eli's keeping watch outside. I promise you, nobody is getting in here." The Driftwood Motel was on the outskirts of Shaky Lake, and its drab 1960s exterior blended seam-lessly into the string of gas stations, taverns, and patches of pine forest that lined the highway leading into town. It was as safe a place as any for Cal and Beth to hide.

Everyone was quiet a moment, the only sound that of the rain—softer now, the gentle tail end of the violent thunderstorm from earlier that night—through the open window.

"Do you have any idea who could have sent the fax?" asked Marge.

Alyssa spoke before Calvin could answer.

"I sent the fax."

All air seemed to evaporate from the room, replaced by a silence so charged that Marge felt it crackle against her skin, felt it lift the fine hairs on her arm. Beth stared at Alyssa, appalled, and Cal's pallor was replaced by a blaze of crimson across his cheeks. Alyssa returned their stares without a change in her expression.

Marge didn't know whether to admire her equanimity or censure her for it. "You *what*?"

Alyssa looked at her, and Marge saw a flash of what looked like distress cross the younger woman's face. Alyssa pushed her glasses higher on her nose and turned back to Cal and Beth. Her face was neutral now, but her fingers were white where she gripped the documents.

"Eighteen months ago," she began, "the Cook County Sheriff's Department identified an uptick in opioid overdoses in the northern Chicago suburbs tied to counterfeit pills. Fake oxycodone, mostly. Sometimes fake Xanax or Adderall. The pills were all laced with fentanyl, which is a synthetic form of opioid that's extremely potent. An amount of fentanyl equal to a grain or two of salt can be lethal. When we tried to dig deeper into the source of the counterfeit pills, we hit a wall almost immediately. Nobody was talking. Even our undercover operations went nowhere. Finally, we got a tip from a woman who said her boyfriend was involved. Apparently he had beat her up one too many times and she had had enough."

Marge felt the familiar surge of terror and outrage that came with each and every story of abuse. She rose from her perch on the end of the bed and went to lean against the wall next to the open window. She needed some fresh air.

"We surveilled the guy for weeks," Alyssa went on. "Then we got a break. He met with a man at a strip club a couple of times, and when we investigated further, we learned that the man he was meeting was named Jack Kowalske."

"My boss," murmured Cal. He turned to Beth and she looked back at him, wide-eyed.

"The CEO of Orion Pharmaceuticals." Alyssa nodded. "Your boss." She paused, as if waiting for Cal to say something, and when he didn't, she went on. "Our theory is that whoever is making the counterfeit pills wants to expand into the world of legal narcotics. Hence, a pharmaceutical company. So we learned everything we could about Orion. About the new product they were developing."

"Salvare," said Marge.

"Right," said Alyssa. "Salvare." She tapped a finger against the stack of paper on the dresser beside her. "It was easy enough to access research data on Salvare. The drug already has FDA approval, so everything is on file with the feds, including study participants' identities. We ran background checks on every participant and found that a surprisingly large number of them had died. Too many of them."

"The ones you flagged in the fax," said Cal. "The handwritten numbers after their names were their dates of death."

"Yes."

Cal looked at Marge, and she saw that his strength was waning quickly. "They lied," he said in a gravelly voice. "They knew the drug was killing people—people it was designed to help." His face twisted with revulsion. "Kowalske and Kevin Allen. They knew and they didn't care."

Beth spoke for the first time. "How was the drug killing people? Was it causing them to overdose?"

"Autopsy data listed the cause of death for the vast majority of the participants who died as myocardial infarction," said Alyssa. "Heart attacks." She hesitated for a moment, as if she wasn't sure whether the other people in the room wanted to—or had the strength to—hear the whole story. "Salvare is an opioid. The same basic chemical as heroin or oxycodone or morphine. Salvare is a synthetic opioid that was chemically engineered to be overdose-proof. When the concentration of the drug in the blood reaches a certain level, the body begins excreting the excess drug. It's like—" She paused and looked a little embarrassed. "Have you ever noticed that your urine is sometimes very bright yellow when you take multivitamins? That happens because your body can only absorb so much vitamin at once, and the rest is eliminated in the urine. It's like a pressure-relief valve. A safety mechanism."

"Safe opioids," said Marge. "That sounds incredible, but wasn't the point to help people stop using opioids altogether?"

"No," said Cal. They all turned to look at him, and it was all Marge could do not to insist on taking him to the hospital. His eyes were closed and his teeth were bared in a grimace of pain. "No, it was only meant to prevent overdoses. It was just swapping one opioid for another, safer one." He stopped and took a few deep breaths before continuing. "Orion would be making money off people's addiction just like criminal drug organizations were, only legally."

"And, let me guess," said Marge. "A month's supply of the drug would cost thousands of dollars."

"Six thousand dollars a month."

"How could anyone afford that?" asked Marge.

"Most health insurance plans would have covered it," he said. "Salvare would have made Orion billions."

"As long as nobody found out that it was causing heart attacks," said Alyssa.

Beth spoke again. "Why would Orion go this far to keep these results secret when people would find out anyway? Once the drug hit the marketplace and people started dying, surely the drug would be pulled off the market anyway."

"Not necessarily," said Alyssa. "All opioids have the potential to cause heart attacks. The problem is that when the researchers analyzed the Salvare trial data, they concluded that people died of heart attacks far more often with Salvare than with any other form of opioid. The FDA would have never approved the drug, so Orion falsified the data." She looked pointedly at Cal. "But you know all about the ways drug companies spin the truth once a drug actually goes to market, even to doctors and other very smart, well-meaning people."

Cal studied Alyssa from beneath drooping lids. Beth scowled at her and seemed about ready to come to her husband's defense, but Cal put a hand on her arm. "You're right," he said to Alyssa. "But why send the fax to me?"

Alyssa smiled. "We profiled various Orion employees—it's a very complex process—and you rated as most likely to blow the whistle." Her smile faded and a deep line appeared between her brows. "I'm so sorry. If I had known it would lead to this . . ." Nobody seemed to know how to respond, and the room fell quiet for a long moment.

Finally, Beth said, "What about Caitlin?" she asked. "What do we do now?"

Cal shifted in bed and hissed in pain when his ruined leg slipped off the pillow. He reached down and fixed the pillow before Beth could help him. "I'll call Kevin Allen," he said. His face was rigid, his lips flat with determination. "I'll call him and tell him I'm in Shaky Lake, tell him that—"

"No," said Alyssa. "They won't just hand Caitlin over. If they find you, they'll kill you, and Caitlin, too."

Beth leaned forward. "You think she's alive?" Her words were more a plea than a question.

"We can't be sure," said Alyssa, "but I think so."

Marge wished she shared Alyssa's optimism. She pushed away from the wall and went to the head of the bed. Cal would end up back in intensive care if he didn't get some rest. "Eli will keep an eye on you tonight and I'll be over first thing in the morning." She laid a hand on Cal's shoulder and squeezed it gently. "We're glad you could finally join us."

36

The rain had stopped a couple of hours ago, and the air drifting in through Marge's bedroom window was fresh and cool. Good sleeping weather, as her father used to say. But she had been lying in her bed, wide awake as Tommy snored, for over an hour; sleep, it seemed, was not in the cards for her tonight. She should have been thinking about the investigation, about Calvin Wallace's reappearance and the disturbing circumstances that had triggered all that had happened in the last few days. An innocent boy, gone too soon. A whistleblower running for his life, for his family's life. A miracle drug that was killing people.

She thought of Ben Sharpe, of Eli, and for the first time, with the world dark outside her window and the air sweet with the fragrance of rain-dampened vegetation, she said it openly to herself: *Thank god.*

Thank god it had been someone else's son in the bottom of that boat. Someone else's tragedy.

The thought of Rachel Sharpe, of the haunted look in the younger woman's eyes when Marge had seen her at the hospital, brought on a flood of shame. She pressed the heels of her palms tightly against her eye sockets, as if she could drive the warm, salty liquid back through the tear ducts. Crying always gave her a migraine, but this time she acknowledged it as a penance for her selfishness.

She turned, propped herself up on one elbow, and reached for the drawer in her nightstand where she kept a bottle of Tylenol. Tommy shifted on his side of the bed. At that moment, her cell phone shot to life with an earsplitting ring. The light from the screen seemed to illuminate the entire room. She didn't recognize the number on the caller ID.

"Hello?" she asked.

"Sheriff?" The voice was an octave higher than the last time she'd heard it, and tinged with fear.

"Tyler, what is it?" She hadn't expected to hear from her informant so soon. She climbed out of bed and retrieved her watch from the top of the dresser. It was nearly three a.m. The bedside lamp went on and she turned to see Tommy propped up on his elbows, watching her. He was used to her getting work-related calls in the middle of the night, but tonight his face was creased with concern. She made a motion of reassurance, then turned back around. She heard Tyler talking to someone, a woman, but couldn't make out their words. "Tyler," she said, louder this time.

"Sorry, Sheriff," he said. He was breathing hard, as though he had been running. "You told me"—he paused for a long breath—"to call you if I saw anything out of the ordinary."

"And?" Behind her, she heard Tommy get out of bed and pad out of the room. He knew when she was going to need a pot of coffee.

"There's this place," said Tyler. "This, like, old building," he said. "It's on the country club's land, but way out in the woods." His voice was muffled for a moment as he spoke again to whoever was there with him.

"And?"

"And," he said, his voice clear again, "I sometimes go there with my girlfriend." He dropped into a near whisper. "I live with my mom, so I can't really, um—"

"Yeah, I get it. And?"

"I didn't think anyone else knew about it," he said. "The cabin, I mean. It's way out there and I only found it by accident last summer."

From the kitchen, she heard the coffee grinder come to life. "Go on," she urged.

He let out a deep breath, and it crackled in Marge's speaker. "I took my girlfriend there, maybe half an hour ago, and I saw someone going into the cabin."

Marge's heart began to thump. "Did they see you?"

"I don't think so. They were already almost through the door. There was a new knob," he said. "I was close enough to see it. Brand-new silver knob."

"When's the last time you visited the cabin?"

"Couple weeks ago."

Marge considered this information in silence for a long time. Tyler spoke first.

"Sheriff, you still there? I hope it was okay to call you. I know it's super late."

"No, Tyler, you did the right thing. What I need now," she said as she headed for the kitchen, "is for you to tell me everything you know about this place."

37

There was something in the storm last night, bringing as it did Calvin Wallace, and later, the call from Tyler Mattson.

Marge balanced a cardboard cup of coffee in one hand while she scrolled through her phone. The back parking lot of the Kwik Trip gas station was deserted, and the only movement outside the truck was a cluster of black-capped chickadees squabbling in the gravel over the remnants of a hot dog bun.

"I don't know what possessed me to take a photo of this," she said, and handed Eli the phone. "It's the original topographical map of the Green Lake Country Club property. A blueprint of what Joe Aiello—that's the mobster who built the place—planned to build. It was hanging on the wall in Andrew Doherty's office." She looked over Eli's shoulder. "Zoom in on the southwest corner."

Marge studied Eli as he squinted at the phone. He was showered and shaved, and the shadows beneath his eyes weren't quite so deep today, despite staying up all night guarding Calvin Wallace. She couldn't help feeling as if maybe the storm had washed away a bit of the bleakness in his eyes. Two banana peels and a wrapper from a gas station breakfast sandwich were strewn across the dashboard of her truck in front of him, and she felt confident that his extra-large cup of gas station coffee didn't contain any alcohol. She'd bought it, after all.

Eli adjusted the screen to examine the map more clearly. "I didn't know the country club property was that big." He scrolled some more and looked at the screen again, then looked up at her with surprise. "Green Lake and Shaky Lake used to be connected?"

"They still are." Marge handed him some photos, warm from sitting on the truck's dashboard in the early morning sun. "The DNR did fly-overs the day after we found Ben and took these photos." She pointed at one of them. "The water's high this year, so you can see the river that flows between the two lakes. According to the map, Aiello planned for a small outbuilding along the river, and it seems the place does exist. Tyler Mattson knew about it and used it as a love shack from time to time. He was taking a girl there last night and saw somebody go into the building. Scared him shitless but thankfully he had the sense to call me."

"You think Caitlin's being held in the cabin?"

"It's hidden from sight by trees, it's not on any current map, it's right on a waterway." She ticked the reasons off on her fingers.

"It makes sense," mused Eli. He reached for the sandwich wrapper on the dashboard and found one last bite of food left. He popped it into his mouth and chewed thoughtfully. "Those Prohibition mobsters needed a backdoor escape route."

Marge nodded. "It was the ideal setup."

Maybe it still is.

She tucked the photos back into her folder and wedged it between the seat and the center console. "We wouldn't need to get a warrant, since it's a kidnapping case," she said.

"You mean we come in through the back door?"

"I've thought it through," she said. "What if someone at the country club is involved in all of this? If we show up at the front door, they'll have time to circumvent our plan."

Eli cocked his head at her. "You think someone at the country club is involved?"

"That call from Caitlin to Tyler Mattson . . ." She took a sip of her cof-fee. "Tyler said he had given the phone to Michael Gilson that morning, and I believe him." She pursed her lips. "I think—"

The truth was that Marge really didn't know what to think about the

Green Lake Country Club. About Michael Gilson. About the enigmatic Andrew Doherty. "I think," she continued, "that Alyssa is right. This case—Ben, Caitlin—is just the tip of the iceberg."

She studied his expression. "If you don't want to do this—the cabin, I mean—it's okay." He was probably one of the most qualified people on the planet to lead a mission like this, in terms of training and experience, but was it a good idea to send him so deep into harm's way after what happened yesterday?

"Yes," said Eli, without hesitation. "I'm absolutely up to it." The look in his eyes begged her to believe him. He turned in his seat to face her.

"Mom."

She looked down before he could see the emotion on her face. She had always considered herself a decisive person. Confident in her decision-making, in her own judgment. But now she was forced to accept that she had made a mistake, that deep down she had known how bad things were for Eli and chosen to turn a blind eye. He was just going through a rough patch, she had told herself. Drinking too much, to be sure, but a lot of people drank too much. Nothing that couldn't be fixed with a little help, maybe a little counseling. Now it was clear: her mistake, her failure to act, to make difficult decisions, had nearly cost her the most important person in her life. She had been lucky, had stopped him from going over the edge this time, but he was far from healed.

"I'm sorry," he said. "I know I hurt you." He put his hand on hers and she squeezed it tightly in response.

She opened her mouth to apologize in turn, but he put out a hand to stop her. "How"—he hesitated, began again—"how did you know where I was yesterday? You know, on the—"

On the cliff.

Marge fiddled with the cardboard sleeve that protected her hand from the scalding heat of the coffee, then took another sip. She had promised not to tell, but maybe it was better he knew. She could still hear the panic in her daughter-in-law's voice as she called Marge from the emergency room.

Marge, you need to find Eli. I think he might try to—

Even now, with her son safe in the truck next to her, Marge couldn't bring herself to repeat the words, not even in her mind.

"Michelle called me," she said, "and I had Alyssa track you by your phone GPS." She had known right away when Alyssa told her where he was that he wouldn't be sitting at the top of a cliff to admire the view.

Eli rubbed a hand over his face and groaned. "I should have known." He looked sidelong at Marge, then gave a puff of what might have been the beginning of a laugh. "You three are . . ." He shook his head, as if to clear it, then smiled in earnest. For long minutes, they sat in silence. The breeze through the truck was beautifully refreshing, as if Mother Nature was doing all she could to set things right. To clear the wreckage of recent years and set the scene for Eli to move toward a life that was worth living. Marge told herself this was possible, refused to accept any alternative.

"Promise me, Eli, that you'll get help."

Eli was quiet for a beat. "I promise."

She studied his face, searched his eyes, and told herself he was telling the truth.

The back door of the Kwik Trip opened and a bony, bowlegged man with a grizzled beard emerged and lit a cigarillo. He caught sight of Marge's truck and broke into a wide smile that was missing several important teeth. He shouted a greeting across the wide expanse of gravel.

"Marge. Eli." He lifted his Kwik Trip baseball cap off his bald head and waved it at the sky. "Hell of a storm last night," he called. "You guys make it through okay?"

"By the skin of our teeth," called Eli out the window. He looked back over his shoulder to where Marge sat and gave her a smile that seemed part apology, part promise. He turned back around, stuck his head out the window, and made a show of examining the sky. "Today, though," he called to the man, "today is shaping up to be one beautiful day."

38

E li sat in the middle of the boat, baseball hat pulled low. He wore a ratty T-shirt with the sleeves cut off and frayed cargo shorts. Alyssa was perched at the bow of the boat in a tank top and shorts. Her ponytail and cheap gas station sunglasses gave her the look of any nondescript vacationer.

"How long we waiting?" grumbled Dan from the aluminum bench at the back of the boat. He sat hunched over, one elbow draped over the tiller handle. "'Cause if we're just going to sit here—" He didn't wait for a response, just leaned over with a grunt and pulled a fishing pole from beneath his seat, then cast his line into the water like this was an ordinary evening fishing trip and not a high-stakes rescue mission. If someone had told Eli a week ago that he would find himself in a boat with Dan Simons and America's most meddlesome FBI agent, he would have assumed they were lying. The plan was for Dan to take them upriver, as close as possible to where they believed the cabin to be. While Eli and Alyssa made their way to the cabin, Marge and Jake would present a search warrant at the front door of the Green Lake Country Club and, if all went to plan, would meet Eli and Alyssa at the cabin. Phil's job was to make sure Beth and Calvin Wallace were safe.

Last night Eli had slept like a dead man, without the usual nightmares, without the terrible, familiar voices. Somehow they passed him by, as if perhaps he had not been on their map last night. As if they had sought out someone else.

Jake.

Eli had been too busy preparing for tonight's mission to talk to him, to see how his friend was doing. He felt ashamed now, especially given all that had happened the past few days, that he had never thought to look past Jake's cheerful, easygoing surface to see what pain he might be carrying with him.

Not alone anymore.

He looked up to find Alyssa watching him. He couldn't see her eyes through her sunglasses, but she wore a quizzical frown; a mixture of curiosity and appraisal. She had a remarkably expressive face when she wasn't performing an official interrogation, as if she stockpiled all her character to use in her free time. Not that this counted as free time, he supposed.

"What?" he asked.

"Nothing," she said. "I just—" She seemed to be trying to fathom something, to work it out in her head. Perhaps she wondered whether he had had anything to drink today.

He had.

In the end, she didn't answer, just made a noncommittal noise and turned back to the paperback novel she was pretending to read.

It was quiet except for the plop and reel of Dan fishing, and Eli wished he had brought his own rod. It would add to the facade, he had told Alyssa, of the three of them just out for an evening boat ride, rather than a slow, precisely coordinated approach to the cabin where Caitlin Wallace might be imprisoned. She had not been convinced, so he had dropped the idea.

Eli checked his watch. It was after eight o'clock. The sun was half-hidden beneath the horizon, and the half that remained blazed red and purple and orange, then, minutes later, disappeared with one final flash of light. Alyssa pulled her sunglasses off and turned to him again. She lifted a brow questioningly, and he nodded back, then turned to nod at Dan.

"About time," said Dan. He quickly reeled in his line and returned the fishing pole to its spot beneath the seat. He fired up the engine, and the mechanical rumble seemed to echo across the glassy, still surface of the lake. It was a gorgeous night; as perfect a summer night as Earth had to offer, and Eli allowed himself to pretend for just a few moments longer that he hadn't found a boy in a boat. That a girl wasn't missing. That all was well in the world.

The cool, damp nighttime air blew across the bow of the boat as they picked up speed, and the sky turned indigo above them as they entered the mouth of the river. After several minutes, Dan slowed the boat and steered it through a narrow channel of cattails and river grass, where the vegetation had recently been crushed by the hull of a boat. They reached the shore just as dusk turned to darkness, and Dan cut the engine.

Without a word, Alyssa grabbed a backpack from under her seat and dropped silkily into the shallow water. Eli followed suit, and, once they were on dry land, he looked back and exchanged a thumbs-up with Dan, who would wait with the boat in case they needed to evacuate via water.

They both donned black tactical clothing—Eli kept his back carefully to Alyssa as she dressed—and organized their gear into various pockets and straps on their persons, then stashed their backpacks behind a moss-covered boulder. The forest was dense and dark, with heavy tree cover; tight with scrub and underbrush, and littered with rocks of all sizes. If not for the path, it would have been nearly impassable, even with their night-vision goggles. After about five minutes of walking, Eli caught sight of the building, a mass of pale gray between the trees. Alyssa was a few paces behind him. They both came to a standstill and ducked behind trees opposite each other along the path. The fieldstone exterior of the building was a patchwork of moss and decay and heavy, sweet-smelling swaths of wild cucumber vine in its full, late-summer bloom. No windows were visible, and the only break in the facade was an arched wooden door, cleared of all vegetation and outfitted with a new-looking doorknob.

Across the path, Alyssa faced him and held up her hands in a question. Eli glanced at his watch and frowned. Nine o'clock. Marge should have been here by now. He pulled his silenced phone from his jacket. No calls, no texts. Alyssa jerked her head toward the building and tapped her watch. Time was running out. Eli pointed to himself and gestured to indicate that he would go first, but she shook her head. She stepped onto the path and he understood that she wanted to go first, that he should cover her. He nodded, then watched, weapon drawn, as Alyssa darted across the clearing and disappeared into the deeper shadow beneath the roof overhang. Through the nighttime hush of the forest, he heard a series of metallic clicks as Alyssa picked the lock, then the soft *snick* of the door opening. She slipped through the door, and, after one more visual sweep of the exterior of the building, he followed.

He felt the blood pulsing through the veins in his neck as he paused just inside the door and took a few deep breaths to slow his heart rate. All was quiet. Marge had likely been stalled at the clubhouse, and Eli remembered what she had said about the possibility of someone within the country club being party to Caitlin's disappearance, about the possibility that the arrival of law enforcement on the secretive club's front doorstep might trigger a lethal change in plans. His pulse took on the sense of a ticking clock.

The air inside the building had a wet, cave-like chill. Something—a piece of furniture, perhaps—sat in the corner, covered with a yellowed fabric. He approached it and gave it a nudge before lifting up the cloth to find an old drop-leaf table. He looked up just in time to see Alyssa disappear though a doorway at the far end of the room. The floorboards creaked and sighed underfoot, and the noise—the sound of his own movement—sent his pulse racing even faster. It did not escape him that his current surroundings bore a gruesome resemblance to another cold, dusty house on the other side of the world; that the shadowy doorway just steps in front of him might lead to something he could never forget, never unsee.

Alyssa's face appeared around the doorframe, and she gestured for him to follow her into the next room. It was small and windowless, with the earthy, fungal scent of old stone and decaying wood; a waft of cold, piquant air drifted upward from the floor and swirled around his knees. Alyssa pointed to a table and two chairs pushed up against one wall, set atop a faded, mildewed rug. She took a few steps closer to the table and crouched down to pull back the rug, then pointed at a spot on the floor where a line ran perpendicular to the wooden boards, nearly hidden under the heavy legs of the table. A trapdoor.

They got on either end of the table and moved it away as quietly as possible; then Eli crouched down and pulled open the trapdoor. The top of a wooden ladder, made of new-looking two-by-twos and bolted to the base of the trapdoor frame, was visible. Eli indicated that he would go first, but again, Alyssa shook her head and pointed to herself. He frowned. The idea of sending her down into the darkness didn't sit well with him, and he balked. Alyssa pointed to herself again, this time with more animation, then reached out a hand and grasped his arm, just below the shoulder. Her hand was warm against his skin, even through his shirt, even in the dank chill of the room. She gave his arm a small squeeze, then shoved him gently away from the opening in the floor. Before he could object, she crouched to the floor, swung her legs onto the ladder, and disappeared into the darkness. He heard the soft *thwack* of her feet hitting the floor. A few seconds later, her voice came through the opening in the floor.

"She's here. She's alive."

Eli's heart struck hard against his ribs.

She's alive.

He dropped to a squat next to the opening, and it occurred to him all at once how very similar going through this trapdoor would be to walking through the door in Al Jalil that had changed the course of his life. He closed his eyes and tried to fill his lungs with air, tried to root his body in the present. For a few awful seconds, he could only press his hand to his mouth and wait for the wave of fear to pass. He knew if he didn't descend through the trapdoor now, if he left Alyssa there in the darkness, he was lost.

"I'm coming down," he called. He descended the ladder in two steps, and, when his feet hit dirt, he started to straighten up and narrowly avoided grazing his head on the low ceiling. At a slight stoop, he joined Alyssa in a corner of the space. Her flashlight stood propped against the wall as a makeshift lantern, and she had pulled her night-vision goggles up to reveal her face. The glow of the flashlight cut through the darkness and illuminated a figure lying curled up on a mat on the floor, buried under a thin sleeping bag. Eli slid his own goggles to the top of his head and took another step closer.

Alyssa fumbled in her jacket and produced a thin, oblong object.

"I think she's drugged," she said. She held up the object, and Eli could see that it was a Narcan pen. He joined her next to the mat and reached out to gently turn the girl on her back. He recognized Caitlin Wallace from the photos Beth had shown him. Her lids parted slightly and she tried to speak.

"Caitlin, my name is Alyssa, and this is Eli. We're here to help." She grasped Caitlin's hand and squeezed. "Can you sit up?"

The girl looked at Alyssa in confusion. "Mom?" She attempted to sit up but slipped back on her elbows.

Alyssa shone her flashlight on Caitlin's arms and looked over at Eli. "See?" she said, indicating a spot on the girl's inner arm. "Injection sites. Both sides." Then she pointed wordlessly to a dark spot on the inside of Caitlin's forearm.

A tattoo of a poppy.

Alyssa pulled back the sleeping bag and lifted the girl's long sundress to reveal a bare thigh, then injected the Narcan. After a few moments, the girl began to squirm and breathe faster. Alyssa threw the Narcan pen into the corner and wrapped her arms around Caitlin. "It's okay, honey. We're here." She pulled Caitlin to a seated position and held something to her lips that Eli recognized as an energy gel pack.

Alyssa inspected the girl all over, as much as possible in the low light. "You're going to have to carry her," she told Eli.

"I don't know where Marge is," he said, "but we need to get out of here now. Back to the boat."

He had just slid his hands beneath the girl's shoulders and knees and begun to lift her when the floorboards above them creaked. Before either of them could react, the intense beam of a flashlight shone down from above. Eli shot to his feet and pulled his gun from its holster.

"Eli, is that you?" called a voice from above. "It's me, Jake."

Eli let out a breath. "We're here, Jake. We found her."

"Thank god," he heard Jake say. "Is she—"

"She's alive." Eli holstered his gun, went to the ladder, and squinted into the bright beam of light. "Where's Marge?" He grabbed the ladder and was two rungs up when he felt the crushing blow of a boot stomp to his face. The force of it knocked him backward off the ladder, and he crashed to the dirt floor. The back of his head hit hard and his vision exploded with stars, followed by a wave of icy, tingling pain. Alyssa yelled something, and he could feel the rush of air from somebody jumping down into the room.

Eli fought to get his bearings. He blinked hard and his vision came back into focus, only to find that it was Jake standing above him with a gun. He had tossed a flare into the center of the room and the amber-red light cast a hideous, hellish glow. The corners of the room darkened and receded in contrast.

"What the hell is going on, Jake?" He tried to sit up. "It's me, Eli—" His words were cut short by a kick to the chest and then the crush of Jake's boot against his throat. Caitlin screamed, and Eli knew without looking that Alyssa had tackled her to prevent her from getting off the mat. Any assistance from Alyssa was, at the moment, being thwarted by a terrified, hysterical kid.

Eli clawed at the boot against his throat, gagged and choked against the pressure, tried to breathe, failed. The edges of his vision blurred from lack of oxygen.

"I'm sorry to do this to you, Eli," he heard Jake say. "We were really hoping it wouldn't come to this."

We?

He heard a click as Jake deactivated the safety mechanism on his gun, and, just as Eli was about to lose consciousness, the weight of Jake's boot lifted. He took a great, heaving breath.

"Jake," he said again, stupidly. His brain seemed not yet ready to acknowledge what his eyes were seeing and his body was feeling. His friend. Pointing a gun in his face.

Not alone anymore.

Jake flicked the gun toward the mat where Alyssa held Caitlin down. "Over there. Slowly. On your hands and knees."

Eli forced himself to breathe, to think, and the circuits in his brain began to flicker back to life.

One game.

Just one game, Jake had said.

The other night, at Babe's. One game of pool with Jake. Then nothing. A hole in his memory, followed by the worst hangover of his life.

Not a hangover.

"You drugged me," Eli gasped.

If Jake heard Eli's words, he ignored them. His face was expressionless, utterly in control behind the gun. The face of a man who could kill a boy, who could steal a girl.

"Why?" asked Eli, and this time, Jake looked down at him.

"Just move, Eli."

"I mean"—his voice was rough, his windpipe still reeling from the blow to his throat—"why *you*?" The man standing above him was his friend, his defender. A good cop. A good *person*. Why would such a person commit such crimes? "Just tell me, Jake."

"Work is work, Eli. Now move."

Eli grunted in pain as Jake's boot made sharp contact with his ribs.

"You killed Ben Sharpe for *money*?" The idea of his friend as a paid thug did not compute.

Caitlin began to wail, and Eli came up on one elbow to look at the two figures huddled together on the mat.

"Get down," Jake snarled. He stamped his boot straight onto Eli's chest again.

In an instant, Eli grabbed Jake by the calf with one hand and smashed his opposite fist against the outside of Jake's knee. He heard a sickening crunch and Jake cried out in pain. Most would have crumpled to the ground, but Jake kept his foot planted on Eli's chest, weaker now, but still heavy as an elephant. Eli looked straight up and saw Jake's face hovering behind the barrel of the gun. He heard a shout, then saw a flash out of the corner of his eye that he prayed was Alyssa and Caitlin fleeing into the darkness at the other end of the room. Jake's eyes flicked in their direction just long enough for Eli to grab the man's uninjured leg. He wrapped his hand around Jake's ankle and pulled with all the force he could muster. He felt Jake's foot twist, and the weight of his other foot shifted off Eli's chest just enough to disrupt his balance. Jake crashed onto his side against the hard floor, and Eli flipped over and slammed an elbow, along with the weight of his entire upper body, against Jake's windpipe. With his other hand, he twisted Jake's right wrist with brutal force, and the gun went flying to the other side of the room. Too late he saw the flash of a knife in Jake's other hand, and felt a sear of pain as the blade sank into his back. He recoiled from the blow. Jake managed to get out from under Eli's grip and shot to his feet. In one fluid motion, Jake grabbed the gun from where it lay across the room and aimed it at Eli. There was a deafening crack, and Eli braced himself for what he knew would be the end.

It never came.

He smelled it first: the stench of death. Foul and all too familiar. Then he saw it. Jake's body, unmoving, on the floor. Then the beam from a flashlight, first on the tattered mess of a man who had once been his friend, and then on himself.

"Eli!" shouted a voice from behind the flashlight, and a moment later, she appeared at his side.

He blinked once, twice, and then the face above him came into focus. "Mom."

39

I told you to wear sunscreen," said Caitlin. "You look like a lobster." She leaned across the boat to touch Ben on his bare shoulder. "A lobster with a farmer's tan." The idea of this, combined with the slap-happiness that comes from being out in the sun too long, set her to giggling, and Ben watched her with a lopsided smile as she laughed.

"You should be thanking me," he said. He pressed a finger against his arm and watched the skin blanch and then turn back to meaty red. "I'm risking skin cancer just so you can have the last of the sunscreen."

She leaned over the side of the boat and splashed him with a handful of lake water, then shrieked when he returned fire. He wagged a finger at her, poised to deliver a mock scolding, then ducked as she directed another spray of water at his face. By the time the battle was over, they were both half-soaked and light-headed with laughter. Caitlin sighed happily and slouched back against her seat at the front of the boat. Ben watched her with something like contentedness as she adjusted the straps of her sundress.

"Is your mom still mad about the tattoo?" he asked.

She traced the poppy on her arm. The curved, scarlet edges of the petals, the ring of black stamens in the center. "She thinks it's symbolic."

He laughed. "Not sure you're cool enough for that."

"Exactly." She grinned and ran her hand across the tattoo one more time. A peaceful lull settled over them, and for long minutes they sat without *speaking, with only the gentle wobble of the boat against the afternoon waves and the cry of birds overhead.*

They had agreed not to talk about bad things today: parents and divorce, the counseling sessions she didn't need, his mom's never-ending problems. They were both only children; no siblings with whom to commiserate or who could share the burden of family troubles.

Four summers of friendship, and, this past year, near-constant long-distance communication, her in Chicago, him in Minneapolis, counting the days until they could see each other again.

Ben looked past her at something on the horizon, and she turned to follow his gaze. A small aluminum fishing boat bobbed in the distance, two men hunched over the small outboard motor. One of the men pulled the start cord on the motor over and over again, but the engine only sputtered and died.

"Think they need help?" Caitlin asked.

Ben nodded and put the motor in gear. He grinned at Caitlin. "Adults, am I right?"

"Completely useless," she agreed. She studied him as he steered toward the other boat, the shape of his shoulders, the way he drummed the fingers of one hand against his bare knee, the gap between his front teeth as he smiled at the two boaters and pulled up alongside. She was struck with a sudden, intense fear that this was all a dream. That Ben Sharpe, her best friend, the person she called when things got bad, might live only in her imagination. That was ridiculous, she thought, and she shook off the urge to reach over and grab hold of him, to lay her hands on his sunburned skin and make sure he was really there.

"You guys need some fuel?" Ben called. He held up the red plastic gas can he always kept full.

"Nah," answered the man tinkering with the motor. His pale, shiny bald head reflected the late afternoon sun, and his horseshoe mustache gave him an almost cartoonish appearance. "She's full of fuel. It's the damn ignition switch."

"Which you were supposedly getting fixed," muttered the other man, just loud enough. His back was to the sun, his face obscured by shadow

and by the slouchy fishing hat pulled low over his forehead. "You're such a dumbass."

The man at the motor looked skyward and sighed. Then he gave Ben and Caitlin a rueful smile. "I'm Bill. This asshole is my brother, Jim."

Ben glanced at Caitlin and she shrugged. "I'm Ben, and this is Caitlin," he said. "We can tow you to shore if you want. I have extra line." Caitlin dug around in the storage box at her feet and pulled out a neatly tied bundle of rope.

The brothers exchanged glances. "Don't think we have much choice," said Jim. He slipped on the pair of sunglasses that had been perched on the brim of his hat and reached across the water for the rope. The angle of the sunlight on his skin changed and Caitlin could see his throat, the pale line of scar that circled around his neck and up under his jaw. She barely suppressed a gasp. Like his head had been cut off and sewn back on.

Jim grabbed the rope and straightened to his full height, and the back-lighting of the sun once more hid his face. "Our truck is there," he said, pointing at a small pier in the distance. "The park's nothing more than a patch of grass and a broken picnic table, but there's a boat ramp." He laughed, and the sound of his voice from beneath the brim of his hat made Caitlin uneasy, though she would have been hard-pressed to explain why. "Don't tell anyone about it, though," he said. "It's Shaky Lake's best-kept secret."

Once the boats were tethered together, one in front of the other, Ben nudged his boat forward and they headed toward shore. It was slow going because too much speed sent the rear boat swinging and slapping awkwardly against the edges of the front boat's wake.

Caitlin smiled at Ben from her perch at the front of the boat. "Lobster," she teased.

"Laugh all you want, Caitlin Wallace," he said. He pulled his sunglasses down on his nose and shook his head with exaggerated gravity. "Just remember me as the guy who sacrificed himself to save your life."

She snorted and rolled her eyes. "People don't die of skin cancer."

"Not true," said Ben.

Laughing, she turned forward in the boat again and let the wind press against her face, savoring every spray of lake water that landed on her, absorbing everything good and storing it away, like an aquifer, to be drawn from in the months to come.

They didn't notice that the other boat was empty of all fishing gear. They didn't notice the men toss aside their life jackets. They didn't notice, as they reached the pier, the men nod at each other and reach into their fishing vests. It was a beautiful day, and all they noticed was each other.

40

Pajama parties. That's what they called these kinds of raids. Late-night surprise visits to penthouses and mansions.

Not all criminals lived in drug dens.

Alyssa looked back over her shoulder at the SWAT team members lined up along the wall and thought of Eli, wished he was here with her in this Chicago high-rise, hundreds of miles from Shaky Lake; the two places were connected by a thread of something dangerous, something shrouded in lies and secrets. The possibility that she might wish him here for reasons that went beyond the purely professional, she chose to ignore.

Eli had assured her via text that his knife wound was healing nicely. The blade had missed his kidney by half a centimeter; it hardly hurt at all anymore, he'd said. She knew, though, that it wasn't the literal stab in the back that had hurt him the most; metal through flesh heals quickly. Jake's betrayal would stay with him for far longer.

For her own part, the thought that she had been so careless, that she hadn't thought to dig deeper into the past of the members of the Sherman County Sheriff's Department, still rankled. Jake Howard was a veteran of the Iraq War, that much was true, but her belated deep dive into his history had soon revealed that the "private security company" for which he had worked after his military discharge was Bolton Solutions, known to the FBI as a private security force in Iraq and thought to provide security for the Balkan drug trade. That a man with Jake Howard's résumé would choose to work as a sheriff's deputy in a place like Shaky Lake was very interesting, indeed.

It had been two weeks since Caitlin's rescue, but Alyssa still rehashed the scene a dozen times a day. The girl was safe. Well, safer, anyway. The Wallace family had not gone home to Skokie. They wouldn't be able to go home for some time, but at least they were together. At least they were alive.

Of all people, it had been Michael Gilson, the elusive country club director, who had helped them. There was a tunnel—nearly impassable after ninety-plus years of disuse—that led to the cabin's cellar. Its existence was a secret—a shameful secret, he had told Marge afterward, a grim reminder of the original purpose of the property—that only a handful of people knew. According to Marge, when Jake hadn't shown up to go to the country club with her, she became suspicious, and even more convinced that Caitlin was being held in the cabin. She had explained the situation to Gilson and he had led her to the tunnel himself, accompanied by his second-in-command, Andrew Doherty.

Without their help, Alyssa knew she would have been dead, rather than standing in the hallway of one of the most exclusive residences in Chicago, moments away from what could be a huge step forward in her investigation.

She tugged at her bulletproof vest, a size too large. It was time.

She gave the signal and two SWATs lunged at the door with a battering ram. Three smashes and the door swung loose.

"FBI, this is a raid!" shouted Alyssa. She felt the rustle of officers brushing past her as they fanned out around the apartment. Again, she shouted, and was met with nothing but the sound of officers shouting "Clear" as they swept each room. An officer emerged from a room to her left and jerked his head for her to follow.

It was a bedroom. High-end everything. Modern, sleek, pristine, but the air was tinged with a familiar metallic smell. The SWAT officer stood at the foot of the bed and pointed to the narrow space between the bed and the wall. She walked across the room and saw a body-sized puddle of blood on the floor, with a very dead Kevin Allen in the center. Calvin

Wallace's trusted coworker, supposed friend, but the single worst person to whom he could have confided the awful truth about Salvare. Kevin Allen had already known the truth and had been willing to go to horrible lengths to help keep it secret. For money. Freckles on the dead man's face stood out against the pallor of his skin, and his red hair was matted and sticky with blood. She looked at the officer and shook her head, then looked back at the body on the floor. She chewed the inside of her lip for a moment, then pulled her phone out of her pocket and began to type.

Allen DOA. Kowalske?

The CEO of Orion. Kevin Allen's boss. A few seconds later, a response text.

Same. Someone got here first.

41

Afternoon light streamed through floor-to-ceiling windows into Rachel Sharpe's lake house living room, and Marge could barely believe it was the same space she had been in only a couple of weeks ago, when she had come in the middle of the night to tell Rachel that her only child had died. The place was pristine. The coffee table was covered with a tasteful assortment of books and high-end bric-a-brac, rather than empty cocktail glasses and bottles of pills. Where drug paraphernalia had sat was now a potted white orchid.

Rachel had been released from St. Anne's Hospital yesterday and had called Marge, unprompted, and asked to meet. She had been unwilling to elaborate on what she wanted to talk about, and Marge had spent the hours since her call in uneasy speculation.

"It's decaf," said Rachel as she handed Marge a cup of coffee. "It's all I had in the house."

Marge smiled. "That's probably for the best." Even now, after Caitlin had been rescued and the Wallace family safely hidden away by the federal Witness Protection Program, Marge had slept poorly. Eli had shared with her what Alyssa had said about Russell Kovach—the possibility that his alibi was bogus, that he might have had a hand in Ben's death and Caitlin's kidnapping—and Marge couldn't shake the feeling of approaching danger.

Rachel settled into an armchair across from the sofa where Marge sat and tucked her feet under her. She looked around the room for a moment, then said, "Chuck wants to keep this house, but I don't see the point. I'm done with Wildwood Clinic anyway."

Marge felt a pang of concern. Surely Rachel didn't intend to go without treatment for her addiction. She thought of the promise Eli had made, that he would get help with his own struggles. As if Rachel had read her thoughts, the younger woman put up a reassuring hand.

"There's a very good clinic in Minneapolis, and I have an appointment there on Friday." She took a sip of her coffee, grimaced, then set it on a glass end table. "Alex Kouris thinks he's the best of the best. Like he's some kind of psychiatric miracle worker." Her tone was defensive, as if she expected Marge to disagree with her assessment of Dr. Kouris. "He's in it for the money." She paused, considering. "Or maybe for the power." She looked at Marge. "Men like that thrive on other people's weakness." She shook her head. "It's twisted."

"You've been coming to Shaky Lake to get care from him for years," said Marge. "I assumed you liked him."

"*Chuck* liked him. Not me." She gave a bitter laugh. "I think what Chuck liked most was the country club membership."

Marge recalled the look on Chuck's face when she'd mentioned Kouris, and it had not been one of affection. She considered whether she might have misinterpreted Chuck's reaction but decided it didn't make any difference at this point. She went on, "Green Lake Country Club? What does that have to do with Dr. Kouris?"

"He's a major VIP there," said Rachel. "And he always manages to get memberships for certain Wildwood Clinic doctors and administrators. He's on the board of directors at Wildwood, so he has a lot of pull there, too. Like I said, he craves power." Marge frowned. She had not known any of this.

"Green Lake is more like a fraternity than a country club," continued Rachel. "All healthcare bigwigs."

Something else Eli had said surfaced in Marge's mind. "If the members are all in the healthcare industry, why are Mike and Kim Beran members?" She was met with a look of puzzlement on the younger woman's face, so she began to clarify. "They own the—"

"I know who they are," said Rachel. There was a long pause as she seemed to work through something in her mind. "I've seen them there, but I don't think they're members. Guests, more likely, although I'm not sure whose guests they would be."

"They talked to a man there earlier this summer about converting their resort into a rehabilitation facility." More information from Eli. "Not a doctor."

Rachel pursed her lips in thought. "Probably Charlie Dawson. He's always lurking around the place."

All of a sudden, the swirl of disconnected facts that had taken up residence in Marge's brain began to meld into something more linear. "Charles Dawson, the lawyer?" He was Russell Kovach's lawyer, according to Alyssa. Caitlin Wallace had picked Kovach out of a lineup and had identified Jake Howard from a photo as the two men in the boat when Ben was killed. She had described, even before seeing the lineup, Kovach's distinctive horseshoe mustache and Jake's facial scars. If Dawson was a regular at the Green Lake County Club *and* represented Russell Kovach, it was a link between Orion Pharmaceuticals and Shaky Lake that Marge hadn't recognized until now. And how did the Berans fit into the mix? "Why would a lawyer be talking to Mike and Kim about starting a rehab center?" she asked.

Rachel shrugged. "I seem to remember that Charlie Dawson is also a lawyer for Wildwood Clinic, and I know they're always looking for ways to expand their empire. I think that's why Kouris was able to get Chuck a membership to the country club. He could help them expand into Minneapolis." She picked up her cup of coffee and put it to her lips. "That's my take on it, anyway."

At first Marge could only stare at Rachel. Gone was the woman she had thought she'd known—the drug addict, the emotional train wreck, the neglectful mother—and in her place was what she realized was the real Rachel Sharpe. The woman Chuck Sharpe had described as smart and capable and compassionate before she had become addicted to drugs. This revelation should have given Marge hope for the woman's future, and maybe it did, but somehow the idea that Rachel knew more, was capable of more, than people gave her credit for just added to the background hum of worry in her mind.

"Chuck and I decided to stay together," Rachel went on. She glanced at Marge, then away again. "He's a good person. He's definitely addicted to his work, but I'm not exactly in a position to point fingers." Her lips settled into a thin line, and Marge saw tears in her eyes. "He cares about me. He cared about Ben. And besides"—she wiped away a tear—"who else is there now that Ben is gone?"

Marge set her cup on the coffee table and crossed the room. Rachel didn't resist when she put her arms around her, and for a long time, she clung to Marge. When her shoulders stopped shaking, she let go and leaned back in her chair. Marge pulled a nearby ottoman in front of Rachel's chair and sat. It struck her again how young the woman was. Early thirties. Young enough to start over. Marge wanted that for her. Wanted it with an unexpected ferocity.

"I'm here, Rachel. If you want me to be."

42

Eli pulled into parking space at the VFW park just before noon and killed the engine. The boat launch was packed with trucks and boats and trailers. Revelers in swimsuits and life jackets lugged coolers and grappled with oversized inflatables, and the sounds of laughing and shouting mingled with the churn of water against boat propellers. Labor Day had come and gone, along with the summer vacation crowd, but enough heat lingered to defer autumn for one last weekend before the lake cooled and the air turned crisp as a carrot.

Andy stood at the end of the pier alongside the empty beach, and Bella waded knee-deep in the sandy water below, a mangled tennis ball in her mouth. The boy had gotten his cast off earlier that week, and the hand that held the fishing pole was pale from four weeks of plaster confinement. His hand was going to be fine, Michelle had told Eli, after Andy's doctor visit. She'd asked after his own wound, and there was a catch in her voice—an emotion he couldn't quite place, but that was loud enough to register over the phone—when he said his stab wound was nearly healed.

Eli pulled his own fishing rod and tackle box out of the trunk and trudged down to the pier. Andy didn't turn as he approached, just angled his casts off to the side so as to avoid snagging Eli with the hook. The boy was just starting to lose his baby fat, and his shoulders were already wide and thick like his father's.

"Hey," said Eli. "Anything biting?"

Andy glanced at him, then turned back to stare in the direction of the red-and-white bobber that floated a ways offshore. He gave the line a few tugs. "Got some bluegill."

Eli set his tackle box on the dock. "Your mom told me you'd be here. Mind if I join you?"

Andy lifted a shoulder. He didn't know—would never know—what Eli had nearly done on the cliff the day of the lawn mower accident, but he was old enough, sensitive enough, to know that his dad was struggling with more than just a stab wound.

"I'll take that as a yes," said Eli. He gave Andy a light jab with his elbow. "Now move over. You're hogging all the space." He felt a wash of pleasure when a smile flashed on the boy's face. He looked like his mom when he smiled.

"You're never gonna catch anything with that," said Andy, eyeing the lure—a vaguely fish-shaped gizmo of iridescent metal and neon-yellow tinsel—that Eli was attaching to his fishing line. The boy nodded at a white Styrofoam box on the dock next to him. "I have leeches."

"Hey"—Eli put up a hand—"you do things your way, I'll do them my way." Andy's smile widened.

Eli lowered himself to the sun-warmed aluminum decking and sat on the edge, feet dangling. He had made it all day without a drink. On impulse, he set his pole aside and reached down to pull off his boots and socks and tossed them next to his tackle box. His still-tender flank complained at the bending movement, but the cool air against his feet felt glorious; a simple, unexpected pleasure that spread throughout his body. He wanted more. Whatever it was he felt in that moment, he wanted more.

"Come on," he said suddenly, and got to his feet.

Andy looked up at him. "Come on, what?"

"Put the pole down," said Eli. The pier shook as Bella trotted toward them, tail held high, tennis ball clenched in her massive jaws.

"But—"

The scab over Eli's stab wound caught on the fabric of his shirt as he pulled it over his head, and he winced and sucked in a breath. The air shimmered with heat.

He tossed his shirt onto the tackle box and glanced down to meet Andy's gaze; rejoiced when he saw the boy's hesitancy fall away, to be replaced by a look of pure delight. Eli barely managed to keep his balance as Bella barreled toward him and jammed the soggy, slimy tennis ball into his hands. He threw the ball and stood back as the dog leaped off the pier and hit the water, then turned to his son with a smile so wide it nearly hurt.

"Race you to the lily pads," Eli said, and then, with a loud whoop, he did a cannonball off the pier. The water closed over his head, and his downward momentum carried him feetfirst toward the soft lake bottom. It was deep enough here to be over his head, and he let himself sink down, down. He relished the sting of lake water against his nearly healed stab wound, and the jolt of water pressure as Andy jumped in a half-dozen feet away. His feet met downy-soft lakeweed, tangled in the long strands, then came to rest against the layer of sediment on the lake bed. He opened his eyes and peered through the gray-green water at the quiet landscape beneath the surface, at the pockets of radiance where the sun cut through the murk, and his wounded body ached with something other than the echo of blade in flesh.

He wanted more, and he was willing to fight for it.

Before he could process the idea, before he could cast aside the feeling, he braced his feet against the silty ground and pushed himself back up to the light.

Acknowledgments

First, thank you to Lara Jones, my editor at Emily Bestler Books. I'm brand-new to this business, but it was clear from the beginning that she is everything I could ever ask for in an editor. Her literary skills and instincts are impeccable, she is a project-management ninja, and she has shown time and again how much she cares about me and my book. She also laughs at my lame jokes and ever-so-kindly goes along with my Chris Evans–related delusions.

Thank you to my brilliant, supportive, and incredibly chill agent, Amanda Jain, who changed my life when she emailed me to tell me she liked my book. That email was the first stop on this incredible, surreal ride, and I'll be telling my grandkids about it someday.

Thank you to all my friends, family, and fellow writers who generously gave their time and energy to read drafts of my book: Justin Kruger, Andrea Pease, Christina Kruger, Jaime Spychalla, Julie Kimmel, Andrea Lerum, Clelia Morris, Michelle Wildgen, Deb Smith, Julie Loeffler, Rankin Johnson, Ben Timp, and especially Amie Hoag. Your feedback was worth its weight in gold.

Speaking of friends, sometimes the universe drops some people into your life who truly get you; whose inappropriate jokes are the inappropriate jokes you love, too; who can commiserate with your every complaint and celebrate even your smallest wins; who listen to your stream-of-consciousness mumbling and take *such* good care of you. Jo Ames and

Amaya Bruce-Allington are, in the words of Anne of Green Gables, true kindred spirits. I can't imagine what workdays would be like without the two of them. Well, I can, actually. They would suck. There are no other people I'd rather be stuck in a small room with for forty hours a week.

I am indebted to the ranks of supportive, trustworthy, and competent people who have helped me develop my story into an actual, published work of fiction: the aforementioned Amanda Jain and Lara Jones, Libby McGuire, Dana Trocker, Emily Bestler, James Iacobelli, Paige Lytle, Shelby Pumphrey, Liz Byer, and Jill Putorti.

Most of all, I want to thank my mom and dad for raising us to believe in ourselves, to believe that wanting it all is okay, to believe that dreams can be achieved if we work hard and take responsibility for our own success.

To my family: How did I get so lucky to have all of you in my life? Andrea Pease, Tim Pease (gone far too soon), Sarah Pease, Cass Crockatt, Cleo and Coleman Crockatt, Sylvia Kruger, Larry Kruger, Christina Kruger, and especially my husband, Justin Kruger, and our two gorgeous, loving, brilliant pieces of work, Rose and Lola.

Finally, to all those experiencing mental health or substance abuse issues, you are not alone. There are people who understand what you're going through and who can help. In the United States, call or text 988 for the Suicide & Crisis Lifeline, or call the Substance Abuse and Mental Health Services Administration (SAMHSA) at 1-800-662-HELP for general information on mental health and to locate treatment services in your area.